BLACK
Wedding

EMMA LUNA

Copyright © 2021 by Emma Luna

First edition

Ebook ISBN number - B099Q2H97Q

Paperback ISBN number - 9798538872046

Hardback ISBN number: 9798483039464

Editing: Proofs by Polly
Proofreading: Moonlight Author Services
Cover Design: DAZED Designs
Formatting: Moonlight Author Services
Chapter Headers: created using stock from DepositPhotos.com by Moonlight Author Services

AUTHOR NOTE

Black Wedding is a dark mafia kidnapping romance that is only intended for readers over the age of eighteen. It features scenes that may be triggering for some people. If you require more information, please contact Emma here:

emmalunaauthor@gmail.com

Emma Luna is a British author and this book is set in London, England. Therefore, British English spelling and phrases will be used. Please remember this and if you do find anything you think is an error use the above email address to report it.

If you want to keep up to date with the latest Emma Luna information, join the mailing list here:

https://www.emmalunaauthor.com

DEDICATION

To Sam

This book is dedicated to you
because without your love and support I would never
have been able to finish Black Wedding.
You have encouraged me every day and kept me going.
You are always there to listen to me moan.
You pick up all the slack when I drop the ball.
Not just the best PA but a great friend too!

Thank you for everything.

BLACK WEDDING

PROLOGUE

Twenty-five years ago, London erupted into chaos when a civil war began deep within the criminal underworld. A new leader was going to come out victorious. The only question is who?

Lester Mullroy and his Family had ruled London for years. To the public, he was just a billionaire hotel mogul, but in reality, he ran the criminal underworld. Nothing happened in his city without his permission. Everyone knew of his illegal businesses, but he is above the law with the police in his pockets. People feared him, and quite rightly so.

Lester allowed smaller gangs to run small areas of London for a price, but he made sure they all profited handsomely. Until they wanted more.

The east and west side gangs banded together with the idea of ousting Lester. They had the manpower and guns, making them a formidable opponent. Lester knew if he wanted to continue to rule, he would need more than just money.

This was an alien concept as he had spent his whole life believing money can buy you anything. Unfortunately, it was no match against the sheer brute force that came from a gang of men full of rage and a desire to take what they think is theirs. So Lester needed to find an army and fast.

This is how Patrick O'Keenan saw a very profitable opportunity.

The O'Keenan Family had wanted to branch out into London for a while. Their main territory was Cork in Ireland, but they were slowly expanding to gain connections worldwide. They had the men and the brutal force, but they had no London connections. Money was what they needed the most.

This is where a young, fresh-faced Shona Mullroy came into the equation.

Shona was Lester's only daughter and the apple of his eye. Patrick's eldest son and heir to the O'Keenan Family business, Vernon, was the right age and the perfect choice to move to London to establish the O'Keenan Family name. The result was the perfect marriage of convenience. Well...it was for everyone except Vernon and Shona.

Together, with Shona's Family money and Vernon's Family army, they created the ultimate Family. It's just a shame they can't stand each other. There is no divorce when you marry for convenience.

Some marriages of convenience develop into friendships at the very least, or sometimes, they can fall in love in the best-case scenario. But Shona and Vernon were not that lucky.

Shona was only twenty when she was forced to marry Vernon. She was a stereotypical heiress socialite that loved to party. She loved spending Lester's money on clothes, partying, lavish holidays and drugs. None of which fits in with the vision of a perfect Irish mob boss wife.

Despite Vernon being only twenty-three, with a playboy reputation, he knew he would have to become the face of the Family and settle down when he married and took over running London. He had been trained his whole life for this.

From the moment they said "I do," they became the perfect image and the Family that everyone feared. Shona was required to attend social events with Vernon or host any that he organised. Other than that, her only job was to maintain the house, which she had cleaners for. But Shona knew her real job was to give Vernon a male heir, and sadly she couldn't employ someone to do that for her.

On paper, they look like the perfect couple. Shona was beautiful, blonde, and busty. Vernon was tall, dark and handsome. Their looks matched, but their personalities were like chalk and cheese. Shona was vapid, selfish, and deceitful, while Vernon was ruthless, narcissistic, and brutal. They hated each other.

Shona hoped that putting off sex with Vernon would increase her chances of getting her marriage annulled. But, of course, Vernon, an Irish Catholic, refused to allow that. Vernon knew he needed a male heir with her.

Vernon laid down the law from the start, ensuring that no matter how she behaved, they would always remain married. She had the choice to become the wife in the most prominent crime Family in the UK and Ireland and gain the respect and worship that comes with the role, or she would be used and abused by anyone Vernon chose. No matter which she chose, Vernon would force her to give him a child.

This was the moment Shona decided to get everything she could out of the marriage. This is how they agreed to have separate wings in the house, to minimise contact. Shona still did everything that was asked of her, attended every function, smiled for every picture, but she was miserable.

Despite their hatred and reluctance, Shona became pregnant reasonably quickly after their marriage. Shona wasn't able to hold off sex for too long, no matter how hard she tried. She hated the idea of bringing a child into their fucked up relationship, but Vernon made it very clear that he would get a child, even if he needed to force her into it. That's when Shona lost the last little bit of fight that she had in her.

Despite not being able to fucking stand each other, their pregnancy united them. Vernon was excited about the prospect of gaining an heir, a mini version of himself. Whereas Shona just wanted someone to love, to give her life purpose.

The birth should have been their most incredible day, but it was their worst. Shona gave birth to a beautiful baby girl named Brianna, Bree for short.

Sadly, Bree was not the boy they craved, but things took a turn for the worst when Bree's labor became traumatic. Shona haemorrhaged soon after birth, and the only way to stop the bleeding was to perform a hysterectomy. Unfortunately, this meant Shona would never have another child, and Vernon would not get his heir.

Despite this trauma, Shona still loved Bree. She raised her to follow in her socialite footsteps and tried to keep her out of the O'Keenan Family business.

To the outside world, Vernon loved and cherished his daughter, but in reality, he was indifferent towards her. He gave her everything he thought she needed, except his love and support. He never saw the real Bree, but that would soon change.

For twenty years, Bree has been in the middle of her parents' drama. Quite literally, since her room is on the first floor in the middle with her parents' wings on each side. She was raised in the knowledge that she was a second-class citizen in the eyes of the Family. No matter how well the women of the Family were treated, they would never be part of the business.

Without a male heir, Vernon was in turmoil. Patrick decided that when a suitable leader was found, he would marry Bree and become the O'Keenan heir. But Bree refused, declaring she would only ever marry for love. What they didn't know is that Bree has a plan. She has no intention of stepping aside to let a man take her place. Screw the sexist rules. Bree is determined to be the first female crime boss and rule over London. This is her story.

CHAPTER ONE
Liam

I creep through the giant mansion, entirely in control of the situation, knowing that I have already taken care of all the security measures. Alarms and motion sensors are disabled, and security guards are drugged with just the right amount of sleeping tablets for them not to bother me. Stupid amateurs always order coffees before the start of their night shift. So it wasn't hard to intercept them.

You see, I have done my research. I know everything there is to know about this house and the movements of the people in it. When the woman of the house goes to bed, she first lets her chihuahua out the back and then takes him up to bed with her. Then she sets the alarm and activates the motion sensors that are around every door and window. She is always the last one to bed.

As I stalk through this giant house, it fucking baffles me to think that the couple who live here have been able to practically separate. They split the house between them, yet they still live like they are a married couple. Going out to events or hosting dinner parties just as if they are happily married. The man of the house does not want anyone outside of their home to know of their separation. People in this business don't get divorced or walk away. They endure it forever.

This house screams money and perfection. Its large, white open spaces are filled with obviously expensive furniture. The home of the O'Keenan Family is well known to everyone of importance. They are a family to be respected and admired, which is why only three people live in a house this large. To the O'Keenan Family, image is everything.

Every other time I had been to the home, I had been here to visit Vernon O'Keenan. His office is on the ground floor and has its own entrance through a door to the east of the property. To the outside world, it looks like he holds his regular business meetings here for a more personal touch. Still, everyone knows it's so he can control the security. He had a large city centre office once until an enemy got inside. Vernon has a gunshot scar to help him remember never to make that mistake again. So, despite hating having people in his home, he was left with no other choice.

The house design was done purposefully to ensure that the men who do business with Vernon could be vetted by security and knew they weren't welcome at the front door. Everyone knew they arrived on time and by appointment only. You mess up, and he doesn't work with you again. It was Vernon's way of letting people know that they worked for him and that he would always be superior no matter what.

The house is so grand they even have several rooms for entertaining guests. There's a giant ballroom where they held parties and an adjoining dining room for dinner parties. It really was the type of house that people literally dreamed about, fucking chandeliers included. But it was all for show. Vernon's way of telling the world that he has power.

However, the entertaining rooms were just a tiny portion of the house. The rest was divided up so that each family member had their own space. Shona O'Keenan, Vernon's wife, kept her space on the west side, as far away from Vernon as possible. She knew she could never divorce him, so she kept away, but I wasn't here for her. The middle of the house is where I'm heading.

I had tried to do as much research as I could on my target, but she has been relatively absent for around four years. Despite being in a loveless marriage, Vernon and Shona managed to produce a daughter, Brianna or Bree, as I have found she likes to be called. So when I was trying to identify something or someone who would be a weakness for Vernon, she is all I saw.

The rumour mill is rife with Bree and her lack of presence in the social circles in which you would expect to see her. Shona maintained the perfect image of a businessman's housewife who attends charity galas and is an upstanding member of the community. That is the role all women in our world are expected to undertake. I found evidence of her training as a debutante but no evidence of her actually becoming one. In fact, it was around the time she should have been announced as a debutante, basically a rich white person's way of saying she is now a woman, that's when she practically dropped off the grid. She stopped appearing in the media and on gossip pages. It's really strange for a girl her age, living in the high society circles like she does, to not qualify or be announced as a debutante. Particularly given that her mother runs the whole damn programme. This should have been my first red flag, warning me that things with Bree are not quite as I think.

Despite Vernon's well-acknowledged displeasure that Bree didn't have a cock, leaving him without a male heir, I knew he cared for her. The pictures I have seen all consist of him smiling adoringly at her, that's all the proof I require. I need something to use as leverage against him, and she is that something.

Vernon O'Keenan underestimated me and thought that he could get away without paying me. I did the job, now I want my money. He has had ample opportunities to produce the cash, and he has failed to respond. So, I am going to make him.

I continue up the stairs, visualising the target and using my night vision goggles to lead the way. I may not know as much about Bree as I would like, but that doesn't change the plan. She is a twenty-year-old girl. The chances of her taking me out are slim to impossible. How much trouble can one small girl give me?

After winding my way through the house, I make it up to the landing overlooking the giant entranceway that I just used to get into the house, ensuring I incapacitated all the security I came across on the way. As I stand outside Bree's door, I take a couple of big deep breaths and mentally remind myself of the plan. Controlling my breathing helps to lower my racing heart and gain control over the adrenaline. One of the first things I learnt for my line of work is that you must be in complete control over your whole body. Having no adrenaline rushing through your body means it will slow down your thinking and reflexes.

Once I am in control of my body, I place my hand on the bedroom door. It's time to take back what belongs to me.

CHAPTER TWO
Bree

Creaking from outside my bedroom door jolts me awake, and I glance over at the clock while listening out for different sounds. The bright red numbers read 3:14am, which explains why it is still dark outside. Instantly, my nerves are on edge as I hear another creak. Most people wouldn't pay any attention to a few minor scrapes in the wooden floorboards, but I was raised as the only granddaughter to two giant crime families, which meant that one of the first lessons I was taught was to constantly be on the lookout for danger. There would always be more low-ranking gangs that wanted what my family had, but if any of them ever attempted to take what we have, none of them had ever gotten this far. We have the best security money can buy.

It was far more likely the noise was either my mother sneaking down to where we now locked alcohol, in the bar room attached to the kitchen, or it could be my father smuggling out his latest whore. The joys of my room being stuck quite literally in the middle. I stopped sticking my head out to check quite a long time ago.

The last time I looked into the noise, I was ten years old, and I opened my door to find my nanny bent over the staircase bannister while my father was balls deep inside. That's when I really knew what an asshole my father is. He had the whole house, so why in the main hallway? I genuinely think I would have preferred to see a rival gang member because at least I knew how to handle those. I had been shown how to shoot at age six, and I was fucking good at it.

Not that my father knew that or that I even had the gun Jimmy gave me. As far as my father was concerned, girls should look pretty, keep the home and children, and keep their mouths shut. Apparently, to be in a crime Family, you couldn't advance past the fucking 1950s because both sides of my family thought that. In fact, I think it's the only thing they have ever agreed upon.

Several times, I have made it known that just because I don't have a cock does not mean I cannot run the Family. The only option for an heir in their eyes is a man. This means that my only job is to marry who they tell me to and pop out babies until I get a boy. When I made it clear how fucking sexist their behaviour is, my father and grandfather told me I had to stay behind the scenes. Unless I was prepared to put on a pretty pink dress and parade around posh social events with my mother, then I wasn't allowed in the public eye, which suited me fine.

Luckily, my father's head of security, and his best friend, Jimmy, did not share the same beliefs as my family. Instead, he believed that everyone, including women, should have the basic knowledge to protect themselves.

Since the age of six, Jimmy has been teaching me about self-defence, including kickboxing and how to fire a gun, both of which turned out I was very fucking good at.

Hearing another noise, this one closer to my door, the louder footsteps had me sure that the intruder was getting closer to my door. That ruled out my dad or one of his fuck buddies since he never made that mistake again. My mother overheard me telling my best friend, Mia, about what happened. The nanny got fired and my father was more careful in the future.

When I was younger, Shona was the perfect mum. She adored me so much, but I think she always, in some ways, blamed me for losing the ability to have more children. She hated that and the fact that she would always be a failure in the eyes of the Families. But I also think she liked treating me like her little dress up doll, which I allowed while I was young, but not forever. As I got older, more independent and rebellious, she pulled away. My father says she is nothing more than a bitter, twisted bitch who is jealous of my beauty. I hated being in the middle of their arguments, I had no idea who I should believe. I didn't think I was anything special. I would have to be pretty fucking gorgeous for a mother to hate her daughter for that reason.

The more I reflect on the shitshow that is my life, the more I question why the fuck I stayed stuck in the middle of my parents' bullshit excuse of a marriage. The truth is that I didn't want to. In fact, I would rather be any-fucking-where else, but the Family wouldn't allow it, and what the Family says is law in this house. Which is how I found myself laying in bed wondering which side of the house our late night visitor was going to head towards.

The sound of the doorknob on my bedroom door rattling jolts my brain out of those speculations and straight into survival mode. Throwing the duvet cover off, I spring to my feet, ignoring that I am entirely naked except for the baggy men's t-shirt I am wearing. The t-shirt didn't belong to anyone important, like an ex-boyfriend, I just liked sleeping in them for comfort. Quietly, I pull open the top bedside drawer, pushing aside my clit sucker—that I genuinely believe has the potential to eradicate the need for men completely—to grab my 9mm Glock 48. The vibrators were at the front of the drawer because they got the most use, but they most certainly are not what I need right now. I'm confident my gun will be all I need.

Nevertheless, I still grab my combat knife in case whoever this is gets too close. I love this knife way more than any girl should, but this is an extra special knife. Jimmy bought me this knife two years ago for my eighteenth birthday. Among all the expensive jewellery and fancy designer clothes and bags, this customised bright purple knife with a 'B' on the handle was the gift I could relate to most. It was more 'me' than anything else. I would have even gone as far as to say it was my favourite gift, if it wasn't for the black Lexus my father got me. Not quite the motorcycle I had asked for, but it's still sexy as fuck.

The door handle is jimmied until the lock clicks open, and that is enough to instantly snap me out of my thoughts. Thinking back to the way my father's face crinkled into a mixture of disgust and anger when I asked him to buy me the bike could wait. Of course, he forbade me from riding, but that just made me better at hiding it from him. Right now, I can't think about anything else except who could possibly be breaking into my bedroom in the early hours of the morning.

As my door is flung open, I run to the nearest sidewall. One of the first things you learn in self-defence is to make sure your back is protected at all times, which is why I plastered it firmly against the wall. No light flooded the room through the open door, as I was expecting. It means whoever is doing this is doing it in the dark. The figure that crossed the threshold of my door has a tall, broad silhouette, but that's all I could tell. It's obviously a man, but whether he is an enemy or not is still open for debate. This is why my arms remain firmly in position; one straight out in front of me, aiming my gun firmly into the centre mass of the man, and the other arm tucked up against my front, with my knife held tight, ready to be used if necessary. As I wait, my heart starts to race. My breathing is accelerated, too, so I hold my breath, trying to prevent the lurker from locating me quicker.

Within seconds he starts to move quickly, but not in the direction of the bed like I expected. When I heard the door handle being moved, I hastily tried to arrange the bed to make it look like I was still curled up under the covers, hoping that's all it would take to allow me to sneak out of the room behind his back. But he looks to be heading straight towards me. How the fuck does he know where I am? I know I'm not making any noise to give away my position. I hadn't even taken the safety off my gun, just in case he heard the click. I need to act quickly, so I decide then that even if this is someone I know, or who works for my father, the dickhead has crossed a line and deserves to be shot.

Clicking the safety off simultaneously, I take a quick but deep intake of breath whilst I hold my arm steady. I then, gently but confidently, push my finger against the trigger. Without hesitation, I aim for right in the middle of his chest. Everything seems to move in slow motion. It feels like I'm watching as the bullet flies out of the barrel and smashes into my target with the exact precision I've been trained to do. The loud bang of the gunshot reverberated through my ears, leaving behind a slight ringing that made me wince.

I know the second the bullet hits because he stops in his tracks; his path towards me stalled temporarily. Taking in rapid, shallow breaths, I try to replace the oxygen I'd missed by holding my breath for so long. I try to slow my heart rate down to think of my next manoeuvre. Far too often, I had been warned that the first bullet, even when it hits centre mass, might not take the assailant down. Jimmy always told me to empty my magazine into the bastards, but I can't do that now. Most people would think that my hesitation is because of my reluctance to take a life, but that isn't it. If the fucker is stupid enough to take on the daughter of a crime boss, then they deserve everything I want to throw at him.

The real problem is that I still don't know if this guy is a friend or foe. My father could be under attack for all I know and has sent one of his security team to protect me. Unfortunately, he still sees me as a delicate little flower that needs protecting. He has no idea what I'm capable of. The last thing I need is some testosterone-fuelled security guard jumping in and thinking he is saving a damsel in distress.

Stupidly, it's my hesitation that sees everything go to shit. While I'm waiting for the mysterious man to drop to the floor, my heart rate returns to normal, but I lose focus of the situation. Instead of falling, after his very brief pause caused by the initial hit, he carries on moving towards me at a fast speed. His temporary stall lures me into a false sense of security, and I close my eyes, which enables him to get the upper hand. My gun is still up, but I have lowered it enough that there's a good chance I would miss him even if I do shoot again.

The closer this guy comes towards me, the more I realise he's most definitely not a member of my dad's security team. When he enters the light surrounding me, I can see that he's much taller than my five-foot-three stature, maybe a whole foot taller, and is dressed in all-black tactical gear. If he worked for my father, he would be wearing a suit. All his security men look the same.

The tactical, high-grade, bulletproof vest he is wearing explains why my bullet didn't even make an impact. But it's the night vision goggles he has strapped to his head that explains exactly how he is capable of advancing through our house undisturbed. This guy was obviously the real deal, and it dawns on me that he must have taken out my father's entire security system, and God knows how many of his men, just to get up here. But the scariest realisation is that I was his intended target all along.

Before I can get my knife into the correct position, a forceful blow knocks the gun out of my hand. At the same time, I feel a firm, muscular arm wrap around my body, holding the arm that I had the knife in tightly to my side. The next thing I know, his opposite hand is raising and aiming towards my mouth. The white cloth the stranger's holding is the last thing I see before everything goes dark.

CHAPTER THREE
Liam

My plan worked perfectly, even with the minor hiccup we had. I expected a bit of resistance, hell, I had prepared for it. I was breaking into a fucking war zone almost. There's more security assigned to the O'Keenan house than some of the royal families even have. These security guards are not overweight ex-policemen who have nothing better to do. Instead, they are at the top of their game and not only are they well-trained, but they also have all the latest technology.

This house is decked out better than Fort Knox, but, in all honesty, it was supposed to be a piece of piss. This is what I am good at. I knew exactly what I was doing and had done all my research on the Family, their house, and the security staff. I knew all of their weaknesses, gaps in their workforce, and how to disable the security system. I should have been in and out in under ten minutes, and I'm sure I would have been if it wasn't for the one thing I didn't take into consideration. Her.

The bright red-haired, petite spitfire was the last thing I had considered when planning. I knew very little about her, but this was not what I had envisaged. She is short, with curves in all the right places. I struggled to find many pictures of Brianna O'Keenan online, which should have been a warning sign. I normally don't do a job without all the information, but this was no ordinary job. This was personal. I assumed this girl would be scared and that I could easily get close enough to have an advantage over her. Just long enough for the chloroform to take effect. I never saw her as a threat. Fuck, was I wrong.

All the research suggested she's a posh little socialite, just like her mother. In the few pictures I found of her, that were a couple of years old, she was dressed head to toe in a ball gown, and dripping in diamonds. Her mother on one side of her, the glass of wine in her hand a permanent feature at all times, and her father on the other side of her. He always looks like the hard-nosed bastard everyone has come to know him as. In almost every picture, his arm is wrapped around Brianna as he gazes at her with a bright smile. The pictures suggest that his daughter is clearly the apple of his eye, which made her my perfect target.

From the moment I burst into this girl's bedroom, I know I have underestimated her. Fuck, I had no idea she even owned a weapon, let alone knew how to use one. She didn't hesitate. She simply took a deep breath and pulled the trigger.

Her shot was precisely on target, hitting the middle of my chest. It hurt like a motherfucker, but she wasn't expecting me to be wearing a vest. Given the accuracy of her shot, I'm relieved she didn't go for my head. But as soon as she momentarily lowers her gun, I realise why she opted for a body shot. She can't see who I am.

Obviously, she knows someone my size shouldn't be letting himself into her room at this time of the morning. I'm guessing her father has been under attack before. Someone who loves his little girl the way he does would ensure that security protected her before anyone else. That's why it surprised me to learn she had no security posted outside her door. Vernon's a cocky twat and probably assumed nobody would get this far.

Capitalising on her momentary lapse in judgement, I ignore the pounding in my chest and advance towards her quickly. Not only do I need to disarm her before she does any more fucking damage, I also need to speed up my exit strategy. No matter how big this mansion is, there's no way that nobody heard the gunshot.

Meaning they will be checking every room in the vicinity of the noise to find out what caused it, and I can't go back out the way I came in.

Walking in through the main door, disabling the alarm, and going up the main stairwell of the house is a pretty ballsy move. Her room is just off the main stairwell, so anyone going upstairs has to pass her room. I managed to incapacitate any security I came in contact with, but there will be more. Going back the same way is an accident waiting to happen. Luckily, I'm a pro and have already mentally worked through all the escape routes I had planned for.

As the tiny girl in my arms becomes limp, I place the chloroform covered rag back into my back pocket and look down at the mass of red hair that is draped over her pale alabaster skin. I feel a very brief moment of regret that I have dragged this poor girl into her father's mess. Then, as I look down at her, I realise she is practically naked. Wearing only an oversized, old Led Zeppelin t-shirt. Typically, on her petite frame, it should stop mid-thigh. However, due to the way she fell into my arms, the shirt has risen and I can see all of her creamy white thighs. Fuck, I can see she isn't wearing any panties. That most definitely is not helping me to concentrate.

I have a lot of experience in these kinds of situations, believe it or not. Despite my preference to leave no one alive, I have been known to acquire live targets as well. Call it kidnapping or acquisitions, I don't care. I will still do it in a professional manner. But the rock hard cock that is currently straining against my black combats is far from professional. Why the hell has my dick decided this is the perfect moment to behave like it's never seen a pair of legs and ass before? I mean, her ass is literally perfect. Curvy and peachy, the exact vision you want to see as you are pounding her from behind. But, despite all of that, she isn't anything new. I'm not exactly a virgin. I've fucked my fair share of women, and plenty with an ass even better than hers, but my dick doesn't care about that.

I need to push this gorgeous girl out of my mind so I can work out how to get us both out of here, preferably without a bullet hole in either of us. My mind is whirling a mile a minute, and I know there is only one option, but for some reason, I'm hesitant. Of course, I know exactly what that reason is. Her. Why the fuck do I suddenly care about making sure she is safe? I'm kidnapping her, for fuck sake!

I understand that the only viable, quick way out of here is through her bedroom window. To jump down onto the conservatory roof beneath, and make a run for it across the large lawn. I have already made a hole in the fence, so I know that as long as I watch out for any remaining security who will now be on high alert, it will be an easy exit. But stupidly, I'm worried about her and I have no fucking clue why. Maybe it's because she looks so small and fragile.

Lifting her into my arms so that I can carry her, the knife and gun she has been holding drops to the floor. I cradle her tightly to my chest and note she weighs next to nothing. I bench press heavier than her on an off day. Yet as I hold her, it feels like I'm carrying precious cargo. I have no experience with babies, but my best friend Kellan recently had a kid. He says whenever he picks her up, it's like handling a volatile live explosive that's as delicate as crystal glass. That's precisely how I feel holding this girl, except she's a fully grown woman who I shouldn't give a shit about. Remembering how tightly she was gripping the hand-to-hand tactical knife before she dropped it, she is obviously no stranger to getting into fights. Strangely, the idea of this tiny yet feisty woman getting into a fight, or needing to use that knife, both pisses me off and turns me on. Her dad is a dick for not protecting her better, and I'm going to make sure he knows it.

We made it off the grounds as quickly as I knew we would. I can see O'Keenan's men running around trying to identify the gunshot's location, and I can hear them responding to one another on the radio I have in my ear that's looped into their security frequency. Their first act was to get Vernon safely into his panic room. No matter how important Bree is to him, the coward always wants to make sure he is safe before anyone else. His daughter was next to be checked on. The delay while they secured Vernon allowed me the time I needed to get away, taking Brianna with me. I can't wait to point that little fact out to the arrogant asshole.

Calling Vernon and telling him it was me who broke through his security and took one of his most prized possessions, taking that opportunity to humiliate him, is next on the agenda. It's fucking time he took me seriously, and he's going to find out just how serious I am. Now this, I'm going to enjoy.

CHAPTER FOUR
Bree

Waking up feels like the most arduous task in the world, and I'm rocking the world's worst hangover. For some reason, I can't even remember what the hell happened last night. It's really unusual for me to get so pissed that I'm like this the next day. My whole body feels like it's held down by lead weights. Even opening my eyes is painful. Fuck, what did I do last night?

Even giving myself a mental pep talk isn't quite enough to help me open my eyes. It's a lot harder than it should be. But slowly, my eyelids start to open, and the bright light flooding into the room feels blinding. I mean, the light physically hurts, and I groan in pain. Shit, I really am in worse shape than I've ever been before. I need some painkillers and quickly. Luckily, I keep some in the drawer next to my bed, alongside my toys and knife, so I wouldn't have to physically stand up. I'm not sure my stomach contents can survive that.

I feel like I'm running the last few meters of a marathon, when really I'm just trying to turn over in bed far enough to get the damn pain pills. Not that I have ever run in an actual marathon before, I just assume it's very tiring and painful. I mean, I'm physically fit, but

I'm not a crazy fitness freak. Most I've ever run is a 5k, and I was happy with that, but right now, my body feels like I barely know how to walk correctly.

I need to stop being a pussy and get my ass in gear so I can take my pain medication and then get on with my day. I'm sure I had something planned, but I can't remember what. I also need to give Mia a call. If I'm this fucked up, she will be even worse. She's the only person I ever drink with, and she knows how to let her hair down. We don't go out often, but when we do, we really go for it.

Keeping my eyes firmly open this time, I roll over, causing my stomach to flip, but not because of my hangover. My vision clears rapidly as I take in the room. I don't recognise anything around me. I jolt up in surprise, or at least I try to. My head starts to spin and I rest it back on the pillow quickly. I may live in a mansion with more rooms than I can count, but I know they all have some degree of floral wallpaper, except for two rooms; my own and my fathers' office. Hell, my mum even decorated my fathers' bedroom, despite never even sleeping one night in that bed. She decorated mine several times over, but every time I would get black paint and paint over it. Finally, after about the fifth time, she realised she shouldn't have even thought about messing with a very stubborn fourteen-year-old.

Eventually, I ditched the black and settled for a gorgeous purple design, but this room didn't have a hint of purple anywhere. The creams and blues, along with sparse decorations, told me this has to be a guy's bedroom. I must have been totally wasted to break all of my rules. I rarely go home with guys, and if I do, I never stay the whole night. It had been close to a year since I had sex with a guy and a few months since I last let Mia drag me out. I have never really been into that lifestyle. It's most definitely a buzzkill knowing my father's men are standing outside the door. It isn't exactly a big turn-on knowing they can hear, which is why I stopped doing it. For some reason, I left all of that at the door for this guy.

Looking around for any clues, I can't see much with

my head on the pillow, so I risk the inevitable headache and nausea and try to sit up, but they don't come. Instead, I feel pain around my wrists and ankles and notice my arms and legs are tied to the bed. Some slackness in the ropes makes me think I might be tied down to prevent me from moving in some kinky sex game. This doesn't feel like it's about keeping me tied up for sex, I think it's about making sure I can't get up off the bed. Looking down, I see I'm in the same Led Zeppelin t-shirt I usually sleep in. I'm fucking relieved I'm not tied to this bed naked. But the fact someone has the fucking audacity to kidnap me is infuriating. What's worse is my father's fucked up excuse for security allowed it to happen. I won't be relying on them to get me out of here. If I can, I will do it myself. I just need to work out where I am and why this asshole took me in the first place.

Take into account the cotton wool feeling in my mouth, the pounding in my head, and the rope around my wrists, it all helps my brain piece things together to try and work out what is going on. That's when I remember the missing information. It all comes back to me like flashes of memories. The noise that woke me up and was followed by the large man that came bursting into my room. I also remember shooting the bastard, but he carried on advancing towards me. He was decked out in full combat gear, which is why the bullet didn't stop him. Instead, it hit him straight in the vest, and that gave him the upper hand.

The last thing I recall is the guy's big arms curling around me and his hand clasping something white over my mouth. Fucker drugged me, most likely with chloroform. I remember the smell so clearly. That sweet scent of acetone that reminded me of the cleanliness smell you get when you go into a hospital. What I want to know is why the fuck he chose me? Stupid question really since I already knew the answer. This could only be because of my last name. But this guy is messing with the wrong girl.

"Oi, you stupid fucker. Get the fuck in here and get me some water, pain killers, and a knife to cut this rope. I promise not to try to stab you with it." I struggle to hide the sarcasm in my voice because I can't even pretend that I'm not going to try to stab this dick with the sharpest instrument I can find when I get free. Of course, if he hands me the knife, that will be even better.

Looking around the bedroom as best as I can, I take in the lack of furniture. There is the double bed that I'm currently laying on, a bedside table with a lamp, two doors, and a chair in the corner. The small table next to the chair has two glasses on it, one is half empty. Some may have used the term half full instead. But I'm not an optimist most of the time, let alone at this fucking moment. Not while some guy has the upper hand over me. The thought of him sitting there, drinking a glass of water and watching me sleep, it infuriates me.

One of those doors is obviously the way in, but I'm not sure if the second door is a closet or a bathroom. Why the hell am I trying to analyse the structure of this damn room? I try to convince myself it's because I'm planning my escape route, instead of what I'm really doing... snuggling into the comfiest bed I have ever slept in. Wow, whatever was on that white rag really has scrambled my brain.

"Get in here, you coward!" I yell, thrashing around and pulling on the ropes, but it isn't helping. All it does is cause rope burns and makes the contents of my stomach slosh around to the point I'm starting to worry they will make an appearance very soon. My head is pounding like a marching band is holding a concert in there, but that doesn't stop me from screaming a string of expletives at the top of my lungs. I figure it is better to shout abuse at my dickhead kidnapper rather than continue moving excessively. That will just result in me being covered in my own vomit.

I'm in the middle of another tirade of swear words that are so creative I'm not even sure they are actual words— apparently, I'm very confident that he is a massive thunder cunt, a douche canoe, and a jizznugget all at the same time—then halfway through trying to invent some new names for him, I hear the door swing open. A dark chuckle fills the room.

Am I hallucinating? I know chloroform can leave

people messed up. Hell, my head aches and my mouth tastes like the bottom of a budgie cage, so they're testament to that. But I have never heard of chloroform causing hallucinations. But, that's the only explanation I can possibly think of to explain why I'm currently drooling over the man who kidnapped me.

Tall, dark, and handsome is like describing the Mona Lisa as simply a painting. It just doesn't do him credit. He's over a foot taller than me, but he doesn't seem too tall because his broad, muscular frame makes him seem proportionate. He just oozes hard, ripped muscles, and they are easily visible, given how tightly his black t-shirt is plastered against his rock hard chest. I mean, the damn thing is nearly tearing at the seams around his biceps. At this point, I can't drag myself away from continuing my perusal of this delicious excuse of a man.

If I thought his t-shirt fit him well, that's nothing compared to how fitted his jeans are. The dark blue denim is stretched so taut across his thighs, I'm mentally begging him to turn around so I can check out his ass. I bet it will be one hell of an ass.

When it finally dawns on me that I'm staring at the guy's crotch, I drag my eyes upward, all while hoping and praying that he has a face that makes me want to stare at his ass instead. He can't be all perfect, I have to find some reason to hate him, besides him kidnapping me, of course. I should have known; I'm not that lucky.

This guy has the face of a God. His black hair is so dark that it shines. It's just long enough to grab hold of when you're running your fingers through it. It flops over his forehead slightly, and it won't take much for it to cover his piercing green gaze. His angular, sharp jaw is covered with a splattering of dark stubble that matches his hair, but it's his dark red, plump lips, currently drawn up into a smirk exposing those pearly whites, that really has my stomach flipping. His smirk is growing the longer I'm stupidly staring at him.

"You called, Princess?" he asks with a rugged drawl that totally matches his appearance. Fuck, trust me to get kidnapped by a gorgeous, cocky twat.

CHAPTER FIVE
Liam

L ooking down at the gorgeous girl I have tied to the bed, I'm a bit annoyed that it's not in the way I want. Her long, wavy red hair falls around her head like a fiery angel. Her pale, alabaster skin makes the blush of her cheeks and the bright rosy red of her lips stand out so much more. I covered the girl in my dark blue duvet cover, but I can't stop thinking about what I know is lying underneath.

Gorgeous, yet sexy, with curves in all the right places. Even though her tits are covered by the oversized, baggy t-shirt, I can still tell she has a gorgeous rack with more than a handful. Her hips and ass have just the right amount of curve that I would love to grab hold of as I watch that ass swallow my cock. Not that I can ever go there, no matter how much I really fucking wanted to. This is a job and nothing more.

Looking at her while she sleeps, she looks like a tiny doll lying there peacefully, but that all changes the minute she wakes up. Her mouth opens, and fire to match her red hair comes blazing out. Hell, I spend most of my time surrounded by asshole men from the army or private security, and some of the words coming out of her mouth would make them blush.

BLACK WEDDING

I can't keep the grin off my face as I walk into the room, and find that she can't stop staring at me, obviously checking me out.

"You called, Princess?"

From the few minutes I spent with her when she wasn't unconscious, I knew she was far from a princess. I mean, she shot me and called me all names under the sun. Not exactly the spoiled little mafia princess I was expecting. In fact, she couldn't be further from that. I really need to start thinking with my brain and not my fucking dick. But, right now, that concept is as hard to grasp as my cock.

"Fuck you, dickhead. You are more of a princess than I am. So how about you get these ropes off me, let me out of this bed, and get me some fucking pain killers. Maybe then I will allow you to keep your cock and balls."

I can't help the deep belly laugh that left me. I can't remember the last time I laughed like this. All I can see is the gorgeous pixie of a girl with the fiercest look on her face as she threatens to castrate me. What's funny isn't how crazy the idea is, it's the fact I actually believe her. I actually think she might be able to pull it off. I'm learning quickly not to underestimate this flame-haired Goddess. There's no way I'm letting her anywhere near my crown jewels unless there's a happy ending involved.

"Sorry, Princess, no can do. I'm gonna make a deal with you, though. I will give you some food, water, and painkillers on one condition. I need you to do me a favour," I ask nicely. I don't need her to cooperate, but for some reason, the idea of doing things the hard way with her is not sitting right with me. She is far too beautiful to wear any scars.

"If you suggest anything that involves your dick going near my body, you will see how serious I am about cutting the damn thing off," she spits at me. I can't help but chuckle once more.

"Relax, Princess. I mean, if you wanna put that smart mouth around my cock, I'm not gonna say no. But, I actually had another use for your mouth in mind." Her face ripples in disgust, and I want to be offended. My cock is most definitely not something to be sneered at, but given I kidnapped her and tied her to the bed, I don't exactly blame her.

"Let me make it perfectly clear, pretty boy. Your dick is going nowhere near me. Ever. So you better get out of here and take care of that hard-on you are sporting using your own hand. I'm not

32

doing any kind of deal with you," she says with a look of both confidence and loathing on her face. I can't help but smile.

"Okay, we have obviously gotten off to a bad start…."

"Ha, no shit, Sherlock," she says, interrupting what she already knew would be a poor excuse for an apology, but I continue regardless.

"I'm not hitting on you. That's not why I brought you here. I'm not going to even bother with threatening you into doing what I want. I'm pretty sure it would just piss you off even more. So I will be real with you, Princess. The sooner you do what it is I brought you here for, the sooner you can go home." I watch as her face settles into a blank unreadable mask, and it worries me. At least when she's looking at me with pure hatred, I know where I stand, but this is a lot more concerning. I have no idea what this woman is truly capable of. A fact I'm sure didn't escape her notice as I see the grin slowly spread across her face. That's when I realise I'm shuffling nervously in her silence.

"What exactly do you need my help with? And before you answer, you should know that I will say no if you call me Princess again." I stop my shuffling and smile at her. Now I know how much it bothers her, I want to call her it all the time, and I will, as soon as she has done what I need her to.

"I need you to speak when I call your father. I'm sure he knows you are missing by now. Your gunshot certainly made sure of that, and since it's been about ten hours since we left, I'm sure he is missing you enough to hear what I have to say," I explain logically.

"T-ten hours? Did…did you just say I've been here for ten hours?" she asks, stuttering over her words and for the first time looking she looks small and fragile. For some reason, I really didn't like that.

"Don't worry about it. It's a common side effect of chloroform. That's why I put you in here to rest."

"How fucking gentlemanly of you!" she hisses. Her venom returned along with a frown, and so did my smile. Turns out, I enjoy watching this red head turn fiery.

"So, if I make this phone call to my father, how much am I worth? What are you ransoming me for?" she inquires, and now it's my turn to frown.

"Nothing he can't afford. I'm only asking for what is rightfully mine. Now, will you make the call?" I reply honestly. I can tell by the inquisitive look on her face that she's not sure if she trusts me or not, but I can also see a gleam in her eyes like she is interested to see what would happen when I tell her father that I have her. Her sparkle dims and I wonder what is going on in that pretty little head to have caused such a change.

"Who are you?" she questions me, sounding genuinely interested.

"Liam. Now, no more questions. Are we ringing your father or not?" I snap. I instantly regret snapping at her, but she is so fucking distracting. I can't let her or her sexy body keep me from my goal. My rock hard dick is already struggling with keeping our roles apart. I don't need more of an excuse.

With a giant huff and a release of air, followed swiftly by a cough and a curse, she finally answers me. "Let's get this over with."

CHAPTER SIX

Bree

I don't know why I'm so nervous about telling my father that I've been kidnapped. There's no denying that I'm the most constant female in his world. Despite his preference for being indifferent towards me, that's still preferable to the way he treats other women. Mistresses, girlfriends, whores, and even my mum know what it's like to be the centre of Vernon O'Keenan's world. At least they do for a short time. He uses them and moves on. Every interaction they have is only for my father's benefit. He's used to being powerful, which is why he has no problem showing them how important he is. If that means treating them like shit or dumping them when he gets bored then so be it.

Many, if not all, have tried to change him. Thinking they will be the one to finally get Vernon O'Keenan to stop playing around, to be serious about his sexual encounters, and most importantly to become the centre of his world for longer than a fleeting moment. They couldn't have been more wrong.

My dad's a very clever man, and there's a reason he's good at chess. It's one game where strategy, and being able to see multiple steps ahead is what you need to win. This makes it hard to surprise my dad or to beat him. Liam may have won this round, but my father will make sure he loses the war. My dad may treat me like I'm invisible sometimes, but I guess this time it will finally put his love to the ultimate test. Will he, for once, be the courageous person I want him to be, and put his only daughter first, or will his pride win out?

I know that to my father I'm the perfect daughter. The girl who, as far as he knows, does as he says, but we both aren't as we seem. I'm really full of fire, and would rather be the Family's heir as opposed to marrying one. I want to rule and I'm capable, but the girl my father see's will never be capable of ruling.

I've gotta admit, I'm a little nervous to make this call. What if he doesn't want to pay for me? Maybe he expects me to get myself out of this mess? I consider whether I should try and manipulate Liam, to explore how this gorgeous excuse for an asshole could possibly be of use to me. Sadly, the drug has clearly messed with my head because the only use I can think of for this sexy man involves him serving me with his tongue or cock. That thought heats me all the way up and I can feel my cheeks flush.

Naturally, the cocky bastard doesn't miss a thing and the little raise of his eyebrow is his way of asking me what's making me heat up. I look away, not wanting to answer and embarrass myself further.

I feel the bed dip beside me as Liam sits down a lot closer to me than I would have liked but his motive was clear as he held out his phone in between us both. I start to tell him my father's contact details, which he made me memorise from a very young age for scenarios just like this. Well, maybe not exactly like this. He didn't exactly cover 'what to do if you think your kidnapper is hot' in kidnapping 101.

Shockingly, before I had the chance to start telling him the number, I realised that he had already pulled the saved numbers on his phone. What is even more surprising is that I recognise the number as being my father's personal number, not one he uses for business. I think there are only a handful of people who know that number.

"Where did you get that number? You better not have gone through my phone, you pervert."

He laughs the more I speak. It's like he gets a kick out of me arguing with him. For some reason, that just winds me up and I feel very confident that if I wasn't tied to this bed I would be kicking him in his crown jewels to see if he gets a kick out of that.

"Relax, Princess. Your phone is still at home where you left it. Like I need your father tracking your phone to find you before I'm ready. We would miss out on this essential bonding time," he says with that sexy smirk on display.

"Do you always have to tie women up to bond with them?" His eyes perk up and I groan when I hear the words out loud. Me and my stupid big mouth.

"I don't have to tie them up, Princess, but it makes things a whole lot more fun. Wanna see how much fun we can have?" His deep gravelly voice is so sexy and seductive.

His gorgeous, playful eyes bore into mine with more intensity than a joke should have, and I felt a shock straight to my pussy. I don't know how long I thought about it, but obviously, it was too long because his face soon turned serious, like he knew I was getting wet thinking about him.

Fuck, what is wrong with me? How messed up does a girl have to be to get turned on by a guy who was threatening my life. Well, it's either that or I really need to get laid. I didn't realise it has been long enough to send me sex crazy.

The way his eyes glisten in the light sometimes is mesmerising, and I know he sees me squirming under his gaze. I need to cut this cocky asshole off before he says something I can't say no to.

"Why don't you untie me and I'll show you how much fun I can have without the rope. In fact, if you give me back my gun, my day will get a whole lot better." His deep responding chuckle ripples through my spine, but I know by the glint in his eye that he can tell I wouldn't hesitate to shoot him...again!

"As much fun as it is to continue this banter with you, Princess, I think we should get on and make the phone call. Don't wanna keep Daddy waiting, do we?"

I huff, but before I get the chance to argue with him he cuts me off by pulling a knife out of the back of his trousers. Slowly, as if he is trying to show me that he doesn't want to harm me, he brings the blade up to my collarbone. He gently trails the smooth yet cool blade across my chest, before finally, the tip reaches my throat. The act is so much more sexual than it should be, and I can feel my breath is trapped. It's like I daren't move or even breathe, yet my pulse still races, but it's not out of fear. Strangely, even with the very sharp tip of the blade, which looks to be a hunting dagger, rests across my throat, I don't feel afraid. Don't get me wrong, I fully believe that Liam would kill me if he wanted to. I just don't think that, right now, he wants to. Let's hope he doesn't change his mind.

CHAPTER SEVEN
Liam

Seeing Bree laying perfectly still beneath my blade does wonderful things to my cock. Obviously, I have threatened before and knife play has never been something I'm into, but at this moment in time, I most definitely am.

Maybe it's got something to do with the fire I see in Bree's eyes, that challenge. She's not cowering or screaming for her life. Hell, she's not even, really trying to get free. All because she's not afraid. She may be the one tied up, but she knows she's the one with the power here. She knows that I need her to cooperate. If she doesn't, I would usually have no hesitation making her, forcing her to see sense. But with Bree, for some strange reason, I can't imagine harming one hair on her fiery little head. I just hope my face doesn't give that information away.

"If you do as I say, this will go smoothly. I don't want to hurt you, but I will do what needs to be done. When I call your father, he will ask for proof of life. That is when, and I cannot stress this enough, Princess, only then are you to speak. Tell him you are alive, tell him you are unarmed, hell, you can even tell him you are being well looked after but that is it. No rescue talks, or code words. No telling him not to give me what I want. Just do as you are told and this will all be over before you know it. Can you do that?" I ask, as I remove the blade from her soft, pale skin. I don't even want to risk breaking that beautiful canvas, even just a little by mistake.

She looks up at me with her big silver eyes, through her long eyelashes and her gaze is one of confusion. Almost like, I'm not behaving like a normal kidnapper would. But the more that thought runs through my mind, the more anger I feel at the idea she may have been kidnapped before.

Fuck, the fury flashes through my body like an electrical rage, I can feel my heart racing and my teeth grind in frustration. I already want to disembowel anybody who has caused this beautiful woman any kind of harm. Then it dawns on me how fucked up it sounds that I'm angry and jealous over a fictitious man who may also have kidnapped Bree. What the hell is wrong with me?

"What exactly is it that you are hoping to gain from my father? Because if you ask me, I will tell you if it's something he will be willing to part with or not," she asks and I can't help the exacerbated sigh that escapes my lips. This girl just will not do as she is told! It's not hard to follow instructions.

She can obviously tell by the serious look on my face that I'm not messing around about this. Her face blanks and when she speaks it almost sounds defeated. "Fine, just get on with it."

While I have her finally doing as she is told, I don't waste any more time. Opening my phone again that had long since gone into standby mode due to lack of use, I quickly dial the number that had been displayed. This is a new phone, so I know he wont recognise the number. Initially, I was worried this might prevent him from picking up, but I need not have worried. After just two rings the distinct Irish twang of Vernon O'Keenan bellows through the phone.

"Who is this?!" he barks, a pleasure as always. Don't be fooled. He isn't answering like this out of concern for Bree, this is his usual manner. Hell, even Bree rolls her eyes at his lack of polite pleasantries. "It's Liam Doughty," I say calmly. I hear a rustle at the other end of the phone followed by lots of swearing. The echoes and different regions of accents tell me that not only am I on speakerphone, but Vernon is not alone. Most likely, he's surrounded by all his closest men. All of which are now cowering in fear over just my name, but I can also hear the shock in Vernon's voice. He thought I had just left it, forgotten all about what he owes me, but he couldn't be more wrong. I was biding my time, planning, making sure my plan was perfect. Waiting for the perfect moment. Now is that time.

"Liam? I-I don't understand. It's y-you? Y-you...you have my Bree?" he asks, his stutter giving away how scared he is.

Her father's reaction obviously has an effect on Bree because I see her physically gulp and start to fidget in the bed, but the real change is in her silver eyes. Before when she looked at me fight and anger laced her gaze, but now her eyes are wide, distrusting, and even a little scared. She obviously knows what it takes to scare Vernon, and since he is trembling at the very sound of my voice and name, she is right to view me suspiciously. After all, she has no idea who I really am.

"I do. Who else do you think would be capable, or have the balls, to break into your house, pass all your security, walk right up to your daughter's room, and take her. Fuck, if I was a different person I could have put a bullet in her pretty little brain while she slept, but I didn't. I've not harmed her at all, but believe me when I say that will change," I spit, as my knuckles turn white from gripping the dagger so tightly. I can't bring myself to look at Bree. Just the idea of hurting her sounds alien to me. Luckily, Vernon doesn't know that.

My family, if you can call it that, are Irish. We were raised to know who the O'Keenan Family was. Patrick may be an old man, but he wasn't ready to hand over the reins completely yet. Besides, he had five boys and didn't know which, if any, he trusted with not only his, but generations of life's work. He had spent a long time expanding his Family's reach worldwide and it would take someone as smart and ruthless as Patrick to continue.

Vernon was the eldest, who Patrick moved to run the London branch. Neil, his second eldest, is by his side constantly, yet still struggles to pick up how to run a business or think on his own. Malachi, his middle boy, got blown up in a bomb attack on the O'Keenan estate years ago. Some say Mal was the favourite, but we all know that just a rumour Patrick started because he's dead and doesn't actually have to hand the position over to him.

Ellian, the second youngest, is in prison for planting the retaliation bomb. Sadly, not only was it in the wrong building, but it didn't explode. Finally, there was Ewan. Patrick's wife had longed for a girl and by the time Ewan came along, she ignored the fact he was born male and did girly stuff with him anyway.

This, according to Patrick, is what resulted in his youngest boy becoming a giant 'poofter' and that no 'fag' would ever run his company. Although, if rumour is to be believed, Neil is gay and wants nothing to do with his homophobic father either. Once Patrick has made his decision the son's can do as they please. But until the old man hands over the reins they are under his control.

"Liam, let Brianna go. She has not and never will be part of my company!" he shouts, the fear obvious by the cracking of his voice as he tries to barter with me. I look over at Bree. I find it hard being in the same room and not looking at her. Her face has twisted from the serene look she had while she was sleeping peacefully. When I checked on her through the camera I installed, after she had just woken up, she was trying to discreetly shuffle and it almost looked like she was making herself comfortable in my bed. I had to look away to just get control of my thoughts and my cock. Poor thing keeps going up and down like a fucking yo-yo, like it can't make up it's damn mind. For some bizarre reason, I liked that she was comfy on my bed. I liked that she looked like she belonged there. She was the first woman to ever sleep in it.

Don't get me wrong, I fuck women when I'm in the mood or not on a job, but I always make sure to go to a hotel or their house. There is a reason this is my sanctuary. I never planned on bringing her here. I had a safe house that we should be at right now. But from the minute she shot me and looked like an angel assassin, I'm sure I've been thinking more with my dick than my head. The plan had always been to tie her to a bed, I just couldn't imagine it being any but mine. A light, gentle cough from next to me, drags me out of my dazed and confused state. Bree was discreetly trying to pull me out of my daydream, I gave her a small appreciative smile. What happens next has my cock standing to attention, almost trying to open my trousers himself, if he could.

I'm sure you're wondering what made my cock behave like a teenage boy who has just discovered porn. All this feisty cretin in front of me has to do is smile. She obviously likes the way I'm smiling at her and she reciprocated. Fuck, her smile literally lights up the room. But the best bit is when she realises she is smiling at me and I was staring straight at her. She shut down, her face back to the impassive mask she has been wearing to show her lack of interest in the situation, except this time there's a reddish, pink blush to her cheeks from embarrassment and I love it. I make a mental note to smile at her more often. I want to berate myself, but

I'm so fucking past that now.

"I will let Bree go when you give me what is rightfully mine. You hired me to do a job, I did it, therefore I have a right to be paid. This is the final warning. Do not make me do something you will regret." My voice is deep, threatening, and laced with the anger I feel over having to go this far. Normally clients don't fuck with me. They know what I can do and that I'm the best at it, so they know not to test me. Vernon's just an arrogant fuck on a power trip.

"Listen here, you fucking idiot, you have no idea who you are messing with here. You better not have hurt one hair on my Brianna's head. Do you hear me? I want to talk to her," he states and I look over at Bree, checking to see if she remembers the rules. I also glisten the knife slightly by turning it so the light hits it. Just a casual reminder of the threat. Not that it bothers her. She just rolls her eyes and looks towards the phone.

"Dad, it's Bree. I'm fine okay, you don't have to worry," she says calmly to ensure her father calms down too.

"Brianna, baby, I have been so worried. Has that bastard touched you? Has he hurt you? If he has I will make him pay with his life. Where are you? What can you..." Before he got the chance to finish his incessant questioning, Bree cut him off. It's a good job she did because there's no way she could remember any more of the questions. He was talking so quickly in an Irish accent that I could barely make out what he was saying.

"Father, please stop. I'm fine. What the hell do you owe Liam? Why can't you just give him what he's asking for?" she asks, more in a demanding tone than I would expect a Daddy's girl to use.

"Brianna, I'm so glad to hear that you are safe, darling. Don't you worry about this nasty business between Liam and I. Daddy will sort it for you. I will bring you home safe," he says condescendingly. Bree's angry response is just as I anticipated. She balls her hands into fists and grinds her teeth in pure rage. I can't help but feel for her, for her own father to underestimate her value in such a way infuriates me, so I can only imagine how she feels. I don't even understand what happens next or why but I have an overwhelming desire to show her that I support her. Gently, I place the knife down between us and slowly trace a hand across her cheek before smiling at her. At first, she looks a bit startled by my touch, then she slowly leans into it. I want her to know I believe in her and that even though I don't know her, I know enough to tell that she is a fighter, not some girly girl who cannot comprehend what our world is like.

Now, instead of pulling on the rope in anger, she pulls on them with her hands out flat as though she is reaching out to me. I almost forget that her father is on the phone and we are in a fucking kidnapping scenario. Whatever this is between us feels more like foreplay.

Her father clears his throat, pulling us out of our moment. Her posture returns rigid and her eyes narrow, like the last minute never really happened. I try to meet her gaze but she averts her eyes, looking at the duvet instead. Just as I sign in frustration at our lost moment, she addresses her father.

"Father, I am not a child. Why can't you just give Liam what he says you owe him? I don't hear you denying it. For fuck's sake, do not piss about fighting this and risking my life, do you hear me?!" she shouts.

"Brianna, what have I told you about using language like that? You are a lady and not part of this world!" he shouts back and I quickly realise that this conversation has taken an abrupt wrong turn.

"Well, that's enough family time. I think you have clearly underestimated your daughter. She has a lot more fight in her than you realise. And she is right, don't waste time, effort, and money doing this the hard way. Give me the million that you owe me, for the job I actually did complete fully. We signed a contract, old man. Do not make me enforce the fine print. Will you pay me what is owed?" I ask sternly. I try to ignore the growl I let out while talking about his poor treatment of his daughter. I also don't miss the confused yet grateful look she gives me.

"Fuck off, Liam. I cancelled the job and you know it. Now, you're behaving like a spoiled toddler. Give me back my daughter or I will kill you!" he shouts and I can hear his rage through the phone. Not that I give a shit. I know I've got the upper hand. Not to mention the hand that's now rested on Bree's thigh and that has her gaze enraptured.

"You booked me to do a job, and just because you decide to call it off whilst I was doing it, is fucking irrelevant. Sadly, when I kill someone there is no going back. If you realise it was the wrong decision then that's your problem. It's black and white. Now, let's talk about when you are going to pay me what I am owed," I say rationally, laying things out simply. I expect Vernon to reply but before he gets the chance, Bree cuts him off.

"You're an assassin?!" she screeches, her eyes bug out wide as she stares at me.

"Brianna, do not speak to that asshole."

"Are you really telling me that you paid Liam to fucking murder someone, then you changed your mind, except you were too late? So instead of saying you made a mistake—oh, now I remember, Vernon fucking O'Keenan doesn't make mistakes. So it must be Liam's fault and you don't reward incompetence. Is that seriously what's happening here?" she seethes, stunning us both into a moment of silence. I now understand how she felt when I stood up for her. It makes me feel fucking indestructible.

"It's not like that, Bree. I informed Liam I no longer wished to go through with the assassination. This is completely fucking unprofessional. I will find him, and I will rescue you. So don't worry too much, baby girl," he explains and I feel my hands grip her thigh tighter as her father disrespects us both.

"I did not find out in time. You left me a fucking voicemail just five minutes before I was due to pull the trigger. I was already in position, prepared, and part of that professionalism means not having my fucking phone on as a distraction. This is a fucking ridiculous situation that we have ended up in, and don't think I won't take it as far as is needed," I slow down my words to enunciate clearer exactly what I mean and how much he should take what I'm saying personally. Except, I can feel that this is spiralling.

"It may only be a million pounds, but as far as I'm concerned it could only be five pence and I still wouldn't pay because I do not owe you jack shit."

"Are you fucking kidding me?!" I shout at her father at the same time as Bree does. It doesn't matter that I told this girl to acknowledge she was alive, no extra bullshit. I'm quickly realising that Brianna is not one for following rules or for being underestimated.

"This is ridiculous! We are getting nowhere. Clearly, my father is not prepared to pay you the million he owed you according to your contract. So what's the fine print, Liam? You have obviously kidnapped me for a reason, and a guy as smart and well planned as you always has a back-up plan, I'm sure." Her face screams of her infuriated expression and whilst this is a massive diss to her father, she is also challenging me. Asking me if I'm prepared to threaten her any further than I already have. It's a question I'm very pleased I don't have to consider.

Brianna is correct in saying that I do always have a backup plan. Luckily, I know that hurting or killing Brianna will not help me. Instead, it will bring the Irish and London gangs down on me, and I can't hurt Vernon physically, since dead men do not pay debts. So I wrote a very clever fine print, just for this type of scenario.

"I told you not to worry yourself, Bree. We will be there to get you soon," he says and then in what sounds to be muffled hushed tones, I heard him ask if they had my location yet.

I can't help the chuckle that escapes my lips. As if he thinks I'm that stupid. I'm routing the call through over a hundred VPNs to hide my location. He will never find us unless I want him to.

"Fine, since you are refusing to pay the million pound fee that you owe me, that automatically triggers the fine print of the contract we signed. If you did not read the small print, that's your fault. Well, and your shit lawyers. He should still have a copy but if he doesn't then I will have a copy sent over. Just in case you can't wait, I will summarise it for you now. It basically said that if you cannot, or will not pay, then you will forfeit fifty-one percent of your official and unofficial businesses. To do this, a marriage will be arranged by Liam Doughty and Brianna O'Keenan. They will then take over leadership of the London firm." I let those words sit in the silence of the room. I dare not even look at Bree, I can only imagine what she's going to do. It's a good job she can't reach the knife.

What happens next, with both of their responses, shocks me into silence even worse than the current noise level.

Vernon's uncontrollable laughter is what snaps me out of my own head. I snap up instantly and look at Bree. She looks furious, just as I was expecting. She doesn't seem like the kind of girl that wants her hand in marriage to be sold. But what really surprises me is that her death stare is not aimed at me. All of Bree's rage seems to be focused towards the unnecessary laughter that is coming from her father.

We both sit there for longer than necessary, listening to Vernon laugh hysterically at a situation that was most definitely not funny. Bree is sat with the same red tinged cheek rage and she almost appears to be vibrating in anger. I think she is going to be the one that loses it and breaks the silence, but she is beaten to it.

"Fuck, Liam. You may as well not have bothered writing a

fine print, and I'm glad I didn't bother reading it. My daughter will never marry a prick like you, and I will never hand over my business to you!" he seethes.

My mind is whirling with how I'm going to respond, but I don't need to because a furious looking Bree pulls herself up, impossibly closer given the rope, but she gets as close as she can and practically spits fire at her father.

"Are you fucking kidding me, Dad?" she shouts exacerbated. I squeeze her thigh to try and get her to calm down but I'm not even sure she knows I'm in the room. She doesn't give him a chance to reply.

"Not only did you fuck Liam over by not paying him, you bartered with my hand in marriage. But it's okay because there's no way I will marry an asshole like Liam, is that what you were thinking? Or maybe you were thinking I won't get married at all? Well, fuck you. I will marry Liam and I will go to my grandfather to request my portion of the Family business, the one I was always told I could have when I get married. You can both fuck off if you think I'm just handing it over. I have been training and this is my time. Together with Liam, I will become the next O'Keenan Family leader and there's nothing you can do about it," she blasts and then sits back staring at me, waiting for me to hang up. Apparently, we don't need to hear what his response is. It would appear I just got engaged to the girl I have tied to my bed. Not a sentence I ever thought I would say. Shit, that escalated quickly. I hang up before any more damage can be done.

Fuck! What's worse is that I'm kind of excited about seeing more of this beautiful vixen. Looks like I'm getting married to my very own firecracker, fuck me!

CHAPTER EIGHT
Bree

Liam is just staring at me like he can't quite believe what the hell just happened. He practically dropped the phone onto the floor when I said the word marry before. I feel like my eyes are flipping all over the room as I try to avoid his piercing gaze, while I wait for his mouth and brain to catch up.

"So, since I'm going to be your wife, I suggest you untie these ropes. Unless of course, you are the type of husband who likes to use these things for fun instead of just for kidnapping reasons," I say suggestively with a wink. He tries to cover his distinctive laughter, but all that happens is he practically breaks down coughing.

"I'm still holding out hope that your father will call back and that I will get my money," he says, looking at me and then pointedly staring, as he questioned whether I thought my dad would be ringing back.

"He's not ringing back, Liam. He doesn't think I will go through with marrying you, or that I want any part of his business. I am just a girl after all." With that, he bursts out laughing and I'm a bit offended, not just for myself but for my gender too.

"Woah, take that look off your face. I'm laughing at the stupidity of your father, not at you. I barely know you and already I can tell that you will kick ass in our industry. How the fuck does your dad not know that about you?" he asks and I stare at him with confused eyes. How does he see me so clearly?

"He doesn't really know me. I've told him a shit loads of times that I want to be part of things, but he never listens. He says I should get an education and then piss it away by becoming a socialite like my mum. I can't think of anything worse!" I'm not even kidding when I say I physically shudder at the thought. I don't drink anywhere near enough to be my mother.

My father thinks I'm not cut out for this type of business, that I can't make the hard calls when they need to be made. He has no idea I can be just as ruthless as him. But that's going to change right now.

"Let me out, now! I promise not to hurt you in any way. If you let me go then together we will make a call that will get us both exactly what we want," I shout.

I can't deny that his gaze looks suspicious or that I am not thinking of how I can get the gun off him and even up the playing cards. But I'm realistic, I know that Liam has opened up a door for me today that I'd never considered. Pulling on the ropes, I give him a pointed stare and I hear him huff as he moves to cut them with his knife, finally freeing my arms. Before I have a chance to overthink things, I punch him hard on the nose. I revel in the delicious crunch I was hoping to hear.

His hands pinch at the bridge of his nose to try and stem the flow of blood.

"What…the…fuck?" he asks, spluttering blood out of his mouth and I can't help but smile.

"You kidnapped me. You didn't think I would let you get away with that, did you? Now stop that bleeding and give me the damn phone."

Much to my surprise he laughs and I recoil slightly because the blood hasn't stopped, and laughter with blood leads to blood splatter that I really don't want all over me. Realising why I recoiled, he reaches back with his free arm and pulls the t-shirt he is wearing over his head, before balling it up and holding it to his nose. As he holds it, he then passes over his phone, just as I asked him, but I don't see the phone right away as I am too busy staring at his glorious bare chest.

He chuckles as he catches me gawking, and he is very lucky

his nose is already bleeding, otherwise, I would have thrown another punch his way. There's a part of me that is led by my lady parts that doesn't even regret staring, he is fucking gorgeous to look at. His chest is bare of hair, which is unexpected given the dark stubble across his cheeks. His pecs are bulging, hard, and completely covered in the most beautiful tattoos. To the naked eye, my skin is bare of tattoos, but anyone who gets close enough will see them. I do plan on getting more, but while I am forced to obey my father, that's one of his rules. I was starting to lose my patience with him and his smothering, chauvinistic behaviour. I had already started formulating a plan, which involved finding a husband to get what is owed to me. The only problem is that the Family only allows males to rule, so whoever I marry would be the face of the organisation. Or at least they would be until we were established and then I would let everyone know I was the real leader. So I needed to find a man who would stand by my side when I needed him, but get the fuck out of my way when it is my turn to shine. Liam seems like the perfect choice.

The mere fact he only ransomed my father for what he was owed spoke volumes. Most people would have been greedy, asked for extra, added on interest, found any excuse to get more. Yet Liam only asked for what he was owed, and he gave several chances for my father to pay before he said he would evoke the contract terms. Don't get me wrong, I am pissed that anyone feels they have a right to barter with my life, but that issue is more towards my father. Although there is a part of me wondering why Liam doesn't want to marry for love.

Staring at me with his soulful green eyes, he holds out his hand to me, trying to pass over his mobile phone that I missed earlier. He mumbles something about using it on speakerphone only. I roll my eyes, but nod in confirmation, dialing the other number I have had memorised since I was a child. He answers after just two rings, and his strong Irish twang warms my heart.

"Who is this?" the Irishman growls down the phone and I can't help but laugh. He has never been one for pleasantries.

"Hey, Gramps, it's Bree," I say cheerily, although I'm sure he already knows what's going on. My father probably had him on speaker when the call from Liam came through.

"Motherfucker. You tell that Irish twat if he lays one hand on your pretty red head, I will find him, cut his bollocks off, and feed them to his mother. Do you hear me?! Can he hear me?" my grandfather shouts, then begins to swear in Gaelic, even though nobody else in the family can speak it. His grandparents were raised in the southern region of Ireland, and they spoke it. He mostly learnt the swear words and a few threats, but none of his siblings learnt it at all, choosing to speak English instead. I'm not even sure his father bothered to learn. He keeps telling me that he wants to teach me, but my dad has always forbidden it. Women should not swear or do anything that is not becoming of a quiet, meek, obedient little housewife. Well, he was in for a shock because there's no way I'm falling into that category.

"Gramps, calm down, please. You know you have high blood pressure. Liam can hear you, and I want to tell you he has not hurt me in any way. Look, I know you always say you don't want to get in the middle of things when I argue with dad, but this time he really is being unreasonable. I don't know Liam, but I know Dad is wrong for not paying him what he is owed," I explain and I can hear my grandfather sigh. He knows whenever I say he doesn't have to get in the middle of our argument that he probably will need to.

"Bree, hun, there is a lot that you don't know. The man Liam assassinated was a very important part of the business, he was essential in getting some of our cargo into the country without it being seen. We had a couple of shipments that were discovered, as well as money going missing, and that could only mean we had a rat. We conducted a lot of investigations and all the signs pointed at the leader of Marcushio Imports as being the one snitching to the cops. So of course we hired Liam to deal with him. We have worked with Liam a lot in the past. In fact, we have even offered him very heavy sums to come on board and work for us full-time, yet he refuses every time. I know your father left word with Liam that the hit was off, but it was too late. That hit has gone on to cause us a lot of shit. Initially, Leon's second in command, Richie, took over the business and tried to keep our shipments moving, and money washed, but then Leon's seventeen-year-old son, Vinnie, soon came along, trying to find out why his father was murdered. He suspects we are involved and has cut off all ties with us, costing us millions in product and fees. We have people we need to supply to, Bree. We need our channels opened again," he reveals, as I try to follow along. This is the most my grandfather, or any member of the Family, has ever included me in regarding the Family business.

"I understand all that, but the mistake is on whoever ordered the hit, surely. They are the one who didn't confirm the data before hiring Liam. He did his job, why should he not get paid for that?" I say sternly.

Looking over at Liam, I see he is piercing me with his green eyes, whilst twirling his knife around between his fingers. Almost like it is a nervous habit of his. I can relate, I am someone who always likes to have my hands busy.

"I do understand, Bree, and I'm sure your father does too. But Liam has stepped over the line by doing this. We have to retaliate. If word gets out that we negotiated or paid him, then your life would be in incredible danger. We would get people trying to ransom you all the time, and they may not be as good to you as you say Liam is," he explains and I groan loudly.

"There will be no retaliation against Liam. I am not calling to discuss the ransom as it is not relevant any more. I am no longer being held hostage. I want to make it very clear I am here of my own free will, Gramps. Liam and I have talked, and we have decided we are going to get married. I want to claim my rights to the business," I said as calmly as possible.

Gramps and I argued over this subject numerous times in the past. The rules of the O'Keenan family have always been that the business is passed down to the first male heir, which is how my dad was given our London based business. They try to keep me out of the majority of business discussions, but I know how it works. Our main base is Ireland, which is the one Gramps currently runs. He needs one of his sons to take over from him when it's time for him to retire, or Grams makes him. Given my uncles are either dead, in prison, or idiots, the decision was always that Dad would move back to Cork when the time was right and that his heir would continue running the London branch.

When the O'Keenan's married into my mother's Family for the money, it was always in the agreement that it would be a Mallory descendant who runs the business. So when my mother gave birth to me, and experienced complications that resulted in her not being able to produce more heirs, they scrambled. Gramps agreed that as soon as I married, the business would transfer into the hands of my husband, with me by his side.

When I was younger, I was forced into dates with suitable boys, assholes who wanted to rule the firm one day. I continually vowed to my family that I would never marry strategically, that

I would only marry for love. But as I got older I realised that was never going to be a possibility. If I wanted to take over and be the first female leader of our Family business then I needed a man who my family approved of and who met all their requirements, but who would step aside and allow me to rule. Liam was part of our world, he was strong, and given his profession he had to be ruthless and protective. He seemed like the perfect choice, but as he stares at me talking through things with Gramps, his confused expression tells me I maybe should have talked to him about our engagement beforehand, not that there was time with my father being a cockwomble earlier.

"Sweetheart, please be reasonable. Think about things. Liam might seem like the right choice right now to get back at your father and his idiot behaviour, but this is still my company. I will not throw it away," he says firmly and I chuckle slightly, rolling my eyes. He may not have said it specifically, but I know what he is thinking when he says 'be reasonable'. I'm surprised my father didn't say it outright before. They think whenever I react or behave impulsively it must be because of my period. Why do men think my decisions are based on some hormonal tantrum?

Did I plan on marrying Liam? No. I wanted to kill him when I first woke up. For as long as I can remember, I have always thought about the best way to get control of the Family business that I am owed, but they will never give it to me unless I randomly grow a cock and balls. So marriage was the only other way. It had to be someone who knew who I was and what I was capable of, making every male I have ever dated in the past off the list. I needed someone who could stand by my side and help me with the business. I am not going to admit I know everything, and there will be areas I need a partner in. When I decided to get married to someone I decided to view it as a partnership. He would stand by my side, help me when needed and protect me when I couldn't protect myself. Liam fit that bill perfectly. I always knew I would have to give something back in return for such a marriage. So for Liam to just want what he is owed, that is something I can give him and more. We can hash out the finer points later, no doubt with Gramps' lawyer involved. Right now, I had to make him see I was serious.

Mentally, I was trying to find the right words to tell my Gramps why this was a good idea in a way he could relate to. Luckily, Liam stepped in.

"Mr. O'Keenan, I'm Liam. I haven't met you in person before so you don't know me, only my reputation. I am the best hitman in the country, possibly even the world. I know you have heard of my family, and know how I was trained. Believe me when I say, kidnapping Bree was the absolute last resort and I never would have hurt her. I had no idea she would be interested in activating the clause in the contract, but now that she is..." Liam says politely, but sternly to ensure that while he shows my grandfather the respect he is owed, he also lets him know he isn't someone who should be messed with. Just as Liam is getting into the real meat of his story, my grandfather interrupts him.

"What clause?!" he shouts. Oh fuck, did Gramps not know about my dad bartering with my life?

"The clause was written into, not just this contract, but every one I have ever had with your family. It covers what happens if full payment has not been received, and all avenues of discussion have been exhausted. It states that Brianna's hand in marriage will be given voluntarily so that I can claim rightful ownership of the London firm," Liam explains.

"What the fuck? Why would you add that as a clause?!" my Grandfather screeches.

"Although I am an independent contractor and I work for myself, my family's lawyer created all the official paperwork. It was only when I made contact with him to seek advice on what to do about Vernon not paying that I was advised of the clause. I didn't know about it before then, and I definitely would never have forced Bree into it. I mentioned it to Vernon as a threat, hoping that he would see sense and just pay me what I'm owed. The decision to go through with the clause was all Bree," he explains and I confirm it, which is why I can hear a loud groan coming from my grandfather.

"Bree, I'm so sorry. I can't believe your father was such an asshole to gamble with your future. I will be having words with him about that. Liam, as for you, I hope you know that this is a plot by your father. He has wanted control of London for years but has been unsuccessful in taking it from me. He thinks getting you to marry my granddaughter is the first step to succeed in that, which it may well be. I don't know how much choice I have in this legally, I will be looking into it. But I need to know, Liam, is this all a plan to give control to your father?" I stare at Liam as his face contorts into one of anger. I recoil slightly, confused by the pure rage that is practically pouring from this man.

"I had no idea my father had any interest in your company. I have not been part of the Family business for many years. I go home occasionally to see my mother and younger sisters, but my father and two older brothers are assholes that I want nothing to do with. So no, I work for me, and now it would seem I work with Bree." he replies, seeming to calm down as he talks and he is now looking at me with an almost shy smile on his face, one I return.

"We have no agenda, Gramps. This may have stemmed from a bad decision made by Liam, and it may have come about because of my father and his fucked up logic, but I really do think this is a good idea. I think Liam and I could run the business for you and be fucking great at it." I spoke with a fire I genuinely felt. I may not know anything at all about Liam, but what I do know, and what I have worked out based on this experience gives me good vibes from him. Yes, he is a dick for kidnapping me and I am not minimising that, but he never hurt me, he never threatened me, not really. I don't even have a bruise from being manhandled, meaning when I was unconscious he carried me with care. I may have got him really fucking wrong, but we will see.

My Gramps doesn't even try to hide his sigh this time, it rings loud and echoes through the phone speaker. "I don't like this. Not one bit. But I trust you, Bree. I know you have talked a lot about joining the business, and I have always deterred you. It was never because I didn't think you were capable, you are very much able to run the business, but there's a danger, and a horror attached to our business that I didn't want you to be part of. I always thought you wanted to marry for love. Has that changed? Because you know that once you marry Liam, that is it. There will be no divorce or re-marrying. You stay with him until you die, and if he dies first you mourn him until you pass too," my grandfather says, sounding very somber. I am still shocked by his statement that he thinks I am capable of running the business. I never knew he thought that.

"I know I always talked about love, but I want to run this business more than anything else. You never know, I may fall for Liam the way you did Grams. Or if all else fails, I can be like my dad and live completely separate lives from him and fuck anyone who moves," I reply sarcastically, causing Liam to splutter and cough on the water he had just started to drink. His eyes had continued to focus on me like he was assessing every word I said. Could I really fall for him? I had no idea, but I do know I want the business and this is the closest I have ever come to it. I'm not throwing it away now.

"Fine. You have two months to get to know each other and to decide if you still want to go ahead. I will come to London then and meet with you both to find out your decision. For now, I will pull back the hit that has been placed on you, Liam." As he says that I start to shout asking who put a hit on him but Liam just laughs, which baffles me greatly.

"Why the fuck are you laughing? Do you want to die?" I ask him and he just shrugs his shoulders.

"Princess, I am the best hitman in the country, which means I know everything there is to know about security and things like that. I also know all of my competition. The only people anywhere near as good as me would be my eldest brother, who won't take on the hit, particularly if my father does plan to use me to get this business. That leaves mediocre hitmen at best, none who stand a chance of even finding me let alone getting close enough to take a shot they won't miss," he explains with a confidence that is very sexy. It does border on slightly cocky, but having the title of world's best assassin doesn't exactly come to people who aren't a little smug.

"Sadly, he is right. We have been trying to hire Liam for years for this very reason. You have my word that the hit is off, Liam. I appreciate that you may not trust me enough yet, but Bree can tell you I'm serious. When I say I will do everything in my power to keep you both safe, I mean it. Brianna is my heart, and you will not hurt her in any way, or I will kill you myself. Also, Bree, if you choose, you can stay in my London home for two months. Get to know each other and decide if you really want to go through with the engagement. After that, if you don't then that is up to you. There will be no repercussions on you, Liam, that Bree herself doesn't order. However, if you decide to go ahead with the wedding, then there will be a handover period where you learn the business. I need to know where you are, Bree, and I am guessing that Liam will not want to give up the safe house he has you in now, which is why I am saying move into my home. You can modify the security as you see fit, Liam," Gramps explains.

I looked over at Liam, his eyebrows are drawn together like he's doing a very complex math solution. My eyes ask him what he wants to do, but he still looks confused. I know he is probably weighing up how much he can trust a family who has lied and deceived him. But that was my father. Gramps is a man of honour and if he promises to protect us, then he means it. Liam nods, just slightly, and I release a breath I didn't know I was holding.

"Send us the address. I will have my tech expert adjust the security settings and then we will move in once he has made it safe. Is that okay?" Liam asks, attempting to compromise with my Grandfather, which I dare say is not something he is used to.

"Absolutely. Let me just say this one thing, Liam. If you hurt my Bree, I will kill you," he growls as he threatens Liam for the second time. Liam releases a little chuckle before staring straight at me. I almost shy away under his penetrating stare.

"Noted, Sir. But can I just say, in the short amount of time I have known your granddaughter, I can already assure you that she doesn't need anyone to make threats on her behalf. She is more than capable of kicking my ass when I deserve it," Liam says cheerfully down the phone, giving me a wink at the same time.

Fuck, did I just get butterflies in my tummy over a guy that kidnapped me? Was it because of that cocky little wink, or because he is the first guy I have ever known who sees the real me and believes in me? The more Liam looks at me with those gorgeous green eyes, and that cocky smirk, the more I know I'm fucked.

CHAPTER NINE

Liam

After spending what feels like forever on the phone with Kellan, my tech expert and best friend, he reassures me that he has assessed and upgraded Paddy O'Keenan house, so that it now runs on his security, not theirs. He did confirm that there was nothing he found suspicious, and it did look like the old man was honest when he said he had no intention of hurting us. He clearly idolises Bree, and it's hard not to.

We have been in my hidden apartment for over twenty-four hours, and I have mostly just been leaving her to herself. I gave her the bedroom, after tying her up I figured it was time to at least show her a little kindness. She comes out to eat with me, or to chill out and watch a movie, but we never really talk. I keep finding myself staring at this beautiful woman walking around in my t-shirts, and wondering what the hell is going on in her brain.

As she walks she carries herself with this easy confidence, and she looks like the ruler she wants to be. Then she catches me looking and she quickly lowers her eyes and blushes, almost like she is embarrassed. Maybe she is. Either way, if I am going to marry this girl, and be involved with this crazy family, then I need to get to now her a hell of a lot better first. I need to make sure she is worth swapping one ridiculous family for another.

Once I had word from Kellan that I was free to move into the old man's estate, I shouted to Bree to let her know we could leave.

"Oh, before I forget, do you need us to go home so you can pick anything up?" I ask her as we are getting ready to leave. I have a large bag full of my clothes and other things, then I have a bag for any work I may need to do.

"No chance. My father will shoot you on sight, whether Gramps has rescinded his kill order or not. I have some clothes at Gramps' house, and I texted asking him to arrange a credit card and new phone for me. So, I should have everything I need waiting for me, but thanks," she said, that slight blush tinting her pale, red cheeks.

"Did you really just say you texted your grandfather and asked for a new credit card and he just sent you one?" I scoff. I knew there were people who lived like that, I just didn't think Bree would be like that. I mean, when I first kidnapped her, I saw her as a little mafia princess, but now I know she is so much more than that.

"It's just for things like food. If I access the money in my bank, my father will trace it. Yet, if I spend Gramps' money he will have the records protected. I always keep a record and pay him back. He goes mad about it, says it's normal for a grandfather to spoil his favourite grandchild." She laughs and it literally tingles through my ears right down to my cock. How does the sound of just her laughing do that to me?

"I hadn't expected you to say you pay him back," I answer honestly and she shrugs her shoulders, almost like she hears that answer all the time.

"I said I will try, he doesn't always accept. Don't judge me before you get to know me because if you do this thing will never work. How about we make a deal? For the next two months, we just get to know each other, like we would do if we were dating almost. Then a week before we are due to meet with Gramps and make the final decision, we will talk about if we are capable of doing this. So no hard stuff until then. Just the 'getting to know you' bit?" she asks, looking up at me through her long lashes. It's not a bad idea.

"So, nothing you wouldn't talk about for the first month of dating. That kind of thing?" I reply.

"Exactly." A smile creeps across her gorgeous face as I start to nervously chuckle. She looks confused by my anxiety and her eyebrows raise in question.

"I would find it easier to tell you that I kill people for a living and come from a messed up Irish crime Family, rather than tell you about some of the girls I've seen in the past." Now her smile returns and as she lightly giggles along with me, I realise her laughter is exactly what I want to hear.

"Well, I'm keen to hear about all the ways you met your past women. I'm hoping kidnap and ransom isn't something you use for everyone," she jokes, and honestly, I'm not sure she really wants to know the answer. I cock my eyebrow, silently asking if this is really where we are starting with the hard topics.

"Maybe we should at least get unpacked first?" I ask and this time she full-on laughs and agrees. She looks so much younger and freer when she laughs. She doesn't appear as serious as I have come to expect from her in just the last day or so. I know she is trying to make it in a very male dominated world which is not going to be an easy feat, she is going to have to come across as a hard faced bitch. But I'm really pleased to know she can turn that persona on and off.

Before I even realise what she is doing, she drops the bag she is carrying. It's only got some random bits of food and household things we decided to bring until we could shop for the rest. She insisted on carrying something and moaned like crazy when I gave her the lightest item. I couldn't exactly give her the case full of weapons that weighed a tonne. As soon as the bag hits the floor she takes the weapons bag off me and places it on the floor, and takes hold of my hand. She starts walking into the main area of the house, pulling me along after her, our fingers laced together and I have no choice but to drop the rest of the suitcases to follow her.

From the second our hands touched, I felt almost like the opposite of an electric shock, and I say opposite because rather than me wanting to recoil and pull away from the sensation her hand causes against mine, I want to pull it close. The tingle against my palm spreads over my entire body and I feel it in my nerve endings, heat chasing through my veins. It also seems to have a direct line with my cock because I feel myself straining against my jeans, begging to be freed. If she wasn't pulling me to follow her, I think my cock would be leading the way and ensuring we follow wherever she wants to go.

Don't get me wrong, I've been with girls in the past. In fact, I've been with a few more than I should have, but it comes along with the lifestyle. I travelled to different cities, scoping out my targets, sometimes for months at a time. In that time, I was able to become whoever I wanted to be and fuck wherever I wanted, to detract from the job I was there to do. I don't say that because I don't like my job as I do. What I hate is that I was never given a choice. Most kids are encouraged to experiment, think about all the different avenues they could explore and all the different things they could become. Not me. I was raised to be an assassin. I was forced into this world. My family decided what skills they needed and I had no choice but to become what they needed. I may work for myself now, but for years I was given no choice. I had to work for my father, until I was brave enough to risk everything and leave.

I was eight when I saw my first kill, and I learnt to turn off my emotions pretty quickly after that. I'm not your typical hitman who is usually sadistic, who doesn't have any idea about emotions, and lives for the kill. That's not me. I kill because it's what I'm good at, and it's all I know, but I have morals. I choose which jobs I take on, and I never kill anyone that I don't think deserves it. I make it quick, never one to torture. I am not someone who typically likes to cause pain in any aspect of my life. Yet, if the need called for it, to protect what is important to me, I would stop at nothing to bring the person responsible down, painfully. My mind instantly flashes to this alluring girl in front of me who is leading me into the biggest kitchen I have ever seen with the most dazzling smile on her face. I would burn the world down to destroy anyone who hurts her.

As she takes me on a tour of the house, I am in awe of the amazing place. I expect to see her grandfather's things everywhere, but there is nothing. Every room we go to seems to be even bigger and better than the last.

"Where are all your grandfather's things?" I enquire.

"Oh, this is just one of his many holiday homes. I can't actually remember the last time he used it. With Gran being unwell, they don't travel much. I was here a lot as a kid, but it has been years. I forgot how beautiful this place is," she muses before continuing to answer my initial question. "He will have sent someone to collect what little things he does keep here when they brought the stuff for me. He told me they left it in the living room, so I will grab it after the tour," Bree replies as she pulls me up the stairs.

There are six bedrooms in total and, feeling gentlemanly, I offer her the large master bedroom. In true Bree style, she laughs. "It's not your bedroom to give away. You didn't think I was going to let you take that massive bed, did you?" she jokes as she points to the large bed in the middle of the room. My mind goes to some very sexy places that include me, Bree, and that bed. I open the en-suite door to continue my tour and try to get my cock to calm down.

The master bedroom has a giant en-suite with a shower big enough to fit about six people. Not to mention the massive walk-in closet that I am sure she will love. I mention this and she scoffs, saying she would prefer the weapons room to that. Fuck, she really might be my perfect girl.

I choose the bedroom right next door to hers and make all sorts of bullshit about it being for security, even going as far as saying that the view and balcony drew me in. It's all lies. I just wanted to be close to her. The desire to get to know her, spend time with her, and protect her echoes through every fibre of my being. Every time she smiles at me, cracks a joke that makes her laugh, or even when she gets snarky with me, I want to fall at her knees and worship her. I have been attracted to women before, but the way I feel about my little firecracker could be my downfall.

Thankfully, we part after the tour so we can both get settled in. We agreed to meet up in a couple of hours for a pizza. I stayed in my room getting unpacked. As I am getting settled in, my tablet starts making a tingling sound letting me know I am getting a video call, and that can only be from one person. Settling on the bed, sitting up with my back against the headrest, I open my tablet and accept the call. I am greeted by the sight of my best friend, looking extremely exhausted, holding onto the most beautiful baby girl I have ever seen. She is only two months old, but she looks so much smaller compared to her daddy's large, bulky frame. Her normally wide, piercing blue eyes are closed and her cute little mouth is sitting open in the shape of an O. She is wearing the cutest pink dress and has a pink bow on the top of her head. She doesn't have much hair yet, and those she does have are so light they almost appear white, which makes it look like she is bald. Even if she was bald, I would still adore this little girl with all my heart.

"Alright, Brother. You are looking exhausted. How's my baby girl doing?" I ask Kellan. He may not be my real blood brother, but I am closer to him than I have ever been to any of my real asshole brothers.

Kellan and I grew up together. His father worked with mine, and after his father was killed working for our Family, he came to stay with us. My father wanted Kellan to join our Family business, but I made it very clear he was to be kept out of it. Kel wears his heart on his sleeve, and it would eat him alive if he had to live my life. Luckily, my father has no idea that Kel is a world class hacker. He is probably the best in the business, but he keeps his talents hidden. He pushes himself, simply because he wants to. Once, he hacked into New Scotland Yard and gave the people who arrested his father's killer a raise. He then wrote to them, anonymously of course, telling them about the back door access he had found, and the code he had written to fix it for them. Obviously, he left a little hole that only he could find. You never know when someone in our business might need to get in.

Kellan has been working with me since I branched off from my family, and started working independently. He hacks security feeds, helps me to assess my clients and targets. He also covers up my hits, making all traces of me even being in that city disappear within seconds. I would be lost or in prison without him. But since Hallie was born he has had a real struggle adapting. Being a single dad is hard, but I know he wouldn't change it for the world. That little girl, my god-daughter, has him wrapped around her little finger without even trying.

"She's a fucking angel when she is asleep. Sadly, this doesn't last very long. The health visitor who came to weigh her and do all her checkups basically said she's a little smaller than average, but that isn't a bad thing. She is consistently growing, which is good. Apparently, this new sleep pattern where she wakes up every two hours to feed is normal. She may be having a growth spurt. It's either that or she is becoming a vampire because the girl has no concept that you sleep at night, not during the day," he says, almost like a whisper. He keeps casually casting his eyes down to check on Hallie, no doubt hoping she doesn't wake up.

"She is not a vampire. If the professional says it's normal then it is. I'm glad Hal's going through a growth spurt, maybe I won't feel like I'm going to break her every time I pick her up if she's a bit bigger," I joke, but it's true. The first time I held her, she was five hours old and weighed just over six pounds. I was terrified, but never has someone captured my heart so quickly. Looking at her perfect, tiny face, with the same wide piercing blue eyes she still sees on me now, I knew she had me. It was almost like I realised for the first time in a long time that I was capable of loving someone. I had forgotten I had a heart until Hallie woke it up. Though now it might be beating for another girl in the room next door.

"I hope so too. Fuck, mate, I am dying here. I don't know if I can do this anymore," my best friend whispers, and I see his face crumpled as the words leave his mouth. I know just saying the words out loud will have slaughtered him, and I think the only other time I have seen his eyes fill with tears was when she was born. He looks at Hallie, like she may have heard him, and that causes him to fall further. I hate seeing him like this.

"Hey! Kellan, listen to me right now. That little girl isn't looking for perfection. She knows you are going to fuck things up as you go. All she needs is for you to be there for her, take care of her, and show her the love she needs. No matter how tired you get, that's not going to change. All she wants is to be loved and cared for. You not only can do that, you have to. She has nobody else," I say firmly. I hate that I am playing the emotional manipulation card, but it's true.

"My mum was here today," he starts and I can't help interrupting him.

"Fuck, I should have known as soon as I saw the bloody bow. If she voiced her opinion that Hallie looks too much like a boy to be beautiful again, I may have to reevaluate my no punching women stance," I grind out, fury rippling over my body. His mother is a right piece of work, and I should have known she played a part in this depressive episode. When I spoke to him yesterday about the security on this place, he was fine. It never occurred to me that he would have had to ask his mum to babysit to do the job. I just had visions of him bringing her, attached to his chest with that sling she loves to be in so much, as he teaches her all about her daddy's job. If I had known I would have taken her. My desire to keep her away from that witch runs deep. She was incapable of raising Kellan, so why the fuck she feels she can comment on how he raises his little girl is beyond me.

"She wants custody, Liam. She said she is going to go to court if I don't sign the rights over. Asshole husband number five, with very deep pockets, has offered to buy the best lawyer in the country to help her fight. She says she is going to paint me as an unfit father. If I don't want to drag Hallie through social service assessments, and court cases then I have to hand her over. I'm fucked," he explains, the tears now falling free as he stares at the beauty in his arms.

"Fuck, I thought I hated that bitch before, but that's nothing compared to what I am feeling now. Look, Kel, we fight this. You have raised that beautiful little girl that you are currently cradling, all by yourself since her piss poor excuse for a mother left her at just five hours old. You are the one that has been there night and day. You are her dad, she needs you. That bitch couldn't even raise you, abandoning you at six years old. Is she going to do that with Hallie too? We are fighting this. I am going to find the best lawyer, and if I have to overpay to buy them out from under her husband then that is what we will do. But you have to fight this, Kellan. Look at Hallie. Could you really live without her?" I ask, already knowing the answer. He may be exhausted, stressed, and broken, but none of that matters when it comes to giving Hallie what she needs.

"You already know I can't. The idea of that cunt raising my beautiful baby gets my blood boiling. But I just can't see the court's finding in my favour. She will find every skeleton I have and use it against me. I can't lose her. Would you really help me? I can't ask you to spend that much money, Liam."

My laughter echoes through the speaker and Hallie must have heard because she starts wiggling in her dad's arms. We both freeze, like she is a bomb that is about to explode. If we stay silent and still, maybe she won't wake up. I can see the plea in Kel's eyes, like he is mentally willing her to stay asleep. She stops wiggling, almost like she had only moved to make herself look comfortable, before letting out the cutest little baby snore. We both stare at her in awe. How this tiny little girl manages to manipulate two guys like us, is amazing. I just know we will be fucked when she grows up.

"Kel, I would throw money at any plan that involved destroying that bitch of a mother of yours. But I would give everything I owned to you and that little angel. So, don't even bother asking. I am telling you, I'm doing it. Why don't you come to the house one day this week and we can brainstorm? I will do some research and speak to some lawyers in the meantime. That sound okay? And if all else fails, I can always kill her," I joke. I should be offended that he doesn't already know I would move heaven and Earth for him, let alone her. I think he is just so scared and tired that he isn't thinking clearly, but I am here to remind him. No matter how despondent he gets, I will be here.

"Thanks, mate. I may take you up on the killing part if things don't go my way. Do I get to meet this new girl? Are you ever going to tell me what is going on? I know you are lying to me. There is no way you are working security and protecting some mafia princess. I know you, there's no way you would take a job like that," he says, his molten grey eyes staring straight at me. No longer filled with tears, they now look suspiciously at me.

I knew he wouldn't have condoned me taking Bree hostage and using her for the ransom. Kellan offered on more than one occasion to simply hack into Vernon's accounts and take what is mine, but I didn't want that. I needed Vernon to give it to me, I was owed it. I shouldn't have to steal what is mine. I would have told Kellan what happened straight after, but things escalated beyond what I had planned. How do I tell him that not only did I kidnap her, despite him telling me not to, but I also agreed to marry Bree?

He will tell me the millions of reasons I should have said no, and honestly, I already know all of those excuses. They streamed through my brain on repeat from the minute the idea was proposed. It may have been in the contract, but Bree was the one who rolled with it. For some reason, I couldn't say no. I wanted to help Bree. I knew she was fierce and determined enough to succeed in this world. She has what it takes to be the queen of our world. Maybe I wanted to make sure I was standing by her side as she breaks down every wall that stands in her way. Or maybe it's just her. Her smile, her snarky responses, her sexy curves, or the blush that spreads across her cheeks when I catch her staring at me. I know the minute Kellen finds out he will accuse me of thinking with my cock instead of my head, hence why I am stalling that conversation for another day.

"I will tell you everything when I see you. Send me a text letting me know when you wanna come over, but give me a couple of days to do my research. Oh, and don't even think about not bringing Hallie. I am missing her already and I only saw her three days ago. If she is having a growth spurt, I might not recognise her," I say, in mock fear. Kellan chuckles, before stopping himself and staring at Hallie again, hoping she doesn't wake up from the movement. She continues to lay there peacefully.

"She will look exactly the same, minus this fucking bow. Besides, now I know her intentions, there's no way I am leaving her with my mother ever again. I hated the idea of her even being in our lives to start with, but I needed the help. Plus, I wanted Hallie to have a female in her life. Too bad all the women we know are massive twats," he ground out. I instantly think of Bree and want to defend her sex, but sadly, Kellan doesn't exactly have a track record when it comes to the women in his life. They all abandon him and leave him lost and lonely. After Hallie's mother, I don't think I will ever get him to take a chance on a woman again.

Kellan must see this flash across my face, a knowing smirk replaces the anger that had been burning bright in his eyes.

"You like this girl," he states, not even a question.

"Fuck off. I will see you in a couple of days. I will tell you everything that is going on then, but if you need me before just shout. Even if you wanna come and stay with me for a couple of days to help with Hal, Bree won't mind." I don't know why I say that final part with such conviction. I don't know anything about Bree really, or if she would be pissed if I invited a single dad and his little baby to stay with us. But there's a part of me that is very sure. I really do need to get to know her properly.

Kellan and I say our goodbyes once Hallie starts to wake up and demands food. I have a lot of respect for my friend, stepping up and caring for a baby on his own. He didn't even want to be a dad. Hallie wasn't exactly planned, but from the second she entered his world, he changed. He became her dad and everything else came second. Sadly, that wasn't what happened with her mother.

Kellan kept dropping hints that he suspected there was more to mine and Bree's story and that he knew I liked this girl. The more he spoke, the more I realised that I don't really know Bree, but I want to. So, let's do this whole dating thing and find out if we are capable of at least becoming friends before we take on all the gangs, and mob bosses that will come for us when they find out a woman is running the O'Keenan London branch. I hope Bree knows that we are in for one hell of a battle, but like she said, that's a discussion for another day.

CHAPTER TEN

Bree

Standing in front of the mirror, looking at myself in the black lace panties and matching bra set I put on, I can't help but shake my head. I am going downstairs, into my own living room, to order pizza and get to know my kidnapper. Why the fuck does that mean I need to wear sexy lingerie?

I try telling myself that it's so I feel confident, that I know I look hot underneath my clothing, and that Liam won't know, kinda like my own little secret. The only problem with that theory is that as I was putting them on, all I could think about was Liam taking them off. What the fuck is wrong with me?

I try to tell myself that this is all based on looks. That I am just attracted to him. His rugged face and rock hard body, but he is more than just my type. If I was to create one guy that was made exactly for me, he is exactly what I would be designing. So, maybe I should just fuck him and get over it? It could just be the attraction and craving that is blinding me. But if I do fuck him and don't want more, how do I then create a relationship with him that could lead to a successful marriage. Which is exactly why I need to think with my head and not the ache in my pussy.

From the few conversations I have had with Liam, I

can tell he is fiercely protective, but he also has a good moral compass which is what I will need by my side in the future. I'm not naive enough to think I won't have to lead by example. I will have to get my hands dirty, and I am more than happy to do that. I know there will be people who step forward to challenge me, and the idea of making my enemies bleed fills me with a buzzing energy. This is what I have waited for, the chance to prove I can live in a man's world. But I'm not just going to live in a man's world, I'm going to take down everyone in my way until I rule over them. There will be no doubt over whether a woman can be in power, I will prove myself. I need to know that Liam will have my back, or this will never work.

Apologising to the ache in my core, and guaranteeing it some vibe time later, I quickly throw on some black leggings and a baggy, grey t-shirt that falls off one shoulder, exposing the tip of my back bra. Giving Liam just that small glimpse of skin, on the off chance he wants to look. Mentally chastising myself, I make sure I am focused on the fact I need to get to know him properly, not fuck him.

Walking into the living room, I notice Liam isn't there yet. I am five minutes early anyway. I grab two bottles of beer that were already stocked in the fridge. I don't even question whether Liam likes a beer or not, he's Irish after all. Pulling out the phone my Gramps left me, I am amazed he got it here in time. I look up the local pizza place's menu on my phone and scroll through, glancing at their options. I don't know why I bother, I always purchase the four cheese stuffed crust. It's the same order every time. What can I say, I like cheese!

While I am drooling at the different pizzas listed, Liam's door opens and as he walks into the room he starts pulling his t-shirt on. Now I am drooling for a very different reason. He is wearing grey sweats, hanging low on his hips, showing off that delicious V containing the most alluring happy trail. I can't even tell if he has a six or eight pack because my eyes are drawn to the mass of dark ink swirls covering his hard chest. His tattoos are beautiful and look like they tell a story, one I am only too happy to stare at for hours and read them fully. I mentally beg for him to take his time lowering his t-shirt, but sadly it is over too quickly. He covers them over with a bright white t-shirt, and I actually pout. I don't know if he realises that they are still slightly visible as the white on his shirt is almost see-through.

Focus, Bree! Get to know him, not his body! I mentally chastise myself once again for admiring his heaven sent body. He flops into the chair opposite my sofa with ease, and he lounges there like the chair was made for him. Considering it's not his house, and I'm almost a stranger, I thought he might feel a bit uncomfortable here. But I am fast learning that Liam is laid back, and could be comfortable anywhere.

"So, I heard there was pizza involved in this little getting to know each other evening. Shall we order first then dive right in?" he asks with that sexy smirk he seems to wear so well. The thought of him diving into my sexy black panties has me distracted all over again.

"Yes…pizza…let's do that," I mutter, unable to form a coherent sentence when all I can feel is my core heating up just thinking of him. What the hell is wrong with me? I know how to control myself. Fuck, I have been training myself to control my emotions and my feelings for years now. It's going to be an essential skill to have when dealing with criminals continuously. So why can Liam break down all the barriers I spent years building?

I place the order on my phone after talking through pizza options. I should have known he would want something like a meat feast. A guy as beefy as him doesn't get that way by just eating cheese. But at least he didn't ask for pineapple. I would have had to demand he leave right away, no matter how much I need him. I can't be married to a guy who likes pineapple on a pizza, or at all ideally.

"So how do we go about this whole getting to know you thing? Obviously, I know how to date, but this doesn't feel like a date. What do you have in mind?" Liam asks me, his arms reaching around to lace his fingers at the back of his head. His biceps bulge against the white fabric, as his muscles tense. I know there are women out there who love a bit of arm porn, but I have never seen it. Until now.

"Honestly, I had nothing planned other than alcohol and talking," I say, taking a large swig of my beer from the bottle. Liam reaches over to his own bottle that I left out for him. He tips the neck of the bottle towards me, in a thank you gesture, before taking a large gulp. Fuck, is everything he does sexy?

"Okay, so maybe like a twenty question style format, or never have I ever when we get really tipsy. Maybe when we are really fucked we can go for truth or dare. I didn't go to university and I didn't really have time to socialise in high school, so that is the extent of my 'getting to know you' knowledge," he explains, playing with the rim of the beer bottle with his thumb. His eyes are downcast as he tells me about his lack of experience with friends. It's almost like he is ashamed.

In the time we had to get ready, I did some research on Liam. I couldn't find much, if anything. He is practically a ghost with no electronic footprint. But I guess that is standard practice for a hitman. So, I called Jimmy. He is the person who taught me everything. He is my father's head of security, but I hope one day he will work for me. He is like a second father to me, and our call didn't go as I had planned.

Sitting on the bed, trying not to imagine what Liam is up to next door, I decide I need to know everything there is to know about him. There's nothing online, so I call the one person who knows everyone and everything there is to know about the people in our world.

"Fuck, Bee, are you okay? I have been so worried about you. I am going to kill that cunt, Doughty. Thinking he can take my girl and get away with it," Jimmy rants, not even bothering to say hello or wait for me to respond. The anger is obvious, but I can also hear the fear lacing his words. He really means it when he says I'm like his daughter. He practically raised me and has been in my life since I was a baby. Growing up he used to call me his Bumblebee. Now, it's just Bee, but we both know what it means.

"Jimmy! Relax, you are going to give yourself another heart attack!" I shout, genuinely worried about his stress levels.

When he had his heart attack last year, I was terrified I would lose the one man in my life who has always believed in me. I should have known he wouldn't give in that easily. He also made it quite clear that despite doctors telling him to reduce his stress levels, and cut down on overworking, he was not going to be following orders. He refused to change his diet. Jimmy's philosophy is that his time is up when it's up, and so he might as well live life to the fullest while he can. Something he has been trying to teach me as well. I just don't ever want to lose him, but he is okay with his time coming. Living in our world, we accept death as a big part of it. To make it to his fifties, with so many targets on his back is a fucking massive achievement. I guess now I am going to have to learn to survive when my targets start to appear too.

"I will relax when you are back home. Look, I know what your father

did to Liam was wrong, but this deal you have going on with him is crazy, Bree. You will get your crown one day, you don't need to marry someone who fucking kidnaps you for attention. Are you crazy?!" he shouts and all I can do is roll my eyes.

"Jim, you know me. When do I ever make a rash decision? You know I have been looking for someone suitable to stand by my side, to help me fight, to rule the business. I know Liam was bang out of order kidnapping me, and trust me when I say I made sure he knows how pissed I was at that. But I'm not seeing him through rose-tinted glasses when I asked for his help. I did it because I could tell he was different. He didn't hurt me in any way. He may be a cocky twat but he was never condescending. He saw the real me from the first moment, and even without knowing it was something I was battling against he couldn't understand how my dad doesn't see my power and determination. After spending such a short space of time with me, he knew I was capable of doing anything. He sees me, Jim. Plus, he never demanded more than he was owed. He isn't greedy or holding me hostage so he can demand money that he hasn't earned. He seems honest and has integrity. I know we have a lot to learn about each other still, though," I state decisively. It is important that Jim knows and understands why I chose Liam.

"I know you don't make reckless decisions, Bee. But I have met Liam a couple of times and I know how much of a charming asshole he can be. He is clearly a good looking bloke, and I don't want that to influence your decision here." He is trying his hardest not to say that Liam is hot, and I can hear how much it pains him to even bring it up. It must be a real fear for him that I am acting on lust and not my brains.

"Look, there is no denying he's good looking, but that is irrelevant. This decision is a business decision and was made with my brain and not my vagina. You have to trust me on this one," I state and I hear the little groan he releases when I say the word vagina. The idea that I even have one is probably too much for him to take. If he thinks about all the guys I let near it he would go on a murderous rampage, so it's best for him to forget or pretend I don't have one at all. I'm still a virgin in his head and will be until I'm married, or preferably until I die.

"Okay, I do trust you, Bee. I just had to be sure. I was so mad that Liam was able to get past all my security. It was my job to keep you safe and I failed. I'm so sorry, Bumblebee." His voice is laced with pain and I can tell he really does feel responsible for this happening to me.

"This is not your fault, Jimmy. Liam is the best in the business, you know that. I'm sure once we finalise our agreement he will work with you and explain the security issues, but I want you to know that I don't blame

you. Hell, even I tried to fight him, managing to get a shot off too. But he was prepared and I got him in the vest. Liam is just good at what he does, which goes into the pro column," I state firmly, ensuring he knows that I mean what I say. He is not to blame and never would be in my eyes. I know my father will be blaming him, my mother in particular. They both hate that I have a better relationship with Jimmy than I do them, but they know they can't afford to let him go. Their security would be a lot fucking worse without Jimmy Neil.

"Pro column?" he asks, clearly pleased we are moving away from what he usually refers to as the soppy stuff.

"Yeah, I am trying to find out everything I can about him. Putting together a list of pros and cons around if he would make a good husband and partner. But he has no electronic footprint. So, I need to know what you know about him. I know you said you met him a few times and I also know that if my father needed an assassin you would be the one to find and properly vet the candidates. I need you to tell me everything," I plead.

"Honestly, I don't know much other than he is fucking great at what he does. But he has a moral compass that not everyone in our world agrees with. If we hire someone to do a job, the reason behind the job is not important, yet to Liam it is. That is part of the reason why he was basically disowned by the Doughty clan. They're an Irish firm that has had their eyes on our London branch for a long time. They have been slowly branching out all across Ireland. The leader, Liam's father, is a hard bastard. He basically started training his children at very young ages to be part of the business. Liam is the middle child, and if my sources are correct he was the most promising of all five. He has two older brothers that are good, but nowhere near Liam's level. They lack the intelligence that Liam has. He then has two younger sisters that he has been protecting since he turned eighteen. He pays for their tuition at a boarding school, which annoys his father as he wanted to use them. Virgins bring a high price, and the fact they are his daughters is irrelevant. Liam put a stop to it before anything happened, but from what I heard, that's what forced Liam to pull away for good. I don't know anything else about him, really. He's intelligent, caring, and a fucking great shot. I know his humanity makes him appealing in the sense he's like a bad boy with a soul. But in our world, I think having a conscience will get you both killed."

The more Jimmy spoke the more I got a clearer view of Liam's past. He grew up in a family with expectations. He's a lot more clever and a lot more skilled than I realised and that intrigues me. But the part of the story that won me over is the love he has for his sisters. It must have *taken a lot of balls to fight against the family that raised you, to fight against everything you are taught to be. His need to protect his sisters rang clearer than any other thing that had been drilled into him. It's that protectiveness that I need by my side.*

"Thanks, Jimmy. I know I should have talked this through with you before I steamrolled ahead, but honestly, I think Liam might be the right choice. I really do. I am going to take some time to get to know him. That way you can be perfectly sure that when we do get married, I am doing it because Liam is the right choice. Please, promise me you will keep an open mind until then. Okay?' I ask, trying to sound as hopeful as possible.

"When you are sure he is the right choice, the one you want by your side for life, then I want to talk to him. I won't give you my blessing until I have spoken to him," he states and I groan. I should have known he would need to interrogate him.

"Fine, but you be nice," I say and he laughs. It's such a deep rumble that I can tell he genuinely means it and that makes me smile.

"I will be as nice as I can to a man who kidnapped my girl. If you decide you aren't going to marry him, can I kill him then?" he asks, sounding more energetic than he has throughout our entire conversation. I shouldn't be surprised, he loves chaos and violence. He thrives on it, and part of the bloodlust I developed came from him. You can't rule without tearing down the world that was there before. Dancing in their blood is the only way to celebrate your rule.

I'm pulled out of my thoughts by Liam clearing his throat and I realise I was too busy in my own head to have answered his question about the 'getting to know you' twenty questions we just agreed on.

"I don't know much more than that. I was basically raised in a crime Family, remember? My father spent most of the time trying to wrap me up in cotton wool, so I wouldn't see what was surrounding me. My mother spent all her time trying to get me out of this world. Signing me up for class after class on things I had no interest in, but would make me more appealing to a rich man who could whisk me away to live the life she never got. Then there's Jimmy, my dad's head of security. He's the only one who sees me. He spent time teaching me about our world, how to fight, how to dominate, and how to rule. Sadly, that didn't really encourage friendships or parties. Me and my best friend, Mia, went to a few, but she is from a really strict family too. So it wasn't easy for us.

74

Most of what I know is from TV. So, after a long ramble, the short answer to your question is that I think the twenty question style works well for now," I answer and Liam laughs. It's a genuine laugh that rings in my ears and lights up his face. I have no choice but to smile. His carefree attitude is contagious. I feel myself relaxing against the sofa. My posture, the one I was taught to maintain at all times in one of the etiquette classes Mum sent me to, goes to hell and I finally relax. Just two friends sharing a drink and having a chat.

"Why do I get the feeling you are not a short answer kind of girl?" he teases and it's my turn to laugh.

"I would apologise, but I am not sorry. I am a talker. You will have to learn to live with it." I spoke the words firmly, but my eyes shone bright along with my smile, letting him know I'm joking. His responding laughter makes my stomach do little flips. I am so fucked.

CHAPTER ELEVEN

Bree

Time passes quickly as we fall into comfortable conversation while waiting for the pizza. We talk about movies I love, but he won't even give them a chance. We bantered over my love of classic crime films like Snatch, Lock Stock and Two Smoking Barrels; any tongue in cheek look at the industry I know all too well. On the other hand, Liam can't stand watching films featuring a hitman, hating how unrealistic they are. Still, as I pointed out to him, it's not like Hollywood can put out an advert for an assassin to liaise with them. As the night goes on, we both start feeling more comfortable with each other.

Once the pizza arrives, we work together to set them up on the coffee table in front of the sofa while Liam replaces our empty beer bottles. When he returns to sit back down, this time, he opts for the other end of the same couch I'm sitting on. My breath hitches as I feel him shuffle closer and lean forward. My brain is going through all manner of thoughts, none of which followed my 'just getting to know him' plan. Luckily, Liam seems to be very interested in the piece of pizza he picks up instead of me. He takes a bite of his pizza and I am entranced as he licks his lips. Watching his tongue trace across his soft lips does crazy things to my insides, I can feel my body lighting on fire. I try to suppress the groan that's desperate to escape, but he must have heard it, and looks over at me with his eyebrow raised in question.

"What can I say? I love pizza," I mumble, trying to think of any excuse to cover up that I was ogling him. I groan loudly and entirely on purpose with the next bite. His eyes widen as the sound registers, and he shuffles uncomfortably. Is it freaking him out? Or is he shuffling because he is just as turned on as I am? I know which I would prefer but I am worried I might have weirded him out. I really should have made my game plan about how to not look like a complete idiot.

"So, we have covered all the easy ones like favourite movies, music, books, food, times of the year, and even weather. I think it's time we go a little deeper, don't you?" he asks, his lips moving to touch the rim of the beer bottle before taking another drink.

"I don't mind deep, you can go as deep as you like," I say, not realising that my words sound like a dirty innuendo until they are out for all to hear. It's like the words leave my mouth before I have even thought about what I'm saying. My word vomit results in his smile turning into a massive, cocky grin. My cheeks flood with heat, the blush colour rising quickly as his questions what I said. His piercing eyes are alive with laughter as he tries his hardest to look like he was taking what I said seriously. He starts to speak, but I soon cut him off.

"Fuck off, don't say anything about what I just said. To answer your original question properly, what type of topic do you have in mind? It is your question to ask next anyway," I speak firmly, shuffling on my side of the sofa, tucking one of my legs under my ass to get comfortable. I'm trying not to notice how we've both shuffled to get more comfortable and that's brought us closer together. The gap between us is so small now.

"I know we said nothing heavy, but I think it makes up a big part of who we are, so I can't ignore it. What made you want to be part of this world? You said your mum would do anything in her power to keep you out of it. Why were you not interested?" he asks, and I smile. This was probably a more straightforward question than asking me my favourite type of music. This was an integral part of me and who I am.

"This is easy. My mum would send me to etiquette classes, dance classes, extra tuition, anything she could think of to make me an appealing prospect. But, believe it or not, men are not exactly banging down my door to date me—" Before I could even finish my sentence, he interrupts me.

"No fucking way. Sorry, but I don't believe you didn't have

guys interested in you," Liam states firmly, disbelieving.

"So, there were two types of guys who were interested. The first was the type of guy who knew all about my grandfather's inheritance. So they basically were only dating me to stand a chance at getting my dad's company. It was a power thing. The second was the bad boys, the ones who wanted to show my dad how big their balls were. They wanted to affirm that they weren't scared of him, and to prove it, they went after the one thing he always said was off-limits. But as I'm sure you have worked out, neither were really interested in me. They either wanted my connections or wanted to say a big fuck you to my family. The first is so obnoxious; they usually hate the idea that I have my own mind. The second was good in bed, but they weren't really there for me either. It all got boring quickly," I explain.

Liam hasn't said a word, so I pull my eyes from concentrating on the beer bottle, my typical shy go-to, and I look straight at him. His beautiful green eyes are boring into me, an angry expression morphing his face. Gone is the usually carefree, cocky smile that I have become used to. Replacing it is a stern scowl that transforms not just his face but also his whole body language. I realise now I am meeting the business side of Liam, the one he utilises when doing a hit. But why is he angry at me? Before I can ask, he steps in.

"I can't believe guys would use you like that. I know I kidnapped you, but that is different. The idea of using you, having sex with you either to get what I want or to get one over on your father just seems disgusting. I hate that they would use you like that," he grinds out, and I can't help but smile.

"Look at you getting all protective. We aren't even properly engaged yet," I joke. But, thankfully, the fun, cocky persona soon returns, and I was so pleased to see it.

"Sorry, I hate to break it to you, but I feel the same way about any woman. They should never have sex used as a weapon against them. It's too much of a personal thing."

"Have you considered, maybe I used them for sex? The assholes that wanted to get one over my father, of course, I knew their intentions. I also know that the ones I did fuck had good reputations, which is why I had sex with them. But, most of the time, I wanted to say fuck you to my father too. So why not do that and get some great sex at the same time?" I ask, and a mixture of emotions flash across his face in response. First, he looks mad as hell, but then there was also a different type of fire burning in his eyes, and I think he might be turned on by the idea of me having mind-blowing sex. Sadly, I embellished slightly.

"Okay, we need to change the subject. I do not want to hear about you having sex with other men," he grinds out, and I chuckle. He stands up, clearly looking for something to do as a distraction, and goes to the fridge to bring us two more beers. His beer was drained, and mine was almost done, so replacements were essential. I need to be careful about having too much, the last thing I want to do is get drunk. I already feel a bit on the merry side, which is probably why more word vomit escapes my lips.

"Okay, so I may have lied. The sex with the bad boys was always better than the dickheads vying for power. Still, none could ever be classed as mind-blowing," I practically whisper into my beer bottle. Finishing the last of the sweet tangy liquid, I quickly swap it for the new one Liam just sat down on the coffee table.

Liam sits back down in the middle of the sofa this time. He's so close to me now that our legs are mere inches from touching. His eyes bore into mine like he is trying to see deep into my soul.

"What do you mean, it wasn't mind-blowing? With any of them?" he asks.

"Woah, you make it sound like I have slept with loads of guys when it's been like six. But no, none of them was what I would call mind-blowing. They were more interested in taking their own pleasure rather than giving, if you know what I mean," I say whilst wagging my eyebrows suggestively, along with a bit of wink at the end. I was trying to look sexy and suggestive, but in fact, I probably looked like I had some kind of eye infection. Fuck, I couldn't do sexy even if I wanted to.

"Hold on. So what you are saying is that you have been with six guys, and not one of them put you first? Please tell me they at least helped you get there in the end, even if they got to the finish line first, so to speak." I can't help but laugh. I love the little innuendos he's using, like he just couldn't bring himself to say the actual words. My thoughts on the subject are that if you can't say it, you probably shouldn't be doing it.

"I'm assuming you mean, did they give me an orgasm even if they came first?" I ask him bluntly. "I have found that men who don't know how to say it can't do it," I tease cryptically, but Liam's cocky face says he isn't going to let me get away with that bit of dig.

"Oh, Princess, not only can I say it, I can do it too. I was just trying to be polite with you, but I won't hold back if you want the real me. So yes, what I'm asking is if the sack of shits you dated before could give you earth-shattering, toe-curling orgasms, whether they had finished first or not." His voice has taken on a new gravely tone that sounds almost raspy. As he speaks, he practically growls. The sound of him talking about the mind-blowing orgasms he claims he can give has my ovaries clenching and my pussy starting to feel wet.

"Never...I've never had an orgasm given to me by someone else," I whisper, hoping the ground will swallow me up. Instead, my admission rings through the air as though I shouted it.

"Fuck, you really have dated a lot of twatwaffles. I have no idea what will happen between us or if we will ever progress to a sexual relationship in our marriage, but I can fucking guarantee that you will come every time with me. I would make sure my tongue craves your taste, my fingers desperate to feel your pussy hungrily grip them for more, and my cock owning all your holes. I would make sure I learnt to play your body like a complex instrument, and only I know how to make you sing. You can rule in public, but I am always in charge when it comes to sex, and whether you want to or not, your body would bend to my will. I would own you." The dirtiness of his words, the hard, sensual look on his face, and the short, sharp breathy moans he releases as he speaks tip me over the edge.

I have never liked the idea of a man dominating me in any way, let alone in a way so personal. Yet the way Liam speaks, like it would be inevitable if we were ever to go down that road, I can believe him. As he speaks, not only do I feel myself getting wetter, I feel my body start to come alive. An electric hum seems to echo along my nerves, spreading throughout my body, warming me more than I needed. I've never had someone turn me on so much with their words. My brain is so befuddled by his words that I literally cannot form a decent sentence.

"Erm...I...what...It's hard. No...not that. Fuck..." What the fuck is wrong with me? The two words I manage to string together make it sound like I'm talking about his hard cock, which of course, gets me looking straight at his crotch. There's no denying he is pitching a tent. I look away quickly, hoping he missed me, but his laughter rings out around us.

"Okay, we have got off track here. I wanted to know why you

choose guns over ballgowns. I think that's a much safer 'getting to know you' topic than one that has you looking at my dick," he laughs. Busted. I should have known he saw me.

"I'm not going to deny it. You know you are hot and are physically my type, but no matter how much I might want to fuck you, that's not what this is about. I need someone who believes in me. Someone who can stand by my side and let me lead, not feel the need to take over. I also need someone who will protect me when I can't protect myself. That is what I am more interested in finding. So, I will answer your question, and then I'm going to bed because I've had a couple of beers more than I should. I'm moving into the land of mistakes," I say, trying my best to sound firm and confident. His smile in response to my rambling is blinding.

"I am willing to take the time to show you that I am all those things. I may have only known you for a short time, but I already see that you are formidable. How your dad has never noticed is baffling, and despite the fact I very much want to fuck you too, we will keep this professional…for now." He practically sings the last word, making it clear we will address it in the future. Hearing that he wants me too, the words rippled over my skin. Fuck, I want him badly, but I meant what I said, business first.

We talked for ages about how I hated my mother's choice of lessons and how I trained in secret with Jimmy. I told him about the blood rush I felt at sixteen when I tortured my first traitor. He tried to report my dad to the police, but what he didn't know is that the police are in our pockets. We own most of the officials in the city, it's how we get away with so much shit. Liam leans closer as I describe the rush I felt using my dagger to draw that first drop of blood. How his screams were like music to my ears and fuelled me further. I drew it out, making sure he felt every ounce of my rage, every bit of the punishment. Right up until he was a sobbing mess, begging for death. Something I was only too happy to oblige.

This is a side of me that nobody but Jimmy knows about, yet as I spoke, I could see Liam revelled in my words, loving the power I could wield in my hands and the fact I wasn't scared of it. Most men would think I'm crazy because I can kill without remorse, but I have my reasons. I have been surrounded by death from a very young age, I became desensitised, and if it's well earned, I'm more than happy to give them what they deserve.

Liam talks about how he has a similar philosophy. He doesn't just take on any job, he only takes on ones that he feels deserve it. As a result, he doesn't inflict the level of violence that I can, preferring to slaughter swiftly and without a trace. That's why he is the best. He is often long gone before anyone even realises that his mark has been killed.

Listening to Liam talk about hits he has done, how he chooses his marks, and what criteria he uses to guide his moral compass is intoxicating. I love hearing him talk about the power he wields over life and death and how he doesn't abuse it. There's something uniquely different about him. When I try to bring up his family or anything about his past, he shuts things down, changing the subject instantly. If his family really is a threat to my crown, I want to know all about them. I will have to work on getting Liam to trust me and open up about them.

We both talk for longer than we agreed, and mutual yawning makes us aware of just how late it is. Checking my watch, I confirm it has gone two in the morning, and we both agree it is time for bed. Liam, ever the Irishman, had drunk at least three more beers than me and didn't have a wobble in his step or a slurred word in his speech. I, on the other hand, was way past tipsy. The happy, smiley, far too affectionate Bree has taken over, which is why I need to get her to bed before I say something stupid. Liam obviously has the same idea. From his standing position, he reaches out to help me off the sofa.

As I stand fully, the wobble from the drinks I consumed is evident. Liam is quick to catch me, making sure he wraps his arms around me to hold me upright. My heart races at our closeness and I feel the heat from our bodies melting together. Ever the gentleman, Liam half carries and drags me up the stairs to my bedroom. He stands me up outside my bedroom door, but I keep hold of his strong arms, not quite ready to let go. I can't help that I am drawn to him, and I don't want him to leave me here.

With hooded eyes, I look up at him, but instead of his signature cocky grin that I have come to like, he looks so serious. He looks like he's brooding, but I don't want to see that. I smile brightly at him and attempt to throw a seductive wink his way so he knows what my intentions are. But in my drunken state, it probably looks more like I have a problem with my eye. As Liam's laughter fills the room my heart starts to swell.

Raising his hand, he finds a stray piece of hair and slowly tucked it behind my ear, his fingers leaving a trail of heat wherever they touch, from my chin, over my cheeks, and up over my ear. Liam's touch causes my blood to rush and meet his fingers, a rouge-coloured blush spreads across my face. I can only imagine how red I must look. I wanted more of his fingers, more of the feel of them against my soft skin. More of him.

"Goodnight, Princess," he whispers in my ear. Shock waves ripple down my spine, heat pooling in my core at the feel of his breath against my skin.

Using my free hand, the one not currently gripping onto the doorframe to keep my balance steady, I reach out and grab a fistful of his t-shirt. He looks down at it questioningly, but before he can say anything, my vagina gives out instructions, my brain no longer calling the shots.

I have to stand on my tiptoes to be able to reach, but as our lips press together, I have no regrets. His lips are soft yet firm. I lick my tongue across his lower lip to gain entry, and I'm instantly hooked on the taste that is all Liam. The soft moan I have no control of ripples out of my mouth and across his lips. My sounds of pleasure act like an electricity bolt striking straight through Liam's body and he no longer holds back. Any hesitation he had about this happening is long forgotten.

Turning me quickly, he pins me with my back firmly against the cold wall, yet the front of my body burns from the proximity of him. His hands feel like they are everywhere, in my hair, holding my face, roaming all over my body in a desperate attempt to pull me as close as possible. I can feel his hardness getting more prominent against my stomach, but it's the way he moves his mouth that really pushes me over the edge. His kisses are brutal, hard, dominant, and yet I crave them. I willingly submit my mouth and let him take my tongue, loving the feel of him abusing them. I want more.

As soon as he bites down on my lower lip, I groan loudly. I can't help myself, I let my hand wander, and just as it sweeps over the impressive bulge in his pants, Liam freezes. We were in our own little bubble, acting on instinct without thinking. My hand travelling south made my intentions very clear and it's obvious they differ from Liams.

He takes a step back, but with his body no longer there to hold me up, the alcohol wins and I start to crumble. Liam reaches out to hold me up using his arm, but his warm body remains a step away. Initially, I feel hurt that he's rejecting me like this, but as he stares into my eyes with a small but genuine smile, I know he's only doing what he thinks is right. It's weird not seeing his cocky, know-it-all smirk, but the idea that our kiss made him smile causes my heart to swell and a matching grin spread across my face.

Liam looks like he is trying to find the right words to explain why he pulled away, but I am silently pleading with him not to say anything. I already know his reasons why the kiss shouldn't have happened and why it can't happen again. But for just one minute, I need to live in the moment of the best kiss I have ever experienced. He gives me a slight nod, understanding what I want.

"Night, Princess," he says, placing a chaste kiss on my cheek. I feel my skin start to burn as my usual blush appears.

Before I even have a chance to say good night, he has gone, practically running into his own room. Leaving me standing in the corridor, my body on fire, my senses craving everything that is Liam Doughty. I want to follow him or have him burst into my room regretting his decision, but I know neither can happen. So I walk solemnly into the bedroom and get myself ready for bed. I already know that those lips and the hardness I felt growing impossibly large against my stomach will be featuring heavily in my dreams. But, for now, I need to remember that the only way anything can happen with Liam, is in my imagination.

CHAPTER TWELVE
Liam

Fuck! I am so screwed. It was a fucking miracle I had even a little bit of self-control, or should I say she did. I don't think I ever wanted that kiss to end, and I didn't plan on letting it until the sexiest moan escaped her lips. Instead of it being the turn on it should be, for some reason, all it did was remind me that we were doing exactly what she said she didn't want to do. I don't know why my brain thought that was the right time to get all honourable. I hadn't gotten my dick wet in over three months. Planning a job as intricate as kidnapping Bree took focus, and now I have the most beautiful girl I've ever seen throwing herself at me.

Had she not drunk her body weight in beer, she probably wouldn't have felt the same. She made it perfectly clear when she was sober that this had to be all about business. Even though I'm not entirely convinced I want to be in this business full-time, hearing her talk about it has me all in. It isn't so much that I want to run the company, I can't think of anything worse. It's more that I want to be there, standing by her side, watching her rule. I have no doubt in my mind she is strong enough to take on the world, but I like the idea of her having someone like myself to stand beside her. Someone to pull her up when she needs it and push others down who think they can take what is ours. I'm not saying I am entirely decided; I did spend my whole life trying to get out of the lifestyle my father forced me into. Can I forget about my shit upbringing and the horrible experience of working for my father, and commit not just to Bree but to the lifestyle I've fought so hard to avoid?

The next couple of days pass by relatively quickly. The following day isn't as awkward as I imagined it would be. She felt guilty for initiating the kiss. I could tell by the blush that spread across her cheeks and the way she lowered her gaze every time I caught her looking at me. It's hard to believe that this force to be reckoned with, the same fiery princess who shot me the first time we met, is shy about a kiss. Then again, if it wasn't for the stubble I had let grow the last couple of days, you probably would have been able to see very clearly that I, too, started to blush when I caught her looking. I hope she can't tell I was thinking about how I have jerked off in bed multiple times, just imagining our kiss and where it could have led. I haven't jerked off thinking about a real woman in a very long time; that's what porn is for, but my head keeps creating sexual situations featuring Bree that are better than any porn clip I could ever find.

We don't talk about the kiss or our obvious attraction to one another, choosing instead to skate around the issue and just cover normal subjects, like our plans for the business and how we will find out who is loyal to us. Or slightly lighter topics, such as activities we can do together to have fun and get to know each other. However, since today's the day Kellan comes to visit and will be staying here overnight, I decide it's a good idea to tell her about him.

She smiles at me as she moves around the kitchen, gathering glasses and plates to bring over to the table now that I have finished setting up the placemats and cutlery. When she walks to the table and I get a chance to fully look at all of her, I almost forgot how to fucking breathe, let alone speak. She is dressed in the tiniest little pyjama shorts you have ever seen. I can seriously see the lower roundness of her ass cheeks, that's how small they are.

She has combined the shorts with her cami vest that stops before reaching the shorts, displaying a beautiful band of pale skin. When she reaches up to get a glass out of the cupboard, I get a delicious view of her belly button piercing. The sight has my dick straining so hard in my sweats, I legit thought they would poke a hole through them. Of course, that is without thinking about how the top of the vest scoops low enough to give off a delicious view of her sizable round tits. They look fucking amazing especially knowing she isn't wearing a bra. I know that because the cami set is a faint blue colour, and I can see the outline of her nipple through it. I pull my eyes away before my dick gets so hard it will never go down.

We sit at the kitchen table; she brings the bacon, sausage, fried eggs, and toast through, putting them in the centre of the table for us to select what we want. I let her get her fill first, then I can polish off the rest.

"So, you've never mentioned anything about any friends to me before. I can't imagine growing up with your family. Making friends had to be hard. Do you have any?" I ask, subtly trying to bring up a topic that I know will lead straight to Kel.

"Yeah, so it wasn't easy at all. I'm sure you did your research on me before kidnapping me," Bree asks pointedly, giving me a knowing look that is half pissed and half proud. Almost like she is pleased I would do such a thorough job. I nod, and she continues, "So, you know I went to Longstaff Boarding until I was eighteen. I didn't want to go there at all. It's a posh preparatory academy where they train you to become little model citizens. Women were taught etiquette while men were taught leadership. I hated the sexist inequalities of the place, but also the reputation I had there. Everyone knew who my parents were. The girls wanted to be friends with me because my mother ran the debutante programme. Only twenty girls from our year when they turned sixteen would become debutantes, and my mother held the golden tickets. Without being a debut, their chances of finding a rich dickhead to marry decreased significantly. Basically, it was the shit in my world. If you weren't a debutante, you were nothing," she spat, her fists clenching into balls as her anger warped her beautiful face into a scowl. I hated seeing anything but a smile on her face.

Well, I love it when she looks at me horny and ready to fuck, but I'm deliberately not thinking about that. I have only just got my dick down to half-mast, and that's the best he could do. It's like just being near Bree, and those ridiculous pyjamas, are a turn on. He is behaving like a teenage cock that's never even seen a pussy before. Great, now I am hard again, thinking about Bree's pussy. What was she talking about again? Fuck, get your head out of the gutter, Liam, and focus on the conversation, I berate myself in my head.

"I'm guessing you didn't want to be a debutante?" I ask sarcastically, the answer already being plainly obvious.

"Fuck, no. I wanted to do anything but. I also wanted to stay away from every bitch who thought being a debutante was a good idea. It was a breeding ground for bitchiness. It taught all about being a decent member of society, and sisterhood, all that other bullshit, but that was just on the surface. In reality, it was a breeding ground for competition, backstabbing, and hatred. Everyone wanted the coveted Princess Debutante, the most promising debut of the year, and the one most likely to marry the richest, most successful guy in the room. That was essentially the only goal for these girls, to find a husband who would trap them into becoming a housewife and a shell that simply pops out babies and follows commands. Everyone assumed that I would be given the coveted spot because my mother was the one making the decision. Sure, she had a committee, but everyone knew it was her vote that mattered. They didn't know that by this point, my mother loathed who I had become and the fact I embodied absolutely nothing that she looked for in a debut, let alone the Princess. About two weeks before she announced who would be debutante Princess, that's when she found out about my extracurricular hobbies with Jimmy. She was so fucking mad," she chuckles.

Just the sight of that beautiful smile on her face makes my face light up too. I like hearing about her past. I never saw her as a debutante. I told her this, and it's her turn to laugh again. I wanted to know about the extracurricular stuff though.

"Well, at this point, I had told him I wanted to run the business. He was the only person who didn't laugh at me or tell me I couldn't. Instead, he told me what I needed to be able to do to not only survive but rule. He showed me my dad's warehouse, where he interrogates or kills people who have wronged him in some way. I learnt how to slice through skin and be comfortable with the sight of blood, to bathe in the screams of pain, and how to turn off my emotions enough to be able to kill someone myself. Not exactly the regular after school club for a teenage girl, but actually, I fucking loved it. I felt more at home with a knife in my hand and blood staining my clothes than I ever did in a ballgown and tiara. But my mother was fucking pissed when she found out...wait, why are you looking at me like that?" she asks me, her eyes boring into mine as she tries to unravel the expression on my face. She doesn't recognise it, but it's awe.

"Sorry, Princess, but this is the face of someone who is in awe of you. I was pulled into this life, made to love it, but you stepped in willingly and excelled at it. It's obvious to me, even if it isn't to everyone else, that you were made for this. Oh, and I'm also a little turned on by the idea of seeing you slicing up someone and bathing in their screams. It's a little more bloody and noisy than I'm used to, but fuck, I bet you would be sexy as hell doing that," I smirked, seeing that blush spread across my little firecracker's face. Who knew a girl that could slaughter a man at sixteen was someone who blushed at a compliment. Fuck, she is the perfect woman.

"That right there, Liam, is why I asked you to be my partner in this thing. Every guy I met before knew about my inheritance and the fact that my husband and I would inherit the London firm. They all wanted the power, and they thought the way to it was by using me. So needless to say, every guy I dated turned out to be a power-hungry idiot who was more interested in kissing my dad's ass than mine," she says. She sounds incredibly seductive at the mention of her ass. Her laughter fills the room as I mutter about them being idiots.

"Anyway, back to your original question about friends, I got sidetracked preaching on my soapbox about assholes," she jokes. "When my mother made it very clear I wasn't Princess debutante of my year, it became even more ruthless as twenty girls all pulled each other down to get to the top spot. There was one girl in the group, Mia, and nobody expected her to make the cut. Sure, she is from a wealthy family, but she was quiet and shy. She didn't excel in social situations, having suffered from social anxiety for most of her life. If she had been more confident, she would have killed them all because she was the most beautiful girl in the group; classic blonde hair, blue eyes, doll shaped features. Everything about her was natural, and she looked like a princess. That made her a threat to the other bitches in the room. They knew if my mum was choosing beauty alone, they were screwed, so they repeatedly targeted her. It started off as name-calling, bullying, even slut-shaming her despite the fact I'd never even seen her have a conversation with a boy. She was really that shy, but of course, guys love a beautiful girl, and despite them hitting on her, she never dated any of them. I stayed back, never got involved, but then I heard their plan to swap her moisturiser cream with a component that essentially was like acid. She would have had superficial burns to her face and obviously had to pull out of being a debutante. I found out the leader was a bitch called Chrissy. I told Mia what was happening, and I secretly swapped the moisturiser with Chrissy's. Her face was a mess, and I made it very clear it was all me, not Mia. Her skin sizzled and burned. It was so fucking awesome to see her get the justice she deserved. What's really ironic is my mum had picked Chrissy to be Princess and was due to announce it that day. Mia and I have been best friends ever since. She isn't part of our world and never will be. Despite me bringing her out of her shell a lot, she is still quiet and shy," she says, and I can't help but smile.

I know I shouldn't like the idea of her burning some bitches face off, but I do. I love that she has a moral compass like mine and would take revenge for the people that matter to her. I am precisely the same with Kellan.

"So what does Mia do if she isn't in our world?" I ask, genuinely interested in the girl who seems to have won over Bree's trust.

"She actually was disowned by her family. She pulled out of the debutante ball, and because she never debuted, they said she disgraced their name. Her family had legendary status, every female had worn the Princess crown, but Mia didn't want that, she wanted a normal life. So, she is training part-time to be a primary school teacher. Mia works babysitting, nannying, tutoring, any work with kids that she can get to help fund herself through college. A lot of what she does is online, so she can work full-time and do a part-time course simultaneously. She is so fucking dedicated to every kid she works with. I know she will be great at it. I have offered her money on countless occasions, but she has refused every time. She wants to do it on her own, and I admire her for that. I think it's hard for her to be separated from her family, though," she says sadly. I can relate.

Believe it or not, before my father instigated all this sibling rivalry, I actually liked my brothers, particularly Finn, my second eldest brother. We used to get on so well, have a right craic together, but that ended long ago. I even missed that dick, Evan, at times. My eldest brother was too much like my dad. He had incorporated so many of his personality traits and was like a mini-version of him. I fucking hated seeing it. We were a close family before he became power-mad and put my sisters in danger. My mood shifted to anger every time I thought of them. Bree must have sensed the shift because she quickly changed the subject with a small, knowing smile. One that said I could talk to her if I wanted, but only when I was ready.

"So, what about you? Any friends?" she asks, and I smile as she walks straight into my plan.

"Well, now that you mention it, I have one best friend, Kellan. He's going through a really shit time right now. He is basically like my brother, and I will do anything to help and support him. So if it's okay with you, I was going to invite him over tonight. I would love for you to meet him, and also, we have a lot we need to discuss," I say, choosing to leave out the part where I already invited him.

"Of course, that's okay. I would love to meet him," she says, just as the deafening ding-dong sound echoes through the room. I smile at her sheepishly whilst giving her the cocky smirk she seems to be so responsive to.

"Okay, so I kind of predicted that you would be okay with it and already invited him. I thought he would be another hour, and I would have time to fill you in with his story, but the shithead is early. I am really sorry, you can yell at me later. But for now, please, can you go and put some clothes on while I open the door. I don't like the idea of Kellan seeing so much of your flesh," I growl possessively as I rise to go and answer the door. She stands up and starts running towards the stairs.

"You are so dead for this!" she shouts as she runs up the stairs. Her eyes may have been glaring at me, but she had a slight smile on her face. I loved seeing her playful side.

"Bring it on, Princess. Do your worst!" I shout back with a laugh. I hear a groan leave her as she disappears up the stairs and I run towards the entrance hall.

Opening the door, I am greeted by my very exhausted best friend, carrying the most beautiful baby in one arm, and what looks to be his entire apartment in his spare arm and even more surrounding him.

"You are early," I chastise Kellan before turning my attention to Hallie. "Hey, Hallie Bear, Uncle Liam is so happy to see you. Come here for some cuddles, beautiful girl," I coo while reaching over to take Hallie from Kellan's arms and walk back into the house.

"Oh, lovely. Don't worry about saying hello to me. And don't offer to help me with this stuff. I've got it!" he shouts sarcastically, but I was too busy staring into the beautiful blue eyes that were so wide and staring up at me. Her little hand grips onto my finger for dear life, and I'm doing everything I can to stop her from pulling it into her mouth to use as a chew toy.

"Well, you didn't have to bring every fucking thing you owned!" I snap in a whispered tone, trying not to startle Hallie.

"Fuck you, Liam. Do you know how much shit a baby comes with? She looks cute as a button right now, but I give her an hour before she has vomited or shit all over her clothes, then another couple of hours before she does it again. Seriously, I go through so much washing I may as well have bought shares in Persil's washing powder. I'm sure Hallie is keeping them in business. It's seriously a race to see who will have a meltdown first, the washing machine or me. I honestly don't know who my money is on," Kellan grumbles as we walk into the living room.

"Fuck me, this place is huge," Kellan says in awe as he finally takes in the surroundings, dumping all the things he has brought off to the side. The bag slung over his shoulder is the only thing he keeps with him as he moves towards the kitchen and opens the fridge. He pulls out a couple cans of Coke, and taking something out of the bag, he starts stocking our fridge.

"What are you doing?" I ask out of curiosity. Hallie takes advantage of the fact that I wasn't paying attention, and now my finger is being used as a chew toy in her mouth. Thank fuck she doesn't have any teeth yet. I can't even bring myself to pull away because she looks so damn content. I hate seeing her cry, so she can have whatever she wants.

"I figured while I'm here, it will be easier to use premade formula. So I bought a few bottles and put them in the fridge. That way, anyone can feed her, and I don't have to worry about sterilising or making up the bottles. They just need to be slightly warmed, and then they are good to go. I do have the powder stuff and equipment for if we run out. You just never know and I feel like I have to prepare for every possible eventuality." He flops down onto the sofa beside me and shoots me a smile when he sees the way Hallie literally has me wrapped around her finger.

I thank him for the can he brought me, take a sip and then place it onto the coffee table before settling back for cuddle times with my favourite girl. All while wondering when my second favourite would be making an appearance.

"Thanks for having us here, Liam. You have no idea how much I need this. You are the only person I trust anywhere near Hallie at the moment. I found out fucking Franscheska, the nanny I hired, was working for my mother; spying on me, going through my fucking computer to get dirt on me," he grinds out, taking a big gulp of the can he is fiddling with while he speaks. I see the turmoil written across his face, and all I can do is laugh.

"Your bitch of a mother is one stupid whore. I can't believe she hired someone to check your computers and spy on you. She may have no idea you are a world-class hacker, but she knows you are good with computers. Does she seriously think you are that stupid?" I ask incredulously.

"I know. I have a state of the art security system that is so good you can't even see the cameras. I also have a firewall, so I knew the minute she accessed the computer. It live-streamed a mirror image of the screen to my tablet, and I saw everything she looked at. I can't believe I let her near Hallie. What am I going to do, man? I need to work, but I don't trust anyone with her. If I can't show the courts I have a stable, reliable support system, then I am fucked. I will lose her." The disparity rang loud, and I know the idea of him losing Hallie is the worst thing imaginable to Kel, and I don't think he will survive it. But the idea that his bitch of a mother, who cared enough about raising him that she ditched him as a child, now thinks she is capable of raising Hallie? Over my dead body.

"That will never happen. Every penny I have is yours. I love this little girl, and I tolerate you," I joke. "She is never taking her away from you. I promise you that. We will find a nanny, and as far as the courts are concerned, I am your support system," I say firmly. I'm about to continue, but soft footsteps and a voice I have come to crave cuts me off.

"You don't know me, but I will stand with Liam as your support system. I also know someone who would be perfect as your nanny. But how about we get to know each other, and I prove to you that I can be trusted before we go any further?" Bree says as she extends her arm out to Kellan. "I'm Bree, nice to meet you." Her smile is blinding, and I catch the knowing smile he throws my way before he reaches out to shake her hand.

"I'm Kellan, and this little beauty is Hallie. If he ever puts her down, you can have a cuddle, but it's unlikely," Kellan jokes, and Bree sits on my side of the couch. There's not much room between me and the arm of the sofa, so she is pretty much plastered to my side, but I don't care. She is looking at Hallie like she is the most precious thing ever, and she just won me over even more.

I finally pull my eyes from the cute little girl in my arms and look over at the beauty sitting next to me. She has changed into a long dark green summer dress with tiny straps on her shoulders. The top of the dress curves like a heart, emphasising the generous swell of her natural tits. Before she sat down, I tried not to focus on how

"Bree, Kellan is a single dad. Hallie's pathetic excuse of a birth mother walked out on them both when Hallie was just five hours old. She posted some papers a week later abdicating all parental rights, and that's the last we have heard from her. So Kellan has been doing everything himself. That's why I said he could stay here so I can help out tonight. Then I'm babysitting this little doll for a couple of hours tomorrow while Kellan does a job for me," I explain. Bree's eyes go through a rollercoaster of emotions, but mostly she looks sad.

Turning to Kellan, she morphs her face into one of determination and a slight smile. He looks confused for a second before she speaks. "You can stay here until we find you a nanny that you trust. I honestly don't mind; I would love to help if I can. But it looks to me like Liam already has everything taken care of." She smiles, and once again, I am in awe of the beautiful heart this girl has. I struggle to combine this version of her with the hard-ass bitch who can torture people with her knife and not care.

"Thank you, you have no idea how much that means to me. But before I say yes, I have to know…what the hell is going on between you two?" Kellan asks, and now it's my turn to groan.

CHAPTER THIRTEEN

Bree

I don't know if I should be offended that he hasn't told his best friend about us and our arrangement, but then again, it isn't something that you can talk about over the phone or via text. I can tell how much Kellan means to Liam and don't even get me started on the tiny little girl wrapped in Liam's arms. It's so clear she means the world to both of these guys.

When I first walked into the room and got a chance to watch them for a bit, I was in awe at the way such a tiny girl who can barely hold her own head up yet has the power to bring these two big, strong men to their knees. Hearing Liam do baby talk and lay her across his chest, fuck it nearly killed me. I legit thought my ovaries were going to explode. So when I heard that she didn't have a mum, and Kellan was going through so much shit, I genuinely meant it when I said we have to help him. He needs to know he has people who are there for him. He already knows that about Liam, but I know I have to win Kellan over if I am to stand any chance of having a lasting partnership with Liam. But how the fuck do you win over someone who has been burnt so badly by women? Honesty is all I have.

"So, to cut a long story short, Liam kidnapped me, and my family refused to pay the ransom. After we talked, I realised this was the opportunity I had been waiting for. I had been looking for someone to partner with, and Liam seems like the perfect choice.

Basically, my Family only allows males to run the company. Still, I'm the only heir, so it was agreed that my portion of the firm would transfer to whoever I marry. But I actually want to rule. So, I needed to find someone who would stand by my side when needed but otherwise, let me rule. Liam has agreed to be that guy. To give my Gramps peace of mind, we agreed to spend two months getting to know each other since this is going to be a lifelong partnership," I explain, deliberately trying to avoid using the term marriage. It's hard enough to explain without labels.

"What the actual fuck? You have no idea how many fucked up things are wrong with what you just said. You!" he shouts, pointing towards Liam. "You kidnapped her when we agreed that was a fucked up plan. What the hell were you thinking?"

I shy away from the anger in his voice, pleased it's not aimed at me. But, oops, I spoke too soon. His piercing blue eyes are now firmly boring into me, his accusing finger now pointing in my direction.

"And you, I don't know if you are crazier than him. Did you seriously propose to the guy who kidnapped you?" The fury in his voice is evident. His shouting causes his stronger Irish lilt to become more pronounced. I wait as I'm not sure he wants an answer. Then, luckily, Liam steps in.

"Look, Kel, the reason I didn't tell you about this is that I knew you would think it was crazy. But you know me better than anyone in the world. In the entire time you have known me, have you ever seen me make a rash decision?" he asks, and his friend visibly sags. The rigid, angry posture he adopted to yell at us soon falls away, and what remains is two beautifully brutal-looking boys having a heart to heart. Despite it being about me, I wanted to leave them to it.

"No, but at the same time, you have never acted so irrationally before. You have spent your entire life trying to distance yourself from the life your father threw you into. You hated the person he made you into. So why would you risk almost a decade's worth of work?" I can see Liam's face scrunch up in displeasure, and the cocky smirk is swiftly replaced by a sneer.

"I had no idea you didn't want to work in this industry full-time or be part of this world?" I whisper, worried he might realise this is not what he wants. But, instead, he takes hold of my hand and gives it a subtle squeeze. The smile I love is back, and his eyes bore into mine like he is ensuring that I understand and take in everything he is trying to convey.

"We agreed not to talk about business. But listen to me when I say this, both of you. Yes, I hated being raised in this world. The things my father put me through nearly broke me, so I do the work I want. I only take on the clients I want to work with. Despite not knowing much about you, Bree, I already know that working with you will be nothing like my father. Yes, you have what it takes to be ruthless when needed, but you are not sadistically cruel. Kellan, I genuinely believe that this woman right here has what it takes to not only rule our world but to do a fucking great job in it. I know I was initially in it for the money, but now it's about giving her the protection she needs. She is going to have a fair few enemies, people who will never accept a woman at the helm," he says firmly, and my heart starts to soar.

Liam was looking at me with a fierceness that I've never seen before. Where our palms are connected, our fingers interlocked, I feel the heat creep up my skin. Like I am drawing warmth and strength from him and the belief he has in me. My heart starts to race, and I can feel my stomach doing little butterflies. Fuck, I really like this guy. I can feel myself subtly leaning forward. It's like he has a magnetic pull dragging me towards him without me even trying. The whole world drops away, and in that moment, it feels like we are alone, and you can cut the tension with a knife.

I notice Liam not only subtly leans closer to me, but his sexy, seductive eyes pierce mine. Looks like we are finally going to take this further without any alcohol influencing us. He licks his tongue over his lower lip, and fuck, that's me done for. He may as well have turned on a tap directly to my pussy, that's how I feel.

"No. Stop that right now. There is a baby in the room. You will not do anything sexual with Hallie in the room, let alone in your arms, Liam!" Kellan shouts, reaching to grab Hallie from Liam. He playfully kicks his leg at Kellan to stop him from getting Hallie.

"Fuck off, you know I wouldn't have sex with you in the room, let alone with Hallie in my arms. I'm not a perve," Liam jokes, but he doesn't exactly decline that he wasn't thinking about us fucking.

"Seriously though, you made this sound like it was a business decision, but what I just saw between you is anything but business. Are you in a real relationship or just taking advantage of the benefits of your business agreements?" Kellan asks, and we both groan together. We have deliberately avoided asking each other questions like these.

"Kel, we are still getting to know each other. We are not in a position to talk about labels yet. But for your information, we are not fucking. The business is the most important part for Bree. It means a lot to her, so we have to make sure the foundations we build will last. I don't think a quick fuck will build a lasting relationship, do you?" Liam chastises his best friend and Hallie coos in his arms.

I look over, and the little girl is so freaking cute. She has those chubby arms and thighs with all the rolls that make little babies look so darn adorable. But it's the way her wide, bright blue eyes that are fixed on Liam that really wins me over. She is looking up at him, just listening to him talk, gripping onto the hand that is not holding mine. She looks like he hung the moon, and she would be pretty content to lay in his arms forever. Girl, I can relate so severely. How the hell am I jealous of a baby? I mentally chastise myself and realise I have completely zoned out, looking at Hallie.

Liam and Kellan are debating whether we should sleep together just to get it out of our system, then we can cut the sexual tension out and focus on the business part of things. Liam isn't exactly telling him it's a bad idea. Instead, he points out we are more focused on building a friendship. However, I did notice that he didn't exactly say no to the sex idea.

Watching the casual banter between Kellan and Liam is so funny. If I didn't know any better, I would say they were real brothers. They are so alike, but yet so different too. It's obvious Kellan is the joker of their little duo. Obviously, only recently choosing to settle down with Hallie. The idea of that little girl's mother abandoning her boils my blood. She is so fucking cute. How can anyone want to abandon her?

The more I focus, the more I realise how exhausted Kellan really looks. He looks so drained, constantly yawning in between arguing with Liam. And don't even get me started on the massive bags under his eyes. So I decide to break up what I'm sure will be never-ending banter.

"Kellan, I know you were saying how exhausted you are. Why don't you go for a sleep? Liam and I can watch this little cutie for you if you'd like?" I ask politely. He visibly sags at my words. At first, I wonder if I've offended him, until he turns the biggest megawatt smile my way.

"I could fucking kiss you right now. Well, I would if I didn't think my bro here would throw down over it," he jokes, looking pointedly at Liam. "Are you sure?" He directs his question to Liam, but I do see his gaze flick my way momentarily. It's obviously hard for him to trust anyone with her.

"I already told you, this is what you are here for. You catch up on your sleep. I know where all her stuff is in those bags, and there are bottles in the fridge. We have got this. I was actually thinking of going swimming. We have a heated pool outside. Can I take her in with me?" Liam asks hopefully, looking to Kellan for his reply.

My brain is exploding. I am silently begging for Kel to say no. I don't think my ovaries or heart can cope with seeing him in swimming shorts, dripping wet, and carrying a baby. This is like the start of any good mum porn!

"Yeah, she loves the water. There are some waterproof nappies and her suit in the suitcase. Enjoy. Oh, Bree, is there any chance you have a bathroom with a massive tub I can soak in? My shithole of an apartment has a crappy bathroom," he moans and before I can answer, Liam chips in.

"Well, if you let me put you in a decent place, you wouldn't have to put up with that shit anymore," Liam snaps, looking annoyed for the first time. I've seen him joking with Kellan, but this looks to be something they have real arguments about.

"Dude, I already take so much from you. I want to provide for my daughter myself. Once I get sorted with a decent nanny, it looks like you are going to need someone a bit more frequently," he asks hopefully, and they both must notice my confusion. Liam is the one that answers.

"Kellan works for me. He is my security guy and is actually one of the best hackers in the world. Something not many people know about. If they did, people like our dads would insist he work for them, but Kel is like me. He has a moral compass and has never signed on full time because he wants to have a say over the type of work he does. He lives in a shithole because the bitch who birthed Hallie took every last penny he had and sold the house out from under him. Kellan will make back enough to sort out a decent place to live after he does a couple of jobs for me. Still, he hasn't been able to yet with Hallie," Liam explains and my urge to help this little family grew so much more.

"Kellan, I have an empty suite upstairs. The room is big enough for you to have Hallie's crib in your room or in the attached living area, whatever works best for you. The suite also has a big bathroom that I'm sure you will love. There is also an empty room next door. Make a list of everything you need to set up a decent computer system. Give your notice on the shithole. You can live here and work for us. When you have made enough, you can get a place for yourself, but until then, having your own space here should be suitable. You will have Liam and me here to help with Hallie. And as your employer, I will buy everything you need to set the room up into a home office. In fact, don't bother giving me a list because I won't have a fucking clue what you are talking about. I will get you a company credit card, and you can order everything yourself. That okay?" I ask, and the look on his face is indecipherable. But Liam's face is easy to read. He is looking at me like he can't quite believe I'm real.

"Are you fucking with me?" asks Kellan, and I can't help the chuckle that escapes.

"No. I promise you can choose your assignments and you don't have to do anything you don't feel comfortable with. You can work around Hallie and can stay here as long as you need to. When you are ready, I can introduce you to my friend, Mia. She is a nanny looking for a regular job, and I think you guys would get on well. But get to know me first, and we will go from there. What do you think, do you wanna work for a girl?" I ask, and this time, it's Kellan's turn to laugh.

"Fuck, Liam. I can see why you like her," he jokes, playfully thumping Liam on the shoulder. The movement jostles Hallie, who starts to whimper, and their reactions make me laugh. Liam looks furious that he would dare to disrupt the little girl who is just laying there idolising him as he lounges on the sofa. Kellan looks terrified, like he faces a caged monster that might have just worked out how to get free.

"Thank you, Bree. I have no doubt you will be a kick-ass boss, and I can't wait to see what you can do…and for the company credit card, obviously. Now, if you will excuse me, I will soak in the bath and sleep until it's time for food tonight. I will cook for us all, it's the least I can do," he says, getting up from the couch as carefully as he can.

Kellan leans over and gives Hallie a kiss on her forehead, which causes her to let out the cutest little giggle. I stand too, offering to show him to the rooms. He continues talking to Liam, reeling off instructions about caring for Hallie. Liam clearly looks like he isn't listening. At some point, between me standing and Kellan collecting his bags, Liam has laid down on the sofa, and Hallie is lying on his chest. Her tummy resting on his rock hard abs. She keeps trying to lift her head up to look at him, but the more he strokes his hand down her back, the less she tries. I tell Liam I will get changed and meet him in the pool soon.

After showing Kellan to his rooms and giving him a mini-tour on the way, we got on well together when it was just us, having a laugh and joking occasionally. I can already tell he's an easy guy to get along with. When I finally get to my room, it takes me a long time to decide which bikini to wear. I don't have any full-body swimming costumes, as usually, I'm here either by myself or with my Gramps, and he doesn't swim. He had it put in years ago just for me. I eventually settle on the most modest one I can find, which is still a black triangle bikini. Small triangular strips cover both nipples; a decent portion of my breasts are on show. The black bottoms are slightly more modest as they have a mid-length curve, meaning they only show the lower curve of my ass instead of the whole thing. I look curvy and hot, but I also look like I am trying to impress, which I certainly am not. However, if that just so happens to be the outcome, I am most definitely here for it.

When I get to the pool, Liam is already there. He is floating around in the water, holding Hallie in his arms as she splashes about. I take a second to appreciate how fucking great he looks covered in water, the rare English sun rebounding off his rock hard body. Fuck, I think I may be drooling. When my gaze finally moves from his body to his face, I realise he is looking at me in the exact same way. Our gazes are heated; he is looking at me like he wants to consume me. I know how he feels. With every step I take into the water, it's like he is pulling me towards him, and my body is only too happy to comply. We are stuck in our own world, drowning in lust and suffocated by sexual chemistry. Hallie manages to break the spell by splashing us both with her hands and giggling loudly. We both turn our attention to Hallie, and our matching smiles reflect how cute this girl really is.

We play about for what seems like ages. Then, after a while, Liam finally trusts me enough to hold her and I don't know who is more scared between the three of us. I don't think I have ever held a baby before, let alone one so loved and adored. I find it comes easily, but I still let Liam wrap his arms around the both of us to make sure we are safe. Being in his arms feels fucking amazing.

It's not long before Hallie starts getting very irritable, and that's when the crying begins. Fuck, how does that beautiful little girl have such a loud, high-pitched squeal? It literally pierces through your skull. I even notice Liam wincing as the pain consumes him also. We quickly get out of the pool and grab towels. I wrap a towel around Hallie and then around us both while Liam runs on ahead to warm up the bottle. I try to keep her outside so she doesn't wake up her dad. I try every move I have ever seen in the movies; rocking, swinging, even bloody singing to her, but nothing works.

Liam lets us know that the bottle is ready, and I head inside. Liam sits on the sofa, making sure to lay down a couple of towels first, so it doesn't get too wet. I pass him Hallie, and when he has her comfortably, I hand over the bottle of milk. I realise we didn't even talk about what we were doing; we just did it. Like we were so in tune with each other, we didn't question it. She finally quiets once the teat is comfortably in her mouth. That is until some fucktard rings the doorbell.

The loud ring echoes around the ample open plan space; I can only hope that the soundproofing in the bedrooms prevents Kellan from being woken up. Liam looks murderous, and I have to say I am with him on this one. But, of course, we weren't expecting anyone, so chances are whoever rang the doorbell didn't do it for anything important, angering the baby for nothing. My palm twitches to reach for the nearest knife. But, luckily for whoever is at the door, Hallie is quickly distracted by the bottle.

I see the t-shirt Liam was wearing earlier, sprawled across the back of a dining room chair, and decide to pull it on over my bikini. At least then I can answer the door in something more presentable. As I open the door, I see that nobody is there, and I release a huff, annoyed that someone hadn't waited the extra minute it took me to get to the door. I am closing the door when I see it, the white box with a black ribbon around it. I pick it up and see that my name is written on it in cursive handwriting. It looks beautiful, but I know I wasn't expecting anything. So very few people know this address or that I am here. And there are only one or two people that would send me gifts. I don't know why but I have an awful feeling in the pit of my stomach. I push it away as I pick up the lightbox and put it on the kitchen counter.

Liam looks over at the box and me, his eyebrows raised as his facial expression asks me questions he doesn't want to risk voicing if he disturbs Hallie. Pulling the ribbon, I slowly unseal and open the box. Before I even realise what I am doing, I let out a blood-curdling scream. It echoes around the house, and Hallie decides to get in on the action, matching my cry with one of her own. Liam jumps up, holding tightly onto Hallie. He hasn't even reached me when Kellan appears, sprinting down the stairs wearing only a very tight pair of boxer shorts. I am so freaked out by the box's contents that I don't even have time to appreciate him.

Kellan demands to know what's wrong, if there is something wrong with Hallie. Liam hands her over to her dad, reassuring him that she is okay. He then runs over, pushing me away to put his body in front of mine. Like he is trying to protect me from seeing what is inside. But it's too late for that.

Liam looks inside to find it lined in clear plastic. Pinned to the bottom of the box is a beautiful Celtic cross, about the size of a book. It's only after a second look that I realise the cross is an exact replica of the one I wear around my neck. Except mine has a rose in the centre, and this one has a pierced human heart. The organ has been pierced through the centre by the lower point of the cross, impaling it fully. Liam pulls out a handwritten laminated sheet, the writing is the same cursive style used on the front of the box. Carefully dripping the blood off the laminated sheet, Liam reads what it says.

"Brianna O'Keenan. This is your only warning. Back away from your claim to the London firm. It cannot be run by a girl; your men will not stick by you. They will never trust you, and you will never trust them. It will only be a matter of time before one of them stabs you in the back. This is me doing you a favour. Give me the firm, and you get to live. But if you decide to go ahead with this shambolic wedding, I will ruin you. I will slaughter you all until your white wedding is invoked with darkness. Everyone will know that it's your black wedding that will be your downfall, and I will take great pride in watching you all fall. So do the right thing and save those you love. Or you will all die."

Liam and I look at each other, our fear now long gone and replaced by anger. If some asshole thinks we will give up that easily, they obviously don't know us at all.

"If they want a black wedding, then that is what we will give them. They think it will be our downfall, that the darkness will suffocate us, but they are wrong. We will have our black wedding, and then we will slaughter anyone who stands in our way," growls Liam as he rubs his hands up and down my arm, clearly trying to make sure I'm feeling alright.

"We need to find out who the fuck sent you that. Bree, I'm going to need my equipment as soon as possible. We need to catch this fucker before he puts us all in danger. And please set up a meeting with your friend. The sooner I find someone to care for Hallie, that will be one less worry I have while I'm working," says Kellan, and I nod, warning it may be a few day's if she is busy. Liam smiles at his friend, pleased he is on board with us. Who knew it would take a heart in a box to help Kellan see he needed to accept help from others.

"Oh, and just to clarify, when you say you are taking the nutcase who sent you a heart in a box's advice, please tell me that doesn't really mean you are having a black wedding. What does that even mean?" he asks, looking confused.

"I think they mean that a black wedding is essentially like a funeral. Everyone dressed in black and mourning the loss of their single life and celebrating the fact they have been forced together. But that's not what my wedding means. I will wear the biggest black dress I can find, and our wedding will unite Liam and me properly. Everyone will fear our dark union as they know the minute we tie the knot, their hopes of ruling die alongside it."

Both Kellan and Liam are looking at me like I might be a little crazy. I'm standing in my kitchen, in a bikini, looking at a cross with a huge heart impaled on it, talking about my big, black wedding. People can say it's a union that isn't meant to be, that it's built on business, not love. But I say fuck them.

CHAPTER FOURTEEN
Liam

The more I stare at the bloody Celtic cross impaled on the human heart, the more I feel murderous. It's not even the threat that bothers me as much as it is the look on Bree's face. Now that she has had a chance to get over her initial shock, she has her game face on and holds the heart like she was the one to rip it from someone's chest. But I saw her face when she first opened the box. Her piercing scream vibrated through my soul, and I saw the look of sheer terror on her face. That urge to protect her and slay all our enemies ran deep.

Kellan took Hallie to lay her down in the travel crib he brought with him and made calls to get some computers delivered. Bree had handed him a black platinum card from her bag, and the look on Kel's face was like she had just passed him a pot of gold. He ran off upstairs. The only thing stopping him from taking multiple sets at a time is the little girl cuddled against his chest. When he reaches the top step, we hear him cursing and muttering something about Hallie wasting quality milk and vomiting on him. I can't help but smile. I never expected my best friend to be taken with the baby when I first found out he was becoming a dad. Now it looks like he was made for it.

Once he has gone, I turn to Bree. She still has the heart in her hand, but now that Kellan has gone, so too is her act. She looks tormented, I walk behind her and cautiously approach her, using my hands to guide her to put the heart box on the side table. When she does, I silently direct her up the stairs. Finally, we reach her room, and I show her in, closing the door behind us. I head to the door in the corner, finding her en-suite and nudge her in that direction.

"Let's get you in the shower, wash away all the blood," I say, turning the showerhead on.

She has a massive walk-in shower, beige and gold tiles lining the wall. The showerhead and pressure settings make the shower look far too high tech for me. I just like to turn it on, make it hot, then turn it off. When I've got the temperature how I want it, I motion for her to go into the shower as I turn to give her some privacy. But instead of letting me walk away, she takes hold of my hand and guides me into the shower with her. Luckily we both still have our swimsuits on. If not, there would be potential for this to go further than we intended.

Letting Bree pull me in, I allow the water to run down my face. Raising my hands, I run my fingers through my hair. I go to rake through from the scalp to the tip again, but Bree's hands beat me to it. She runs her fingers through my hair, and I can't help but moan. I have always loved people running their fingers through my hair. I open my eyes to find her standing right in front of me. Luckily the blood had long since fallen away from her fingers. Her eyes stare into mine; the terror she was feeling is now replaced by the fire she seems to reserve only for me, and fuck do I love seeing it.

"I don't know if this is a good idea, Bree. I saw how freaked out you were," I say gently, not wanting her to feel any shame.

"Of course I am freaked out. It was a fucking human heart. But what freaked me out were the details they knew that nobody should know. They know we are getting married, but they also know about this necklace I wear every day. It's a Celtic cross that I had handmade. Mia designed one for her and one for me. We got them made, and this necklace is one of a kind, but now there is a massive replica on the side table in the kitchen with a heart impaled on it. It has to be someone we or I know," she murmurs as her arms stroke down my back, her fingernails scraping as she goes. A shiver ripples down my spine, and no matter how much I chant about football stats or think about nonsexual things, I can't control the way my dick strains against my shorts. It's like it is reaching out to her.

"We will find who it is, Princess, and I promise you will have your revenge," I state firmly, vehemently sure that I will keep that promise.

"Can you help me forget?" she asks, looking up at me through hooded eyes, her fingers gripping onto my hips.

"Princess, if we do this, there is no going back. I don't know what will happen, and I can't make you any promises if we do this," I murmur.

I can hear my cock shouting at me for cock-blocking him, but I have no choice. We have to clarify this. I have never been in a relationship before. I fuck and move on. She wants us to have a working relationship and mix sex in with it too. Maybe we can be married with benefits, but there's also a chance it could all come tumbling down around us.

"I'm not saying this makes our marriage real. Our business relationship will always come first, but I want you, and I am done ignoring it. This is just sex. Afterwards, we go back to how things were. Agreed?" she asks.

Rather than reply to her, I let my body do the talking. I turn her so that she is against the wall to the right of the showerhead. As soon as her back hits the wall, and she is firmly pressed in using the hardness of my body, I raise my hands to thread through her hair. Taking a handful near the scalp into a fist, I pull slightly. A light wince leaves her, followed by a moan. Looking down at her, I watch as the water drips off her lips, her eyes look almost black with passion. I waste no more time before pressing my lips against hers.

Her lips are so soft at first, but as soon as her brain catches up with her lips, she reacts. Her arms wrap around my neck, and she pulls me into her, her lips forcing themselves against mine until the kiss is almost bruising. I swipe my tongue across her lower lip, demanding access, and she instantly obeys. My tongue is punishing, demanding control, but hers battles back just as furiously. She claws at my back, grinding her hips against my thigh, trying to get impossibly closer. We are already so close that the water can't even drip down between our already connected bodies.

Using my hands, I rake them all over her body, running them up to her arms and down her back. I waste no time in undoing the fastening to her bikini top and removing it to expose her fucking amazing tits. Kissing down her neck, I find a sweet spot just over her clavicle. When I suck on that exact spot, she moans loudly, scraping her nails down my back and kissing the same place on me. Fuck, I had no idea it could feel so good to have someone sucking on my neck. I knew we were leaving marks on each other, but neither of us seemed to give a shit. I was too preoccupied with touching these fucking amazing tits.

I waste no time, using one hand to tweak one of her nipples while I move my mouth over the other. Her nipples are so responsive, and the moans that fill the steamy shower cubicle are guttural and almost animalistic.

"Fuck, Princess, I need to taste you. Can I?" I look up at her and the expression on her face almost slays me. She looks sex drunk, and I really fucking hope she gives consent quickly because I am struggling not to just take what I want.

She doesn't respond, but instead, she takes what she wants, fisting a handful of my hair into her hand and pushing my head down. I let her lower me until I am kneeling below the Goddess in front of me, kissing my way down her body. My fingers graze along the same route as my lips as I pull her bikini bottoms down. Next, I gently crook her leg over my shoulder, exposing her sweet pussy right in front of me. Determined to take control, she uses the hand currently gripping my hair and pulls my head until it is exactly where we both want it to be.

Using my fingers to gently part her sweet pussy lips, I flick my tongue over her clit. She jolts as though I electrocuted her, and a loud groan escapes her lips. I can't resist looking up, and fuck, I almost come there and then at the sight of the beautiful woman before me. Her back is arched off the shower wall with her head thrown back in ecstasy, water dripping over her body and making me want to taste all of her.

I like that Bree isn't shy, she knows what she wants, and even though she doesn't use her words, there's no doubt. The problem is, I want to hear her words. Normally, I would stop until she tells me exactly what she wants, and begs for it. But I think this time I might give her a free pass. I'm not sure I can stop tasting her even if I wanted to.

Flicking my tongue across her clit quickly, her fingers close even tighter in my hair, and I don't hesitate to give her more.

Using my tongue I lick across her slit, making sure to dip my tongue into her waiting hole before returning to her clit. As she continues to writhe, I take my finger and thrust it into her.

Now it's my turn to groan. Her pussy is so fucking wet, but I can still feel how tight she is. It's like her walls are clamping down on my finger, determined to make sure I don't stop, which of course, I couldn't even if I wanted to. I piston my finger in and out a few times, making sure she is prepared for me, and when I'm sure, I add a second one. Together, my fingers piston in and out of her pussy while my tongue flicks against her clit. Her juices flood into my mouth, and her sweet taste is fucking addictive.

"Oh, please don't stop," she moans and fuck me; my other hand goes straight to my dick.

"Oh, don't worry, Princess, I couldn't even if I wanted to," I say as I flick across her clit even faster.

I can feel her orgasm building, her moans become more frantic, and her grip on my hair is almost bruising. Her pussy walls clench even more, and she seems to be getting even wetter if that's possible. She continues to mumble about what she wants and that she doesn't want me to stop. Finally, bringing out her sweet voice is like music to my fucking ears. I fist my cock and stroke from the base to the tip, making sure to apply the amount of pressure I know I love. Pre-cum leaks from the tip, and I gently spread it across the head, making sure not to use too much pressure as it's so fucking sensitive.

It doesn't take long until I am on the edge of coming, and I am determined to feel her flood my mouth before that happens. As my fingers hit deep, I make sure to tilt my fingers, trying desperately to find that spot, the sweet one that I know will push her right over the edge. It doesn't take me long before I feel it, and soon after, she falls right over that cliff. Her pussy spasms and grasps onto my fingers, so I hold still while her moans and groans echo loudly. Her taste floods my tongue, and I can't get enough of it. I lap gently at her clit, trying to soak up as much as I can.

Fuck, it's too much, and I can't stop myself from exploding all over my own hand. I groan against her clit, and in response, her pussy spasms even further, her whole body shaking thoroughly. Her legs start to shake, and I have to let go of my cock and take my fingers from her pussy so I can place my hands on her hips and ensure she doesn't fall. Setting her foot down, I slowly stand, making sure to kiss my way back up, sucking lightly on both her nipples before reaching that spot on her neck again. She pulls me up until I am back to towering over her and the look on her face almost slays me.

She reaches out to take hold of my cock, but I move her hand aside, stroking my hand through her hair. She looks at me like I just took her favourite toy away, and fuck. I almost cave and let her have whatever she wants, but this wasn't about me. This was about me helping her to forget.

"I want your cock. I want you," she whispers into my ear, almost as though she is afraid of telling me exactly what she wants.

"Fuck, you can have whatever you want, Princess. But not right now. This, gorgeous, was just for you," I say as I press my lips against hers.

Her tongue sweeps over my lips, demanding access, and I can tell when she finally tastes herself as she groans into my mouth. Fuck, I'm getting hard again, and my willpower to make this all about her is waning quickly. So instead, I turn her around and start to gently wash her hair. I run my fingers through her long luscious locks, and it amazes me that I have never done this for a woman before.

We both take time to wash each other, trying to avoid each other's more sensitive parts, so we don't end up fucking like rabbits in the shower. Turning off the shower, I lift her up and wrap us both in towels. Making sure we are both dry, I gently lay her on the bed before pulling the covers over us. She rests her head against my chest, another new for me, and I gently brush the hair out of her eyes. We fall asleep like that, and I choose to ignore how fucking comfortable I am with her tucked against my side and with her leg hitched over mine.

We are both awoken from our sleep by the mobile ringing on the bedside table right beside my head. I reach over, confused when I don't recognise the name and number on the phone, for that matter. That's when it comes back to me that I am in Bree's room, and she is still lying against my side. She sees me looking at the phone and reaches over, taking it from my hand and giving me the most beautiful smile.

"Hey, Jimmy, what's going on?" She pauses, clearly letting the guy finish before telling him she will meet somewhere in thirty minutes. I look at her questioningly.

"Jimmy, my dad's head of security. I sent him a text last night after you fell asleep. I couldn't sleep until I knew something was being done, that people were looking into it for us. That was him telling me he has a lead. I'm going to get some answers," she says. I can tell by the way she is looking at me that she is waiting for me to tell her she can't go or to ask her more questions. I know how she operates though and remember that she is not to be fucking messed with, so I let it go and sit up to get dressed.

"Okay then, let's go meet Jimmy." If she thinks she is going without me, then she has another thing coming. If we are doing this thing, then we are doing it together. After tasting her sweet pussy, I know I am all in.

CHAPTER FIFTEEN

Bree

I don't even bother trying to tell Liam that he can't come along. I want him to see the other side of me, the one I don't let anyone see. The side that people don't think I am capable of having. But that's okay, I love being underestimated because the underdog always wins.

The threat really caught me off guard because it was so personal. Whoever sent it knows a lot about me, or there's a snitch in my father's company. That's who we are going to have a little chat with today. Jimmy has suspected for a while that Art is a turncoat, that he swapped to work for a rival firm, but nobody has any proof. We are working on rumours and accusations, but you can't be too sure in our line of work. So I plan on finding out.

Obviously, my life has been threatened numerous times before. I mean fuck, I was kidnapped just a couple of weeks ago. It feels like Liam has been in my life for so much longer, and he was never a real threat. I mean, he could have been if he wanted to be. I've never seen Liam in action, but I have seen him focused, and the rage on his face when he saw the threat let me know exactly what he is capable of. I know that together we will put this threat to bed, and then we will exemplify whoever is responsible. We have to make a point, so nobody else thinks about trying this and to make sure that they take our reign seriously.

Pulling up at the warehouse, I climb out of Liam's BMW. It's sleek, black, and rumbles when the engine starts. This car is perfect for him; it's like him but in vehicle form. It looks perfectly normal, but when you turn on the engine, it roars to life, rumbling through your body before soaring along the open roads. It doesn't look like it's powerful, but as we know, looks can be deceiving. He walks towards me with that sexy, cocky grin that quite literally melts my panties. I try desperately not to think about how it felt with his tongue on me earlier. Fuck, he has a talent, but when he said he didn't want or expect anything in return, he had me. I already knew the guys I had been with before were fucktards, but Liam just confirmed it. I have never had a guy make it all about me and my pleasure, and fuck did he make sure I was screaming and moaning with pleasure. I have never been given an orgasm by someone else, and he managed it on the first attempt. I was literally knocked off my feet.

It was supposed to be a one-time thing, a way to get him out of my system, but all it has done is leave me desperate for his cock. But since we didn't go all the way, I was not classing earlier, no matter how fucking epic it was. Yeah, that makes perfect sense. It only counts if he sticks his cock in, which means we still haven't got it out of our system. Perfectly logical! I'm still in shock he managed to give me a fucking earth-shattering orgasm on the first attempt. He puts the other pussies I dated to shame.

Liam reaches over and grabs my hand, lacing our fingers together. We look like a real couple, which is precisely the look we are going for. I don't miss the way his gaze slips over my body, taking in my appearance. Given how his eyes become hooded with lust, he is obviously a fan of my work ensemble. I am wearing some old ripped jeans, a dark vest top and my favourite leather jacket, paired with my favourite black motorcycle boots. I look like your classic rocker girl, but there isn't exactly a dress code for running a crime Family. My father and grandfather are always in their suits, dark and foreboding. I am not a suit kind of girl, and neither is Liam. He is wearing a similar look to mine, and fuck, does he make distressed jeans and a tight t-shirt look so fucking hot. I'm not even trying to hide my staring. His cocky smirk becomes even more prominent, and I just roll my eyes at him. He knows he is fucking gorgeous, but I don't mind letting him know a bit more.

I guide Liam towards the door. The signs surrounding us are for a toy company that is owned by my father. It's a front for imports, but you have to have somewhere to conduct business. The large metal building is on the edge of an industrial estate. The nearest factories are far enough away that they never cause us any issues. We don't want any too close or they may become suspicious. Not that it matters, my father and Gramps have greased enough palms to ensure that nobody looks too closely at our business.

Jimmy, obviously having seen us on the CCTV, comes out to meet us. Jimmy is tall, burly, and stern-looking, but that's just the face he keeps for other people. I get to see the relaxed smile that is rarely seen. His greying hair is short, and a matching lightly cropped beard spreads across his chin. The crow's feet and bags around his eyes are a reflection of his age, but made worse by the stress of the job. He is only fifty-eight, but he looks a lot older. I smile when I see him, dropping Liam's hand so I can greet Jimmy with our usual hug.

Pulling me close, he whispers in my ear while making sure to keep me wrapped up in his arms, "Missed you, Bee. How are you doing?"

He lets me go, and straight away, I reach back to take Liam's hand in mine. It's like I am drawn to him, desperate to maintain some form of contact with him. But, now that shit is getting real, I realized on the drive over here that even though I know I can do this alone, I don't want to. I want to know that no matter how bad shit gets, when I get home with Liam I can take off the mask. I don't have to be Brianna, leader of a crime Family in front of him, I can just be Bree. The girl who plays twenty questions while getting drunk and eating her body weight in pizza. Liam is about to see the brutal side of me in action for the first time. What if I scare him off?

"I'm doing good, thanks. I need to find out who is threatening our reign before we have even gotten married, though…Which reminds me…Jimmy, meet Liam Doughty. Liam, this is the guy who raised me. He's like a father to me, Jimmy Neil." I stand between two men who shouldn't mean so much to me, but they do. Jimmy stepped up to be my dad when I needed him the most, when my own father didn't give a shit. Liam is the one who stepped up to stand beside me. He believed in me before he even got to know me. These men get me, but will they be able to get along?

"We have met before," spits Jimmy.

Liam starts to speak but is quickly interrupted. The loud thump

114

of skin on skin startles me, and it takes me a few seconds to realise that Jimmy punched Liam in the face. I take a step so I'm firmly in the middle, preparing to break up a fight but knowing, in reality, I stand no chance. These are two big guys, and if they throw down while I'm standing here, there's a good chance I will get hurt, even if it is by accident.

I'm startled when I hear Liam laugh, his hand cupping his bleeding nose. I listen to it more clearly as he pulls his hand away, revealing some blood, but luckily his nose doesn't look broken. "I guess I deserved that," he chuckles.

What the hell? If I wasn't confused enough with Liam's reaction to being punched, I am even more baffled when Jimmy stretches out his hand to shake Liams. I am looking between them like the world's most bizarre tennis match, my eyes flicking from one to the other. I am waiting for the fight that never comes.

"I appreciate a man who can admit his mistakes and take a punch." Jimmy is still holding out his hand, and I know it is the utmost disrespect to refuse the handshake. But I also know Liam's hand is covered in blood.

Wiping one of his hands down his jeans, he reaches out and shakes Jimmy's hand. "I don't regret kidnapping Bree, but I am sorry because I can see how much she means to you. I never expected things to go this far, but now that this is happening, you need to know I am all in. I will stand by Bree's side, no matter what."

Jimmy nodded, but his face still held that look of suspicion. He struggled to trust people in everyday situations, so this was even worse. But I know Liam would win him over, he's just that type of guy. He won me over while I was still tied to his bed. Fuck, maybe we need to get those ropes out again. No, focus, Brianna!

"You talk a good talk, but time will tell. Don't forget, boy, that I know all about you and your family. You abandoned your blood and said you didn't want to live this life, but now you do. Why?" Jimmy asks sceptically.

Liam chuckles, pulling his hand away to find his nose has now stopped bleeding. He uses the hem of his t-shirt to clean himself up, and I try to ignore the flash of abs I get when he lifts his top. "My father's a psychopath. I am in this life; I never left. I just follow my own standards. Blood is important to me, my family is still my family, but that doesn't mean I have to follow his words as gospel. I genuinely believe Bree has what it takes to make the right kind of changes. I follow her because I choose to. Even if we weren't getting married and sharing the role, I would still follow her," Liam says, taking my hand in his.

His cocky smile is back, and I can't help matching it. "So, now that you have interrogated Liam, can we get to the real reason we are here?" I say, practically bouncing on my heels, desperate to get started.

I can feel that telltale feeling of blood lust invading my senses, my heart racing as adrenaline floods my system. Jimmy nods and leads us into my father's warehouse. We walk through the fake setup, the rooms that look like they really could belong to a toy factory, before getting to the backroom. My room.

It's a large room covered in what I'm sure used to be white tiles. Now they are stained in various bodily fluids and grime. The floor even has a handy drain to allow for it to be easily cleaned after usage. Along one wall is a table made for DIY tools but littered with all manner of instruments that can inflict pain. Not that I bother much with those. There's also a tatty, orange sofa that looks like it has seen better days, but it serves its purpose as somewhere for people to sit while they watch the show. There's even a small fridge next to it that I know the guys always keep stocked with beer. Of course, sometimes there can be hours between the person being captured and the interrogation beginning, so I don't blame them for wanting somewhere kitted out.

My attention is drawn to, as always, the chair that is padlocked to the centre of the room. Tied to the chair is a young guy, probably only a couple of years older than me. I have seen him around my father's office before. I know he is one of his dealers. His name is Art.

His jeans are tattered with graffiti paint, and his t-shirt is ripped, revealing his severely malnourished body. His face is sullen and almost grey. His eyes look sunken and lifelike, his cheekbones prominent. Seeing me staring at him, he attempts what looks to be a smile, but all it does is expose his blackened, chipped teeth, which are few and far between. Clearly, Art doesn't just deal drugs. He looks like he uses more than he sells.

"Well, well, if it isn't Princess Brianna. To what do I owe the pleasure?" Art slurs his words, clearly not yet down from his latest hit.

"It's Art, isn't it?" I ask, and he nods enthusiastically. "I am here to ask you some questions. If you answer correctly and honestly, you can leave here with a free hit on me. On the other hand, if you lie or don't tell me what I need to know, I will make this difficult for you."

His high-pitched laughter ripples through the air. "What the fuck you gonna do, Princess, or should I say whore. I have heard the rumours."

As he says the word whore, I hear Jimmy growl from my left, and see Liam step forward to make sure he is right beside me on my right. Yet neither of them interfere.

Pulling my knife out of the holder in my back pocket, I grip it in one hand, and with the tip placed against the finger on my other hand, I twirl it around. Making sure Art can see the blade and how sharp it is. "Tell me, what have you heard?"

"That pretty boy over there kidnapped you, and you were so wet for it that you not only opened your legs, you said you would marry him. So now, he and his fucked up Family will be running the London firm. Your daddy is not happy with you at all," he practically sings, not realising he is giving me what I need every time he opens his mouth.

"Who said the Doughty's will be running London? Everyone knows that Liam left his family years ago," I ask, taking a step closer to Art. He just laughs at my question, exactly what I expected him to do.

"Come on, Princess. I didn't have you down as a stupid cunt. Of course, he is working for his family. Everyone knows Desmond is after the London firm. He will never take the Irish side from Mr. O'Keenan, but this firm is weak and only getting weaker." As he finishes, I step forward until I stand right in front of him and kneel down, one knee hitting the floor. Now I am looking straight at Art. I slowly lift my knife and drag the blade down the back of his left forearm, right from the elbow to the wrist. I make sure to do it on the back of the arm to ensure I don't hit any significant vessels, but it causes enough damage.

Art's high-pitch screams fill the air as he shouts profanities and begs me to stop, his body is physically shaking. My body reacts to his screams and blood loss with an intensity that makes my heart race. Adrenaline is flooding my veins, and my pulse is beating in my ear. The sensations bring my body to life, and I love the power it brings me. It makes me feel seven feet tall, and fuck, do I want to hold onto it.

"Call me that again, and I will create a matching line on the

117

opposite arm. Understood?" I ask, not really looking for a reply, but of course, Art answers. He begs me not to hurt him anymore. I want to laugh at how quickly he changes his tune. But then again, we already knew he was a rat. We just need to know who for.

"What I want to know from you, Art, is who you work for? I know you are no longer loyal to my father, which means you are no longer loyal to me. So I want to know who you are working for? Who is making moves against us?" I ask.

"Whoa…I-I don't know where you heard that, but I am not a rat. I am loyal to you and your dad. You have to believe me," splutters Art, while rocking back and forth, trying to get free of the ropes that bind him securely to the chair. He stands no chance of getting free until we decide to release him.

"Oh, Art. I thought I said you would be honest with me," I say as I take my knife and draw a small but deep line across his right upper chest. It bleeds but not too heavily. It's more to cause intense pain than anything, and it does its job.

Art, crying and sniffling, now looks like even more of a mess than he did before. "Nobody wants you to rule, Brianna. I'm sorry, but that's true. Even your father is determined to put a stop to it. You have more enemies than you even know about!" he screeches, spit and snot flying everywhere.

CRACK.

The sound of flesh hitting flesh causes me to stumble backwards, and I feel Liam take hold of my shoulders to help me back up into a standing position. Apparently, Jimmy hit Art across the face, which now has blood pouring everywhere. Jimmy tells Art to pull it together and to answer my questions, but it has the opposite effect. Instead of calming him down, all it does is make him more hysterical as he tries to spit the blood out of his mouth. Fuck, I think he may have just spat out one of the very few remaining teeth he has left.

Looking across at Jimmy, I tighten my gaze, making it very fucking clear I am not happy with the intrusion. I did not ask for his help or his interference, nor was it needed at this stage. Guys like Art don't respond to violence, if anything, that pisses them off, but they do respond to fear. It's the fear of what I could do to them that makes them sing like a canary.

Sensing my displeasure, Jimmy holds up his hands in an apology and steps back. I continue with my questions, kneeling back down to make sure I can maintain eye contact with Art. It's easier to tell if he's lying this way.

"So my father doesn't want me to rule. What has he got planned to stop me?" I ask, and before Art gets a chance to answer, Jimmy cuts in.

"Bree, your father, isn't planning anything, He may not believe you can rule, but he listens to the old man. If your grandfather declares that you and Liam can rule after you are married, then that is what will happen. He follows the rules." Jimmy steps towards me as he speaks, and whilst I don't see this as a wrong move, Liam obviously does as he angles his body so that he can put himself in front of me if needed.

Both Jimmy and Art are watching the showdown with interest, wondering if Liam is really willing to put himself in danger for me. Of course, I already know he would; it's just the type of guy he is. What bothers me is that the man I have viewed as a father figure for all these years is suddenly looking very shifty. He is acting defensive and abrasive, which he never usually does with me. He's lying about something, and I want to know what.

Gently touching Liam's arm, I indicate that it's safe for him to step back, that I have got this. "If my father isn't planning anything, then why are you getting so defensive?"

"Because, Brianna, I brought you here to interrogate a rat. Yet all you seem to be doing is looking for more reasons to get angry at your father. So, of course, this asshole is going to say your dad is involved. That way, he doesn't have to name who he really works for. Fuck, Bee, didn't I teach you better than this?"

Wow, that cuts harder than a knife. His words make complete sense, yet my body is telling a different story. Jimmy has always told me to follow my gut, and right now, my gut is screaming at me not to trust Jimmy. I feel like my world is caving in around me as the one man I have trusted my whole life stands in front of me, chastising me. I avert my eyes quickly so nobody can see the tears that are starting to well up there. I need to push aside all emotions.

Feeling Liam place his hand on my shoulder, it's like he is passing his energy over to me, telling me he believes in me. The fact he hasn't stepped in or said anything speaks volumes. He knows I can handle this.

"You did, I'm sorry," I say to Jimmy, avoiding eye contact so he can't tell how insincere my apology is. I then turn my full attention back to Art. "So, who are all these enemies you were talking about earlier? And if you mention my father, I will slice your throat slowly" I sneer, making sure the threat is clear.

"I-I don't...I don't know the details," Art stutters, and I smile.

Taking my knife, I slice identical lines across each thigh. The blade is so sharp it goes straight through his jeans and into his skin, drawing a nice trickle of blood. The screams and pleas for me to stop echo around the small room. But Art doesn't know it's completely soundproof. We could have a room full of police next door, and they wouldn't know he was in here.

As I start to slice the second leg, Art tries to talk, but I have already begun, and I am not stopping until they are symmetrical. But I listen to his cries, hoping to pick up something useful.

"Please...please stop. I will tell you everything. There's a new gang on the streets. They are recruiting people from different families, trying to get as many rats as possible. Everyone knows that if the O'Keenan Family weakens, even the slightest, the Doughty's will exploit it. But the fact you two are uniting has everyone shit scared. They hate how powerful your families already are separately, let alone what it would be like with the O'Keenan's money and Doughty's ruthless behaviour. When people are scared, they try to capitalise," he whimpers. I watch as the blood drips down his body and feel that tingle of power rushing through my body, it's a heady, intoxicating sensation that I crave. I start to answer him, but Liam speaks for the first time.

"That's bullshit. Everyone knows I'm not with my father, that I don't work for the Family and haven't for a long time." Art has the nerve to chuckle.

I slice quickly across his lower abdomen, probably a little too close to his dick, given the way he yells and attempts to jump back while being tied down. Now it was my turn to chuckle. The stupid fucker made the cut worse. Who tries to jump while there's a knife piercing his skin. He's lucky little Art didn't suffer, instead, his happy trail is a bit less happy though. I, on the other hand, am a lot happier and feel a lot lighter. I don't know what it says about my personality that I love to cut people up and watch them bleed, of course, only if they deserve it. And right now, Art deserves it as I hate the way he was laughing at my Liam.

Whoa, did I just say my Liam? Fuck. I need to get my head screwed back on and worry about the feelings I'm developing for him some other time.

Art's whimpering stops when I pull the knife away, and he addresses Liam again, clearly understanding my warning. "Sorry,

Sir." He bends forward like he is really trying to bow, having realised Liam's fundamental importance and how fucked he is. "People are idiots. They think you leaving your family was all a ploy. They are laughing at the idea of a female boss. No offence, Brianna, Miss. I think you will be a great boss, but others do not feel the same way. They think it's all a ploy to make it look like you're the leader, but really, the Doughty's are pulling strings behind the scenes."

I look over at Liam, his face is a mask of indifference. Knowing not to show emotions in these scenarios is one of the first things Jimmy taught me, but right now, I want to know what is going through his head. Is there really a chance the Doughty's are trying to take the Family business from within? I have never had reason not to trust Liam, and I sure as fuck won't be starting now. We will need to have a very serious fucking chat about how real this threat from his father is. Given the way his eyes flick from me to Jimmy, I'm guessing he wants to know how significant a threat my family could be. Fuck me. Could my dad hate the idea of me ruling so much that he would threaten me, put me in danger? The simple fact that I don't know the answer speaks volumes, and I need to look into that. But that doesn't explain who this new threat is.

"Okay, so we have established that both my family and Liam's are against our wedding and us ruling. Fine, we get that. But I also notice you are using our families to get out of explaining who the real threat is. Who recruited you?" I ask calmly.

"I don't know. I don't know anything! I refused to be a rat. I work for you, I promise!" Art screeches and the desperation almost hurts my head.

"We both know that is a lie. So I am going to give you two options, and you better take the right one. However, I would prefer the wrong one, personally," I mused, thinking of the blood dripping all over Art's helpless body.

A cough from behind pulls me out of my musing. Jimmy knows me so well, having done this with me lots of times before. "Option one, you tell us who this new fish in town is, and I will give you a kilo of smack to do whatever the fuck you want with it. You want to smoke it, snort it, fucking bathe in it, I don't care, but your intel better be good, or you will pay back the cost plus interest and damages. Option two, I will continue to cut along every area of your body until you are singing the correct name and begging me to stop. Still, by that point, you will have angered me. So, I will put the word out that you are done. Nobody in this town, shit, in this country will sell to you again. You will have no choice but to go cold turkey and withdraw. You will also find no work amongst me or any industry associated with me. Blocked means you are done. So, what will it be?"

The luminous lights that fill the room glisten off the bloody knife as I twirl it in my hand, letting him know what my preference is. I hear Jimmy walk away, closing the doors to the room as he goes. All eyes are focused on his departure, but it's not long until he returns. He is carrying a brick of uncut snow, showing Art that we are not pissing about. I can see the concern in Jimmy's eyes; he is not happy I am offering up over fifty thousand pounds worth of product. Still, he doesn't see the big picture.

The shit Jimmy is holding in his hand right now is uncut, pure, and Art is not used to taking the good stuff. Our product is legit, and my Gramps ensures they don't water it down with anything dangerous, but we still dilute it. Mainly for the money, but also so these assholes don't overdose and kill themselves. There's no regular income from a tweaker if they are dead. So, I will let Art take one hit from the good stuff, and when he is out of it, I will arrange for someone to steal back our product. So, Art gets the best hit of his life, and I get my heroin back. It's all good.

Looking at Art, I can see he is still contemplating his options, hoping option number three will pop out of thin air. Bored with how long he is taking, I take a firm grip of my knife's handle, and without warning, I slam the blade down into the top part of his thigh. The blade penetrates right through skin, muscle, and fat until it reaches the hilt of my handle. Art's screams fill the room even worse than before, and it's like music to my ears.

"I'm sure by now you can tell that Bree here is very serious. Now, if you don't want her to twist the knife even further into your flesh before moving onto the other parts, I suggest you start talking." Liam doesn't look at Art as he addresses him. Instead, his gaze is firmly on me. His dark eyes blaze with desire, and he is looking at me like he has never seen me before. I feel naked, like my body is heating up with every lingering glance. He is turned on by watching me, and fuck if that doesn't hit me in all the right places.

"You're fucking psychopaths, both of you! Fucking bitch, no wonder people are trying to kill you!" Art screams and I audibly tut. What a fucking idiot. Why the hell would you antagonise the girl holding the knife in your thigh.

I start to slowly turn the knife, and at the same time, Liam raises his arm and punches Art in the side of his cheek. His fist must have connected with Art's nose because the crunching and snapping sound can be heard, loudly indicating the break in Art's nose. Blood sprays from his nostril, hitting both Liam's hands and spraying across my chest as I was still kneeling in front of Art. His screams echo around the room, but his speech is practically unintelligible. Blood, sweat, and tears are all mixing together to form just a mumble of bodily fluids.

"I'm sorry, I don't think that is the answer she was looking for. If you call my girl a bitch or any other unpleasant name, not only will the drug offer be off the table, but I will let her cut your dick off. And as you so politely stated, she is a psychopath who would do it," Liam spat out. Of course, the idea of me being a psycho isn't one that scares him all that much.

"Fine. His name is Vinnie Marcushio, but you didn't hear it from me. Now can I take my shit and get out of here?" asks Art, hopeful that his torture is ending, but I'm more concerned with addressing the curse words that come out of both Jimmy and Liam's mouths. Clearly, this is the name of a guy I should already know.

"Who is this guy?" I ask, standing up and pulling my blade with me as I rise. The slice of it leaving Art's leg is divine, and his screams are worse than when the knife went in. Blood spurts from the wound in all directions, and it's clear I hit a major artery when I went in. "Put your finger in the hole in your leg, or you will bleed to death," I add before looking between Liam and Jimmy for answers.

They both look to be really fucking disturbed by this news, and I feel like I should have heard this name before; he is clearly a significant player. Fuck, I hope this isn't a sign of how fucking terrible I am going to be at this whole leader thing. I mean, I don't even know who my enemies are. I must have voiced that last part out loud because Liam takes hold of my hand, staring intently at me like there's a message he is trying to get across with his eyes.

"This isn't because of you, Princess. This is all your father and me. Vinnie Marcushio is the son of Leonarda." He looks at me like I shouldn't know that name, and when it becomes clear I don't know what he is talking about, he continues, "He is what started all of this; he's the reason we met. He was your father's money man, washed the cash for him, and he suspected your father was guilty of ripping him off. He showed me everything I needed to convince me that I would take the case, but then minutes before your father realised he was innocent, it was too late. I was making my move, and all forms of communication were turned off, so I didn't get caught. Your father faked all the evidence he showed me and then refused to pay me, even going as far as telling Vinnie, his son, that he played no part in his death."

I can literally feel my mouth hanging open with every word Liam speaks. Given how Jimmy is shaking his head and pacing like a caged lion, I know he is telling the truth. I can't find the right words. Unfortunately, Art doesn't seem to have that problem.

"This is why your father's men are jumping ship like it's the Titanic. Your father is a lunatic, clearly a trait you fucking inherited." I'm in no mood for this shit. I take my blade and quickly slice two lines on either cheek, long and deep. This is a sign that is synonymous with my Family. It's the sign we have been carving into rats since we became a firm many years ago. Sometimes it does more for your reputation to let them live and send a fucking suitable warning to everyone else that you won't be crossed. Everyone will know Art is a rat now, and nobody will want to work with him.

"So last week, when word got out that you two were getting married, we got a threatening message from Vinnie. He was drunk and ranting about how he wouldn't stand by and let Liam gain power. When Leo was killed, he came to us asking if we knew anything. Your father told him Liam was working for his father and was trying to bring down your Family to gain power. He had no idea that you and Liam would end up forming this fucking alliance. He just thought he could pass the blame onto a rival Family and hopefully take your father down a peg or two, Liam. Like I said, though, we didn't know that by doing that, it would place a target on your back, Bree. He clearly thinks this is Liam's big plot to take over the Family and is determined to stop it," explains Jimmy.

"You are both wrong. He knows you killed his father. He knows because he was the one hacking your files and stealing your money. He hated his father being a slave to the O'Keenan's and felt that the Marcushio's have what it takes to be their own crime Family. This is just him taking out the competition and getting his revenge at the same time," Art discloses, further solidifying his status as a rat. I don't think he is even aware he just confirmed the actions of his new boss or that he was working against the Family. Asshole.

"Then we will just need to make sure we take him down before he gets to us," I assert, standing tall and firm in my resolve that this fucker will pay for trying to bring down my family and me.

I nod to Jimmy, signalling that I am done here, before leading Liam away from this building. The feel of his hand against mine, the blood of our enemy smudged between them, is a heady sensation. That, combined with the way he is looking at me, makes me realise I made the right choice in choosing Liam as a partner and that I am so fucking screwed. I am falling for this guy, and I don't know if I want to stop myself.

CHAPTER SIXTEEN

Liam

Fuck! I knew she was a badass, but I never really knew how much until just now. I don't think I ever questioned that she would be more than capable of getting her hands dirty if she needed to. Still, I just assumed I would be the muscle of our little partnership. Instead, she blew that theory so far out of the fucking water that I don't even think it's wet anymore. If it wasn't for her family's ridiculous rule that only men can lead the Family, then she wouldn't need me at all. I don't know why but that's a fucking terrifying thought.

Walking out of the warehouse in comfortable silence, the sexual tension continues to grow between us. Bree's eyes keep flirting over me, and whenever she catches me staring, looking at her in amazement, she turns her head. It's like she is worried that after everything I just saw, I would want to run in the other direction away from her. I don't.

As we reach the car, I quickly scan the surrounding area and see that we are very much alone. I note a couple of security cameras, no doubt belonging to Vernon, that I will need to get Kellan to take care of later. But right now, I need to show this girl exactly how I'm feeling.

Taking hold of her shoulders, I spin her abruptly, pushing backwards simultaneously until her back presses hard up against the car. I move with her, making sure to stay as close to her body as I can get. Her tiny gasp is like music to my ears, and I don't give her a chance to do anything else. Using one hand, I fist it into her hair, giving me complete control over her head, while my other holds onto her hip to make sure her body goes exactly where I want it to.

I press my lips firmly against hers, they feel so soft under mine, and I waste no time in dominating them. She moulds against my touch, her body pressing against mine. Her hands grip the front of my t-shirt, the blood of our enemy smeared across us both. It should be disgusting and gross, but if anything, it's even more of a turn on. I waste no time in swiping my tongue across her lips, demanding access that she willingly gives. Our tongues intertwine, and it feels as though they are desperately trying to pull us impossibly closer. Her taste is sweet yet with an edge that is fucking delicious, and I want to keep tasting all of her, but I know we can't risk too much outside her father's warehouse. I don't want any of her men, or her family to see me fucking her in a car park.

I'm literally getting ready to pull away and tell her we need to take this home behind closed doors when she moves first. Her lips kiss along my jaw, right up towards my ear, and as her breath hits my sensitive skin, I can't help the groan that leaves my lips. My little vixen makes things even worse by taking one of her bloodstained hands and grips my cock tightly through my already strained jeans.

"Fuck me hard and fast against the car," she whispers into my ear, sounding like every guy's fucking wet dream. My brain thinks up all the reasons why this is a fucking bad idea, and I push each and every one of them away.

Knowing that I need to act fast, I spin her around and pull her ass against my denim-covered cock. Her tits are pushed up against the car window, and her back is arched. She looks so fucking beautiful. I wish I could see what she looks like in this position completely naked, how hard her nipples get if they touch the cold glass without the clothing barrier there, but I have no problems making the most of what I have in front of me.

Kissing down her neck, nipping gently along her ear, I get ready to devour her. "Are you sure about this, Princess? There will be no going slow or gentle." Fuck, I really hope she doesn't stop me. My cock is so constrained right now I think I genuinely might die of these blue balls if she calls it off, but in this small space of time, she has come to mean a lot to me, and I respect her too much to think

127

with my cock completely.

Luckily, her response is to thrust her ass against my denim-covered cock, but I need to hear her say it, and as soon as I tell her that, she wastes no time in telling me exactly what she wants. "Please, Liam. Please fuck me, right now. I need it hard and fast. We can do it slowly another time, but not now. Now I want to fuck all the adrenaline out of my body."

With every word she speaks, my cock gets harder and my heart starts to race. This girl really is something else. She is my dream girl, and I plan on giving her anything and everything she will ever want. However, the brief pause while my brain and cock admire the beauty that's currently moulded between the car and me is long enough for Bree's insecurities to enter her head.

"Unless you don't want me like this, covered in blood. I know I can get a bit carried away...." I cut her off with a firm spank to her ass. The spank is cushioned due to her jeans but the yelp that escapes her lips tells me it had the desired effect. "What the fuck?!" she yells, and I can't help but chuckle.

Pulling her trousers down to expose her sexy, white ass, I gently massage the area on her right cheek that has a slight tinge of pink to it. Her responding moan confirms that she likes to be spanked, information I will happily store away for another playtime.

"You looked like a fucking badass in there. You just confirmed that you don't need me for my skills. But that doesn't mean I don't want to be here because I do, no matter how much that might scare the shit out of me. Right now, I have to fuck your sexy pussy. It will be rough and fast, and you will love every minute of it. Then when we get home, I will make sure to do things right. I will worship every part of your body before taking you in all your holes until I own you. I want you to crave me. That sound good to you, Princess?" I ask as I dip my finger gently between her folds and find the answer for myself. She is dripping wet, and I have to bite my lip to stop myself from moaning.

Nodding her head, I quickly remind her that she must use her words to get what she wants. Removing my cock from its denim confines, the head is bulbous and deep purple as it bulges in desperation, pre-cum leaking from the tip. Not that I need to get it any harder, but I still fist my shaft a couple of times, preparing it for her. Stroking it over her ass crack and trying not to imagine how tight and fucking divine it would be if I could take her ass too, but there will be plenty of time for that later.

EMMA LUNA

"Yes, that's what I want. Please...please, Liam. Fuck me." Her voice is deep and full of lust as she begs and pleads with me to give her what she wants. The begging is like music to my ears, and I didn't think I could get more turned on than I already am, but shit, she sounds so hot. If I had time, I would make sure to drag this out, make her really desperate for me until she had no choice but to beg and plead. Yet another thing to add to our ever-growing sexual bucket list.

Giving in to her pleas, I give her exactly what she wants and slide my cock into her soaking wet pussy. I'm not a small guy, and even though she was definitely wet enough, I want to take my time. Once the head is in, our heady breaths mix together in a primal need, and she tries to push her ass backwards to fully impale herself on my cock. I grip her hips in both hands, ensuring that she stays in place. Kissing and sucking on her neck as a distraction, I slowly push my cock further into her hot, tight pussy. She feels like velvet, tightly gripping my dick, making it harder to push the last inch or two in. When I finally bottom out, she moans, telling me she loves how deep I am.

After a couple of seconds, giving her time to adapt to my size, I start to move slowly at first. It's not long before the sensations overwhelm me, and I can't help speeding up. I piston in and out of her dripping cunt, and it feels like my cock is wearing a glove that fits perfectly. Don't get me wrong, I have enjoyed fucking girls in the past, but this feels different, better, and as much as I don't want it to end, I also know I can't take it slow. Not just because we were in a public space, that aspect fell away when she begged me to fuck her. The problem is the way her tight walls squeeze my cock, begging me to take her faster. Of course, I'm only too happy to oblige.

The air around us fills with the noise of our bodies colliding, our skin slapping together in a frenzy. Bree's responding cries of pleasure and pleas for more drive me crazy. My balls start to throb in that telltale sign that I am getting close. The tingles start in my balls before slowly spreading up my spine, and I feel as though all my muscles are coiling like they are preparing for something. The anticipation consumes me, and I feel my heart start to race. Still, I try to ignore the tingling and concentrate on ensuring Bree gets to the finish line before I do.

Given the way her breathing is becoming more erratic, her movements are less coordinated and more frantic. It's clear she is close. Her pussy is getting wetter with every thrust, yet it still feels like she clenches her walls tightly around my dick.

Reaching around, I push my hand down the front of her body and reach between her soft folds. Finding her hard nub, I gently rub the pad of my thumb across the sensitive point. That is all it takes for Bree to lose control. Her panting becomes desperate, and her muscles become rigid as she desperately tries to push her ass hard against me, trying to hold me in place. With the way her greedy pussy is gripping my dick, there's no way I could escape even if I wanted to.

Minutes later, Bree starts to fall apart, her orgasm ripping through her body. Her moans are deep and swallowed by my lips as I turn her head and devour her mouth. It's not the most accessible position to kiss in, but it feels as though we are working on instinct. Finally, her pussy starts to spasm and heats up around my dick. I didn't think she could get wetter, but I feel a small gush of fluid around my cock as her walls milk my cock.

It's not long before I fall after her, my body becoming rigid before my climax hits, and I lose control. The tingle in my balls spreads over my body, my nerve endings feel like they are on fire, and I'm being electrocuted. My heart is pounding erratically, but it seems to match the pulsing coming from my cock. I feel as though I am no longer in control of my body, having handed the reins over to the primal desire and just allowing myself to live in the moment.

It's not long before our orgasms subside, but we both remain there, breathless and lost in the sensations. I can still feel little spasms in her pussy, and I know if I stay in there much longer, I won't stay soft for long. Pulling out slowly, Bree gasps, and I feel her body sag against the weight of my arms. I hold her up with one arm wrapped around her body while I use the other to pull up her jeans. Looking down, I have to bite my lip to stop the whimper that is embarrassingly trying to escape. Seeing my cum dripping out of her red and swollen pussy has to be the sexiest thing I have ever seen, and I can feel my well-used dick start to harden again. I quickly tuck it away and start thinking with my brain instead of my cock. That's when the panic sets in.

"Fuck...I am so sorry, Bree. I wasn't thinking," I mutter as I turn her around to face me. Her face looks flushed with a light sheen of sweat covering her, and her hair sticks up at all angles from where I held onto her and manipulated her head to meet my needs. She looks properly fucked and it's probably the most beautiful I have ever seen her look.

As the words register, her face drops, and I instantly hate myself. "Do you regret it?" she whispers, and I feel my heart crack. Her eyes cloud over as they fill with tears she refuses to let fall. I couldn't hate myself anymore right now if I tried. I never want to see pain on her face again, especially caused by me.

"Are you kidding me? Bree, that was without a shadow of a doubt the best sex I have ever had, and I am already counting down until I can fuck you again. So why would you think I regret it?" I ask.

Her eyes meet mine, and she looks at me curiously, like I am a puzzle she is trying to crack. I know I look confused, but that's because I am. "I should be asking you that? You are the one who just said you were sorry we fucked and that you weren't thinking. Just what a girl wants to hear after being fucked hard against a car!" she shouts.

"Woah...no. Princess, you have got this all wrong. I said I was sorry because I fucked you without a condom. I was pissed because I have never done that before. I'm normally really good at remembering stuff like that. No way in hell do I regret fucking you, Bree," I explain, as a mixture of determination and guilt seeps through my voice. I stand tall and maintain eye contact, so she knows how serious I am. Hell, I'm not even sure how much I care about the condom. I loved that my first time bare was with Bree, but I definitely do not want to knock her up.

Her body relaxes, and she starts to chuckle. Her lips part, and she throws her head back like she is relieved. "Thank fuck for that. I thought you regretted having sex with me, and I really hoped that wasn't the case because I bloody loved it, and I need more. So much more. Don't worry about the condom thing; I forgot too. I have never forgotten before either, but my brain wasn't exactly doing a lot of logical thinking. I am on the pill and am clean, so you don't need to worry. I kinda enjoyed being able to feel you bare," she purrs the last sentence, and that's all it takes for my cock to start to stand to attention once more.

"I'm clean too, and don't you worry, I already made a list of all the sexy things I need to try with you. I'm going to fuck you so much that you and your pussy will be begging for a break. Now, let's get home." I pull open the car door next to her and guide her into the passenger seat.

Just as I am getting into the car, my phone vibrates in my pocket, and I take it out to see a message from Kellan.

Kel: I thought you were going to interrogate a rat, not fuck in the car park. A bit of warning would have been nice. I really didn't need to see your pasty white ass!

Fuck! I should have known he would hack into the warehouse security cameras to watch my back. I know I should be grateful, but I'm more concerned with the girl sitting next to me who just read the message over my shoulder and now looks pissed.

"Bree, take a deep breath and let me explain," I say softly, hoping to reason with her enough that she doesn't take her knife to mine and Kellan's balls.

"You can explain why your pervert of a friend was watching us have sex or how he managed to hack my father's security?" she screeches.

"Okay, so your father's security is an easy question. Kellan had to hack into their security to help me kidnap you. He left a back door open so he can get in and access any security system operated by your father's team if he ever needs it. That includes this facility. I didn't know he was watching. He would have logged in to make sure we were safe, and as soon as he saw what was happening, he would have turned it off. He will also have deleted the footage. But I made sure to position myself between you and any camera. So nobody could see you, and that's exactly how I wanted it. I could have bent you over the hood or fucked you on it. I had all these things in mind, but this was the only place I could keep you out of sight. I'm sorry. I will bollock him, I promise," I explain, taking hold of her hand and desperately hoping she can see how serious I am.

"You really did that to make sure I was protected?" she asks incredulously.

"Of course. I don't want anyone seeing your sexy body but me."

I wait for her reply; she seems unsure about what to say, but before I know it, she leans over and presses her lips against mine. It is a sweet kiss, her lips soft yet firm as she takes what she wants. It's over far too quickly, and I feel my stomach flip. Her kiss is like a drug, and I am desperate for more.

"Thank you. Nobody has ever been that considerate or said that about me before. I'm not really sure how I'm supposed to respond," she muses, confusion clear on her face, and I can't help the chuckle that escapes.

"That response was perfect. Now, let's go home and find out all we can about the fucking Marcushio's so we can take them down. Can't have anybody trying to ruin our black wedding, now can we?"

Now it's Bree's turn to laugh, and I love the way her face lights up and how carefree she looks. It makes her look so beautiful. "Why do people keep calling it a black wedding?" she asks as I start the car and pull out of the driveway.

"It's an old term used by some members of our faith who believe that marrying for any reason other than love taints the sanctity of marriage. It's also an ancient ritual performed in times of crisis. Two people who have never met before getting married in the hope of warding off whatever plague's befalling the community at the time. But that concept has been adapted over the years. It now basically means a marriage of convenience or arranged marriage. If we were to do it properly, we would get married in a graveyard, and both wear black. It would also be funded by the community, so their good deeds will be recognised, and the plague will end, bringing around good fortune. Or at least that's the story my mother always told me." She listens intently, turning her whole body to face me as she takes in my story.

"Let's do that. Let's have our black wedding. If people want to talk and say we are cursed or whatever, then let them. I think the moral of the story is that actually, a black wedding might start off as arranged or frowned upon. Still, actually, the aim is to bring prosperity and happiness to those two people. That is our story. I don't know where this relationship is going, and I know getting married prematurely without ever having a date sounds crazy, but who knows the future. Maybe we were always destined to get married; this is just expediting things. Maybe we will hate each other in a couple of weeks, I don't know. But I do know that there is nobody else I want by my side as I take on my enemies and prove I can run this Family."

I can't help but smile with every word she says. This girl really is something else. I have no idea if I would eventually want to marry her if we dated normally, but this isn't a normal situation. This is fucked up, and I know I could be potentially tying myself to someone for life, only to split up with her and still have to pretend. But right now, all I can see is how happy she makes me and how fucking amazing she is.

"I have no idea what will happen between us on a romantic level, but I am very fucking excited to find out. I know we could be risking the business relationship, and when we marry, there's no going back. But right now, the idea of being without you is not something I wish to think about. So we are going to get married and be a fucking amazing business team, and in the meantime were are going to continue dating and seeing where this thing leads us. Speaking of which, I am taking you on a date on Friday night."

Her smile lights up her face, and she doesn't need to speak to know she agrees with every word I just said. Most girls would want to know all the details, but not Bree. She is happy going with the flow and seeing what happens, exactly the type of girl I like.

We drive the rest of the way in companionable silence. Finally, we are greeted at the door to our house by Kellan and a miserable Hallie. Her face is a disturbing mixture of red and purple, with crease lines warping her usually angelic face into something demonic. Her wails could be heard from outside the house, and I can tell why Kellan looks so frazzled. He is trying to sway her and reassure her to quieten her cries. He is pacing up and down the corridor, trying to get her to calm down.

"What's wrong with my baby girl?" I ask Kellan.

"She is hungry, but I am waiting for the kettle to boil. In the meantime, she is trying to burst my eardrums."

Before I even have a chance to say anything, Bree steps forward. "Here, let me take her while you go and get the bottle ready. Does she need changing?"

Kellan looks from her outstretched arms to me, and I give him a slight nod. I know it's not easy for him to trust women right now, but I would trust Bree with Hallie. He knows if I trust her, then he has no reason not to. I'm almost as protective of Hallie as he is. Acknowledging my reply, he hands Hallie over to Bree and almost instantly, she stops crying. Letting out a few whimpers to know she is still hungry, she looks a lot less purple, which makes me very happy.

"I've just changed her, thanks. Looks like you have a magic touch," Kellan says. I detect a slight note of jealousy in his voice, but my hardened stare soon softens that.

Bree leads Hallie over to the couch and settles down with her. She places Hallie's belly against her own. Hallie turns her head and rests it down on Bree's chest, looking content. Her face has returned to the angelic looks and her mouth settled into that cute little O shape she makes when she is hungry. As Bree strokes her back and smiles down at Hallie, I can't help but acknowledge the fluttering in my stomach. I imagine her holding our baby, and I want to smack myself. What the hell is wrong with me? We barely know each other, and yet I imagine her with my kid. I really am screwed.

Not wanting to be exposed to that anymore, I walk into the kitchen to talk to Kellan, but he speaks before I have a chance. "You are so fucked," he states. There's no judgement there; it is merely a statement.

"I don't know what you are talking about," I reply, although I sound a little less sure of that when the words come out than they did in my head.

"You are falling for her. It's obvious. But don't worry, she is equally as fucked," Kellan states as he shakes the bottle of milk he just made for Hallie before placing it in a bowl of cold water to cool it down.

"I don't want to talk about it. I have a job for you." I explain all about Art's confession and ask Kellan to find out all he can about the Marcushio's. We need to learn as much about what they are up to as we can. He agrees and is so excited he is practically vibrating with excitement.

After clarifying precisely what I need him to find out for me, we walk back into the living room. Hallie is still lying peacefully on Bree's chest, looking around at the world, as Bree quietly talks to her, telling her how beautiful she is. Kellan sits down, and Bree hands Hallie over to him for her feed. She guzzles the milk like she has never been fed.

Together we sat for a while, just talking. Bree and Kellan take the time to get to know each other, and as time passes, they become more relaxed the longer they talk. They discover they have a lot in common, and I learn that Bree enjoys football and video games. They share banter over their rival football teams and discuss tactics for Call of Duty. As they start to grow more friendly, I feel myself begin to relax. It's crucial for me that the two most important people in my life get along.

Our bonding session is interrupted by the doorbell. Bree gets up to answer it as Kellan puts Hallie to sleep in the Moses basket in the corner of the room. He is practically walking on tiptoes and holding her like a live explosive that cannot be jostled.

"What-" I start to speak, and he cuts me off instantly with a very firm yet whispered shush.

"If you wake her up, I will slice off your balls." Clearly, Kellan's sleep deprivation is making him a little crazy. So when I offer to watch Hallie while he gets some sleep, he practically jumps with excitement.

Before he can run off to bed, we are interrupted by a loud, high-pitched squeal coming from the hallway. Bree! I waste no time taking off in her direction, and I can hear Kellan's footsteps close behind mine. Finally, we reach the door, where Bree stands in the open doorway, looking white as a ghost. She is staring intently down at the welcome mat, her hands covering her mouth in what looks to be an attempt not to vomit.

As soon as I reach her, I grab her arm and pull her behind me. I make sure to put my body between her and any possible danger. I see Kellan take a protective stance next to her, too, as we both assess the threat. At first, I don't see anything, but then I look down at the mat and see what freaked Bree out so much. Lying on the mat is a giant black rat with a dagger pierced through the middle. Blood is seeping from the wound on the dead rat, and it's clear this has just happened. In addition, there is a note attached to the rat.

Never trust a rat.
If you go ahead with this black wedding, you will be sorry.
No female will ever rule London.
Quit now, or I will rain pain and suffering down on you
and all your supporters.

I look over at Bree, who has quickly gained control of her emotions. She is no longer shaking with fear; now, it is anger. "I don't give a fuck how many times they want to threaten us. We can take on anyone, right?" she asks, and I almost want to chastise her for even feeling like she needs the confirmation.

"Too fucking right. We are doing this," I assert, and she smiles.

"You are both fucking mad. But, I'm in," adds Kellan with a shake of his head. He would follow me into the fiery pits of hell, so I had no doubt he would stand beside us for this fight.

"What do we do now?" Bree asks, and that's an easy response.

"Kellan is going to have a lie down while I watch Hallie. Then I am going to fuck you until you forget all of this shit. Oh, and I have a date to plan." She smiles at me with her big bright eyes, a look of mischief seeping in. Fuck, she looks so sexy.

I am pulled out of the little bubble we seemed to have created for ourselves when I feel a punch against my arm. I look over at Kellan, who is shaking his head. "No fucking while you are looking after the baby. I am trying not to screw her up too badly, and that definitely won't help."

Both Bree and I laugh at Kellan as he trundles off towards the stairs, mumbling about being serious and not wanting to send his daughter to therapy later in life. When we finally hear he is up the stairs, I close the front door and place both hands on Bree's cheeks, stroking them gently with my thumb. She looks up at me, her beautiful eyes full of lust and admiration. I lean forward and gently place my lips against hers. I pull away quickly, intending for it to just be a light, comforting kiss. Instead, her whimpers have me rethinking.

"Are you okay?" I ask, and in response, she stands on her tiptoes to reach me. Using her arms that she wrapped around my neck, I let her guide me until our lips meet. This time it's a more prolonged, deeper kiss. We both pull away as things start to feel a bit more hot and heavy than they should while we are babysitting.

"I'm good. I'm going to go and take a shower before Hallie wakes up. I tried to make sure she wasn't lying in any dried blood before, but I'm unsure how successful I was. I won't be long. Then we can pick up where our lips left off as we plan to take down our enemies and go on our first date. What a weird sentence," she adds, chuckling before giving me one last sweet kiss. I watch as she walks away, knowing full well how truly fucked I am and not caring one bit. I want Bree, and I am not walking away.

CHAPTER SEVENTEEN

Bree

Time seems to pass so quickly since the day at the warehouse. Liam was true to his word, and we have fucked in every position imaginable, but yet my body still craves him. He knows how to play my body like an expert musician, and only he can make me sing. I have never felt the way I do when he fucks me. I knew I was missing out on something with the other guys. After listening to other women and the media, I knew what I should have been experiencing, but I just didn't. None of the guys before had ever made me orgasm, yet I can fall apart on Liam in seconds. It's literally like he knows all my body's sweet spots, and he makes it his mission to use them all.

But it hasn't just been about the sex this past week. We have also spent time getting to know each other. Going swimming, watching movies, going for walks, and just chatting like a regular couple getting to know each other. Things have become so easy between us, and I know that my feelings for him are getting stronger with each passing day.

Things have also been going well with Kellan. He has his own rooms set up in the house for him and Hallie. He has gotten a lot more comfortable with me looking after her, even leaving me with her by myself. I know that is a big step for him, and after learning more about the women in his life who have fucked him over, I am not at all surprised. The more time I spend with him, the more I can see how close he and Liam are; they are practically brothers.

I was shocked to learn how much I have in common with Kellan and how much fun we have hanging out together. I'm amazed by his talent. He literally can hack into anything unnoticed. It's like a superpower that he doesn't abuse. Liam said he used to hack into high-security sites just to prove that he could, but now he has something to live for. He can't raise Hallie from prison, so he only hacks what he needs to. The best thing I ever did was bring him on board.

In between getting to know each other, Liam and I have been chatting with employees of my father, finding out what they know about the Marcushio's and testing their allegiance to me. I've had to use my knife a few times, but primarily people are loyal to the O'Keenan Family name. A lot were not keen on a woman being involved in the Family business, but I can show those with time. A few also didn't trust Liam wasn't working for his family to try and overthrow me. However, we both agreed that for those people, as long as they show us loyalty, then we can earn their trust. Things were really starting to look real now.

The warehouse had become almost our second home. We interrogated so many people there, and we literally fucked against any surface. With Hallie being at home, we are limited to how loud we could be, and Liam loves to make me scream. So, the warehouse has become our place where we can screw to our heart's content and be as loud as we want. I think Kellan might be getting a little bit annoyed with how much footage he keeps having to delete. But after he caught us fucking on the living room sofa one night, there's nothing he hasn't already seen.

The week passes by quickly, and as our Friday night date approaches, I start to get nervous. We have done the whole getting to know each other thing while we have been living together, and we have mastered the sex, if I say so myself. But now we need to find out if we can date like a normal couple. I have been on many first dates before, but never with someone I am already developing feelings for. I really don't want to fuck this up.

Previously, I hadn't wanted to know any details, but apprehension was getting to me by Friday morning. All Liam would tell me is that we were leaving at 6pm, there will be food, and I need to wear trousers and sensible shoes. This sent me spiralling while I tried to work out what we could be doing, where he was taking me, and most importantly, what the hell do I wear?

Now that I am dressed and ready to go, I feel a lot calmer. I opted for skinny jeans that make my ass look amazing, my trusty converse, and a black vest top that curves low enough to show my cleavage. I'm wearing light make-up, just enough of a dark smokey eye to make them pop, and a creamy red lipstick that makes my lips look plump and enticing. My ordinarily straight hair is curled in long red waves pinned back, so only a few sweeping strands cross my face. I can't remember the last time I was this excited about a date.

Once I am ready, I walk downstairs to meet Liam. From the moment I woke up tied to his bed, I have always found him attractive, but never more so than how he looks right now. He sits on the sofa wearing a pair of dark ripped jeans and a plain black t-shirt that hugs his muscular body. His dark hair, which usually flops in whatever direction it feels like, is now carefully styled into a spiky look. He looks almost the same as he would typically, just a bit more stylish. But what really has my ovaries exploding is what he is doing. Currently, he has a little ball of pink curled up in one of his arms, while he has a picture book in the other, and he is reading to her. She is paying absolutely no attention to the book and is instead watching Liam like he hung the moon. I know how she feels.

Kellan runs past me, his hair dripping wet and water droplets rippling down his exposed chest. Unlike Liam, who only has a few tattoos, Kellan is covered in them. He looks like an inked God, and although I have no interest in him sexually, it doesn't hurt to look.

Obviously, I stared for just a bit too long because Liam clears his throat to get my attention. "You, go and get your coat," he instructs me before turning to Kellan, "And you, start wearing shirts around the damn house, please."

Kellan just chuckles and takes Hallie out of Liam's arms. Her responding grumble tells everyone precisely who her favourite is in this house.

"You have some competition here, Bree," he says, and now it's my turn to chuckle.

"Oh yeah, I know that. By the time Hallie is old enough to give a shit about boys, Liam over here is going to be old and wrinkly, so I have nothing to worry about," I joke. Both boys stop dead in their tracks, all the colour draining from their faces.

"Fuck!" says Kellan, almost as a mutter to himself. I look around for the danger they are seeing, and I have missed, but I don't see anything, so I ask them what is wrong.

"Well, for me, you scared the shit out of me by saying I will be old and wrinkly when we both know I will be a gorgeous silver fox that still fucks as good now," Liam postures, and I can't help but chuckle. On the other hand, Kellan still looks like he has seen a ghost and is staring at Hallie.

I look over at him, waiting for his reason, but instead, Liam continues. "You just reminded us both that at some point, this little ball of pink is going to want to date boys, and I am rethinking my assassination moral code, whereas Kellan is trying to decide when is a good time to start warning them off."

"Is now too soon?" he asks, his face staring intently at mine. Following my initial chuckle, I quickly realise he is serious. He drops down onto the sofa, cradling his head in his hands.

"Listen, you have about thirteen years before you have to worry about that sort of thing. But let me give you some advice as a girl raised by an overprotective father, just leave her be. My father didn't leave me alone and tried to tell me who I could date or marry. He had my whole future planned out for me, and so, of course, I rebelled. I wanted to be my own person and make my own choices. I mean, they did turn out to be quite a good choice, but to my dad, all he will see is that I asked my kidnapper to marry me to rebel. So, give her a break, okay?"

"There are so many things wrong with that sentence. Firstly, did you really just tell me that my sweet baby girl will start showing an interest in guys at thirteen?" Kellan asks, and as I shake my head, he lets out a very audible sigh of relief.

"No, silly. Thirteen is when she will start going on dates. She will start liking boys from around nine or ten, depending on how soon signs of puberty show and her period hits," I explain, but clearly, I said the wrong thing as Kellan jumps up with Hallie in his hands, and both he and Liam start pacing like a caged bear.

"Oh my God. I don't know what I'm going to do. In the space of five minutes, you have reminded me that not only will she be at risk of being kidnapped, thanks to the shit business we are in. But, she might also want to marry her kidnapper. Oh, and then you reminded me I only have about eight or nine years before I have to worry about boys and puberty and periods. I think I just aged like fifty years in one conversation. I don't know how to do this. How the hell do I talk to her about boys, or puberty, or periods? Fuck, I can't raise a girl by myself." Kellan may have started off feeling very jokey about the conversation, but the more he joked, the more his fears rose to the surface.

Liam told me all about Kellan's mother fighting for custody and that she doesn't think a man can raise a young girl alone. Her main argument is that Hallie needs a girl in her life, and both Liam and Kellan have always said that is not the case. That Kellan can be both mum and dad, but he doesn't look so sure right now.

Liam starts to reply, but I shake my head, cutting him off. This is my mess to fix, and I walk over to Kellan, taking his free hand in mine and looking him straight in the eye so he can see my fierce determination as I speak. "You listen to me, Kellan. You are never going to be the perfect dad because he doesn't exist. You will mess up. You will do and say the wrong things from time to time. Hell, there will be times when she hates you, but that's good. It means you are winning at this parenting thing. Don't you dare think you can't do this by yourself because you absolutely can, but you don't have to. Whether it's help buying her first bra, or her first tampon, or talking about periods and sex, I will be there to help. When Liam and I agreed to get married, even if this relationship stops working, we will have to remain amicable as friends and as business partners. The O'Keenan's have a no divorce rule, which means you are stuck with me. We may have only known each other for a couple of weeks, but I have enjoyed getting to know you, and I know you already know how much I adore this little girl. So, you never have to do this alone. Okay?"

"So you will bail us out of jail when we murder the first guy who tries it on with her?" Kellan jokes, and I feel my whole body relax. I never intended on freaking him out. If I have learnt one thing from spending the last couple of weeks with him, it's that he is a great dad.

"Don't be stupid. We won't get caught," jokes Liam before turning to me. "Come on, beautiful, we have a date to get to."

He reaches out and takes my hand before leaning in and giving me a short but fucking fantastic kiss. I know it's his way of promising more is to come. Before I even realise what I am doing, the most cheesy giggle escapes my lips, and I throw my spare hand up to my mouth to try and disguise it. I sound like a lovesick teenager going on her first date. Sadly, I did not hide it well, and Kellan starts throwing around stupid teenage girl jokes before Liam stops him and pulls me towards the door. Just as we reach it, he stops, turns around, and leans over to kiss Hallie, who is still curled up in Kellan's arms. She almost looks like she is trying to reach for Liam and grumbles when Kellan stops her. She may only be a couple of months old, but that little girl has got the cutest personality, and I am so looking forward to watching her grow.

When we get in the car, I can't take the anticipation any longer. My knee is bouncing with excitement, and I turn my body to face Liam as he peels out of the driveway. "So, you're gonna tell me where we are going?" I ask nicely, and he chuckles.

"Nope. You are just going to have to wait and see." He sees my responding pout and starts to laugh.

We joke about it for the duration of the car ride, and I am amazed once again at how easy it is with Liam. He genuinely is one of those easy-going, easy to be around types of guy. I always joke that he is so laid back that he is almost horizontal. Given my hyper organised and full-on mode that I can get in when I am thinking about business, I need someone like him to balance me out.

We have been driving for around twenty minutes when Liam's phone rings. It's connected to his car through Bluetooth, and the vehicle announces it's an unknown number. Liam looks worried, and I tell him to answer it. He looks reluctant.

"Nobody has this number. It's protected and encrypted by Kellan. So, you, Kellan, and my sisters are the only ones who know this number, and if it was any of you, your names would have come up," he explains. But I tell him to answer it anyway.

Hitting the answer button, Liam sounds wary as he greets the caller. He was right to be cautious as a technologically altered voice begins to talk. "Liam, congratulations on your upcoming wedding. Who would have thought you had the balls to infiltrate the O'Keenan's and try to take over power that way. You're a lucky man. Bree is definitely a looker. Given that ivory tower, her daddy has been keeping her in, I bet that ginger cunt is really fucking tight. Have you had a sample, or are you waiting for your black wedding day?"

"Who the fuck is this?" Liam growls, his knuckles start to turn white as he grips the steering wheel tighter. His posture becomes rigid, and if looks could kill, this caller would be very dead and buried.

"Just an interested party. But since you clearly don't want to disclose any details about that sweet ass, I will get to the point of my call. We have all heard the rumours that Bree thinks she can run London for the Family, but that will never happen. Even if Gramps O'Keenan will do anything for her, Vernon will not let that happen. Personally, we do not give a shit about them; we want to rule. We want to take out the O'Keenan's and rule for ourselves. We have no issue with you, so we are giving you an option. Help us take down the O'Keenan's, and we will let you walk away with your life, or you can stand with Bree and burn with her and her family. But know this, you will never be in power. So...what will it be?"

Liam places his hand on my knee to get my attention before raising his finger to his lips, instructing me to remain quiet. I give him a quizzical look with my eyebrows, but he remains firm.

"Why should I trust you? I don't even know who you are," Liam asks. At first, I am pissed he is even entertaining this asshole, then I realise he is trying to get more information. My anger is redirected to the dick on the other line.

"You don't need to trust us. Just know we are a better option than the O'Keenan's and their little bitch, Brianna. Although we are not as pretty to look at," the voice jokes, and I can feel my heart racing as I ball my hands in and out of fists.

"So, you don't want me dead? You just want me out of the way, yeah?" Liam quizzes.

"We have no issue with you. But we will slaughter everyone linked to the O'Keenan's before we take power for ourselves," replies the mysterious voice.

"Can I negotiate for Bree's life? Can we walk away from the power and let Bree live?" Liam asks, and I start to shout at him, but Liam quickly covers my mouth to prevent anyone from hearing me. Clearly, he doesn't want the person on the other end to know I am here, but like fuck if he thinks I am going to just sit here and let him take what is mine.

"Why? Do you have feelings for Bree? We heard this was a black wedding, a marriage of convenience. Is that not true?"

"It started out that way, but now it's real, and I will not let her die," Liam speaks with such conviction that it's hard for me to tell if he is just playing along or if he means what he is saying right now. Does he see our wedding as real? Do I?

I physically shake my head, pushing all thoughts of that out of my mind, and trying to pull myself back into the conversation. However, the voice seems to be having a moment of contemplation, the silence continues, and I chance a look over at Liam. He looks furious, more so than he did when the voice initially threatened me.

"If you can get Bree to hand over to us, then we will let her live. But you only get one chance at this. When the time is right, and her Gramps has signed the paperwork to make her official, we will send you the same papers. Sign it over and make the announcement within twenty-four hours, and we will let you both live. If you don't, you will both die. Painfully. Do not double-cross me, boy. Do you understand?"

Liam agrees, and the call ends. I look over at Liam as he pulls over at the side of the road. He starts slamming his hands against the steering wheel and cursing loudly in what sounds like multiple languages. I wait for him to calm down a bit before I reach over and gently touch his shoulder. It's not much, but just enough to let him know I am here.

"Are you okay?" I ask. It sounds like a stupid question, but what else is there to say?

"No! Now we have another fucking enemy," he grumbles.

Taking hold of Liam's hand, I wait for him to turn to look at me. "It doesn't matter. We can fight them all. What makes you think this isn't the Marcushio's?" I ask although I think I already know the answer.

"If it was them, they would want me dead. So this has to be someone who doesn't want me dead, and I had an idea who it was from the beginning, but his last sentence confirmed it," Liam says, his face suddenly looking drained.

"You know who that was? How?" I have so many more questions, but I try not to overwhelm him.

"I think it was my father. I suspected when he gave me the chance to live, but then he called me boy at the end. That's always been what my father says to me. It's his way of reminding me that I will always be the child in our relationship and will never be able to take him on. Only someone who cares about me would compromise with me," Liam muses, and he does not look happy with his theory, but I think he could be right.

"What are we going to do?" I ask because I am not sure this is an enemy that Liam will take on, but I will not let someone destroy the perfect life I have built.

"I will deal with my father another day. I will text Kel now and ask him to look into the call for me. But for now, we will go on our date and pretend this shitshow didn't happen. Sound okay?" he asks as his face morphs back into the smile he was wearing before he took the call.

There's a part of me that wants to say no to the date and to go home. To find out whatever we can about what our enemies are planning. At the same time, I've been looking forward to this all week, and Liam has gone to so much effort to plan the most amazing first date. It may have got off on the wrong foot, but I sure as fuck will make sure we enjoy the rest of the night.

CHAPTER EIGHTEEN

Liam

It may not have quite been the start that I wanted for our first date, but I was determined to make sure Bree had a good time. I had planned this perfectly, and the idea that it could have been ruined by that bullshit phone call is pissing me off.

A part of me knew it was my father from the minute he started talking; he is synonymous with using those damn voice machines. But when he offered to spare my life if I walked away, that's when I really knew it was him. My father hates me. There's no doubting that, but he would never kill me unless he had to. It would kill my mother. If I refuse and leave him with no choice, he will move against me; he can argue his case for that. But he knows there is no way I will step aside and give him power. That's the last thing that a lunatic like him needs. London would be so much worse if the Doughty Family gains any kind of power, which is why people are wary about me. They think I am secretly working to hand power over to him, but if they knew me at all then they would know that is the last thing I wanted even before I met Bree. Now I have her and her safety to think about. She is my priority, and I sure as shit will not let anyone take her from me, especially my family.

As I drive the remainder of the way, we sit in silence, but I want to get back to the fun and banter we had before the call. I want to remove the concerned scowl that Bree is currently wearing. I know she is considering all the scenarios and working out what we will need to do next in her head, but I need to clear all that out. I need her to be in the here and now…with me.

"Have you worked out where we are going yet?" I ask playfully, taking hold of her hand whilst using the other to drive.

I chance a glance over at her and see her taking in our surroundings. She will be able to see very soon where we are going. "The beach?" she replies, her pitch rising at the end and turning her guess into more of a question.

"No, that's too far away," I tease.

"Can't you just tell me?" That adorable pout she uses when she isn't getting her own way reappears, and I want to kiss her so badly right now.

"Nope. Keep guessing," I sing, knowing I am winding her up but I can't help it. I love seeing her pretend to be annoyed. I know she really wants the surprise, that's why she hasn't asked about it before now.

Her gaze scans the surroundings again as she mutters about me being an asshole, just loud enough for me to hear. I see the first signs of our destination and keep casting glances over at her to see her reaction when she realises. I also try to keep an eye on the road so we don't die before getting to our destination. I know the moment she sees it because her whole body language changes. She sits up straighter and leans forward; her leg begins to bounce, which I have learnt she does when she is excited. The plastered pout on her face is quickly replaced by the biggest grin, and her silver eyes shine and glisten against the headlights of the cars zooming past us.

"We are going to the funfair?" she asks, almost in disbelief.

It might seem like a trivial date for some people, but not for Bree. I remember one of the first getting to know each other nights we had, and Kellan was there. He was telling her all about when we used to go to the funfair as kids. We would ride the big wheel, challenge each other at dodgems, just generally have a laugh. Kellan once ate so much cotton candy and doughnuts that when he threw up after going on the dodgems, it was a pink coloured vomit. Bree listened intently but never added in her own stories, so we asked if she had any. She was really sad when she told us she had never been to the funfair. Her mum thought it wasn't ladylike to have fun, and her dad said the security was too risky. Basically, they just wanted to tell her who she should be. I wanted to show her that with me, she can have whatever she wants. If I can give her the world, then I will.

"Yeah, Princess. That okay?" I ask, already knowing the answer.

Thankfully, I just manage to park the car and as I turn the engine off, she takes off her seatbelt and throws herself into my lap, kissing me hard. Her hands grip my hair tightly, pulling at the ends as she sweeps her tongue across my bottom lip, demanding access. I let her take what she wants, gripping her ass to pull her closer onto my growing erection. She shuffles slightly to get more comfortable, trying to swing her leg over until she is in a straddling position. However, there is not enough room between me and the steering wheel. Her movement causes a deafening and continuous burst of noise as she accidentally sits on the horn.

The noise scares the shit out of us both, and she jumps back onto her own seat as we both start to laugh. Our chuckles turn into a full belly laugh as we look at each other laughing. Reaching over, I give her a light kiss before pulling back and adjusting my cock so it's a bit more comfortable.

"Come on, Princess. Let's go for a ride," I joke, and she rolls her eyes at my lousy innuendo.

Getting out of the car, I run around to open her door but find she has already let herself out. She then reminds me that she is an independent woman who doesn't need men to hold her door open. While she mutters about feminine rights, I take hold of her hand and lead her to the entrance.

Buying our tickets, we walk inside, and I see her mouth is wide open in admiration. This is nothing new, but for someone who has never been before, it's a sight to behold. The lights, the music, the shrieks from the rides, but it's the laughter that rings out the most. Everywhere you look, people are having a good time. Couples on dates, families having quality time together, friends having a night of fun. Everyone is enjoying themselves, and as I watch Bree take in all the sights and sounds, it's like I see it all through new eyes.

"Where do we start?" Bree asks.

"Wherever you want, Princess. What takes your fancy?" I ask, and her eyes light up again.

"Well, I definitely want to try all of these food stalls over here. So I am guessing we should go on all the rough rides first because as funny as a pink vomit story is, I do not wish to experience it," she jests.

"Okay, so it depends on how aggressive you want to start.

If you want to go for it straight out the bat, then something like slingshot, twister, or loop rage. They do anything from sling you in the air, spin you around, and go upside down," I explain, and when she starts to go a little bit white, I decide maybe starting off with that is not the best idea.

"Alternatively, we can start with the mid-level stuff like waltzers, crazy frogs, or octopus, which are thrill-seeking but nowhere near as aggressive as the others." I wait for her to answer as she looks around.

"And if I want to start really slow?" she asks tentatively, and I smile.

"Then I have the perfect thing for you," I say before taking her hand and pulling her over to the dodgems.

We queue up, and her eyes light up with excitement. She watches the riders who are already on and laughs along with the people having their turn. As we get closer to our turn, I notice her reading the warning board, and she frowns.

"This says we aren't allowed to deliberately bump into people. That looks like half the fun," she asks, looking confused as she glances between the signs and the bumping clearly happening right next to us.

"Yeah, nobody follows that rule. They have it in place so that they cannot be held liable. Just try not to hit any kids too hard," I explain, and she chuckles before turning her mischievous gaze my way.

"Oh, they are safe. But you...I'm coming for you," she threatens with a sexy as fuck smirk on her face.

As soon as the ride attendant lets us in, Bree runs to the purple car she has selected in the corner, choosing colour over practicality. On the other hand, I carefully saunter to the luminous yellow one that is directly behind Bree. She looks around at me and catches the grin I have on my face, her eyebrows raise in question.

"Rookie move, Princess. Never choose based on colour. Always go for the dodgem directly behind your target. That way, you can get in at least one hit."

Just as I finish talking, the music starts, and she speeds off, trying to get away from me, but I bide my time. She makes the first corner, and just as she is making the second, I make a quick left turn. Cutting off the corner and ramming full speed into the side of Bree's pretty purple dodgem, it then sandwiches her against the wall.

"One - nil, Princess. Bring it," I joke, and she laughs before speeding off.

Several manoeuvres later, when the score is four-nil to me, she finally manages to get behind me, and the girl holds no prisoners. Putting her foot down entirely on the accelerator, she speeds right into the back left side of my car. This causes us both to spin and laugh loudly before I hear her shouting, "Four-one, I'm making my comeback."

She did manage to make her comeback, and eventually, she got her fourth hit just as the music stopped. As I helped her climb out of her car, she couldn't stop giggling. A little boy, who looked to be about seven or eight years old, stopped us on our way out.

"That was so cool. You looked like a fiery assassin charging into people. I know you were keeping score. I think she wins because she got a few hits in on other people," he says before his mum pulls him away, muttering an apology that Bree is quick to squash.

"Don't apologise," she says to his mum before turning to the little boy. "Thank you. I think I won too, but you were terrific as well."

His mum smiles, and the boy's face lights up before he runs off, pulling his exhausted-looking mother with him. This is what happens when you mix children and sweets; you get hyperactive kids.

"Looks like you have got competition, Liam, and I don't just mean at the dodgems," she jokes.

Silencing her quickly, I pull her body against mine and press my lips against hers. It's searing and passionate but full of the promise of more. I pull away far too quickly, deciding that a fair full of other people and kids is probably not the place to get hot and heavy. But I want Bree to know it is on the agenda, which is why I lean forwards and whisper in her ear, "Later."

Her breath seems to catch, and she smiles that shy but knowing smirk at me. "Where to next?" she asks.

We spend the next couple of hours wandering around the fairground, going on all the rides. The cute little carousel where we were the only adults that didn't have kids, to the slingshot that had us sit in a ball before shooting us into the air. I'm sure Kellan would have been able to hear her screams all the way back at home, but as soon as we landed and our feet touched the floor, she was back to giggling. I think we literally laughed and smiled the whole way round. We posed for selfies, played hook-a-duck games, and she scared the shit out of the guy running the shooting stall with her incredible precision. He made the mistake of asking if she wanted me to shoot for her. He said she had a better chance of winning something. Instead, she won the grand prize, and that's how I ended up having to take a four-foot bulldog wearing a union jack t-shirt back to the car. Apparently, we are naming him Gerard. After a few arguments about him taking up too much room, I finally just gave in and carried the damn stuffed dog.

We stuffed ourselves with hotdogs, doughnuts, cinder toffee, and cotton candy in between the rides. I had bags of sweets and delicious treats that I also took back to the car, including a very nice stick of rock in the shape of a large cock for Kellan. In addition, I won Hallie a giant, pink teddy which I know she will love. I was just grateful I managed to talk Bree out of choosing the goldfish. She felt Hallie would be more stimulated watching a goldfish. Until I reminded her that goldfish require actual care, Kellan is only just managing Hallie and himself, adding in another life, and he might crack.

A loud tannoy announces that the fair will close in ten minutes, and Bree looks a bit sad. "So we can fit in one more ride. What will it be?" I ask.

She looks around, taking her time to analyse her options. There are only a couple of rides that we haven't done. Some we have done multiple times because she enjoyed them so much. I will say yes to whatever she chooses. Still, I really fucking hope it's not the slingshot because I just ate a massive footlong hot dog and whippy ice cream, and I really want to keep that inside my stomach.

She starts pulling me quickly towards the far side of the ride. I must physically look terrified because nearly all the rides in this section will most definitely make me lose my dinner. "Relax, I want to go on the Ferris Wheel," she says with a smile as she pulls me into the very short queue. It's coming up for midnight, and the crowds left a couple of hours ago. The wait times are minimal now, and we are getting seated in the carriage in no time.

As the ride starts taking off slowly, Bree takes hold of my hand. "Thank you," she says with a squeeze of my hand and a bright grin.

"You don't have to thank me, Princess. If you want something and I can get it for you, then I will do it. I would give you the world if I could," I reply, looking away from her. I don't know why, but I feel vulnerable at this moment, alone above the stars.

Emotions are shooting through my body as I try desperately to grasp what I am feeling. I have never felt like this before. I have never felt like I might not be good enough for a girl, but with Bree, I don't think anyone will be good enough in my eyes. She is perfect.

Bree takes hold of my cheek and forces me to look at her. "Hey... all I want is you. I told you about me not having gone to a fair before weeks ago, and not only did you remember, you made it your mission to change that. You have made a little girl's dreams come true today, so don't you ever think any less of yourself. But there is one thing you can do to help make a grown woman's dreams come true," she states.

Before I can ask her what she means, she leans towards me and presses her lips against mine. As with all our kisses, what starts off sweet ends up being sizzling and sexy, full of passion. When we finally pull apart, we look around and see we are stopped at the top of the Ferris Wheel, looking out at the stars and the lights of the nearby towns.

"Now you have made my dreams come true," she mutters, and I ask what she means. "I've always wanted to be kissed amongst the stars at the top of a Ferris wheel." Her smile is incandescent, her fiery red hair illuminating in the moonlight with the bright lights from the fair hitting her at every angle.

"I'm a lucky guy," I say, giving her a sweet but short kiss as the wheel starts moving.

"I'm the lucky one. You are a pretty great guy, Liam Doughty. Kidnapping aside, obviously," she jokes just as the ride pulls to a stop at the bottom.

The ride operator looks horrified at her words. He's looking at me like I'm a psychopath, and he is considering jumping me. He looks like he is in his mid-teens and has absolutely no muscles and several patches of acne dotted across his face. Although he would stand no chance with me, I respect that he is concerned enough about Bree to consider it.

"I didn't mean that how it sounds. It's an inside joke between us. I can promise you I am not being held hostage or in any danger. He's my boyfriend," she explains and as she says the last word, I feel my body tensing.

Nobody has ever called me their boyfriend before, I never go that far, but really, we are so much more. Technically we are engaged, but that was supposed to just be for business. I think when Bree calls me her boyfriend, that's how she really sees us, and for once, despite how much it freaks me out, I am all in. I have no idea if we together will cause more harm than good, but I think I am falling for the fiery redhead. I will burn down the world around us as long as we can stand together through it.

After being shuffled out of the fair by the bosses who were closing, we climbed into the car, and I felt myself release an audible sigh I didn't know I had been holding. We had been on our feet, going from ride to ride for around four hours, and I was so bloody knackered. I look over at Bree to see her shyly trying to hide her yawn. Then, with a smile, I start up the engine and start the drive home.

We had been driving for around half an hour when Bree finally plucked up the courage to speak. She had been casting glances at me, looking like she wanted to say something since we got in the car. I was just waiting for her to see how long it would take her.

"Did it bother you when I called you my boyfriend? You kind of froze?" she whispers, looking down at her leg that has started to bop, this time out of nervousness.

"I'm not going to lie; the word caught me off guard, but not for the reasons you are thinking. When I heard it, I waited for myself to freak out. I have never been a boyfriend to anyone before, never wanted to be, and whenever a girl has suggested it in the past, I would bolt. So, yeah, I was waiting for that moment, but it never came, far from it. I think I actually may have liked being called your boyfriend," I explain. I know she believes me because her restless leg stops moving, and she tucks it under her bum as she turns as much as her seatbelt will allow so that she is facing me. The smile she has worn all night is now firmly back on her face.

"It just slipped out for me too, but I didn't regret it like I thought I would. I have feelings for you, Liam, really fucking strong feelings, and that scares the shit out of me. I planned on just keeping this a business deal, no emotions, but that is so fucking far out of the window that I don't know what to do." The words rush out of her mouth like she can't entirely control what she says, but they need to be heard.

"I have feelings for you too, Bree. As far as I am concerned, this doesn't change anything except make it better. I have never dreamt of getting married or anything like that, so doing it for a business arrangement and to help you out seemed like an easy decision. But after talking it through with Kellan, I would have said no to anyone else, but with you, it was easy. So maybe we need to just go with the flow and see where things go. If this turns into a real marriage, then that's a bonus. But, at the moment, I get to marry my friend and the only woman I have ever thought was capable of ruling her own syndicate." I speak with confidence and conviction, making it clear I mean every word I say.

"I think I am one lucky lady," Bree replies, and I can't help but lower the tone.

"You are a very lucky girl, Princess, and when we get home, I am going to show you just how lucky with my tongue, my fingers, and my cock."

CHAPTER TWENTY
Liam

I'm awoken by a gentle touch, and my brain tries to quickly catch up with what I am feeling. I don't know how it knows, but my body knows it's in no danger and that I can stay relaxed. I realise instantly why that is; I can smell him. His peppermint, coconut, and just a hint of petrol, plus something that is all Liam. I feel almost encapsulated by his warmth and his scent, and as I open my eyes, I realise why.

I must have fallen asleep on the drive home, and instead of waking me when we arrived, he was now carrying me into the house. His arm is tucked under my legs, with the other around my back, while he lets my body lean against his muscular chest. I leave my head resting there, just listening to the sound of his heartbeat. If I stay like this for too much longer, it will drag me back into my slumber, and I want to give him the chance to make good on the promise he mentioned before I fell asleep dreaming about it.

Climbing the steps to the front door, I start to wonder how he is going to get the keys and open the door without putting me down. I suspect he knows I am awake given the way my hand has been stroking his chest, but it's like neither of us wants to speak for fear it might burst the bubble we have thrown ourselves into. But before either of us gets the chance to make a move, the door flies open to reveal a very flustered looking Kellan.

Don't get me wrong, he usually rocks the dishevelled look, but this is so much more. His hair is all over the place like he's been running his hands through it constantly. The bags under his eyes look even worse. The frown lines look like they have been there so long that they will be permanent from now on, but I hope not. I have always thought his cheeky personality and looks were part of his charm. Whenever he decides to get out into the dating world again, women will go crazy for a guy as great as Kellan. Except right now, he looks almost scared.

"Where the fuck have you guys been? Why were you not answering your pissing phones?!" he yells, his eyes wide and almost feral looking.

Liam must have seen the same thing I did in Kellan's expression as he carefully lowers me into a standing position. All thoughts of exhaustion are long gone, replaced with the adrenaline coursing through my body at the possibility of danger.

"We put the phones away after that fucked up call earlier. We didn't want them to ruin our date," Liam explains, making sure to keep our fingers interlocked. It may not seem like much but just feeling his fingers gripping onto mine is everything.

"Well, while you two were enjoying your fucking date, I have been here dealing with your father and his men, Bree," he spits, anger coursing through his veins as he continues to pace.

Both me and Liam are equally stunned when he says it was my family causing problems; we had been expecting Liam's. Liam tries to calm Kellan down and persuades him to come into the living room to explain what happened. Kellan refuses to move.

"Your fucking family put my baby girl and me at risk today, Bree, and I will not forget this. I am going up to my room, you can deal with this shit, and we will discuss this properly tomorrow. If I stay any longer, I will say or do something I know I will regret," Kellan says, and both I and Liam shout after him, but he is in no mood to tell us what is happening. We look at each other warily. I think there would only be one reason Kellan wouldn't come into the living room to have a sensible conversation with us, and I really hope I'm not right.

Leading Liam through into the living room, I am not shocked to see my father sitting on our couch, lounging across it as though he owns the place. He is dressed in his usual black suit, with a blue tie today. That's the only part of the ensemble that he changes. His dark black hair is slicked backwards, undoubtedly to cover all the missing patches where he is going bald. To the outside world, my dad looks like an overweight, slimy businessman who does well financially but has nothing else in his life. They would be right. They must have parked their car around the corner or Liam and I would have spotted it out front.

Accompanying him, as always, is Jimmy, who is sitting on the only lounge chair, and Mouth, who is pacing near the dining table. Mouth has worked as my dad's personal bodyguard for a little over ten years, I think, and I still have no idea how he got that ridiculous nickname. But whenever I call him Malcum, his real name, he never responds.

"Father, it's gone one in the morning. What the hell are you doing here?" I asked incredulously.

"Well, Brianna, when I got here at nine, it was a slightly more reasonable hour, but apparently, you had a prior engagement. Do you really expect to be able to run this Family if you can't find the time for a business meeting?" His voice is strained like he is trying very hard to remain professional. This theory is backed up by how his eyes keep flicking between Jimmy and Liam, both of which would not tolerate him speaking to me like shit.

"I figured that since you haven't handed control over to me yet, I am not in charge yet, nor did we have a meeting booked. So why did you break into my house and threaten my guest?" I sneer, taking a less than impressed glance at the gun resting on his knee and the two attached to the shoulder holsters he is wearing. I know Jimmy will be packing, just a bit more discreetly.

"Given that this house still belongs to me, I think you will find you are the guest in my home, and that idiot is a stranger." At his words, I, of course, aim my gun at him; he's lucky I don't shoot him and his smart mouth. My father scoffs at my actions.

That threat is all it takes for Liam to take a step in my father's direction, but before he can say anything, I make sure to cut him off. Of course, no good can come from him shouting at my dad in anger, but that doesn't stop me. "Are you fucking serious? He is here, alone, with a baby, and you threatened him!" I shout, feeling my rage starting to boil under the surface.

"My enemies still have children, Brianna. Don't be so naive. Until I could be sure he wasn't a threat, I approached him as the enemy. If you do not start acting like that, you will quickly get yourself killed in this business. This is a prime example of why women shouldn't be given any power. They're too trusting." He throws the last part out there, waiting for the men in the room to agree with him. Mouth does instantly, but Jimmy and Liam stay quiet. I can feel the rage vibrating off of Liam from here, and the cold mask on Jimmy's face annoys me. I know in front of my father, he has to remain silent or just agree with him. But I want him to, for once, stand up for not only me but my gender as well.

"As much as I would love to stand here and get life lessons off you, it is a bit too late, don't you think?" I sneer, my disgust at his actions dripping off every word.

"Obviously not, Brianna, or you wouldn't be here whoring yourself out with two men. Please tell me that baby is not yours?" my father asks, and all I can do is laugh at the absurdity of that comment.

"When the hell do you think I had time to not only have a baby in secret but also to hide it from you for nine months?"

"I have no idea, Brianna. I feel like I don't know this version of you. Some slut so desperate for a power she can't handle that she is willing to whore herself out to two men. But not just any men, rivals." His words hit me like a truck. My dad has never talked to me like this before. I have never seen him look at me with such hatred or disgust. Tears start to fill my eyes, and I do everything in my power to push them back.

"How fucking dare you? You do not get to come into the house that Patrick offered to us as a safe space, waving a fucking gun around and insulting Bree. Now, say what you came to say and then get the fuck out. You are not welcome here with that attitude." Liam is firm and strong, his disgust at my fathers comment evident on his face. I am not used to having someone stand up on my behalf, and even though I definitley don't need anyone to fight my battles for me, I am fucking glad he is on my side.

"So you are the trigger happy assassin that thinks he can marry my daughter. Tell that asshole Desmond that he will have to try a lot harder if he wants my turf," my dad hisses, staring hard at Liam like he is something off the bottom of his shoe.

"I am not being dragged into a war of words with you. Everyone knows Patrick is the one who makes the decisions, and you will be made to go along with them. Of course, I will prove to him that I have no allegiance to my father or family, but I don't need to prove shit to you. As it happens, I really do like your daughter and not that you seem to give a shit, but I can

159

promise her a good life," Liam explains. I think my heart may actually burst from excitement. I can't believe he is standing in front of my father, telling him that our marriage has the potential to be real.

"You are not marrying my daughter, and that is the end of that discussion. But since your grandfather seems to want to indulge your every whim, I am supposed to hand over some key responsibilities to you. So, you can start by finding out who jumped and stole our shipment. We lost thirty AK47s, and they are now in the hands of one of our enemies. My money is on the Doughty clan, and it does appear you have an in with those thieving scumbag twats. I want you to interrogate whoever you need to, but most importantly...find me those damn guns. You have one week, and then I will get involved. Understand?" he asks as Liam and I cast glances at one another, stunned into silence.

Unable to form actual words, I nod my confirmation as my father stands up to leave. As he reaches the door, he turns around with his usual smug face staring straight at me. "Oh, I forgot. If even just one member of my Family gets taken out by an AK47 slug, I will wipe out the entire Doughty clan, whether they are guilty or not. And don't think I will miss those pretty little beauties you have stashed up North. Freya and Ryleigh, right? So you better solve this before there are any casualties," he threatens, but he has pushed Liam over a line he should have known better than to cross.

Liam lets go of my hand and charges my father, pushing him out of the door until my father is on the ground outside the house. Liam jumps after him like a caged animal who has finally found freedom. As he pounces, Mouth and Jimmy draw their weapons and firmly aim them at Liam. All I have on me is a knife, and nobody wants to bring a knife to a gunfight.

Pulling Liam back, I quickly push him behind me and stand between Liam and the bullets. Don't get me wrong, I am short enough for them to go over my head and still hit his, but neither of them will risk my life.

"We get your fucking warning, Father. Now get the fuck off my property!" I shout before turning my back on the guns. Of course, some would say that was a stupid move, and under normal circumstances, I knew my father or his men wouldn't kill me, but I couldn't say the same for Liam. So getting him back into the house was my number one priority.

By the time I manage to push Liam back inside, which in itself is not an easy feat given the muscular advantage he has over me, I could hear their car speeding off. Taking his hand, I lead him into the living room. Whilst we were outside, Kellan had come downstairs, carrying a very awake but surprisingly quiet-looking Hallie. There are three beer bottles fresh from the fridge sitting on the coffee table. He leans over and grabs one before taking a very long swig.

Liam seems to deflate and calm down just at the sight of Hallie, and as he sits down next to Kellan, he instantly starts stroking Hallie's bare foot. I can hear her coo from all the way across the room. I flop down onto the empty lounge chair that Jimmy had occupied not even ten minutes before. I feel as though all of the fight oozes out of me, and the pressure mounts. I know I can deal with it and take on all my enemies, but that doesn't mean I can't allow myself just one minute to feel the fear and let it overcome me. I need to feel it so that I can move on and use it.

"I'm sorry, Kellan," I whisper. It's barely audible, but all eyes find me, so I know they heard. Liam tries to tell me it isn't my fault, but Kellan remains silent. The silence says it all.

After a few minutes go by, he finally speaks. "Don't be. But things are really heating up around here. Is your friend still interested in babysitting? I have a lot of work to do, and I need someone to help with Hallie…and before you two offer, this shit is getting real. You need to take these threats seriously. You know what you need to do, right?" The last part is addressed to Liam, and his responding groan speaks volumes.

"Of course, I will give Mia a ring in the morning," I say.

"Please text me her details so I can check her out beforehand," Kellan asks, and I can't help but roll my eyes.

"Kellan, we have been friends for years, but fine, if that will make you feel better. So what is this thing you need to do that has you oh so very annoyed, Liam?" I can't help but ask; not knowing is making me anxious. My leg is bobbing up and down faster than a kid on a pogo stick right now.

"I need to go back and see my family," Liam mumbles, and I know a mask of confusion is evident across my face.

"I thought your family banished you. You can't go back, can you?" I ask, genuinely curious as to how he can get around that. Banishment sounds pretty final.

"That is why he looks like someone just pissed in his cornflakes. The only reason he would be allowed back is to introduce his family to his new bride-to-be," Kellan explains. His face is wrinkled with annoyance and intense concentration. They both seem to be trying to find a way out of this, but I don't understand why. There's no better way to scope out the competition than from the inside. I choose to ignore the part that says I only want to do this to learn more about Liam and his childhood. That's just a happy bonus.

"So, what's the problem?" I ask, not entirely sure why they hate the idea so much.

"The idea of you in the same room as my father makes my blood boil, Bree. He is dangerous, and I would really prefer if we came up with another plan," he explains as he continues to stroke and play with Hallie's tiny feet.

"That's bullshit. I was raised around danger; I can handle myself. Besides, I need your father to meet the next leader of the O'Keenan Family's London firm. He needs to know that I do not see him as a threat, and if he wants to continue and avoid a war between the two clans, he will respect my leadership. I can't show him that if I am hiding behind you, Liam," I point out, speaking with passion and confidence. If I am honest, I'm trying to avoid allowing the fear to seep into my voice. Fear is a weakness I cannot afford.

"Girl has got some balls. Looks like I am booking two tickets to Ireland," sings Kellan as he raises his beer bottle. "Here's to us trying not to go to war," he toasts with a laugh, but Liam and I say cheers anyway. We need all the luck and good fortune we can get if we are going to escape this mess unscathed so I can actually get to walk down the aisle.

CHAPTER TWENTY

Liam

After several long and painful days of arguing with Bree, I finally agree that she can come to Limerick with me. The idea of having her anywhere near my psychotic father has been winding me up all week. No matter how much Bree, Kellan, or even my own damn brain tried to convince me she can handle it, my protective instinct just couldn't take it. In the end, I agreed because common sense won out.

Over the past week, we had several more run-ins with Family members to discover their loyalty and who our enemies really are. They all sing similar songs about wanting to be loyal to Bree, about my father approaching them, and about knowing someone who has defected to the Marcushio's. But unless they all know the same people, which is impossible since they all come from different business strands, their stories are just a little too similar.

There have been cases where I have genuinely questioned whether we have interviewed that person before. The stuff coming out of all of their mouths was almost identical; it is hard not to think they were coached. But then the question becomes, by who? And which part exactly are they lying about?

It's a common tactic that if you want to throw people off your lie, you make sure to tell a few more so that people don't know which one is the lie. Is this Vernon, and they are never going to be loyal to Bree? Is this my father, and he really has been approaching people intending to get them to turn sides? Or is this the Marcushio's stealing people right from under our noses?

The problem is we have too many enemies on all fronts. It becomes too complex to deal with all at once. So, we are dealing with my father first. That's how Bree and I found ourselves in a car sent by my father, driving through the countryside from Shannon airport to my family estate on the outskirts of Limerick.

I watch as Bree takes in the beauty of the surroundings and the twang in my chest reminds me of exactly how much I have missed Ireland. Obviously, there are neighbourhoods I am not all that fond of, namely anywhere my father rules, but the area in itself is beautiful.

Ireland is well known for its greenery and idyllic scenery, and Limerick doesn't disappoint. The old-time feel to all of the buildings makes the town look older than it is. I can see Bree's eyes light up as we drive past the well-maintained cream and moss coloured bricks of King John's Castle. It's a legendary tourist spot on the western side of Ireland. People come from all over to see the castle that has housed many sieges over the years. Although it has recently been renovated, much of the external structure remains the same. Evidence of our developing brutality and new forms of weaponry has become apparent with each battle it represents.

"It's so stunning," Bree mutters, and I can't help but agree with her.

My father and his pompous grandiosity have been attempting to buy the castle from the Shannon Heritage company that owns it. He believes he will defeat and tackle any enemy he chooses if his base is impenetrable. Thankfully, they said no, repeatedly, much to my mother's pleasure. She indulges most of my father's whims. That's what tends to happen when you are being abused; you would rather work with your abuser rather than risk another beating. But she always hated the idea of lording what we had over the poorer areas.

I see the look on Bree's face when we make it out of the main, beautiful, picturesque version of Limerick and enter the slums. This is an area on the edge of the town full of people living in the poorest situations; often, they have no money and no other options. The crumbling council houses are built in a standard way. Still, to avoid them looking like the shit they are, the council painted them different bright colours. But now, all you can see are old shitty houses with crumbling bricks and awful, dull and chipped paint. The general foreboding feeling, in addition to the house colours, is not the only thing that tells me we are deep in the deprived neighbourhood; it's just the idea in itself. It's almost like you can smell the poverty.

The area was made famous in the film Angela's Ashes Based on the memoirs of a man living in the tenements in the 1930s and 40s, and while the area has generally improved, it is still the rougher and less affluent part of the city. Poverty, filth, vermin, and desperation are rife here and is painfully evident from the minute you arrive in the area. Somehow even the weather seems bleaker, more cloudy and likely to rain. Yet, in the bright tourist area of Limerick, the July sun shines bright.

Bree recoils slightly from the windows as she takes in the houses that have more crap dumped in their lawn than a recycling plant. Only a couple of people are milling around, and it's clear they belong here. They look withdrawn, gaunt, and generally unkempt. I know if we come through this area in a couple of hours when the town has woken up, the roads will be filled with unruly children, people doing drug deals out in the open, and even people shooting up right next to the kids. But the police stopped interfering in Limerick business a long time ago. This is how my father makes his fortune by ensuring that poverty remains, and he has a steady flow of repeat customers.

It's not long after leaving the slums, we turn onto my family estate. The large wrought iron gates, moulded in the centre into the shape of a D, swing open as the driver confirms who they are. If the gates weren't a giveaway on what to expect, then the stupidly long driveway allowed you to take in the massive land area that the estate is built on.

The old Georgian property, named Fedmore House, was built around 1880 and belonged to the parish. My father bought it around seventeen years ago, just before Ryleigh was born. In typical Desmond fashion, he couldn't leave the beautiful, idyllic house as it was. He needed the place to look big and extravagant, his ultimate display of power. So he expanded the already reasonably sized mansion by adding two extra wings, making the building into a horseshoe shape. He added a swimming pool, cinema, astroturf pitch, and the more he built, the better he looked, but we never got to see any of those things.

My siblings and I were assigned rooms on the furthest side of the western wing. My mother had rooms in the main building and generally could be found in one of the casual rooms in the main house while my father has the entire east wing with its own entrance, so we wouldn't be able to interfere with his business dealings. Unless we were summoned, of course.

We all had regular times when we would have to present in the east wing to get to the shooting range, spar, or whatever else my father had planned for us that day. He never saw us as his kids; we were simply pawns in his quest for power. So, the closer I got to arriving at the main entrance, the more my anxiety was starting to kick in.

Nobody except Kellan knows I suffer from anxiety. In the two years since I was banished from Limerick, I have managed to get it under control. But just the thought of coming back here, the resurfacing of all those horrible memories, is causing my heart to race. My palms start to sweat, and I hear my breathing rhythm change as I begin to hyperventilate. It's the worst thing I could have done, as it then makes all my other symptoms worse. My vision starts to blur, and my mind no longer even sees the horrible scenes of the past as it turns black. But that doesn't matter; the panic has already taken hold. If I don't get control back soon, I will faint.

I feel Bree take hold of my hands, and she keeps one firmly in hers, but the other she places on her chest, right over her heart. "Feel my heartbeat and listen to my breathing, then just copy what I am doing," she whispers, making sure my father's driver doesn't know what is going on. To a casual observer, it looks like a couple having an intimate moment. Still, in reality, it's my girl throwing me a lifeline.

Feeling the beat of her heart and listening to the inhales and exhales of her breathing, I let myself get lost in Bree. I let all the good things that I get from being with Bree consume me, pushing away past memories. Soon after, I feel a sense of calm overtake my body, and my rigid, tense muscles finally start to relax.

"You really hate it here, don't you?" whispers Bree.

"You have no idea."

We finally make it to the top of the ridiculously long driveway, driving past the stables and outhouses, where many regular house and security staff live. Growing up, my brothers and I had more fun there than we ever did in the main house until my father found us and beat us all for it.

The car stops, and the house butler, Manuel, is there in seconds to open the door for Bree. He would generally come around and do mine afterwards, but I get out myself before he gets a chance. Then, taking a deep breath, I look up at the grand doorway and see my mother and Finn, our middle brother, standing there waiting for us. I take hold of Bree's hand and lead her towards the welcome committee. I know I don't have to worry about our bag, as Manuel already has that in hand.

"Mother...Finn...you didn't have to come to the door," I say with a forced smile.

"Oh, nonsense. My baby boy is home. Of course I would come to greet him," sings my mother as she runs down the stone stairs and throws herself at me.

Using my free hand to catch her, I hug her painfully thin body whilst making sure I don't let go of Bree's hand. My mother eventually pulls back with a smile and turns to face Bree. My mum is a little woman, coming in at just under five feet, and she is painfully thin. But that is to be expected when your regular diet consists of chocolate, gin, and antidepressants. It's hardly a healthy balanced diet, but it's what she needs to get through the days here, so who am I to argue. Despite the general aura of depression and sadness that oozes out of my mother, I can tell that the smile she uses for Bree and me is genuine. That makes me happy.

Despite my mother not being a great mum growing up, I don't blame her, and I don't hate her the way I did when I was younger. I used to wish she would stand up to my dad, that she would fight him and fight for us, but she never did. It bothered us all for a long time growing up, but I saw how much shit she took from my father for us as I got older. He may have still abused us horrifically, but it could have been so much worse. I just wish she would have had the guts to leave with me when I got myself and my sisters out, but she said that while ever one of her children remains under Desmond's roof, then so will she.

"Mum, this is Brianna O'Keenan, but she goes by Bree," I say to my mum whilst gesturing towards Bree before repeating the gesture in the other direction. "Bree, this is my mum, Siobhán."

I smile encouragingly at Bree as she returns the smile and reaches for my mother's outstretched hand. "It's lovely to meet you, Mrs Doughty. You have such a beautiful home, so grand." Bree's gaze flicks around the bright green lawns that expand beyond the house as it sits on almost sixteen acres of land.

"Oh, none of that nonsense, Love. Call me Von; that's what most people call me. You are even more beautiful than I thought. Fire hair to match a fiery personality from what I've heard," my mum jokes, and Bree laughs.

"I hope you haven't heard anything too bad," Bree replies as my mother begins leading her up the path, but the door is blocked by my eldest brother, Evan, who now stands next to Finn.

They are both standing there with their hands on their hip, essentially guarding the entrance to the house. Evan is almost a twin version of me, except his physique is leaner from all the running he does, as opposed to the muscles I have. Growing up, people used to think we were twins, as we were born just ten months apart. The scowl and stiff posture don't match his usual fun, outgoing personality. However, Evan is precisely how I remember him. At twenty-six, he is the oldest child, three years older than me, and has been groomed since birth to follow in my father's footsteps. As he stands there in a suit, anger rippling through his body and a look of disgust on his face that is aimed at Bree and me, I no longer see the brother I once loved. Instead, all I see is a younger version of the man I have hated my whole life.

I also see the danger directed straight at Bree, and I pull her behind me, so I am directly between her and whatever is about to happen. I stare daggers at my brothers, making it very clear that I will face whatever they have planned, but they will not touch one hair on Bree's beautiful head.

"Enough of this stupidity. Boys, move out of the way, please," my mother says, suddenly sounding very tired.

"You were banished, Liam. What makes you think you can step foot back in this house again? And to bring the fucking O'Keenan bitch, you must be suicidal," Evan spits out, and I can see the fury etched on his face. One hand keeps clenching into a fist while the other hovers precariously over his gun. But we both know I am a much better and faster shooter than him, and I am armed. He would be down before he got his finger on the trigger, which is why he is throwing threats around.

Taking a few deep breaths, I try not to let the anger consume me as I reply, "Bree here is my fiancée, and you will show her some respect. You know that mother insisted he included exceptional circumstances to the banishment, and introducing my fiancée to my family is on the list."

"If we are following the rules, that means the girls should be here," Evan states.

"They will be here in the morning and will be staying for tomorrow night only because of the party. After that, we are all out of here. And the girls sleep together in the room next to mine. Is that clear?" My voice is stern as I make my demands very clear.

When Desmond added the exceptional circumstances clause into the banishment, he couldn't just give my mother what she wanted; he had to try and capitalise on it. So, the only way I can return it is to bring my sisters back too, which is why I have avoided this place for so long. I need to keep them safely away from Desmond and his friends' wandering eyes and perverted hands.

"We would never hurt the girl," said Finn quietly, almost like he was afraid to speak, but he wanted me to know that. I gave him a genuine smile before turning back to Evan, who is clearly running things around here now.

"Fine, but no hassle. The first sign of trouble, and I will not hesitate to kill Bree, do you understand?" Evan asks me, and I hear a little laugh coming from behind me. Evan obviously hears it too, and his face morphs into a look of deep displeasure. "Something funny, Hair?" Evan added, looking straight at Bree.

She doesn't even ask me what the word he uses means, having already deduced it was an insult given the way he spat the word in her direction. On the other hand, I know very well that he just called my girl a whore, but before I can even take a leap forward to beat on the little gobshite, she pulls me back. This time she puts herself in front of me, and I see the smile on my mother's face. Firecracker is definitely an excellent way to describe Bree.

"Sorry, I was just laughing at your incorrect assumption that you actually could kill me. I may be a girl, but you would be wise not to underestimate me. I come here in peace, not as the future leader of a rival syndicate, but as the girl who is about to marry your brother," Bree calmly explains, and Finn visibly relaxes. He tries to hide the slight smile, but I see it. My favourite brother is definitely still in there, even if Evan is lost.

"We all know that this is just a business deal, so don't come in here pretending like your black wedding is real," Evan grinds out, clearly annoyed that Bree has the balls to stand up to him. It's not exactly something we are used to seeing. Women don't live in our world and they most definitely don't argue with men in high ranking positions. As my fathers heir, Evan is second in command

and doesn't take shit off anyone.

"Actually, we may be getting married for business reasons, but we are in a real relationship. It may not be traditional, but it's ours. We came here to share it with you, not to be vilified before we even have a chance to step in the building," replies Bree, as my mother takes over her hand and leads her up the step towards Evan.

"Fine. Father wants to see everyone in his office. Right now," he adds, and with just one word, everyone around me seems to freeze. My mother looks dejected, Finn looked terrified, Bree looked apprehensive, and I was on edge as Evan basques in our fear. I had hoped we would settle in before facing him, but sometimes it's better to not put bad shit like this off. So as I take a big deep breath and squeeze Bree's hand in reassurance, I pull my posture back and clear any sign of emotion from my face. Then, remembering the training from long ago, reluctantly, I converted back into the shell of a man my father insisted I become. I only hope that once Bree sees this side of me, she doesn't run a mile. I have faith that she will pull me back from the dark place my mind has to occupy whenever I'm in this house.

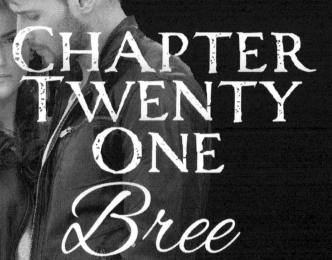

CHAPTER TWENTY ONE
Bree

As we walk through the opulent entrance corridor, I am in awe of the house's beauty. High ceilings, original features, and bright white walls give off a sleek, clean appearance. The hall leads into a large welcoming room. The most enormous crystal chandelier I have ever seen is hanging above us. The sweeping staircase is covered in white and grey marble, making it look lustrous and grand. Evan leads us to the right, and we all follow in uncomfortable silence.

The further into the house we get, the darker the decor becomes, and our moods begin to match as well. With every step we take, each Doughty seems to change a little more. They all have rigid, straight postures, like someone has shoved a pole up their ass, and they have no choice but to stand tall. Yet, they don't hold their chin high. Instead, they are all looking towards the floor. The more I glance at Liam, I watch as his eyes glaze over, and it's like I am watching them all turn into mindless zombies.

We reach a closed door, and Evan knocks twice, loud and firm, before returning his demeanour to match that of his family. As soon as Evan's fist connects with the door for a second time, Liam gently pulls me behind him and lets go of my hand. I try to grab it again, but he doesn't let me. Finn takes a step towards us, and at first, I am worried. I haven't been able to read whether he is a danger like his older brother or a victim like his sweet mother. But as he stands side by side with Liam, both blocking me from the danger behind the door, I decide he maybe is a victim. Although, there's still a chance of him turning, I will need to remain vigilant around him.

I open my mouth to speak to Liam, mostly asking for his hand back as I need to feel his warmth and strength, but as soon as the first sound leaves my lips, both Liam and Finn turn and shoot me with the most evil stare I have ever seen. At that moment, they look like twins, with the same dark and dangerous eyes.

A loud booming voice with a heavy Irish lilt shouts through the door, breaking our staredown. "Enter!"

Evan opens the door, and one by one, we file into the large office. The feminine, lustrous white decor that fills the house is nowhere to be seen in this room. Instead, dark mahogany covers the walls, the bookshelves, and the large desk that takes up most of the room. It's dark and foreboding from the minute you enter the room.

Liam's father, Desmond Doughty, sits behind the large desk, leaning backwards in his wide office chair. There is only one seat on this side of the desk, and I wait for Von to take it, but nobody does. Instead, Desmond stares at us all with large, dark eyes. Desmond looks good for his age, he is what some girls would refer to as a silver fox. He clearly keeps in shape and looks well-groomed in his posh black suit. His grey hair and matching beard are trimmed stylishly and distract from the dark eyes and slightly too large nose, not to mention the frown lines. But when you look at him, you don't see any of that. Instead, it is just the evil scowl that accompanies his sinister stare.

With Desmond's slight nod of the head, Evan takes the only seat in the room, and my conscience tells me I should say something. But, luckily, the sensible part of my brain is winning today, so I keep quiet and remain hidden behind the boys.

"I see the prodigal son has returned," Desmond sneers towards Liam, who just remains still and silent. "Why don't you introduce me to my new daughter-in-law? That's the reason you're here, isn't it?"

"Father, this is Brianna O'Keenan." His voice remains monotone as both he and Finn take a small step to the side, revealing me to Desmond. Although, I notice they both remain partially in front of me, and make no move indicating I should approach him to shake his hand. Especially since he didn't offer it. It doesn't escape my attention that Liam doesn't introduce Desmond. Maybe it's some weird power thing? I will stay silent until I know what is going on.

"Hello, Mr. Doughty. Nice to meet you," I reply, trying to sound as cheerful as I possibly can in a room full of monotone zombies.

From the second Desmond gets a glimpse of me, his dark gaze that was already sinister takes on an even worse tone. His glare reminds me of how a starving person would look at a chocolate cake, like he wants to devour me. Liam clenches his fist in front of me, but I'm the only one who sees it because Liam is always in my line of sight. To Desmond, his clone army is still standing perfectly still, void of anything, but I saw Liam's flicker of emotion. That protective instinct he has towards me is still there, so I know I can bring my Liam back.

"Well, well, well. Aren't you a pretty little thing? Thank God you look more like your mother than that eejit of a father you have. Though the red hair is unexpected. Maybe your mother was friendly with a redheaded member of staff?" he asks, and I know there is no point in replying to his bullshit. He is just trying to wind me up. Liam seems to quietly release the breath he is holding when he realises I am reluctantly staying silent.

"They have come to celebrate their engagement. I have arranged the party for tomorrow, as you instructed," says Von, her voice shaking as she speaks. I want to move to her and give her my strength, but I am quickly learning that if everyone else is as still as a statue, I should be as well.

Desmond looks at his wife with a sneer. Clearly, there is no love between them. She quickly averts her eyes and looks as though she wishes she had never spoken. Liam obviously is not happy with the way Desmond treats Von. His fist has almost turned white from all the tight pressure, yet he doesn't move, and when he speaks it is still emotionless. "You didn't need to throw us a party or go to all that trouble for us."

Desmond laughs, deep and insincere. He sounds like a stereotypical bond villain. "Oh, don't be an eejit, boy. The party may have your name on it, but it is all for me. To show my business colleagues about our new alliance," he sings, smiling sadistically at Liam.

"And what alliance would that be, father?" Liam asks. His voice almost remains neutral except for the slight growl he tries to hide as he says father.

"Well, from what I hear, your marriage means that you will inherit the London firm from Vernon. So that means the Doughty's will finally have a stake in the English capital," he jeers, looking very pleased with himself.

Liam starts to respond, but I cut him off. If I don't assert my dominance now, I never will. "I'm sorry, Mr. Doughty, but I think you have the wrong information. I will be inheriting the London firm, and Liam will be ruling with me, but I will be the one in charge. Of course, if you wish to develop a working relationship with me and my people, we can look into that. But you are wrong to assume you will automatically get power because of my feelings for your son."

As soon as the words leave my lips, chaos ensues. Von, standing right next to me, lets out a frightened cry as Desmond stands up in a roar. Evan copies his father but sounds a little more unsure of his actions before facing his family. Finn audibly groans but takes a step back in front of me, a move that is mirrored by Liam. Except Liam doesn't make a sound and still looks just as hyper-focused as before, only now his gaze looks to have a little more light, and they are aimed straight at Desmond.

"How dare you come into my house and disrespect me?" he barks, and I notice Von shrinks back a little, as does Finn. On the other hand, Evan is wearing an evil grin, looking as though this is going exactly how he wanted it to.

"I didn't cause you any disrespect. I merely stated that I will be taking over from my father. I am not asking for your respect as I believe respect is earned. You may not like this arrangement, but that's how it is," I say firmly.

Desmond slowly contemplates his reply, but instead, Liam addresses him. "We are here, like you asked, to announce our engagement. That is all. You can't use me in a play for power because I am no longer part of this family, and that is well known. Bree will lead the London firm, and she will be fucking great at it." Slowly with each word, I can hear my Liam coming back to me, and as soon as he swears and Desmond's eyes narrow, I know he is fully back.

"Why don't we all go and get freshened up? Then, we can meet for dinner at seven in the main dining hall," Von whispers, her voice shaking. I may not know much about how Liam was raised, but I am starting to get the picture pretty fucking quickly.

We all part and agree to meet back up in a few hours. Finn leads us to the opposite west wing, up the grand stairs, and as we walk down the long corridor, I watch both boys transform before my eyes. They start to relax, slouching more as they talk to each other. The banter and laughter come easily between them. It quickly becomes clear Finn is much more like Liam than Evan, which is good because I'm still considering stabbing the eldest brother for his whore comment earlier.

Finn walks us to the very end of the corridor, pointing out a room opposite which he indicated was his, and the one next to him was Evan's. Next to our room would be the room for his sisters when they get here tomorrow. I am excited to meet them; I know how important they are to Liam. As Finn shows us around the room, he opens a cupboard to reveal a secret fridge.

"I didn't know what you would like, Bree, so I just stocked it with lots of chocolates, some cream cakes, a bottle of red, white, and rosé wine, some diet coke, and of course Liam's favourite, beer. If you want anything that isn't in there, I can get it for you," Finn states, looking at me with a big, bright smile. As he hands me my favourite chocolate bar with a cocky smirk that matches Liam's, I can't help but smile. This one is definitely the charmer of the family.

CHAPTER TWENTY TWO
Liam

"**H**ow are you doing, Finn?" I ask, unable to resist any longer.

When we first got here, and he was standing guard at the door, I thought my father had got to him and managed to corrupt him like he did Evan. But then he stood beside me to protect Bree, and I knew my big brother was still in there. The problem is that we all have to play a role here, pretend to be the person my father wants us to be and just hope the whole time that we can come out of it when the time is right.

Finn exhales loudly before plopping himself down on the bed. "It's a fucking nightmare, Liam. I should have got out when you did," he groans as I sit down next to him. I see Bree take a seat on the sofa in the corner near the fridge as she demolishes the chocolate bar Finn gave her. She looks a bit uncomfortable, like she wants to provide us with some privacy, so I smile at her. I love how she is so kind and caring to the people who matter to her, and it's great that she now includes the people who mean something to me.

"Why didn't you?" Bree blurts out before covering her hand and mumbling an apology for asking an invasive question.

"Don't ever apologise for that. There's too much censorship in this fucking house as it is. This wing has always been our safe space. And to answer your question, I'm ashamed to say I was afraid. I had no money, and Liam was using all he had to look after the girls. He didn't need his big brother to be a burden either," Finn admits, although he doesn't make eye contact with either of us as he speaks.

"Fuck that. You would never have been a burden. What con has he got you doing now? It must be bad if it has you reevaluating the past," I ask, and Bree looks very interested in the conversation now. She has been desperate to learn about my past, but some things are hard to explain.

"Don't judge me for this, okay, Bree?" he says to her before turning back to me. "Do you remember Mrs. Windslow?" he asks, and I rack my brain for where I have heard that name before.

After a few seconds of thinking, it finally comes to me. "You mean the old secretary from St. Mary's?" I ask for confirmation. If it's the person I am thinking of, she was a lovely older lady at our junior school who used to work for the headteacher. She's the person Mum would ring when one of us was sick. I haven't seen her since we moved to secondary school-aged eleven, so that's almost twelve years ago. No wonder it took me a while to think of the damn name.

"Yeah, that's the one. Well, Dad found out she not only owns a considerable property but has a big retirement fund and life insurance payout. Plus, she has no relatives. Currently, her money is being split between the church and the Pug Welfare and Rescue Association. Apparently, she likes pugs and Jesus," he explains, and I am trying really fucking hard to get five when I add up four and four. Because there aren't many reasons he would need to know this information, but I hope it's for a different reason than the one currently running about in my head.

"Please tell me you aren't doing what I think you are?" I ask him, but he remains silent, just shaking his head. Further confirmation of what I already know.

Fuck! It's times like this I really fucking hate my father and the power he wields over others.

"Sorry, I may be being stupid or naive, and you can tell me to sit quietly in the corner with my Cadbury's, but I have no idea what you are talking about. I would love an explanation," she says, looking sheepishly at the second chocolate bar she just started on.

I can't help but smile at how cute she looks tucked up on the sofa, her knees crossed as she looks at her chocolate lovingly. Fuck, I'm actually jealous of a chocolate bar. What the hell is wrong with me? Finn catches me looking and gives me that knowing smirk.

Asshole.

"Growing up, we were all given a role, a talent that we were told to foster. Liam was a fucking good shot, so assassination was his bag. Evan hasn't always been how he is now, but my father has influenced him far too much. Desmond loves to cause pain and suffering. Evan has slowly been turning off his emotions more permanently and has become so fucking angry that it's scary. Whereas my talent is that I'm a good liar and manipulator, and when you add in my looks and charm...well, ever since then my father has essentially been using me as a honeytrap scam," he explains, and Bree looks stunned. Although he is fucking great at his job, I know my brother so well that I don't ever have to worry about him lying to me. I know all his tells. I will have to let her in on Finn's secret's so she can feel safe in the knowledge he isn't ever manipulating her. Not that he would, my brother hates his job.

She's sitting on the sofa with a chocolate bar in her hand, raised as though she will put it in her mouth until something stops her. She literally sat open-mouthed like a fish, gobsmacked. I can't help but chuckle at how fucking cute she looks. Finn joins in with the laughter too, and that's all it takes to snap her out of it.

"Wait! So...so how old is this woman exactly?" she asks, and I see Finn grimace.

"She is a very young seventy-two," he whispers, and now it's my turn to look shocked. I hear Bree choking on her chocolate in the corner.

"Fuck me. I was thinking she was in her sixties, and even then that was bad," I say, and instantly regret it when I see the look on Finn's face.

"So, what...you have to marry her? Are you having sex with her?" Bree asks, her voice becoming more high-pitched as she asks Finn questions I never saw coming.

"We are dating at the moment, and yes, I am supposed to marry her immediately so we can get the will in my name. Unfortunately, she is starting to lose her marbles a bit. If we don't move quickly, her consent will be questioned. And no...I can't bring myself to sleep with her, but I am going to have to if I want her to believe that this is real," he explains, sounding more and more dejected as he speaks.

"Fuck!" Bree and I both say simultaneously before looking at each other and laughing. I can almost hear Finn rolling his eyes.

"That's not even the worst part," Finn adds. "Her nurse is

McKenna Lowry."

"Fuck, you are really screwed," I add, not really needing to state the obvious, but it comes out anyway.

"Before you ask, Red, McKenna and I were best friends growing up. When we were sixteen, she told me she liked me. I liked her too, but I had just been given my first mark, and it was one of her friends. My father told me that I couldn't have girlfriends unless it was in secret, away from the mark. She deserved better than that, and so I told her I didn't feel the same way. I ripped both our hearts out, and we haven't spoken to one another since. She is still just as fucking gorgeous now, you know," he added, looking at me for confirmation. I shake my head. There's no way I will sit in front of my girlfriend and tell her how hot McKenna was growing up. She was hot, but she only had eyes for my dick of a brother.

"I know this might seem like a really stupid or obvious question, but can you not say no?" Bree asks gently.

Finn stands up, facing away from her, and raises his t-shirt. At first, I get ready to bollock him for undressing in front of my girl, but then I see the look on Bree's face. She looks horrified, but all I can see is his ridiculously tight abs. I stand up to see what Bree is staring at, and my anger bubbles over; a murderous rage fills me.

All across Finn's back are strips of red and exposed skin in various degrees of healing. Some look to be cuts, others bruises and given the shape and size, I know exactly what caused these wounds. It seems like he was whipped with both ends of the belt and the buckle end appears to have done some fucking messed up shit to his back. It looks as though the skin has been pulled away to reveal pink flesh. The varying degrees of healing basically means this is a regular occurrence.

"Why the fuck is he beating you every day?!" I shout.

Exacerbated, Finn sighs before he starts to mumble. "I have my instructions, Liam. This is my motivation. Every day I don't seal the deal, I get another ten lashes."

If I thought I was angry before, nothing prepared me for my little spitfire. Jumping to her feet, she walks to Finn to check on his wounds, gently using her fingertips to assess them. She may have no medical training, but she has been swotting up on first aid. She figured we have so many enemies, it might be essential to know. Plus, with a baby in the house, it's even more critical.

"Finn, some of these look really sore," Bree says as Finn pulls his t-shirt back down in our typical avoidance fashion. We all learned to take shit like this long ago, but I always hated seeing my siblings going through it. I hate it even more now.

"Look, forget I ever said anything. I'm gonna go and take a shower before the shitshow starts. I will be back to meet you at like ten to. Is that enough time?" Finn asks, and I say yes.

As he is going to leave, he throws his head over his shoulder to address Bree. "It was nice to meet you, Bree. I hope this place doesn't ruin you."

As Finn closes the door, I stand up and go and sit on the sofa next to Bree, leaning forward to give her a kiss once we are on the same level. As soon as her lips touch mine, things become heated between us, and before I know it, she is sitting on top of me, straddling my thighs, my hands gripping her ass and her neck to hold her close.

As our kiss breaks, I look her in the eyes and continue to use the hand that isn't on her ass to stroke her face. "Are you okay, Princess? I know this has been rough, but it's only a little over twenty-four hours and we can go," I ask with a sarcastic chirp at the end.

"I thought my family was bad, Liam, but your family is batshit crazy," Bree jokes, and I can't help but laugh. I am most definitely not going to disagree with that.

"I'm an assassin by trade, Princess. You can't have thought I was raised by good people," I add, and she laughs.

"True, and normally I would totally jump on the opportunity I have right now to talk about your past, but I hope it will come another time. Because right now, I want to sit on my knees and see how much of your cock I can swallow to distract you from where we are. Is that okay?" she asks through hooded eyes as she slowly slides down my body until she is kneeling before me.

"You can suck my dick anytime you want, baby. You don't need an excuse," I reply as she pulls my growing erection out of my jeans.

"That's good to know. Now shut up so I can see if I can deep throat him. I was a bit gutted last time that I didn't quite manage it." She pouts as she licks the tip.

I'm fucking glad I have already agreed to marry this woman because she is most definitely a keeper.

CHAPTER TWENTY THREE

Liam

The evening passes by in a blur, and I am on edge the entire time. My muscles are coiled tight, my posture rigid, and my face is constantly an emotionless mask. I feel the darkness of the past creeping into every corner of my brain. I am reminded of why it was crucial to get out of this place before I lost myself.

Now I have a new plan that involves getting Finn the fuck out with me. Hearing him talk last night reminded me of how much I used to protect him when I was here. He may be my big brother, but our relationship has never worked that way. Finn isn't built to withstand pain the way I am, and despite a lot of attempts on my father's part, he can't get him to turn off his emotions, which means he will never be any good at this business. This is something I am fucking pleased about. The longer I sat at dinner last night and watched Evan interacting with my father, the more I realised I had already lost one brother. But, you can be fucking sure I'm not losing another.

Every time I thought the darkness of this place was going to consume me all over again, Bree was there. A touch of her hand against my skin, a squeeze of my hand, or a chaste kiss. Not to mention the fucking tremendous blow job last night. It's like for every piece of darkness that comes with this house and this family, she shines an even brighter light and reminds me of my new life. It may be full of fucking unknown enemies that want to take it from us, but being here just reaffirms precisely what I already knew. Nobody is taking Bree and our life from us.

Morning arrives far too quickly, and I am filled with a fresh dread; my sisters will be home any minute. Just as I am thinking of that my phone vibrates.

Ryleigh: We are nearly there. Remind me again why the hell we have to be here?

Freya: Don't listen to her. She's just grumpy because she was out last night and has a hangover.

Ryleigh: Fuck you.

Freya: Despite the fact that I know you will have already read the above message, eejit here wants me to erase it and tell you she is so pure and well-behaved that she doesn't even know what alcohol is.

Ryleigh: Fuck you. I am a fucking angel compared to you. Or do you wanna tell him about the blow you did and Big G?

Freya: I'm going to fucking kill you.

Liam: GIRLS!!!

Liam: Please, just chill the fuck out. When will you be here?

Liam: And what the hell is Big G?

Freya: About five minutes, I can see that ugly ass gate.

Ryleigh: It's not a what; it's a who.

Liam: I will meet you at the door, do not get out of the car until I am there.

Liam: And we will talk about the drinking, drugs, and Big fucking G when you get here.

"Fuck!" I shout as I spring out of bed, pulling on some nearby boxers and sweatpants.

As soon as she hears my desperate yell, Bree comes charging out of the bathroom. She holds her toothbrush like she might be able to use it as a weapon while wearing only a sexy purple and black lace panty and bra set.

"What is it? Are we in danger?" she asks, scanning our surroundings.

"No, my sisters are at the gate. I need to get down to the entrance before my dad or Evan does. Also, it turns out my teenage sisters have discovered alcohol and drugs in the three months since I last saw them…And someone called Big G," I say incredulously, hating the idea that my sisters are growing up. It was hard enough to prepare them for puberty or when Finn and I had to go and buy them their first bras, but this is something completely new. I thought they were good girls.

While I have a meltdown trying to find a t-shirt in the bag I bought, Bree runs back into the bathroom and finishes whatever she was doing. She walks back out looking as gorgeous as always. Only now, she is rocking the tightest pair of leggings and a baggy t-shirt that hangs off one shoulder, giving me a little peek of the fantastic push-up bra she has on under there. She strides over to me, pulls my hand out of the bag before instantly handing me a white t-shirt to go with the grey sweats. I don't miss the way her eyes appraise my body as she watches me pull the t-shirt on.

"Don't look at me like that, or I won't be able to make it downstairs in time," I threaten with that knowing cocky smirk I know she loves.

"You know, I think any guy looks hot in sweats, but right now, you look good enough to eat," she purrs as she slides up to me.

Throwing her arms around my neck, her fingers work their way into my hair as she pulls my head down so our lips can touch. Like normal, the kiss starts off sweet, but as soon as our lips touch, it's as though all thought is erased from my mind and all I want to do is consume her. Her tongue demands access, and obviously, I oblige, but the resulting moan that escapes from us both as our tongues meet brings me to my knees.

A vibration noise comes from the surface next to us and pulls us both out of the little bubble we get into when we are around each other. Like the whole world falls apart, and all I see is Bree. I reluctantly pull away and read my phone before cursing loudly once more.

"What's wrong?" Bree asks.

"Evan is on his way to the door. Finn is with him and doing his best to put him off. But if Evan knows, then that means so does my father. I need to get down there. But don't think I will let you get away with getting me all excited with no time to act on it," I tease. She bites on her lower lip while trying her best to look innocent. It doesn't help my growing hard-on in the slightest.

"Sorry, babe. I didn't mean to get you all worked up. Oops." She torments me as she deliberately bends over in front of me to tie her laces.

Her gorgeous, round ass is pushed up in front of me and fuck, it does nothing to help my now very strained cock. She knows she is teasing me when I have no time to give her what she knows we both need, but I can give her a little taster. As soon as my hand connects with the plumpest section of her ass cheek, she releases a little yelp before jumping up and turning to face me. Her hand tries to touch the sore area on her ass, but my hand beats her to it, and I gently caress the place I just spanked.

"What the fuck, Liam?!" she shouts, and I can't help but laugh.

She may sound annoyed, but I can see the flush in her cheeks and the fire in her eyes. There's no denying she enjoyed it. "Don't pretend you didn't like that, Princess. We both know that if I was to touch you right now, your pussy would be dripping wet. But don't worry, that spank was just a taster of what is to come later. You have been a naughty girl trying to get me all hot and bothered when you can't do anything about it. So, later, I will make you so desperate to come you will be begging me. If you are a good girl, I might even let you. Now, come on," I say before taking hold of her hand and dragging her out of the bedroom, ensuring I close and lock the door behind me.

Kellan has the security cameras hacked, and I have my own sensor that I hooked up above the door as soon as I got here. So I get a notification to my phone every time the door is open, and it immediately activates the cameras we have in the room. They don't record until they are activated, and I can deactivate them. You can't be too careful around here. I wouldn't put it past Desmond to have cameras or recording devices set up in the room so he can monitor us. He may not have looked like it, but he showed me just how scared of Bree he really was yesterday. Now I just need to find out if he is responsible for taking the AK47s, where he is keeping them, and what exactly he is planning. Something tells me straight up asking him will not work, which is why I have my own bugs supplied by Kellan. I just need to work out how to get them into his office.

Bree and I run through the house as I pull her behind me until we reach the front door. We get there just in time because things are starting to kick off. Finn is blocking the front door while Evan attempts to get past him to open it. My mother is standing nearby, just watching the boys fumble and argue like they are teenagers. I am actually impressed with Finn's strength. He appears to be holding his own against Evan, which definitely would not have been the case before I left. From the way he is ducking and diving before getting the odd push in and blocking everything Evan throws his way, it looks like he has been training in some form of martial arts.

Luckily, we arrive just in time as a booming voice fills the hallway and brings everyone to a standstill. "Stop!" My father's thundering voice ripples around us, and it's like he has a controller and presses pause because every one of us stops mid-motion. "Stop fucking about and open that door. I want to see my girls," he taunts, looking directly at me with a smirk.

After all this time, that fucker still hasn't realised that he will not be able to touch a single hair on their head for as long as I am breathing. Finn stands out of the way, but looking at me, he makes no move to open the door. He is looking for my confirmation, I give him a slight nod, and he allows Evan to get to the door handle. Evan holds the door open, and my father walks out first. Evan follows him out, as does Finn. My mother remains frozen in place. Bree and I walk over to her.

"Why did you bring them here, Liam? They were safe," she softly cries, and it breaks my heart.

"I promise you, I will keep them safe," I explain vehemently as my eyes scan between my crumpling mother and the car outside. My father is currently threatening the driver, telling him to open the doors for him, but this driver doesn't work for him. I paid for the ride and paid him a fuck tonne of money to only open the car doors to me. But my father's already nonexistent patience looks to be wearing thin.

"Go. I will stay with your mum," Bree whispers before pushing me towards the door. I smile gratefully at her before running out the door.

BANG!!

The gunshot rings out loud, and chaos ensues. I turn back to check on Bree to see her push my mother around a corner. She takes out the gun she must have stashed in her leggings and takes position around the corner. Ready for any danger, but also protecting my mother.

Luckily, I remembered to pick up my gun as we left the room, so I slid it out of my ankle holster before looking at where the danger came from. Finn has hit the floor but doesn't look injured. Instead, he is keeping himself safe as he's obviously unarmed. Rookie mistake in this fucking house.

Evan stands next to my father with his gun out, pointed straight at me. On the other hand, my father is leaning in through the now broken window, so he can open the car door. I quickly realised that my psychotic excuse for a father got so impatient waiting for the driver to open the door that he actually shot him. The young man I had hired to drive my sisters is slumped over the steering wheel, blood running through his bleach blonde hair and down his face. Given the amount of blood and brain matter splattered across the passenger side window, there is no question that he is dead.

High-pitched screams from the car's back seat pull me out of the haze I am in, and I propel myself to the passenger side back door. My father has the doors unlocked, but I need to get there first. I pull the passenger side back door open before my father has a chance at the other side. Having already worked out who is opening which side, both girls are huddled against my door. From the second I open it, they practically fall out. I help Ryleigh out first and then Freya, making sure I put them both behind me, keeping my gun aimed at my father. That's when I see Evan.

Unfortunately, it is two against one. My father approaches from the rear side of the car, his gun aimed at me, as Evan comes from the opposite side with his weapon also pointed at me. Knowing my father is much more of a threat, I keep my gun aimed at him, but I know I'm in the shit here.

Before I can think of a plan, I see Bree come flying down the stairs, her gun firmly trained on Evan, and she plasters herself against my side. Then, using her free hand, she curves it behind her to ensure my sisters are firmly tucked between the two of us. Part of me wants to kill her for putting herself in danger, but the other part of me wants to fucking kiss her. Not only did she put herself between me and Evan's shot, but she also ensured my sisters were firmly hidden and protected. Fuck, I love this girl.

Wait, what? I love her? Fuck, I mentally chastise myself. I need to get my head back into the game. I will come back to this another time, when I am not being led by adrenaline and how hot she looks holding a gun.

"What the fuck? You did not have to shoot him!" I shout at my father, who simply curls his lip up in a sneer.

"I gave him an instruction, and he refused. I will not accept any disrespect in my own home, boy. You may think you have big bollocks over in London, but this is Limerick. This is my territory, my rules. Now, step down. I will not ask again," he spits out.

I feel my hand almost start to lower out of instinct alone until I hear the soft cries from behind me. My terrified sisters remind me of why I am standing up to this asshole.

"Why don't we all lower our weapons? The girls are scared, and I don't think this is quite the welcome they were expecting," states Bree from behind me.

My father and Evan both growl at the same time. They are not used to having a woman who is willing to stand up to them. But they are very much mistaken if they expected Bree to stand in the corner cowering like my mother currently is. Bree is someone who loves with all her heart, and if she cares for you, she will think nothing of risking her life for yours. She shows no fear and will throw herself into anything. Basically, the opposite of how every mafia princess is raised. Girls in our world are taught to remain silent and scared. Not to defend themselves or speak their mind. So Bree is precisely the type of girl my father hates, which is a good thing because he is a fucking pervert. He won't be interested in a girl who can fight him.

"You do not get to make demands in my house. Do you want to end up like him?!" my father shouts, pointing over at the man behind the wheel with a hole running through his head.

My sisters began to cry again at the mention of the body nearby, as did my mother. I look over at her and see Finn has crawled over and is standing in front of her. He might not be armed, but he will protect our mother if things start to go to shit.

"We both know you can't kill me. If you do, the entire O'Keenan Family will rain holy hell down on you and will wipe out any trace of your existence. And before you say anything, that is not a threat, it's a certainty. So, unless you want to curse everyone who has ever come into contact with you, then I suggest we all lower our weapons, and we can welcome the girls peacefully," Bree states.

There is no threat in her voice, nor does it shake. She simply affirms precisely what would happen. She is the apple of Patrick's eye, and even Vernon would want to get revenge for Bree. My father knows it would start a war, but he is still determined to save face in front of all the employees gathered around the grounds. They obviously heard the gunshot, and it got their attention, but they are not stupid enough to get too close. They have seen my father lose his shit before, and everyone is in danger until he drops the damn gun.

"Look, I will put mine away first, then Evan. We go one at a time, so you know we are serious," I say as I put the gun into the waist of my sweats. I will put it in my holster when shit has calmed down more, but I know one of the girls can get it if they need it. Both girls have been trained to shoot with me. Freya is a damn good shot too. The problem is that even though they can shoot if needed, they don't want to. I have sheltered them from this shit for so long, it's like they aren't used to it happening anymore. Which is why they are so upset. I should be pleased that the loss of a human life still gets to them, but I do need them to toughen up just a little, at least around Desmond. He will tear strips off them if not.

Once the gun is away, I look over at Evan, waiting for him to lower his weapon, which he doesn't. Instead, he looks over at my father for his permission. With a slight nod of the head, Evan follows the instructions like a good little lapdog and puts away his gun. My father then looks towards Bree.

"Your turn, Pox. Gun away...but don't think I will forget this," he threatens, and Bree just laughs.

"You forget, I may have been born in England, but my family is Irish, and I spent every summer in Cork. I know what Pox means, and I may be a nuisance, but you need to take what I say seriously. I am not kidding around when I say I want to rule the Family, and I am not afraid of you. At some point, we will have to discuss whether you want to be my enemy, or see if we can work together, but now is not the time for that. So, I will put the gun away, and I hope you have the balls to stand by your word and do the same." Bree stands firm as she tells my father exactly how she plans to handle their business relationship. I had no idea she planned to talk to him about an alliance, if he turns out not to be the enemy we are looking for, of course. I would have told her she was fucking crazy.

Desmond looks like he is physically shaking with rage, but I know he will put the gun down. Bree called his word into question, and although my father is a psychopath, he is very strict about promises. If you commit, there is no backing out. He puts the gun into his holster, and as the final threat is removed, I let out a breath I didn't know I had been holding.

"Get your sisters settled in. We will meet for breakfast in twenty minutes. And Bree...we will have that meeting after. Understood?" he asks, and Bree is quick to confirm.

Before I have time to object, Bree takes hold of my arm and indicates we should take the girls inside. I am pulled out of my anger by the silent sobs coming from my sisters, and the overwhelming need to protect them forces me to push them into the house. Finn already has mum in the house, and the girls are quick to run as far away from Desmond as they can.

I take them up to the room next to us, as I instruct Finn to help Mum calm down. Once the girls, Bree, and I are in their room, I close and lock the door. My fingerprint lets the sensor know it's me and that there is no danger yet. As soon as the lock turns, my sisters crumble. Freya falls to the floor in front of the bed, her head against her knees as she folds herself, making herself as small as possible. Her tears flow freely.

Ryleigh, on the other hand, throws her arms around my neck, gripping onto me like I am her final lifeline. Her sobs echo around the room, and I wrap my arms tightly around her, stroking her back and whispering reassurances into her ear.

I look over at Freya and watch as Bree sits down beside her, mimicking her position. Freya casts a glance at the stranger sitting next to her, and seeing the small smile Bree aims at her, Freya gently lays her head on Bree's shoulder. Bree looks over at me with her smile, and I know for sure what I felt earlier wasn't just an adrenaline rush, heat of the moment thing. I fucking love this girl, but I need to find the right time to tell her.

Eventually, I manage to get Ryleigh seated on the bed that Freya is leaning on, and their tears begin to dry up. Silence fills the room, but I just don't know what to say. I'm the one that dragged them here and made them witness that horrific incident. If I hadn't returned, they wouldn't have had to either. It's my job to protect them, and I failed. So how do I find the words to say I am sorry?

Before I get a chance to say anything, Freya lifts her head and addresses Bree. "You must be the bride-to-be?"

"Yeah...sorry it wasn't a great first meeting. I'm Bree," she mumbles, clearly not sure how to talk to my sisters right now.

I can tell by the slight shake of her hand that she is trying to hide, the pink tinge on her cheeks, and the way she is chewing on the inside of her lip that she is nervous. She knows how important my sisters are to me, and it's obvious she is worried they won't like her; she doesn't have to be.

"You are kidding, right? Girl...you are a badass. The way you stood up to that asshole. We have been trying to learn how to do that for years. I'm Ryleigh, by the way." Ryleigh states as she pulls herself away from my hold, looking embarrassed by the wet stain she left on my t-shirt.

"I'm Freya. I don't know how you have the balls to do what you just did, but thank you," my eldest sister says as she holds her arms out, asking permission to hug Bree. She quickly obliges, and it's not long until my youngest sibling throws herself on the floor to get in on the group hug. Their joint laughter is like music to my ears.

As they pull away from the hug and start to giggle, I feel my heart starting to fill even more than before. How has a girl I never saw coming managed to fit into my life so perfectly?

"Before we go down for breakfast, can I ask something? Why does your father do this to you?" Bree asks, and both the girls look away as though they are embarrassed. They have no reason to be.

I start to answer, but Freya cuts me off. "When we were younger, we were literally both his favourites. He adored us and showered us with more love than he did all the boys, more than we thought he was capable of. Then one night, when I was about fourteen, Dad was drunk, ranting and shouting at Mammy. Normally, she just lets him get on with it, but she was equally as drunk this one night and couldn't take any more. It turns out that night was the anniversary of the death of their child. She would have been born before me, after Liam. Evan was only four at the time, so none of them remembered there was a baby. Apparently, Mammy did not take the baby's death well, and to cut a long story short, she had an affair. During this drunken argument, Mammy let slip that we are not really Desmond's daughters. She has never revealed who our father is, which is a good decision because Desmond will have him slaughtered. But since that day, he stopped seeing us as his daughters, and we became a commodity. He has to benefit from our existence somehow, and he decided that sex is our only asset. He also knows that he can use us to get to Mammy, which is why

EMMA LUNA

he drops a lot of sexual innuendos when she is around. If Liam hadn't gotten us out when he did, we would have ended up worse for wear as Desmond was planning to auction off our virginity," Freya explains, and with every word she speaks, I watch as the girls change. Freya and Ryleigh look more embarrassed as they try to avert their gaze from her, but Bree, her face, morphs more and more with anger. I can almost feel the anger vibrating off her from here.

"Fuck, that's so fucked up. Has he ever tried it on with you?" Bree asks sheepishly like she's not sure if she should get that personal.

"No way. I think there is a part of him that still sees us as his daughters. But his pride is what's controlling him now," explains Ryleigh. "I can't wait to get the fuck out of here."

Finally, a statement we can all get behind. A knock on the door pulls us out of our moment, and Finn walks in, reminding us of our breakfast appointment. Then Bree and I need to find out exactly what my father is planning, and if he is the person responsible for the threats.

191

CHAPTER TWENTY FOUR

Bree

Listening to the girls talk about their horrific experiences makes my blood boil. I hate that anyone would treat them like that, but to get it from your father is something I just can't understand. He raised them for most of their life. I have learnt very quickly that blood isn't always thicker than water. The bonds we choose for ourselves are often the strongest. Thankfully, they will always have Liam, and now me.

Thankfully, breakfast passes by in a blur. It was very uneventful, which for this family, I have quickly learnt, is a novelty. We all wait for Desmond to dismiss us, as nobody can leave the table without his prior approval. As everyone else goes off to their respective rooms, he instructs Liam and me to his office. Liam takes my hand and gives me a small smile. That's enough for me. It tells me my Liam is very much here, and that he's not the zombie in Desmond's office from yesterday.

We approach the door, two big burly looking men with shaved heads and stern but vacant expressions are guarding either side of the entrance. Desmond instructs them to wait outside, which is good for us. He at least doesn't plan on using his security staff to try and kill us. Sadly, that doesn't mean he isn't going to lose his shit and kill us himself.

There are two chairs in the room this time, and he instructs us to each sit, which we do as he slumps into his large, luxurious leather seat behind the desk. I feel his piercing black eyes boring into my skin, almost like he is trying to kill me with just his eyes. But, unfortunately for him, that sort of shit stopped intimidating me a long time ago.

"So, what is it you want to talk to me about?" Desmond asks, indicating with his hand that he gives me permission to speak freely.

Taking a deep breath, I make an on the spot decision that I need to just be honest. Of course, Liam will be pissed because he coached me on what to say, and this is practically the opposite, but I have to do this my way.

"So, I know that men don't recognise me as a leader, I don't give a shit about that. I will prove myself with time; that's all I can promise people. I won't ask for your trust, but you can sure as fuck trust that I will earn it. I will prove myself to everyone, but to do that, I need to be given a chance. I know I have several enemies. I have enough threats to know I am being targeted by more than one group. What I need to know is who I focus on first. So, how much of a threat are you to me?" I ask, making sure to keep eye contact at all times, so he knows how very fucking serious I am.

His laughter rings through the room as he throws his head back before looking at me again. "I will always be a big threat to you. It is no secret that I want London, and you are naive if you think people won't capitalise on your weakness, using this handover time as a time to attack. However, I can assure you I have not got any outward plans to attack you. Believe it or not, I have no intention of slaughtering my son. He may be a pain in my ass, but I made his mother a promise, and unless I am forced, I will not break that promise. Besides, Evan reminded me that if I wait for you to provide me with a grandchild, then my family will be in power anyway," Desmond added. I don't know which part of that statement freaked me the fuck out more.

"So you want to work with us? Suppose you are willing to accept me as the leader. In that case, I will agree to a truce, and we will open lines of communication to have your family working with mine. Not only will this give you more reach and a financial boost, but you will also have links to London," I offer, my heart racing as I do.

I try not to glance over at Liam, but it's difficult to ignore the shake of his head and look of annoyance on his face. Desmond, on the other hand, now is wearing the biggest, and quite frankly most disturbing, grin I have ever seen. "And what makes you think I won't use that to gain more power and overthrow you?" he asks, and I can't help but chuckle.

"I fully anticipate that is what you will do, but as I mentioned before, I only want to fight one enemy at a time. So, I offer a temporary truce to you while I take out the Marcushio's, and then you and I will have our time later. You will never rule London, and Liam will never side with you. So one day, our fight will come, but that day is not today. Do you agree to a truce?" I ask, my voice hitching slightly at the end as doubt starts to creep into my mind.

Initially, I thought Desmond would never be someone who would honour a truce, but then Liam told me earlier that his word is the most important thing. I know he will try to stab me in the back one day, and when that day comes, I will be ready. But until then, I need him to keep his word while I take out the Marcushio's.

"Fine, Your Highness. You have a deal...for now. But we will have our day," he states, and I reach my hand out to shake his.

As our hand's touch, his face turns into a leer, and his eyes wander down to my cleavage. He keeps hold of my hand as he licks his lips, eyes still ogling my tits. Liam coughs deliberately to get Desmond's attention. Desmond makes sure to shoot a smirk in Liam's direction before letting go of my hand.

"Now that that is sorted, you need to give back the guns," Liam states, and Desmond looks at him in confusion,

"What guns?"

"The AK47s from the shipment you hijacked," Liam explains.

I watch Desmond's face as Liam explains what he means, and the confusion remains on Des' face. When he denies that he has the guns or knows anything about the guns, I believe him. There's no way he could have hidden his reaction that well. This guy wears his emotions with pride. He doesn't try to hide them; instead, he owns them. Looking over at Liam, I see he believes him too.

We don't linger with Desmond for too long, wanting to get the fuck out of his office as quickly as possible.

"I will text Kellan to tell him the Marcushios are armed, and we need him to locate the guns like yesterday. While he is working, wanna go back to bed?" he teases with a very sexy wink that almost brings me to my knees. Literally. Like, right here in the corridor.

"Fuck yes. Let's go." I pull him along with me as we practically run back up to our room.

The engagement party approaches quickly, far too soon for my liking. I know I am going to be the one on display, that people are going to be looking at the new O'Keenan leader. For quite some time, there has been speculation over what would happen when Gramps became too old, and Dad would be pulled back to Cork to run the Irish syndicate. Nobody ever suspected I would be capable of leading. Instead, they thought I would be forced to marry someone who would rule. Now I need to show them that I don't need a man by my side, and even though I choose to have Liam with me, he is not the boss. I am.

Liam waits patiently for me to finish dressing. His mother ordered the dress for me, and it arrived today. When I first put it on, I instantly wanted to take it off. Never have I put clothes on and felt naked. But the more I looked at it, the more I realised I love it. The silky black material flows over me like a second skin, all the way down to the floor. The front of the dress droops, almost like a roll, exposing my cleavage. My leg is visible thanks to the slit up the side that stops mid-thigh, but the bit I find incredibly sexy is the back. The spaghetti strings hold the dress up as the back of the dress droops all the way down to my lower back in a U shape. If I had a tramp stamp, it would be on view for the world to see.

Once I admitted I would wear the gorgeous dress, I decided I needed to have hair and make-up to match. Hours of pampering later, and I am waxed, plucked, and ready to go. My smokey eyes make my silver eyes sparkle, and the deep red lipstick plumps my lips perfectly. I curl my red hair and pin it back off my face but arrange for the curls to fall down my right shoulder, ensuring the back of the dress is visible.

Taking a deep breath, I open the door, and for a minute, I get to take in the mouth-watering view in front of me. Liam hasn't heard the door open or seen me yet, so I get to stare at him. I have always thought Liam was akin to a Greek god, but he almost kills me in a suit. My heart is racing as I take in his rugged stubble, all the way down to his tailored black suit. His mother picked out a red silk tie to match my dress, and he looks fantastic. The tight trousers hug his ass, and the white shirt is just see-through enough that I can see his beautiful abs. I am one lucky woman.

Liam catches me staring at him, and I wait for him to joke with me about it. He usually makes a joke about how I find him irresistible, and the cocky Liam that I love comes out. But that doesn't happen this time. Instead, he unapologetically stares back. His dark eyes rove over me, and it's like his eyes are on fire. Everywhere his eyes touch, my skin begins to heat up under the scrutiny.

"Fuck, Bree, you look gorgeous," Liam states as his eyes continue their lazy perusal of my body.

"You like?" I ask as I slowly turn around, making sure to stick my ass out slightly, so it really accentuates the missing back of the dress. I also cock my hip and place one hand on it, making the thigh slit very visible.

"Oh fuck. I wanna fuck you so bad right now," Liam groans as he adjusts the growing erection in his pants, no doubt trying to make it more comfortable.

"Later. First we have to mingle and stop people from trying to kill us."

Liam grabs hold of me and pulls me until my body is plastered against his. I can feel his hard cock straining to get free, and I am so tempted, but this is work time, and I need to get my head into it. His lips brush against mine, and I am such a goner. The taste of him is intoxicating, and I run my hands up his chest and then around his back, making sure to stay under the jacket, so I can feel more of him. His hands explore every inch of my exposed back, feeling lower and lower until his hands slip beneath the fabric.

"Are you not wearing any panties?" he whispers in my ear, his voice a low rumble that I feel in my stomach.

"Nope. Wouldn't want any panty lines, would we?" I ask seductively, and he giggles.

"You will be the death of me, or my blue balls will. Either way, let's get to this party because the sooner we get there, the sooner we can leave, and the sooner I can fuck you in this dress," Liam purrs and fuck if I don't physically feel myself getting wetter.

Liam pulls away before going to the safety box on the side, putting in the code until the lid flips open. He takes out his preferred gun of choice, checks it, and once it's full and the safety is on, he places it in the special pocket in his inside jacket pocket. Looking down at my outfit, I curse when I realise I have absolutely nowhere to hide a gun. So when Liam takes out and prepares my weapon, I ask what he is doing.

"This will be strapped to my back. You will not be leaving my side anyway, so if you need it, you take it. Do not hesitate to use it because none of the assholes here will hesitate. Okay?" he asks me, and his face looks so severe. I want the sexy, cocky Liam back.

"Is this like the crime Family version of you carrying my purse? Are you my bitch now?" I joke, giving him my best serious face, but I can't keep it up.

His face is a mixture of uncertainty and annoyance, and when I start to laugh, it quickly turns into that sexy glare he gets when he is getting ready to pounce. He is like an animal stalking his prey and just waiting for the right time to go for it. I can't help it if I like winding him up.

"Don't think I haven't forgotten the spanking I owe you from earlier. You just added more onto the tally, and yes…I am still keeping count and will be doing so all evening," he growls.

As I stand there with my mouth open and my panties dripping, I can't help but ask, "How many am I up to?" Although I'm not entirely sure I want to know. What I do know is the evil smirk on his face tells me that as the figure is rising, my ass is going to be deliciously sore.

"You don't want to know, but you should be good tonight if you want to be able to sit down tomorrow, that is," he jokes as he pulls me out of the room.

Walking together down the corridor, I let Liam lead as I still have no clue where anything is in this house. He has taken me on a bit of a tour, but I just got more confused. Until we get onto the main corridor where our bedroom is, I have no sense of direction. Then, as we turn a corner, we hear a voice calling us from behind. We turn to see a very suave and sexy looking Finn, dressed in a suit, running towards us.

"Look at you looking all debonaire," I say to him as I reach over and straighten his light blue tie. It compliments his navy blue suit and white shirt perfectly.

"Are you kidding me? I could have turned up stark bollock naked, and nobody would even realise because they will all be looking at the new queen in the black dress. You look hot, Red," Finn jokes, and he must stare at me for a little bit longer than Liam is comfortable with because before I know it, he slaps him playfully around the back of his head.

"That's my fiancée, you perv," jokes Liam as Finn mutters

about him being an asshole for ruining his hair.

The boys banter back and forth until we reach what looks to be a small reception room, but given the noise coming from behind the double doors, it seems like we are near the party.

"Is this the entrance to the party? Are we late? Nobody is going inside," I ask, wondering if everyone is already here.

"This is the door used for the grand entrance. Basically, we will be announced as we walk in, then we will walk down a set of stairs, and the party is on the floor below. There's a public entrance downstairs. We can go out into the gardens from there if you ever need some fresh air," Liam explains, and I am grateful. Growing up in a Family like mine, you learn the escape routes pretty quickly, and it's reassuring to know that Liam was raised the same.

We wait for a few minutes, and it's not long before all the Doughty's are gathered in the room. Freya is dressed in the most beautiful sky blue ballgown that accentuates her blonde hair and blue eyes. Ryleigh is the more rebellious one of the two, and she is wearing a short, purple dress that is tight like a corset on top but flies out like a ballgown below. It stops mid-thigh, exposing the most beautiful tattoo of a woman's head and her brain is filled with books like a library. This is clearly the first time anyone has seen the tattoo since everyone's shouting at her about it. She has dyed her hair bright purple in the few hours we were apart during the day. I think she looks fantastic, and I make sure to tell her that.

Von is dressed in the most elegant, long silver ballgown. She looks almost regal with the way she holds herself, and with her arm wrapped around Desmond, this is the closest I have seen them since I got here. Both Desmond and Evan are dressed all in black, looking like twin versions of each other. Both of them leering at me most disgustingly. I can feel Liam by my side getting ready to say something, but we talked about this before we came. Neither of us is going to do anything to risk the truce we have in place.

A girl enters the room dressed in a short black skirt and a tight black shirt. Her shiny black hair is pulled back into a simple ponytail low on the back of her head, and her eyes remain averted at the floor.

"I'm sorry to disturb you, Sir. Manuel sent me to inform you of the order of introductions," muttered the girl towards Desmond.

"Well...get on with it then, you eejit," Desmond sneers, and I feel Liam recoil beside me. Out of the corner of my eye, I notice that Evan appears to look uncomfortable. He's bouncing from one foot to the other and generally looking more shifty than usual.

"Sorry, Sir. You and Mrs. Doughty will be announced in five minutes, then there will be a five-minute break. Then Evan will accompany Freya, followed quickly by Finn accompanying Ryleigh. There will then be another five-minute break before Liam and Brianna are introduced. I have my headset on and will be informed when you are to go," she explains, and everyone shifts around the room, so they are standing in the correct order and with the right person. But other than that, nobody acknowledges that she even spoke.

"Thanks for that," I say to her. All eyes turn to me like I had just taken a shit in the middle of the room.

"Please, do not address the help, Bree. Only I talk to them, isn't that right, children?" he asks all his children. However, his gaze is aimed directly at Evan, which is odd because he appears to be the only one that blindly follows Desmond anyway.

Everybody mutters some form of confirmation at Desmond's question, then the girl indicates it's time for Desmond and Von to enter. As the doors open, our room is filled with a roar of applause as they enter the Ballroom. I try to look around at the room, but after seeing the massive hanging chandelier, I figured it would be better if I didn't see any more.

As soon as the doors close behind Desmond, the atmosphere changes. All the kids start to relax again, including the girl sent with the instructions. I am shocked when Liam begins talking to her. "Teigan, what are you doing here? I thought you went off to university."

She smiles at Liam, but it's clear that there is no light behind her eyes. Even with a smile on her face, she still looks so sad and lost. I feel like I want to hug her or save her, but I have no idea what to do.

"It's a long story, but I work here now. So you really shouldn't be talking to me. Your dad has spies everywhere," she practically spits the last part, and I can't help but notice the way she looks at Evan as she says that. I'm not surprised; I wouldn't put it past him to report back to Desmond about the staff.

In quick succession, she announces the two sets of siblings, and they enter to much softer applause. However, it's still apparent there are a lot of people in the room below us. Now that it's just me and Liam left, I am starting to get nervous. I can feel my hands begin to sweat, and as I fidget from one foot to the other, I'm tempted to begin pacing the room. Liam squeezes my hand to calm me down.

"Tee, I'm so sorry you are stuck here. What happened between you and Evan?" Liam asks, and that stops my anxiety straight away.

"Did you date Evan?" I ask Teigan incredulously, and she chuckles.

"We dated all throughout high school, and he wasn't as much of a dick back then. Then, I went off to university, and he stayed here to work for his father. My Evan disappeared the day he never showed up to move away with me," she says, her breath hitching as though the story still makes me sad.

"I remember that Evan was supposed to go with you, but then he just didn't. He changed after that. So why did you come back?" Liam asks, and Teigan shakes her head, looking even more dejected than before.

"My mum got sick; I came back to help her. She needed some treatment that was only available in the US, and I needed money fast. The bank wouldn't take a risk on a student with thousands of student debt and no job, so I came to the only person I knew who would give me the money. I had the tickets booked and was all ready to go, but then mum passed away. I couldn't get my money back, and Desmond wouldn't let me move out of the town to try and find a job. He said it would be the same as running, which he offs people for. He insisted I work here and work off my debt. By the time I am about a hundred years old, I will have probably paid off the original debt, but my grandchildren will be paying the interest. He has me bent over a barrel, and boy does he fucking know it," Teigan explains, and my heart breaks for this beautiful girl.

"What did you study at university?" I ask, genuinely curious.

"Would you believe it if I told you criminal psychology?" she asks, and I can't help but laugh.

"Please tell me you didn't want to be a pig?" pleads Liam, and the lightest laugh escapes Teigan's lips. It causes her face to light up slightly, and I see a hint of the girl she once was.

"No way. I wanted to work with criminals, people with psychotic tendencies, things like that. Help them to learn to manage their behaviour and basically how not to go to prison," explains Teigan.

A short sharp laugh escapes me. "Well, Evan could really use your help there," I joke, and both Liam and Teigan mutter in agreement.

"You know, he used to be funny, kind, and easy-going, but the more time he spent with Desmond, the more he became his clone. I fucking hated it, and I hate having to spend every day watching him morph into this version that I can't stand," she murmurs, her voice laced with sadness, and I feel Liam sag beside me. Teigan clearly has never got over Evan.

"I know what you mean. I wish I could have got my brothers out when I helped my sisters," Liam groans, a wave of sadness washed over him, and I can hear the genuine regret in his voice.

"Don't think like that. They are men and not boys. They are older than you, and you are not responsible for them, okay?" she says but interrupts us before we can reply. "Shit...you're up."

Then with no time to prepare, the doors open, and I walk into the wolves' den, clinging onto Liam as though he were my life raft, which in a way, he is.

CHAPTER TWENTY FIVE

Bree

Walking down the stairs, I feel myself gripping onto Liam, who feels equally as tense. As I look down below the giant chandelier, I can't help but feel intimidated by the sheer grandness of this place. It is legitimately like an old fashioned dance hall. Like the rest of the house, it is bright, airy and covered in marble. However, the features in this room all appear gold, like it's been made to look more opulent than the rest of the house.

There are round tables set up with chairs covered in bright white tablecloths with black runners. In the centre of the tables are the most beautiful arrangement of black flowers. There are so many different shades of black with the odd splash of white and green to help the black flowers stand out more. I notice that there are black and white calla lilies in the bouquets as well as black roses. The arrangements allow the room to shine, and I can't help but think this looks like a wedding reception. I also make a mental note to take a picture of the centrepiece bouquets because I would love to have that when I get married.

When I finally stop taking in all the details around me, after noting where the exits and the bar and food are, I finally allow myself to be in the moment. The noise of the applause reaches my ears, and I belatedly look at all the people standing below. There must be over two hundred people, and all eyes are on us.

I instantly notice the people who work either for or with Desmond because they are all dressed in the same black suit with a black shirt look that both Desmond and Evan are wearing. They look like a mini-cult that are all following their leader, but it's good for me because it points out who my potential enemies are. Everyone else in this room is still an unknown, and I notice Liam scanning the room and analysing the threat in the same way I am.

Desmond steps forward as we reach the final step with his hand outstretched to help me down. I reluctantly hold my hand out to comply, plastering a big fake-ass smile on my face and trying not to cringe as his skin connects with mine. Then, keeping hold of my raised hand, he leads us to the centre of the dancefloor, where Von is waiting with a microphone. As soon as we arrive, she immediately stands by Desmond's side and gives him the microphone. Now that we are in position, I try to pull my hand away, but he simply tightens his grip on me.

Liam, noticing my tension, squeezes my other hand in reassurance and softly begins massaging the back of my hand with his thumb. It's such a delicate touch, but the sensation is incredible. It instantly relaxes me, at least, as much as I can be with where we currently are.

"Welcome, everyone, and thank you for coming to help us celebrate the engagement of my youngest son, Liam, to his beautiful fiancée, Brianna," Desmond announces loudly. He uses the microphone to point to us as he announces our names. He pauses slightly to wait for the applause that starts after my name. Given he doesn't drop the microphone, he clearly has more to say.

"My wife, Siobhán, and I are so thrilled to be gaining such a gorgeous new daughter into the family. Most of you know that Liam is no longer an official member of this Family, but that is strictly business. When it comes to personal family matters, we will always be there for our children. Even when they choose to marry the enemy," Desmond adds with the most sadistic chuckle. The laugh is replicated by all the people wearing identical suits to him, but the joke falls on deaf ears to everyone else. Which sadly means Desmond feels the need to carry on and talk more, much to my chagrin, and Liam's too if his slight groan is anything to go by.

"For those of you that don't know, this little firecracker is Brianna O'Keenan, daughter of London boss Vernon. When she and my son marry, together, they will take over the running of the

London firm. So, I want to clarify to everyone here tonight that the O'Keenan's and their businesses are off-limits for now. Bree and I have talked, and we have come to a mutually agreed-upon truce. I obviously cannot guarantee that one day that will change, but their wedding will go ahead undisturbed for now. Is that message understood?" he asks the room, and a chorus of 'yes' rings out around the room. I then notice that Desmond nods towards Evan, who, along with two other men, leaves through the service entrance door. I know Liam saw the same thing because his thumb stops massaging my hand and his whole body becomes tense once more. His muscles coil the same as mine, and we are both preparing for whatever it is that Desmond has planned.

"Now, the reason I ask you all to confirm this is because I did put the word out this morning, only to find that one member of the Family decided to go rogue." Evan comes back through the service doors as he speaks, followed by two men dragging a barely conscious, bloodied man into the party. As I turn to see where they are taking him, I notice a couple of men setting up some plastic sheeting on the dance floor behind me.

"What the fuck is going on?" Liam whispers towards his father, but I'm not even sure he hears him speak. He is too busy glaring at the man being dragged in, his dark eyes taking on a whole new vicious look. He releases his grip on me to step towards the man being dragged into the room.

"This is Lucas, he works for me, and has a desperate need to move higher up in the Family. He thought that taking his own initiative would impress me. He was wrong." He then turns to Lucas, forcing Liam and me to step back so he can approach him. The plastic sheeting crumples loudly under Desmond's footsteps, and the silence around the room is deafening. I notice some of the people closest to the dance floor begin to step back.

Liam looks around, and when he finds Finn with his sisters, he subtly tells him using hand signals to take the sisters out of the room, which Finn quickly does. I'm glad Liam was able to get them out of here. Nobody should have to witness whatever will happen here, but young girls are a definite no. Sadly, there are many other teenagers who look around Ryleigh's age here with their parents, and I watch as some of the parents try their best to shelter them. Everyone knows that shit is about to go down, but leaving is not an option. Liam warned me that Desmond is a bit theatrical, and if he sees people leaving he would take that as a personal insult.

Desmond and the people he has working for him would identify weakness straight away. This party does not need to escalate any further, and I already saw how trigger happy Desmond is.

"Lucas...tell Bree and my son, Liam, what you had planned," Desmond says into the microphone. He addresses the crowd instead of speaking directly to Lucas. This is all a show for him, and we are his little puppets playing a game.

When Lucas doesn't answer him, Evan punches Lucas straight in the abdomen, and with a loud groan, he falls forward, bending at the middle as his legs try to give way beneath him. If the two men weren't holding him up, he would have collapsed to the floor to wrap his arms around his stomach. But, instead, the painful area remains exposed only for Evan to punch him again in the same spot. I start to step towards them, but Liam holds me in place. With a subtle shake of his head, he makes it clear I shouldn't interfere.

Lucas starts to talk, but amongst the tears, blood, and sweat, it's really fucking difficult to work out what he is saying. "I-I didn't...I didn't know...about the rule," he cries.

Desmond steps right up to Lucas and finally lets go of my hand. He uses his now free hand to fist into Lucas' hair and pulls his head back. Lucas has no choice but to look up at all the guests, and with the microphone Desmond has thrust into his face, there is no way everyone won't be able to hear him.

"I'm...I am s-sorry. I planted a bomb under Liam's car. I didn't know...." His words trailed off at the end, becoming a bumbling apology mixed with more bodily fluids than I usually like to see when people are talking.

The sadistic smile returns to Desmond's face. He theatrically stands forward, his arms wide as he addresses his waiting audience. "See...he admits to disobeying my order. However, his reasons for doing so are irrelevant. If my security team had not seen him planting the bomb and managed to safely disarm it, not only would my son and Bree be dead, any other members of my family that were close by could have been caught in the crossfire. Including me."

Liam's face slowly morphs from one of concern to anger as his eyes darken and his brows wrinkle. Rage vibrates through his body, and I can feel the tension in his hand. I try stroking him with my thumb the way he did mine, hoping that has the same soothing effect as it did me. Sadly, it doesn't, and I know his mind will be overcome with thoughts of what could have happened if Lucas' plan had been successful. I know exactly how he feels because that rage is overcoming my body too.

No longer am I standing here feeling sorry for the bloody young man in front of me. Now, as I stand here thinking about his blatant disregard for my life and the safety of people I care about, the blood lust starts to ascend. The idea of someone hurting Liam alone makes me crazy, but when I think that he could have harmed Freya, Ryleigh, and Finn, I become murderous.

"Normally, I would be only too happy to take care of this problem myself, but I think Brianna deserves a chance to show you all the type of leader she plans to be. So, Bree, the floor is all yours," Desmond states as he hands the microphone over to me.

"Bree, I can sort this out if you want?" Liam whispers into my ear, but we both know that would be the worst thing I could do. That would be telling people that I need Liam to do all my dirty work, and they instantly will have no respect for me as a leader. But, I made a promise to Desmond that I would earn his and everyone else's respect, and this is the first step in doing that.

"Do you have a gun? Obviously, I don't have anywhere to keep one in this dress," I joke, making sure to smile at the audience as I used my hand to direct all eyes to my dress.

The idea of having people perving over my body in this dress is not a pleasant one. Still, I have never killed someone in front of a room full of people before, let alone ones that are judging my every move. Whilst I am like this, I can school my face, making sure to replicate Desmond's sadistic smile. The more of a psychopath they think I am, the less likely they are to challenge me. But when the time comes for me to end Lucas, I have no idea if I will be able to school my features for the performance. The majority of the men in the room are the people that matter in our world. If they are too busy looking at my body to notice my face, then that's precisely the kind of distraction I need.

I know I could have gone for the gun Liam told me to use, but I had a reason behind that. Firstly, I have no idea how the rest of the party will go, given we have got off to such a bloody start. So having an unused, concealed weapon in hand that nobody knows about can only be a good thing. Also, it helps me to see who offers me the use of their gun. Not only because it tells me who is carrying and where, I can also get an idea of who wants to show loyalty to me. It has to be someone who trusts me because if they give me their gun, it leaves them unarmed and vulnerable.

You only do this if you trust that the person you are giving the gun to won't turn around and shoot you.

I expect to get one or two responses, so both myself and Liam recoil in shock when around twenty men step forward. Evan shouts at everyone to get back and to stay off the dance floor. The men who are charging forward instantly stop and fall back into place with the guests they came with. While, much to my surprise, Evan takes out his gun, takes hold of the barrel, and offers the handle of his weapon to me.

"I assume you know how to use this?" Evan asks sarcastically, causing Liam to snort in response.

"She is probably a better shot than you are, Ev," Liam jokes, and I'm shocked to hear the use of a nickname. Liam soon masks his face again, blanking off all emotions that flashed forward for a short time. It was like a little glimpse of the past, what the boys were like when they were younger and how they had fun together. Evan must see it too because, for the first time since I met him, I see a genuine, full-faced smile. It's initially a bit unsettling to see him looking happy instead of the broody asshole he usually is. It actually lights up his face and makes him look much younger than his twenty-six years.

Taking the gun off him with a smile, I hand the microphone over to Liam, so I can check the barrel of the gun. I run through all the safety features, making sure to take some deep breathes too. At the same time, I consider what the fuck I am doing. I hold my hand out for Liam to give me back the microphone, remembering that this is a performance after all.

"Lucas. You don't even know me. So tell me...why do you want me dead? Explain it to me," I ask casually, and I hear chuntering from around me. They think I am weak; what they don't know is I have a plan.

"I was just following orders! I have nothing against you personally," he cries and once again, the muttering happens.

"And who gave you that order?" I ask with a smile, holding the microphone out, ready for his response.

"Well...it was my boss Jasp that told me, but I'm sure he got it from high up," Lucas sobs, fresh tears rolling down his face as the room explodes with jeers. Lucas obviously didn't realise that he just ratted out his boss in front of the entire Family. Well...I say he didn't realise, he did as soon as people started shouting at him. I can't help but smile as my plan plays out perfectly.

"Desmond, did you inform this Jasp person that you had put an amnesty out for my family and me?" I ask Desmond, making sure I keep my performance as theatrical as he did.

The room that was only a second ago filled with mutterings and taunts was now deathly silent. You could have heard a pin drop as I held the microphone in front of Desmond, waiting for his reply.

"Of course, I passed on the information," Desmond growls, just as I expected him to.

"Is Jasp here tonight? Jasp, please step forward." The room is silent as people look around for the person who should be stepping forwards. All eyes go to a group of men standing off to the side, and it is painfully obvious which one is Jasp. He looks like he must only be about twenty years old, and there's a good chance he may have just pissed his pants. But I can't show any mercy.

I wait for several long minutes for him to step forward, but he doesn't. Not until Desmond's loud command rings through the room. Without using a microphone, his instructions for Jasp to move forward could be heard by everyone, and it's clear Jasp's refusal to step forward angered Desmond.

"Jasp, hi. Thank you for coming forward...eventually. What I need to know from you is whether you told Lucas here that I was off-limits or not?" I ask, and I hear a slight chuckle coming from Liam, who I am pretty sure has just worked out my plan. Other than that, the room remains silent.

"I...I think I told him," Jasp mumbles into the outstretched microphone, clearly unsure of what answer he should give.

Unfortunately for Jasp, there is no good answer here. If he says he told Lucas, he let the attempted assassination go ahead and didn't warn someone. Or if he didn't tell him, then he failed in his duties. But personally, I was hoping for lucky option number three, which would have been him telling me that he didn't know. That way, I would have had proof Desmond didn't plan to instigate the truce. So I am genuinely shocked to find out he did.

"So, what you are telling me is that you knew I was not to be harmed, you passed that information along to Lucas, and yet he still went ahead with the plan anyway? Did you know about his plan?"

Jasp's mumbles his denial about knowing anything about the assassination attempt. Having heard this, Lucas calls out that Jasp is a liar, and it echoes around the room. Blood sprays from his mouth as he shouts about Jasp knowing everything and that he told him to go ahead with the plan anyway. It was already in motion, after all. They planned to deny knowing the kill order had been rescinded.

"Well, I think that is evidence enough for me. Jasp, please, will you stand with Lucas," I sing, the fake sadistic smile back on my face.

Jasp doesn't move, instead choosing to look over at Desmond. Desmond looks baffled and stares at me like I'm a book he can't quite read yet. This is a prime example of why you should never underestimate someone. I give Liam the nod, and that is all the instructions he needs to grab the young man and drag him over onto the plastic sheeting. Jasper, obviously feeling brave, tries to bite Liam's arm. Liam quickly pulls his arm back and punches Jasp in the gut. He doubles over, and his groan fills the room. He is lucky Liam hasn't done more damage.

"Bree, what the hell are you doing?!" Desmond shouts at me in the lowest whisper his voice can produce. He doesn't want anyone to see him questioning me and my methods, but he doesn't like how things are going.

"You told me to handle this however I would normally, so that is what I am doing," I reply sternly before turning my attention back to the audience. My hard-faced, sadistic smile, bitch face is ready.

"As far as I am concerned, both of these people not only risked my life but the lives of Liam and his family. That is a crime that cannot be forgiven. Lucas, for planting a bomb and threatening our lives, I have no choice but to sentence you to death. Jasp, for failing to stop an attack you knew about and disobeying your boss' orders, you are sentenced to death." I rush the words but make sure to state them clearly and with purpose.

As soon as I say the last word, I hold my gun up, aim and fire two shots. The first hits Lucas dead in the centre of his brain, and the second leaves a matching hole in Jasp's head. The screams and pleading that started as soon as I told them their sentence became silenced in an instant. The crowd also becomes deathly silent, following the initial shock of the gunfire. As I look out over their faces, I see a mixture of shock, horror, sadness, but mostly I see fear. By killing Jasp too, I proved I will not stop at the person responsible. I will punish anyone who even plays a part in the plot. Tonight, while I may have scared the shit out of many guests, there are also quite a few with whom I just gained some respect, and that is the most significant achievement.

Handing the gun back to a shocked Evan, I give the microphone back to Desmond, who looks at me like he has just seen the real me. The genuine smile he has on his face is scarier than the fake sadistic one. As soon as I hand it over, I walk straight over to Liam's side and take hold of his hand. He instantly begins to stroke his thumb over the back of my hand again, trying to calm my racing heart and my nerves.

"Well...at least we know Queen Bee has a fucking great aim. Let's get that trash out of here boys, please. Now, the party can really start. The buffet is open in the adjoining room, the bar is free-flowing. So eat, drink, and for fuck's sake, dance. Start the music!" Desmond shouts, and as soon as he does, music fills the air and people begin their mingling.

It's funny how people can go straight back to the party and pretend like everything is perfectly normal. Like it is a very regular occurrence to have two bodies removed from the dance floor. I watch as they roll up the plastic sheeting, making sure no blood seeps out onto the dance floor. I know I probably should feel some hesitation or sadness that I took two lives just now, but I don't. They were a threat to Liam and me, and they clearly did not respect the truce. Therefore, they would always be a threat. I feel much better knowing I took care of them myself.

"Well, that was unexpected. You just went up in my eyes, Queen Bee. Some of my boys can't shoot as good as you did," Desmond praises me, and all I do is smile. With a slight nod of the head to indicate he is done with our conversation, he walks away to begin his socialising.

"Wanna get a drink?" Liam asks me.

"Fuck yes, a bloody strong one, please," I reply, and his responding chuckle warms my heart. I love hearing him laugh, particularly in this house, as this is definitely the place laughter went to die.

Liam leans in and suddenly presses his lips against mine. Using a hand on my lower back, he plasters his body against mine. I deepen the kiss, making sure my tongue sweeps along his, savouring the taste that is all Liam. I hear some whooping and catcalls that pull us out of our kiss, a clear sign we had taken things a little too far than what's allowed in public.

As Liam slowly pulls away, he kisses my neck before whispering in my ear, "That was so fucking hot, watching you in charge like that.

You have no idea how hard I am for you right now."

I feel his words deep in my core, my pussy getting wetter at the thought of his cock straining to be free, right here, in front of everyone. I can't wait for this fucking party to be over so we can get to the entertaining part of the night.

CHAPTER TWENTY SIX

Liam

Thankfully the rest of the evening passes by uneventfully, but then again, when you start a party by shooting two people, things can only get better after that. I still can't get the vision of Bree out of my head, as she holds the gun perfectly straight, not a shiver or shake, then she pulls the trigger. I was already struggling to gain control of the constant erection I've had since seeing her in that sexy black dress. Then add on her fire as she unapologetically showed everyone the type of leader she really is, and my dick was screwed. This erection is never going down.

All night, as we mingled, ate, talked, and danced, I was painfully aware of how much my body craved my girl. Watching her dance with Finn was the final straw. I knew there was nothing between them, and she was just being friendly with him, but horny me did not see that. Real me liked the fact my girl and my brother got on well, but horny me just saw her teasing me, and I had reached my limit for the night.

Just as the song is about to finish, I stride over and grab Bree's arm before pulling her, slightly more aggressively than I would usually, towards the nearest door. We had gone through the servant's entrance, which is good as there would be less room to be interrupted. Opening the second door on the left, I smile at the thought that the place hasn't changed since I was younger.

As young boys, Evan, Finn, and I used to run riot around these halls. We loved to explore each and every room. We always found new hiding places and new spaces to explore with a house as big as ours. So I knew when I opened this door that it was one of the servant bathrooms.

Pulling Bree inside, I quickly lock the door behind us.

"What are we—" Before Bree has a chance to complete that sentence, I push her back against the door and smash my lips against hers. The kiss is rough, bruising, and rushed as I try to devour this beautiful demon.

Even though I know I am acting a bit caveman-like, taking what I want, Bree is only too happy to give, and before long, her tongue is battling with mine. Her hands make the first move as she shucks off my jacket, followed quickly by my tie. Then, one by one, she opens the buttons on my shirt, making sure our lips remain connected. Once she has my shirt off, it's my turn to retake control.

Pulling her forward off the door, I gently manipulate her body so her back is plastered against my body. Then, reaching round to the front and slipping my arms into the loose fabric around her cleavage, I cover her breasts with my hands and gently start to knead them. As I kiss along the side of her neck, over her collarbone, I quickly turn my attention to her sensitive nipples. I alternate between squeezing them tightly and rubbing them softly, driving Bree crazy. The mixture of pleasure and pain causes her to cry out in a delicious moan as she grinds her ass back into my already strained cock.

"Do you like that, Princess? Do you like it when it hurts, or do I need to rub it and make it better?" I moan into her ear.

"Yes, please...I need more," Bree pleads, and I am only too happy to oblige.

Taking my hands from her gorgeous tits, I reach down and pull her dress up above her hips before sliding it off her body completely. I throw the dress out of the way because it's just a piece of fabric without my girl in it. She is what makes it look so good. But nothing compares to the sight of seeing her in nothing but the pair of black stiletto heels she is wearing. We both look at ourselves in the mirror in front of us, and I am shocked by what I see. We both look wanton, our hair dishevelled, and our lips bee-stung. We haven't even got to the best part yet.

"Fuck, you look so gorgeous. I will fuck you over this counter, and you are going to watch in the mirror. I want you to watch as I pound into your sweet little pussy, and destroy you for all other men," I groan into her ear as I suck hard on that sweet spot on her neck. Her breathy moans of confirmation are all I need to hear.

Using my feet, I kick her legs further apart, making sure they are spread out wide. I guide Bree into the position I want her in, laying over the marble sink countertop next to the sink, her nipples pressed against the cool marble, with her ass up in the air. Not only is her ass at the perfect angle, when she arches her back, it exposes that pretty pink pussy I have come to love. I can already see it glistening from here.

I use my finger to gently stroke down her slit, confirming she is just as wet as I thought. Her moan is guttural, and her hips buck up like she is desperate for more contact. Something I am only too happy to oblige. Kneeling down slightly, I swipe my tongue over her slit, tasting her juices and swirling my tongue around her clit. Luckily I was holding onto her hips as she bucked again, her legs becoming more wobbly. I continue licking until I am sure she is nice and wet, and I use my finger to confirm. As my digit slides into her hot waiting hole, Bree's groans ring out loud. I make sure to spread her juices all over, making sure she is nice and ready.

"You like that, Princess? Tell me what it is you want," I ask as I continue to gently stroke my finger in and out of her tight channel and spread her juices over both her holes.

"Your cock," she mumbles, her eyes locking onto mine in the mirror. She is biting her lip; her fists in front of her are clenched tightly as the anticipation builds.

"You want my cock? Tell me where. Use your words, Princess."

I can tell by the despondent groan that she is not happy I am forcing her to beg. Bree knows that while I will happily let her be the queen and stand by her side out there, in the bedroom, or bathroom in this case, she knows I am the one in charge. So while she may look at me with a deathly stare or try bucking her hips in demand, we both know she only gets what she wants if I think she has earned it.

"Please...please. I need your cock. I need to feel all of you in my tight cunt. I am so wet, and it's all for you, Liam. Please fuck me," Bree pleads, her desire dripping off every word, and of course, I am quick to give her exactly what she wants.

Knowing she is ready enough, I quickly plunge my cock deep into her waiting pussy, ensuring that tight, wet channel takes all of me. When I am balls deep, our moans echo around the room, and I pause just for a second to give her time to adjust. Or at least, that's what I tell myself. It's not at all because I need to take deep breaths and gain some control so I don't blow my load the second I move my cock.

Bree, always the impatient one, starts to move her hips as she clamps down onto my cock with her pussy walls. Fuck, that is definitely not going to help with the coming too soon issue. Her pussy fits my cock like a glove, and I feel it squeeze around me just to confirm my thoughts.

The sound of my hand slapping against her sexy ass is like music to my ears, and the responding yelp has me chuckling.

"Remember, Princess. You rule out there, but I rule in here," I growl into her ear as I stroke that delicious pink handprint on her ass.

"Fuck—" Before I give her time to finish whatever sentence was most definitely about to get her ass in more trouble, I start to move my dick in and out.

I start off by going slow to savour the moment, but I'm fighting a losing battle. Her pussy is too sweet, and my cock is already addicted. So I decided to take this hard and fast.

Holding onto her hip with one hand, I use the other to fist her hair into a ponytail, giving me a stronghold before I pull back on her hair. Doing this not only brings out the most delicious gasp as her hair twinges at her scalp, but the pain adds to her pleasure. It also means that as I pull back, she is forced to look at her beautiful, arched body. The curve I am causing in her spine pushes her tits out towards the mirror and changes the angle of her pussy. This allows me deeper and deeper access to that sweet spot.

It doesn't take long with me pistoning deep into her before Bree begins to show signs of getting closer to that edge. The tilt of her pelvis to meet my thrusts become uncoordinated. Her breathing becomes erratic as she pants desperately for gasps of air. Her moans become inaudible, and her pussy feels like it gets wetter with each thrust. Ensuring she is sandwiched between the counter and my hips, I know that I need to keep her locked in place because as soon as she orgasms, those sexy legs that are already starting to shake will give way.

I feel her getting closer, and if I bite down on my lip any harder to stop myself from coming, there's a good chance I might bite the damn thing off completely. Although, I am very aware that our departure will be noticed soon, if it hasn't already, my brain really doesn't fucking care right now. I want to try something, and she is in a perfect position; I can't turn down such a good opportunity. So I watch as she starts that build-up, doing everything I can to help her get there, including sucking on that sensitive spot on her neck that I know will help get her there quicker. Then just as I know she is about to reach the start of her orgasm, I pull out.

You have no idea how fucking painful that was for me to do, but I have a plan.

"What the fuck, Liam?!" Bree squeals as she keeps eye contact with me through the mirror.

"You weren't about to come just then, were you? I thought you knew you had to ask for permission first, Princess."

Bree begins to reply, no doubt with something that is a healthy mix of sarcasm and swearing. So I decide to help her ass remain a nice pale colour, and instead of the spanking she deserves, I use my finger to gently stroke along her slit. Her resulting moan is delectable, and as I look down, it's no wonder the head of my cock looks angry, purple, and swollen. It desperately needs to get back into Bree's warm hole.

"Please, I will ask first. I promise. Just fuck me again...please, Liam." Her words ring clearly as she begs me, loud and desperate. I can hear the slight shake in her voice, that desperate craving for her impending orgasm.

Quickly, I plunge my cock back into her waiting cunt, and it feels so fucking good. Her pussy is tight, wet, and warm, and it's a fucking miracle I have lasted this long. Bree hasn't fully come down from her peak yet, so it doesn't take too many fast and deep strokes before I feel her getting there again. I know when I hit that illustrious special spot deep inside because Bree becomes almost frantic with need, only this time she uses her voice.

"I-I...please...Liam. I need...I need to come, please." Her words sound like breathy pants that become more frenzied the closer she gets. Looking in the mirror, I watch as she bites her lip in between words while her hands grip tightly onto the counter.

"Not yet, Princess. You haven't earned it yet," I whisper into her ear, and I watch as her body lightly shudders from the feel of my breath on her skin, loving the feeling of how tightly her pussy clamps when that happens.

"No...I can't hold it. I have to come. Please...what do I...

what do I need to do?" she pleads, and I smile, pleased that my plan has worked out the way I wanted it to.

"Do you want me to give you the best orgasm you have ever had?" I whisper, and her screams of confirmation leave her lips before I have even finished the question.

Using the hand that was holding her hip, I make sure my other hand that is clutching her hair remains in place so I can watch her as I encourage her to experiment with me. I gently swipe my fingers through her slit alongside my cock, making sure to get it nice and wet. Once I am sure it is, I gently stroke my finger all the way to the back of her slit, making sure to cover her asshole in plenty of her juices. Once I know it's covered, along with my finger, I gently press the tip of my finger against her waiting asshole, making sure to watch her face in the mirror as I do.

Her eyes fly open, and she reaches back with one hand, gripping onto my wrist, so of course, I stop. "I've never...I've never done anything there before. I don't know...." Bree's voice trails off as her eyes meet mine in the mirror. Her hesitancy tells me she is stopping more out of fear than anything else.

"Do you trust me?" I ask her, and I don't have to wait long for her to reply with a yes. "Take some nice deep breaths and relax. I won't hurt you, and if you really want me to stop, just say dodgems. That can be our safeword," I whisper into her ear.

Bree's face morphs into a smile before she removes her hand from my wrist, laying back over the counter and exposing her asshole to me once more. She takes some big deep breaths before addressing me through the mirror. "I'm trusting you, Liam."

As soon as the words leave her mouth, I start moving my cock again slowly as I press the tip of my finger into her puckered asshole. As soon as it passes the first tight ring and the tip slips inside, Bree lets out a long, frenzied cry as she feels her pleasure increase. After the initially hard part, the rest of my finger slides in easily. Once I have it fully impaled, I take a few seconds to allow her to adjust.

If I thought her pussy was tight before, now it is even worse, or should I say better, because it's so much better. Given the way her pussy is having minor little spasms, as she prepares to reach that delicious edge, I know she can feel a difference too. Once I am sure Bree is okay and happy to continue, I try to coordinate my thrusts. As I pound my cock deep into her pussy, my finger does the same thing in her ass.

"Please...oh, Liam...fuck...I-I-I...I need to come. Now!" she yells frantically, her hips become uncoordinated, and her sweet cunt starts to tremble in anticipation.

Usually, I would make her properly beg me. That was more of a demand, but my cock might literally fall off if I delay any longer. I am ready to blow my load right now, but I want Bree to fall first. So, as I continue my assault on her sweet, wet hole, I add a second finger into her asshole. The feeling of being stretched by two fingers and a swollen hard cock is too much. Her body begins to push her over the edge.

"Open your eyes, Princess. I want you to watch as you fall apart with my cock in your pussy and my fingers in your ass." As soon as I give the order, she obliges straight away. At this point, she doesn't want to risk me taking away what she needs to come.

Our eyes lock in the mirror, and I watch as her orgasm consumes her. Her body starts to shake, her pussy quivers too, as her high-pitch groans of pleasure seem to reverberate all around us. I feel my cock getting wetter as it, along with my fingers, become trapped as her ass and pussy both clamp down hard. I hold still, letting the sensation of her climax work its way through her body, but the feeling of her pussy gripping my cock is too much. With a loud grunt, I blow my load deep in Bree's cunt.

The deep coiled build up in my muscles seems to be replaced by the feeling of being electrocuted as I judder with the intense sensations overcoming me. I have never felt an orgasm that strong or lasted for that long. It felt like I couldn't stop coming, and neither could Bree. She was coming down from her orgasm when mine hit. The feeling of my cock exploding deep within her was enough to push her back over the edge with a smaller orgasm. There literally is nothing better than feeling your girl falling apart on you.

As we both come down from our orgasms, our frantic panting is the only noise that can be heard. I gently pull my fingers out of Bree's ass first before pulling my spent cock out of her pussy next. Keeping her bent over the counter, I grab the nearest towel and gently use it to clean up the mess we both made. Her pussy is so sensitive that the roughness of the towel causes her to whimper.

I'm not sure if the sensation is too much or she is becoming more turned on. But I can't think about that now because we really need to get back to the party.

We both dress again in silence, casting glances at each other to see which one will break the lull first. With a small, shy smile, Bree slides on her dress and takes the opportunity to talk while her face is covered. Clearly, she is embarrassed about whatever she is about to say and doesn't want me to see her face. She doesn't have to worry about that sort of thing with me. She can tell me anything. "I really enjoyed that. Do you think maybe one day, when I'm ready...maybe we could try your dick instead of your fingers," she mumbles, and I can't help the grin that spreads across my face.

Completely ignoring her embarrassment, I instantly reply, "Princess, are you asking me to fuck you in the ass with my big, hard cock?" I try to keep my voice as playful as possible, to hide the deep need I have not to throw myself in dick first right now.

"Not straight away. Your dick is massive. We need to build up first, like maybe with a butt plug or something. Then when I'm ready, we can try your cock," she explains. Her embarrassment dissolves slightly when she sees how very fucking into it I am. A beautiful girl like Bree offering her ass for fucking, why the hell did she think I wouldn't be interested?

"Fuck, yes. I'm so in, Princess. And now we have a safeword; I might bring the rope back out. I can't wait to tie you to the bed again," I groan as we both check our appearance in the mirror.

Whilst we may look presentable, it is painfully evident that things got hot and heavy. Bree's hair is unruly and no longer styled the same as before. I seem to have pulled out all the clips as I used her hair to hold onto. Our lips look swollen from the abuse they took during our passionate kisses, and our cheeks are both flushed with pinkness. An obvious sign we have both been exerting ourselves, but I am past the point of caring if people know. We are at our engagement party, for fuck's sake, we can celebrate any way we want. And what I want right now is to get this damn party over and done with so I can take my girl back to our room and make a start on stretching out her tight hole, ready to take my cock.

I notice she is staring at me, the cutest expression on her face as she bites her lip. A new flush of rouge creeps up her cheeks, and

I know she is thinking naughty thoughts. I smile my knowing cocky smile at her, and her resulting eye roll makes me chuckle.

"I can't wait until we get home. I want you to tie me up and fuck me in the ass so badly. I'm going to order some toys for us to play with as soon as we get back to the room, and then by the time we get home tomorrow, there will be lots for us to experiment with." Her voice trembles slightly with each word. I know she is sure of what she wants. The problem is still with her apprehension over telling me what she wants, what she craves. She still gets a bit embarrassed, but she is getting much better.

I chuckle at her words, loving this new sexually adventurous Bree. "Fuck yes, let's get back to the party for another ten minutes or so and then say our goodbyes. I have plans for you, and I really don't want an audience," I whisper as I pull her out of the bathroom. Her carefree chuckles ring out like bells as we subtly walk back into the party like we never left.

The rest of the night passes by in a blur. We each dance with people who ask us, but always make sure to squeeze in a few dances with each other. I use that time to whisper in her ear, telling her all the little things I plan on doing to her. It's also a good time to steal some short passionate kisses, little promises of more to come.

After about an hour, when we are getting closer to midnight than either of us would have liked, Bree starts to yawn and moan about how much pain her feet are in with the torture devices she calls shoes. Don't get me wrong, she looked hot as fuck when they were the only thing she was wearing in the bathroom, but they do not look fun to walk in. So, it's not surprising that the longer the event goes on, and the more Bree is on her feet dancing, the more she moans about her feet hurting. Finally, I made the decision that it's time to leave.

First, I need to find Finn to make sure he gets the girls to their room safely. I look around the room and find him leaning against the wall talking to Mckenna. They look like they are having an argument. Their hand movements become more animated and heated, and I don't know whether my interruption will be welcomed or not, but I interject anyway.

"Sorry if I am interrupting. Hi, Mckenna, it's nice to see you again. You look great," I say with a smile.

Mckenna looks over at me, and her face instantly changes from the wrinkled, stern, angry face she was aiming at my brother, to smiling at me. "Liam, don't worry, you weren't interrupting anything important. I can leave."

"No! Stay...please," Finn shouts, but Mckenna just shakes her head.

"There is no point in us having the same fucking argument over and over again. I work for your girlfriend, and that is it. You disgust me, and while you continue to work for your father, that will not change. You are not the Finn I once knew. So, unless it is related to my employment, I need you to stay away from me. Every time you talk to me, it just hurts. You hurt me. I can't take any more." Her voice breaks, and tears well up in her eyes. Finn looks like she just stabbed him in the heart, his posture slumps, and he looks broken. As Mckenna walks away, he just remains still.

"Finn, go after her," I instruct, taking hold of one of his shoulders and physically shaking him to get his attention.

"There's no point. She made that pretty fucking clear, Lee. I don't know what to do. I really do have strong feelings for her, but I can't do anything about them. Not unless I leave the Family business," he grunts, clearly feeling sorry for himself.

"Well, leave then."

A deep, sarcastic chuckle released at my response. "And do what? Where would I go? I have no fucking money," he cries, complaining the same way he did when I tried to get him to leave with me and the girls.

"Listen to me, Finn, because I am only going to say it this one time. If you love someone, you will do anything for them. Even if that means facing a fear and doing something you really don't want to do. But you do it because they are worth it. So you need to decide if Mckenna is worth it. You might make an enemy out of Desmond, but you might not. You need to decide if she is worth the risk. If you think she is, then you can come to London with us. Bree will find you a job. One that doesn't force you to whore out your dick for money that you never see. You can keep your cock in your pants and earn money that stays in your bank. We even have a few legit jobs that we can find if you really wanna go straight. There are options open to you, Finn. You just have to decide if you are going to take them. How badly do you want Mckenna? That's the question you need to answer, and when you know the answer to that, then the question of what would you do for her will be the easiest fucking question in the world to answer."

Finn listens to me as I talk, and I can see him casting a glance at Bree, who is standing behind me, not wanting to leave my side but also trying to give us some privacy.

"Would you do anything for Bree?" he asks, and I can't help but chuckle.

"Finn, I am in the middle of the lion's den wearing a fucking suit. I brought my sisters back to a place I physically fought to leave. I said I would never work for one Family, that I just wanted to do the assassinations that I wanted, but now I am all in. Bree is my life now. So yeah, I would do anything for her," I exclaim proudly, not even a hint of hesitation in my voice. I hear a sharp intake of breath from Bree as she hears me talk about all the things I would do for her. How strongly I feel for her.

"Look, Finn, you need to think about it. I am here if you need me. Bree and I are getting ready to head back to our room. Please, can you make sure both girls get home safely? And we can meet you at breakfast tomorrow," I ask, and he nods his head. He is in deep contemplation, and I honestly have no idea what he will do.

Finn has always been terrified of our father, which is why he never comes with me when I offer to get him out. He thinks that the revenge Desmond will seek will make it not worth his freedom. But now he has a reason to fight; I just hope he chooses to get free. I hate what this family is doing to my siblings. It may be too late to save Evan, but I can still save Finn.

We say our goodbyes to all the people who matter before heading back to the room. As soon as we are far enough away from the entrance that the music can no longer be heard, Bree stops and takes off her shoes. She holds onto them and moans with satisfaction as her bare feet touch the cold marble.

Not wanting her to get her feet dirty and cold, I sweep Bree up into my arms, and she chuckles as I carry her like a bride back to our room. Once we are safely there, I lock our guns away safely, and she checks her phone. Desmond instructed us that phones were not permitted in the event, and so reluctantly, we left them here. The longer she stares at her screen with a blank expression, the more worried I get. As she puts the phone down, her face scrunches in annoyance, and a loud groan fills the room.

"What's wrong?" I ask, my mind whirling with all the possibilities. We are fighting enemies from all fronts, and I don't think we can take another hit. I hate the idea of anyone threatening my girl, and now that we have ruled out my father, we know it has to be the Marcushio's sending the death threats.

"It's my Gramps. He is coming to London in a couple of days. He wants to sit down and meet with us to see if he will grant permission for our wedding. Looks like we're getting to know you time is up, and we need to decide if we are all in or not."

As she speaks, I don't reply and instead, walk over to the cupboard beside my bed. I take out the box I stored there for safekeeping before stepping back and standing in front of Bree. I see Bree's eyes follow my movements from her standing position beside the bed. I take a big deep breath to try and steady my nerves. I was waiting for the right moment to be perfect, but as with everything that Bree and I do, it is spontaneous and in the moment.

I need Bree to know how totally fucking serious this is to me, so I make sure my face shows no hint of the nerves I am feeling, and that my eyes never leave hers. I gently lower one knee to the floor and open the box as I speak. "Brianna Elouisa O'Keenan, we may not have met under the best circumstances, and our relationship may not have progressed the way it normally would, but that doesn't matter to me. We are not normal. We are extraordinary when we are together, a force to be reckoned with. I want to stand by your side as you conquer this world, not just as your business partner but also as your husband. I know we still need to get to know each other a lot more, but we have forever to do that. What I am trying to ask is, Bree, will you spend your forever with me? Will you do me the honour of becoming my wife?"

I watch as tears fill her eyes, and she usually blinks them back. Her desperate need to remain in control of her emotions at all times, but not this time. Now she stands frozen, her tears streaming down her face freely, as she looks between me and the glistening diamond ring I am holding towards her.

Silence passes for a long time, and I don't know whether this is a no and I should get up or not. My heart is facing so quickly I can hear the blood rushing through my ears. The hand holding the ring starts to shake, and I can't hide the disappointment from my face. As soon as my smile switches to a frown, that seems to be the motivation she needs to speak.

"You want to marry me for real?" she asks, her voice sounding so unsure.

"I wouldn't normally propose to a girl this soon, but we have a different set of circumstances. But yes, Bree. I want to marry you for real. Do you want to?" I ask, hopeful.

With a loud squeal that I am pretty sure sounds like a yes, she launches herself at me. Since I am on one knee, with one arm already in use holding a ring box, nothing stops the momentum. We end up crashing into a heap on the floor, but Bree just smiles as she straddles me, her lips pressing against mine in a frenzied attack.

Reluctantly I pull away, my free hand stroking the hair off her face and tucking it behind her ear so I can see all of her face. "Is that a yes?" I ask, holding the ring in front of her.

Taking hold of the ring box, her face lights up in wonder as she removes the ring from the box. Holding the ring up in front of her, she turns it around, examining it closely before placing it onto the ring finger of her left hand. As the ring slides on, she lets out the cutest little squeak. "Yes, I will marry you."

My heart pounds in my chest, and my stomach starts to feel like it's flipping. I know that I should be freaking out right now or regretting what I just said, but the truth is, I have no regrets. I fucking love this girl, and now I have plucked up the courage to tell her that I will marry her for real, not just for business. I just need to take that last little step and tell her how I feel. But that will have to wait because I have lots of other plans for my lips tonight. I want to devour every inch of my fiancée's delicious body.

CHAPTER TWENTY SEVEN

Liam

Breakfast in the morning is relatively quiet and uneventful. Most of the family are in a sombre mood or living with their hangovers. When my father puts on an open bar, everyone makes sure they enjoy it. Shortly after breakfast, it's time for us to say goodbye and head off. Except for the shootings at the beginning of the party, our visit has been less memorable than I was expecting. And a lot less violent. I am still suspicious of my father and his motives, but I know if he puts his word on the line, then he is serious. So, my family isn't a threat for now, but that might not be the case forever.

Finn comes into the bedroom under the pretence of helping us carry our things, but given I have one case, he is obviously hanging around for another reason. I'm about to call him up on it, but Bree shakes her head. It's weird how she knows what I am thinking at times.

"It has been so lovely meeting you, Finn. You really have to come to London some time. Of course, you are always welcome to stay with us," Bree declares whilst holding her arms out as an invitation for a hug.

My brother and Bree have grown so close over the last twenty-four hours, and the more time they spent together, the more they got on. It's the same with my sisters. She is easy to love, and my siblings fell just as quickly as I did, but in a slightly different way, obviously.

"Well, you better reserve me a room then because I will have to come over for your black wedding. If we go on gossiping about all the people in the room last night, it will be quite an event. Are you really getting married in a graveyard like the legend states?" Finn asks animatedly as he pulls Bree in for a big hug.

With a roll of her eyes that matches mine, she starts to chuckle. "I love that people know more about a wedding we haven't even planned yet than we do. But I don't think we will be getting married in a graveyard. A church seems a bit too traditional for us too, don't you think?" she adds, looking straight at me.

"Princess, I will marry you anywhere you want, but I do agree a church doesn't really suit us. Anyway, Finn, can you go and get the girls, please? We have to go."

Almost as soon as Finn leaves, we hear a knock on the door. Looking at each other to confirm we aren't expecting anyone to knock, I shout to inform them they can come in. As the door slowly opens, I am shocked to see a very sombre looking Evan walk into the room.

"Evan, hi. Are you okay?" Bree asks, after several seconds of waiting for me to do the welcoming, but I can't. I just don't know what to say to my brother anymore.

"Can you guarantee that whatever I say stays between us?" Evan asks, his voice more of a plea than a question.

His usually put-together look is dishevelled, and he looks like he is spiralling. His ordinarily dark, piercing eyes look hollow and lost. He no longer looks like a mini version of our father, just a lost young guy who needs help. I give him the promise he is looking for, as does Bree.

"I need you to find a way to get Teigan out of here, Liam. Desmond told her last night that she isn't making money back quick enough, so she needs to move to a higher paying job. He informed her that she will be transferred to work in his underground nightclub, Shades, next week. We both know that it's just a sex club, and she will have no choice but to sell her body. I can't let that happen. He knows I still like her; that's why he's doing this. It's his way of making sure I fall in line," he cries, his desperation soaked into every word.

I have to admit that I'm shocked. Not only did I think Evan was a lost cause, but I also had no idea he still had feelings for

Teigan. If Desmond knows he likes her, then, of course, she will always be at risk. He knows that if Evan is ever going to leave the Family, it would have been for her, he nearly did it once, and I think he has regretted it ever since.

"I had no idea you still liked her. When you didn't leave with her, I thought you made your choice," I add, desperate for more information before I decide if we are risking our necks for him.

"It's a really long and fucking messed up story, but the short version is that I still care about her. There is no way I can stand by and watch her get sold to the highest bidder night after night, get fucked in front of everyone, or get sold permanently as a fucking sex slave. You know what Desmond is like. The debt is his, and he will get it reclaimed in any way he can."

"We will help you," Bree states firmly, and I can't help the groan that escapes. I wanted to make sure this wasn't going to put the truce at risk and also that we can trust Evan before we agree to anything. Too bad my girl is a crusader, determined to free everyone that needs her help.

"Well, we need to talk about it to sort out specifics," I add, and Bree rolls her eyes.

"But, Evan, I will only get Teigan out if you agree to come too," Bree states and this time, it is Evan's turn to groan.

"I can't leave, it would be suicide," he cries, and honestly, I'm not sure he is wrong. Out of all of us, he is the one that knows the most when it comes to my father's business dealings. He is being groomed to take over the business one day. So he knows too much. If he were to leave and start working for the enemy, us, his life would be in grave danger.

"We will protect you. Look, someone once told me that when you find the person who truly matters to you, you will do anything for them. Even if that means risking your life, theirs is more important to you. But, sometimes, to get what you want most in life, you have to take a risk. So, when you are ready, you can move to London and come work for me, then I will make sure Teigan is safe," Bree states, and I can't help the little chuckle that escapes when I realise she is quoting my own words. It's the same speech I gave to Finn the night before.

"I can't right now. I can't explain, but I need you to help her," he pleads, and as I look over at Bree, she looks so sad. I know she wants to help him, but in this instance, the thing that will help

227

him the most is if he helps himself. I can't let Bree be the one to hurt him. Their relationship is still building and has a chance, whereas Evan began hating me a long time ago.

"I'm sorry, Evan, but Bree is right; this has to come from you. We can help you both get out, you stand a chance at a real life with her, but you have to choose it. You have to want to choose her. Our offer is open anytime you change your mind," I say with finality, and his face morphs from one of desperation to anger. His piercing gaze fixed directly at me.

"Fuck you and your offer. I will find another way. But know this, if something happens to Tee in Shades, it will be on you for not helping her," he spits as he shoulders past me.

"That isn't fair, Evan. We want to help; we really do. But you are the reason Tee is here, and you are the reason she will have no choice but to work in Shades. When you stop acting like a child and accept responsibility for your actions, we can help you. But until then, you can blame us if you like because we know we offered," Bree states firmly, and for a second, I thought she had got through to him. He froze and listened to every word she said, and just as I thought he was going to turn around and ask for help, he storms out, slamming the door as he goes.

Only minutes later, the door bursts open again, and I can't help the groan of frustration that escapes. We are never going to get out of here if we don't leave soon. Even people using private planes, courtesy of Bree's grandfather, still have to leave on the flight time they request. I will not miss this flight and be stuck here.

Utterly oblivious to me or my annoyance, my two sisters come running in and launch themselves at Bree. The three of them hug each other and look genuinely sad to be leaving. We are taking them back to London with us, and from there we have a driver taking them back to school from the airport.

"I'm going to miss you so much, Bree. Please tell me we can video call regularly, and talk all the time?" Freya sings, linking her arm into Bree's. Although it's clear she is happy with the way my sisters are behaving, she looks confused. She has only ever had Mia as her friend; this girly behaviour is all new for her.

"Yeah, when can I come and stay in London? I want to go around the shops and see a west end show. There's so much more to do in London," Ryleigh adds.

"Yes, we can talk regularly. You have my number. Just call or text if you need something, and I will be there. But, we have to go now because your brother looks like he is going to burst a blood vessel if he stares at his watch any harder," Bree jokes while looking poignantly at me. With a smile she turns back to my sisters. "Seriously, would you girls do me the honour of being my bridesmaids?"

The shrieks of excitement from both my sisters are loud enough to be heard outside. I will be astonished if Bree hasn't burst an eardrum. It's not normal to have such a high-pitched sound bellowed into your ear. Despite the ear damage, I can't help but smile. I had no idea she would ask them and seeing how happy they are and how much they love me just affirms I made the right decision agreeing to marry Bree. She doesn't even hesitate to show my sisters the same care she would to any of her friends. That fact she likes and gets along with my sisters is fantastic.

As I reminisce about proposing to Bree, I remember the way she rode me afterwards. Her sexy body bouncing up and down on my cock whilst wearing the ring that tells everyone that this girl is mine. It was fucking mind-blowing. Strangely, it was more intense than the usual hard, fast, and rough sex that always seems to overcome us. Last night we were in no rush. We wanted to savour the moment. I didn't just fuck her; we made love for the first time. And even if that means I need to hand in my man card and be labelled a pussy, I will take it because it was the most intense, mind-blowing orgasm and I'm desperate for more.

Finn storms in several minutes later and practically has to round up my sisters and Bree, cajoling them along like he is herding cattle into a pen. They are so distracted by the shiny diamond on Bree's finger that it makes walking and staring difficult. By some miracle, we manage to get to the front door fairly quickly. The car is waiting for us, and as Finn and I go to load the bags in the boot, I take the time to talk to him alone.

"Are you coming?" I ask, and he just looks down at the ground, kicking some little gravel pieces by his shoes.

"I can't," he whispers, and I roll my eyes.

"You can. You are choosing not to. The offer will always be open. Don't let Desmond ruin your life," I add, and Finn looks even more upset. His gaze remains fixed on the floor; his body language is slumped. He seems like a guy who gave up a long time ago, and I want to shake him. I want to give both brothers the power to fight back, but they have to take the first step.

Desmond and Mum come out, followed shortly by a very dejected looking Evan. My mother hugs and kisses us both before offering her help with wedding planning. She even offers to come to London to help, which is met with a look of disapproval from Desmond. However, Bree says she will definitely ask for help if needed. Then my father steps forward as if he wants to see us off as an average family.

His actions make me want to laugh out loud. I don't think I can ever remember a time when my father hugged me or told me he loved me. Desmond isn't capable of showing emotion unless he somehow benefits from it.

"Well, Queen Bee, it was very nice to meet you, and I have to admit I am pleasantly surprised. You are not at all what I expected. Before I met you, I would have laughed at a female leader, but now I have met you, I am not so sure. I am willing to see what you can do, which is why I agreed to the truce. It will give me enough time to see what type of leader you are, then work out if I would be better off being on your side or taking you out. Only time will tell. I look forward to the wedding," he states as he holds his hand out for Bree to shake.

Holding her hand out, she clasps his as she speaks. "Don't forget this truce is also a trial period for you and your people. I only work with people I can trust, and I will need to decide if I want to work with you or not. So consider us both on trial."

His evil laugh rings out as he drops his hands. He nods at me, indicating that he will not be giving me the same level of goodbye as Bree. I am still excommunicated, and he has not forgotten that. I motion for everyone who is leaving to get into the car. My mother stands off to the side, gently weeping as the girls refuse to hug her. She failed to protect them, and that's a difficult thing to forgive.

"Bye, girls!" my dad shouts with a sarcastic voice and wave of his hand.

Not one of them replies. I climb into the car, and as I shut the door, I look over at both of my brothers. Gone are the depressed faces from earlier. The boys who were brave enough to ask for help are long gone. In their place stands two fucking zombies.

Both stood bolt upright, their faces empty masks that display no emotions, their eyes dark and hollow. Between them and my sobbing, trembling mother, my heart breaks. My father is responsible for so much damage, and he doesn't even care.

I stare at them continuously, lost in my own mind as I try to think up ways to help them. Ones that don't require me slaughtering my own father. I'm pulled out of my daydream by a soft hand touching my shoulder from behind. Then I feel her soft breath on my neck as she leans forward from the back seat to talk to me.

"You can't save them, Liam. They have to want to save themselves. You offered to help them; that's all you can do," Bree whispers against my skin, and I feel a bolt of electricity run straight down my spine into my cock. How does this girl manage to turn me on with just a breath of air against my skin?

"Thank you," I reply. Although, I'm not sure exactly what it is I'm thanking her for because she has done so much for my family and me. But right now, this car can't take me away fast enough. I want to get back to our house, to see Kellan and Hallie, and to settle into our new lives together.

CHAPTER TWENTY EIGHT

Bree

The next few days after we get back from our trip to Ireland pass by in a blur. It feels like we are finding new threats every day or hearing about recent tragedies. Father is on the warpath after one of his drug runners, a fifteen-year-old boy, was shot down by an AK47. Liam and I have been given the responsibility of finding the gunman. But if we knew where the fucking guns were, we could locate the gunman. Even Kellan is coming up stuck.

Every day he tries something new, but he becomes convinced that my father and Jimmy lied to us. That they gave us wrong information of when the guns were taken and where from. Kellan has tracked every road in and out of the building, even pulling up old sewage plans so he could be sure they weren't smuggled out underground. He has scrolled CCTV, as well as hacking into several personal cameras. He believes that either the guns were never there to begin with, or they never left. He is currently tracing back to see if there is proof the guns ever arrived, not just at the safe house but also into the country. We know what ship they should have come in on, and if we can follow them off the boat, we should be able to track their actual journey.

All of this means more work for Kellan, and he is pissed that my father lied. I, on the other hand, expect that sort of shit from him, but not Jimmy. He is usually honest with me, even if he knows it pisses me off. I need to confront him to find out the truth, but I have slightly more important things planned today.

As I sit there bouncing Hallie on my knee, my heart swells every time she lets out the cutest little laugh. She occasionally looks at me with a smile, but her gaze is permanently fixed on Liam if he is nearby. I'm not sure if he is a general baby whisperer, but he definitely has the magic touch when it comes to Hallie. In the middle of the night, when she screams like a banshee and tries to wake up the entire neighbourhood, no matter what Kellan tries, the minute Liam touches her, she calms down. The problem then becomes putting her down because she screams again, so Liam is severely sleep-deprived at the moment, but he doesn't seem to care. He still carries on as usual and always has a smile for me.

Kellan comes running down in a rush, as always, and I take a moment to appreciate the fact he has dressed up. He is wearing smart dark jeans and a dark blue shirt with the sleeves rolled back to his elbows, showing off his tattoos. He may be a computer geek, but there's no denying he has muscles that are clearly bulging in that tight shirt. His usually relaxed face and carefree smile have gone, replaced with a serious expression.

"Liam, your girl is perving on me again!" Kellan shouts as he winks at me. With my free hand, I flip him the bird, and he chuckles.

"Why are you all dressed up?" Liam asks.

"Because this is a job interview. Just because she is a friend of Bree's does not mean I will give her the job, nor does it make this any less formal. You want me to trust this person with the most important thing in my life, to trust she will be safe and well looked after with this person. So, yeah, I'm taking it seriously," Kellan states as he moves to the dining table, where he sets out a glass of water and prepares some pieces of paper.

"I don't want you to hire her for me, Kellan. I truly believe she will prove to you that she is good enough," I argue, but with a sweeping hand gesture, he dismisses me, and I can't help but roll my eyes at him. Then again, I can't imagine what it feels like to be hurt by all the women in your life. It's no wonder he doesn't trust people. Hallie only deserves the best.

The doorbell rings, and Kellan stands to go and answer it. He takes a few big deep breaths, almost like he is nervous, before turning to look at me, Liam, and Hallie. "You can stay here as long as you don't upset the interview process. If you do, you are out, understand?"

Even Hallie laughs, although I suspect she is just copying Liam. Kellan mutters something under his breath before he goes to answer the door. I hear talking, introductions no doubt, before I watch my friend Mia walk into the room. She goes to approach us to say hello, I assume, but Kellan interrupts her.

"Please, don't pay them any attention. If they become too disruptive, they can leave. We will get on with the interview, and you can speak to them afterwards, does that sound okay?" Kellan asks, using a posher voice than I have ever heard him use before.

"Of course, I am happy to get started," replies Mia.

Mia takes off her coat, and I almost groan. I have always been jealous of her figure. It is literally the perfect hourglass shape with decent sized tits. Girls with skinny waists don't often have the curves to match. Combine that with her five foot six height, which in heels makes her a giant compared to me, and she is basically a supermodel.

She has those perfect high cheekbones that everyone craves, lips that always seem to be plump and inviting, and the brightest green eyes that always seem to glisten. Her long blonde hair usually hangs down to her waist, but today is pinned back into a butterfly clip. She is wearing a tight, knee-length, black pencil skirt and a soft lilac blouse that has been tucked into the skirt. She is dressed to impress.

I notice that I'm not the only one looking at my friend as she places her jacket on the back of her chair. Kellan looks like he is mesmerised by the very sight of Mia as he watches her every move. I'm guessing he isn't just looking at her as a potential employee anymore. They both sit down, and as soon as he realises Mia is also looking at him, the mask descends. Kellan looks away, picking up the papers in front of him, before starting the interview.

"Thank you for meeting with me, Miss Whitlock. Is it okay if I call you Mia?" he asks, and I hear Liam snort from beside me before not so subtly trying to disguise it with a cough. Kellan flicks the evil eye at him, and we know we are in the shit now. Mia confirms that she will reply to her name and Kellan continues. "Let's jump right in then. Why do you want this job?"

Mia sits up straight and keeps eye contact with Kellan the whole time as she answers him. "I love working with children. I am working and training at the same time as I get my childcare qualification. I love being a nanny. I like getting to know the children I work with and learning about their personalities. Every baby responds and learns differently. Once I have figured that out, helping them is a whole lot easier. I have heard a lot of good things about Hallie and you. I would love the opportunity to get to know her and to see if I can help her grow up."

Mia talks with passion and conviction with each question Kellan throws her way. No matter how stupid or ridiculous they are. Just as I can feel them getting ready to close things up, confident that there is no possible way he can turn down my girl, Kellan picks up the piece of paper in front of him. As he speaks, it is like he has been waiting to get to this bit, and I already want to groan with disbelief.

"Mia, when I asked you if you have any known criminal connections, why did you lie?" Kel asks, and this time Mia looks shocked. Her eyes dance around slightly like she is unsure exactly where to look.

"I didn't lie. You know about Liam and Bree anyway," Mia stutters defensively, but with a shake of his head, it's clear that's not what he means.

"You know I'm not talking about them. Do you want to tell me, or shall I tell you what I know?" Kellan asks, this time pronouncing his words loud enough for me and Liam to hear. Mia looks very unsure and a little intimidated. I have never known her to lie, and thank fuck because she is shit at it. Her discomfort is evident from across the room.

"What do you...think...you know?" she asks. The pauses before and after make it pretty fucking clear there's so much more she isn't saying.

"Your father, Mortimer Whitlock, his accountancy firm is another one of Vernon's money men. But your father is so much worse than washing dirty money. He is a pervert and a rapist. But none of the cases ever went to trial. Even though the girls were all fucking underage, they were paid to drop the case and refused to testify," Kellan spits, and I can't help but recoil. I know her dad is an asshole who does business with my dad, but I had no idea he's that much of a nonce.

Mia's face starts to crumble, and she looks as though she may cry, her chin trembling slightly. Her voice was strong and animated when she spoke before, but now it's barely above a whisper, monotone, and sad. "I have detached myself from him. That's why I'm doing this job to pay for school. I could have taken his blood money handout, but I refused."

With a shrug of his shoulders, like he doesn't give a shit about Mia or that he's hurting her, he continues. "What about Kyle Fratacello?" Mia freezes at the name. Kellan waits for Mia to unfreeze and talk, but she seems lost in her own mind. The only movement is a single lone tear that trails down her cheek. When she doesn't speak, Kellan starts talking again. "Kyle runs one of the northern syndicates but works for Bree's Family overall. What I want to know is what happened that summer you spent with him just after turning eighteen. A marriage request form was submitted, but you never went through with it. I couldn't find a marriage license on file. What happened? Are you still engaged to that psychopathic piece of shit?"

Mia remains still, but now her tears are falling freely, and she begins to sob. She doesn't answer his question, and Kellan just rolls his eyes. On the other hand, I cannot stand by while my best friend sobs her heart out just a few feet from me. So I hand Hallie over to Liam and approach Mia. Kellan starts to stop me, but I give him a fierce glare making it fucking clear I do not intend on being messed with.

Putting my arm around Mia's shoulders, I pull her into me. "Hey, Mia, it's okay, darling. I'm here. Shush, you don't have to cry anymore," I whisper in her ear before turning my attention to Kellan. "What the fuck do you think you are playing at? I said you could interview Mia, not fucking interrogate her."

"Maybe you don't know her as well as you think, Bree. I saw the look on your face when I said the name, Kyle. You had no idea that your best friend almost got married to a fucking wannabe gangster nearly twice her age. I'm sorry for upsetting her, but I have to think of what's best for Hallie. Any unknown criminal connections put her at risk. Fuck, being around you two recently feels like I am in the middle of a war, and I cannot have my daughter caught up in that. I want someone to care for her so that I don't have to worry about her while I'm working for you. I don't want to have to continuously wonder if my employee is working for my mother or if they have links to Hallie's past," he says poignantly. He's clearly referencing any ties to the woman who birthed Hallie and doesn't deserve to be called a mother.

"That was over three years ago, and no, I don't know exactly what happened, but I do trust Mia," I say, looking straight at Mia as I stroke the hair out of her face and wipe the tears from her eyes. She gives me a small smile, and I am just pleased the sobbing has stopped.

"Well, I don't. So, I'm sorry, Mia, but I won't be hiring you," Kellan says firmly and I look over at Liam. He just gives a slight shoulder shrug, effectively telling me to keep my nose out of Kellan's decision. I huff, not happy that I can't fix this.

"That's not a problem. I'm actually glad you didn't hire me. I don't want to work for an asshole who would rather trust a fucking piece of paper than a real person. What you have there is one small piece of a much larger story, but you didn't think about that. You didn't think about the psychological trauma you may have caused by bringing up a time I have spent three years and a fucking shit load of money going to therapy to get over. So no, I don't want to work for such a massive dickhead, no matter how adorable your daughter is. Just know that researching someone's name on the computer does not give you a full story," Mia explains as she stands. Her whole body is trembling with fear, but her voice stands tall as she talks. With every word she mentions about trauma and needing therapy, I feel like my brain is about to explode. How could my best friend be in this much pain, and I never saw it? She begins to leave, but I take hold of her arm to pull her back to me.

"Mia...wait," I start, but she cuts me off.

"I didn't tell you because I couldn't. When I find the right words, you will be the first to hear them," she whispers.

"How did I not notice? How could I not see all this pain?" I ask, although I am not sure if I expect her to answer. She reaches around to hug me, pulling me in tight.

"I didn't want you to see. You saw what I made you see. It's not your fault. You are not to blame in any way," Mia cry's once more causing her voice to hitch.

"Mia..." I start, my voice raising slightly at the end, making it obvious I intend to ask her some questions. She knows all my tells, and that's why she's looking very apprehensive. She indicates for me to ask whatever I need to, but first I want her to know I'm here for her.

"Mia, do you want or need to talk to me about this shit? Should I be worried?" I ask, genuinely concerned about my best friend, right now.

"I don't talk about it. Not to anyone except my therapist. Maybe one day I will open up to people, but that day is not today. Okay?" she replies, her mood becoming more sombre. I need to bring back the bright and bubbly best friend I have come to love.

Just then a thought enters my head, and I know this will never make up for whatever trauma she has gone through, but it may act as a distraction. "Will you be my maid of honour?" I finish, and the smile that brightens up her face is exactly what I wanted to see. As she is leaving I make a joke about insisting she wears a bright pink dress to the wedding. I am pleased when Mia starts cursing and telling me there's no chance in hell she's wearing any pink. When she finally leaves a few minutes later, thankfully, she goes with a smile and looks a lot more relaxed. I understand Kellan has to be protective over Hallie, but not at the expense of other people's feelings.

When I walk back into the room, I am ready to tear Kellan a new asshole, but he has taken Hallie upstairs. Luckily, Liam calms me down and reassures me he bollocked Kellan enough for the both of us. Looks like my idea of setting up my friends so they could help each other out was a massive mistake, or maybe it was a blessing in disguise.

Perhaps having whatever this is, out in the open will help Mia and me become better friends, more talkative with each other. I thought we were close before, but obviously she hasn't shared a lot of important parts of her life with me. It might be through fear, or pain, but she should still have told me. We need to fix that, but at a later date. Only time will tell, if our friendship can be fixed. But for now, I enjoy a moment curled up on the sofa with Liam while we spitball ideas for our wedding.

CHAPTER TWENTY NINE
Bree

For several days after the shitshow of an interview, I tried to reach Mia, but she has reverted into her shell. She has sent me the odd text here and there, but it's not like her to not reply to my messages. My mind whirls with all the possibilities of what could have happened in her past. What things she hid from me, and why. The more I thought, the more I spiralled. Was I really such a shit friend that I didn't notice my friend going through a hard time? I knew she was unavailable during the summer holidays while we were at school. Still, I thought it was because she was with family. That's what she always told me.

On top of dealing with my overactive imagination, Kellan's walking around with a face like a slapped ass. I have no idea why he is moping when Mia is the one who left here in floods of tears. Liam says he is ashamed of what Kellan did, and that's why he is acting out. I don't think he knows how to cope with being in the wrong.

In addition to their meltdown and the constant array of worsening threats making their way to our house, we also have to deal with my Gramp's imminent arrival. He gave me plenty of warning, which was both a good thing and a bad thing. Good because I could prepare, not just myself but Liam too, but bad because the anxiety is killing me. He will be here any minute, and I think I have actually worn down the carpet where I have been pacing up and down the corridor.

His car arrives, and Liam walks over to meet me. He had been sitting on the sofa watching me pace back and forth. If he's nervous, he definitely doesn't show it. He kept out of the way because he knew nothing would settle my nerves. I jump when the doorbell rings, even though I knew it was coming, I just couldn't help it. My nerves were practically shot at this point.

Liam chuckled. "Relax, Bree. He is just your grandad."

I look over at Liam, giving him the evilest stare I could muster. He deserved to be glared at for underestimating Patrick O'Keenan. He may look like a pleasant old man, but he is far from it.

Taking several deep breaths, I pull open the door to welcome my Gramps. To anyone observing, it looks like an ordinary girl welcoming her grandad. He looks just like you would expect someone who plays golf five days a week to look; dark, smartly pressed trousers, sporting polo shirt, and a flat cap that is hiding the bald patch on the top of his head. The rest of his hair is thinning and grey, his face wrinkled but sunkissed from lots of trips abroad. He pulls me into a hug, and that smell of sandalwood, cigars, and lavender transports me back to the summers I used to spend in Cork. My Gramps is obsessed with lavender, convinced it helps him to relax and sleep. He has it in his bath products and even uses an aromatherapy mister to infuse it into the air while he sleeps.

Releasing the breath I didn't know I was holding, I squeeze him tightly before inviting him into the house. Kellan has taken Hallie to the local park since we don't want to expose her to any more potential danger. Not after she tried to pick up the last "gift" sent to me; a voodoo doll made to look like me with several cuts all over its body. The news of our engagement party seems to have confirmed to people that we are seriously getting married and therefore they are upping their threats.

We get settled on the sofa after the introductions, and welcome drinks have all been sorted. I can tell Liam is a bit more on edge than he usually is. He isn't slouching on the sofa in the way I have come to expect.

"Well, I have to admit, I thought I would want to shoot you, Liam. I guess there was still a part of me that thought maybe you were being kidnapped, or this was all happening under duress. But it isn't, is it?" Gramps asks with a reluctant sigh as he takes a long swig of the coffee Liam prepared for him.

"No, it isn't, far from it actually," I reply with a smile as I take hold of Liam's hand. It's not something I've done for show. I genuinely like to be touching him. His closeness gives me a strength I didn't know I had, probably thanks to how much he believes in me.

"You have taken these two months as I advised, and I am guessing you have come to a decision."

Before I get a chance to answer Gramp's questions, Liam cuts me off with his own answer. "I want to thank you for encouraging us to take the time to get to know each other, Sir. We made some swift decisions, a lot based on rash emotions. So taking the time to think things through and get to know each other was the best thing we could have done. So, I think we have to thank you for that, Sir," Liam addresses my Gramps with respect and a smile, his thumb stroking my hand, that small yet intimate gesture he knows I love.

"Please, call me Paddy," my Gramps adds, and I can't help the massive grin that lights up my face. My Gramps obviously sees it because he rolls his eyes, trying to downplay the gesture, but we both know it is huge. There are very few people close enough to my grandad to be allowed to call him by that nickname. In fact, his highest level security guard, who has worked with him for around ten years, still only calls him Patrick.

"Paddy, thank you. First, I want to apologise in person for the way this thing with Bree started. I took my frustrations with her father out on her, and that was wrong. It was also wrong to include her hand in marriage in any contract. I can assure you that we have discussed this issue, and I have constantly been trying to make things right with her since day one," Liam says, looking genuinely upset. I had no idea he still held guilt over what happened between us.

"That was more my father's fault than yours, Liam. He was the one bartering with his daughter's happiness," I growl. I had no idea that my father was so ruthless that he would risk me and my future.

"Yes, that was a regrettable turn of events. However, are you telling me that the legal implications of the contract are no longer a factor here?" my grandfather asks, staring straight at Liam whilst maintaining his relaxed posture in the comfy armchair.

"I can promise you that as far as I am concerned, that contract never happened. The more I got to know your amazing granddaughter, the more I realised what a beautiful, special girl she is. We may not have started this thing in the most natural way, but now our relationship is very much real," Liam states proudly, and I feel my heart grow impossibly larger. How is it that he builds me up even further with every word that comes out of his mouth? It's like he knows exactly what to say to make me feel better about myself and give me confidence.

"Wait...so you are together for real?" Gramps asks incredulously.

"Gramps, I know this is slightly unexpected given our last call, but this is all thanks to you. You told me to get to know Liam, and I did. What I found was a kind, caring, and amazing guy. He gives me the determination and courage I didn't even know I needed. I have always known I have what it takes to run this Family, but with Liam by my side, I'm even more certain I can do it," I explain, and I am shocked to see him genuinely smile.

"I knew as soon as I opened the door and saw you as a couple, it's like there's a chemistry in the air between you. You move around each other like magnets that are being drawn together. Now, all I need to know is if you are good enough for my granddaughter, Liam." His voice sounds almost romantic and whimsical as he talks about us, like soulmates that are made for each other. Maybe we are? I feel as though a part of me is drawn to Liam, a part of me that wasn't awake before he woke it up. Fuck, I sound like I'm part of a cheesy rom com movie.

"I don't think anyone will ever be good enough for Bree," Liam states and receives a responding chuckle from my grandfather. "But I can promise you that I will spend every day making sure she is happy and safe."

My Gramps scoffs at the last part, and my eyes widen in shock like he questions whether Liam could really keep me safe. Out of everyone I know, he is the one I trust the most with my safety. "Liam, do not be so naive as to think that keeping Bree safe will be an easy process. If she gets her own way and takes over running my company, there will be enemies at every turn. What I want to know is how much of an enemy your father really is?"

With a short giggle that he tries to hide behind his hand, Liam addresses my grandfather. "My father will always be a threat. He wants to rule London; he always has. It has more connections, better shipping lines, and the cops are easier to bend than the Garda. But when we went to Limerick recently, he talked to Bree and agreed to a truce. My father may be many things, but he never breaks his word. So, for now, he is no threat at all, nor are the people that work for him. But don't be fooled into thinking that the time will not come when he rescinds the truce and attacks. We must be ready at all times, but I do have an inside link to his organisation, so hopefully, we will get some internal feedback before that happens."

As Liam explains our recent trip to Ireland and his psychopathic father's newfound love for me, my Gramps listens with an indecipherable mask. I've always hated when he gets like this, and I can't read his emotions. But there is a reason he is the leader of the most prominent crime Family in the world; closing off his feelings is essential. Who knows, maybe one day in the very distant future, I will be the one running the entire empire, but right now, that idea is daunting. With factions worldwide, London may be the largest, even compared to the original Cork branch, but there are still others. The second-largest after Cork is surprisingly in Canada, and I'm not even sure I know them all.

Liam shakes me, causing me to snap out of my daydream, and I realise that my Gramps and Liam must have continued talking while I zoned out. But now they are asking me a question. It's painfully obvious I missed it, so Liam asks me again. "I was just telling your grandfather that my father is not a threat right now, and he asked if I was a secret member of the family. So I explained how hard I fought to get out, alongside Freya and Ryleigh, and continue to fight for Evan and Finn."

"He's telling the truth, Gramps. He is most definitely not working for his father," I confirm, much to my grandfather's delight.

"Very well then, I guess we have a date to run. Pick a date within the next two months, and tell me where and when you want it held. Your mother will help you with all the arrangements, Bree. I will ensure you get your chosen venue even with it being so close to the date." As he speaks, I notice no reaction from Liam, but I am more than a little shocked.

"Why two months? What's the rush?" I ask.

"Because, Bree, talk of your impending nuptials is already

causing unrest. We have guns on the loose that could be used against us, not to mention that we can hardly take care of business if you are distracted by a bloody wedding. Plus, I am getting too old for this shit. I want to retire, and spend some quality time with your grandmother. Also, do you know how much golf I could play if work didn't get in the way?" I don't think he meant it as a joke, but I couldn't help but laugh. His job doesn't interrupt his life too much for someone who already plays five times a week. He asks why I laughed, and I fill him in on my internal thought. Liam makes a sweet comment about not wanting to wait to marry me anyway.

Fuck, why does my heart feel like it's going to explode every time he talks?

"How do you like the house?" Gramps asks in general, but I know he is aiming the question more at Liam than me. I used to stay here regularly; he knows I love it here.

"You have a lovely house, and we love it here, thank you," Liam replies, and my grandfather smiles with a nod of the head.

"That's good because I am gifting it to you as a wedding present. So you can do what you wish with the place now. This is supposed to be for your wedding day, but I want you to have it now," he explains, holding out an envelope which he pulls from the document bag that he brought with him.

Taking hold of the envelope, I not so gently tear the page open, and sure enough, written across the top says 'Transfer of Deed'. My eyes start to mist over, and emotion clogs up my throat as I tell him thank you for such a beautiful gift.

"This is very generous, Paddy, but we can't accept something so extravagant," Liam finishes his sentence, and I shoot him my best pissed-off expression.

"Speak for yourself; I love this house," I snap at Liam, much to my grandfather's amusement.

"Never mind that, Liam. It's my gift. Besides, Bree's grandmother, Clodagh, wants to spend more time at our summer property in the south of France. So we'll have a lot less need for this house. Bree has always wanted it, and since you will need a firm London base, you can keep it. Now, before I leave you both to continue with your wedding planning, what I want to know is...who are the people putting your life in danger, and what is your plan to stop them?" Gramps addresses me as soon as he finishes instructing Liam about the house.

"We believe the threats are coming from the Marcushios. He has made contact, making it very clear he wants revenge for what happened to Leon. We are gathering information at the moment, doing recon. We won't move, or should I say, I will not go to war with them until we know everything there is to know about him. But I can assure you, his little acts of rebellion as he tests the waters are being shut down all over the UK. If he tries anything, we will know," Liam explains, his voice confident and very sure of himself. He doesn't see the Marcushio's as an issue, but they are.

"We have reason to believe that Vinnie may have been planning to gain power long before the shit with his father went down. He was the one stealing from you, and that's why Dad thought it was Leon. All the signs pointed to him, but it was Vinnie all along. So I think until we make an active plan to take him out, he will always be a threat," I add onto the end of Liam's statement.

"Liam, you disagree? I caught that little shake of the head," my grandfather asks, always the perceptive one.

"Honestly, no, I agree. I think Vinnie is emotionally unstable since the death of his father. He holds some guilt that his actions caused his father to get killed. But, from what we have heard, he was planning this out long before Leon's death. So, of course, his death would have an impact. But I did a lot of research on the family before the hit and have done a lot since, and I do not see these threats as coming from him," Liam states, and my head flies around to face him quickly.

"Why have you never said this to me?" I ask, my voice becoming a high-pitched squeak.

Liam takes a deep breath before turning his body slightly to face me, making sure I see his face clearly as he talks. "I didn't want to worry you until I had proof, but I couldn't lie to your grandfather."

"So, who do you think is sending the threats?" my grandfather asks the question that's sitting on the end of my tongue.

"This is just a theory, and it lacks any real proof. I acknowledge that the Marcushios should remain a person of interest, not to mention any new enemies that crop up. Originally, I suspected my father, but I don't think it is after talking to him. I think there's more chance of him being obvious about his threats. He wouldn't try to disguise them," he explains, and I shake my head in agreement. Then he looks at me with a wince, and I know he is worried about whatever he's going to say next. I indicate for him to go ahead.

"There is a part of me that is wondering if this is Vernon. A lot of the threats have had a personal connection to Bree, something only someone close to her would know," he mutters, and my heart starts to race. I never even considered him. He wouldn't threaten his own daughter. Would he?

"I have to admit that I have been wondering that too. Ever since the first threat with the cross, I have wondered if he is involved somehow. I hope that he is not, but I think it warrants more investigation...which I will do. Of course, you are free to investigate and deal with the Marcushios, wipe them all out as far as I am concerned, but leave Vernon to me. Understand?" I feel as though I am sitting there in a blur, my mind whirling with Gramps and Liam's words.

The afternoon passes quickly while we finalise all the details of how the business will transfer over to us after we get married. It's so strange to see my Gramps and Liam actually getting along, which is definitely what starts to happen by the end of the day. They are having a laugh and a joke together, but I can't get that statement out of my head. My mind is continuously assessing every threat, looking for that connection between it and my father. Liam is right; they are there.

Trying to ignore that suspicion now it is there is difficult, but as we part, we agree that no action will be taken until after we marry. We agree on a date and a venue. After a very handsome bribe from my grandfather, we got the place we wanted. So, in just twenty-five days, I will be walking down the aisle and marrying the man I never saw coming. A man who has become my everything. I can't wait to be Mrs. Doughty.

CHAPTER THIRTY
Bree

The wedding day arrives in no time, after what feels like a chaotic five-day build up. Every day my ecstatic mother would arrive on my doorstep at the crack of dawn. Either to finalise another wedding detail or whisk me off somewhere to look at all the things she had in mind for a wedding. So, when I completely ignored her and told her exactly what I wanted, she almost had a mini-stroke. She hates all of Liam and my ideas, but we do it our way or not at all.

Nobody was safe from her reach. I took numerous phone calls from both Liam's sisters and Mia, as my mother was harassing them for their measurements so she could order the bridesmaid dresses. She even came over with a personal baby shopper so that Hallie could try on some gorgeous flower girl dresses. Her reach knew no bounds as Desmond even called me to say that she was being unreasonable and wouldn't let him pick who sits at his table. With the number of people coming, he is lucky he even got a table.

Liam and I had a vision of an intimate ceremony, where it was just us and a few of our closest friends and family, but nobody else wanted that. Desmond wanted at least half his employees, as did Patrick. Not to mention the associates we have to invite to not piss them off and accidentally start another war. One is enough.

The Marcushio's have been strangely quiet since the wedding

preparation began. Well...if it is even them sending the threats. They seem to have almost disappeared, and Liam thinks this is further proof that my dad is involved, that Gramps must have confronted him about it, which is why they stopped. Although we couldn't rule the Marcushio's out yet. So, we kidnapped Richie Ricardo, former second in command when Leon was alive.

It was actually the easiest interrogation I have ever done. He sang like a canary without me even having to get my knife out, since he no longer has an allegiance to the Family. He was supposed to be in charge if anything happened to Leon. Leon only wanted Vinnie to take over when Richie thought he was ready, but Vinnie is a typical know-it-all teenager who wants it all. So, it was the perfect opportunity to set the Marcushios up as not just a rival Family, but the Family. His stupidity knows no bounds, and Richie even admitted to us that the longer Vinnie has any kind of power, the more danger everyone will be in.

After a lengthy discussion, not only did Richie strengthen his allegiance with my family and me, he also helped us with information about Vinnie and his plans. Strangely, he is sure that Vinnie doesn't have any weapons since he called Richie only two days before, asking if he knew how to get any. Vinnie is definitely looking to arm, but he isn't armed yet. This further supports Kellan's idea that my father still has the guns and has been playing us for the beginning, sending me on a wild goose chase. But why?

When I'm not wedding planning, I seem to spend every waking moment thinking about what my father could be doing. My mind goes from best to the worst-case scenario in a flash. Initially, I can't help but think he is making his move against who he sees as a rival, but then Liam reminds me that I am not just his daughter but his only child. Would he really kill his child? So then I think of the best-case scenario, which doesn't end with my death. Maybe he just doesn't want me to marry Liam? Sadly, no matter what his agenda is, and what he plans to do, I will be ready. He is in for a shock if he doesn't think I can see all of my enemies, and I have a plan to weed them all out, but first, I have to get ready to go to my own wedding.

Since our wedding planner from hell couldn't agree with what we wanted to happen, we all decided to compromise slightly. I was never a girl who dreamed of having a wedding. It never really entered my head until I started to fall for Liam. Before, it was just going to be another business transaction, another contract to sign, but then it became more. The longer Liam and I thought about it, we realised we somehow wanted Ireland to be represented in the wedding. The thing I love most about Ireland is the beautiful architecture and green spaces. So after some research, we opted for Farnham Castle as our venue. Not only was it not far from London, but its adaptability and flexibility meant that we could cater to what everyone wanted.

So in just under half an hour, I will be walking to the gorgeous Lantern Room, which is a beautiful, bright room lined with a wall of stunning arched windows. We have chosen to have it laid out with black lace bows secured around them and black flowers lining the aisle. I chose all the flowers that Von recommended. My mother and her bonded nicely over the bouquets. Although I have had to rein them in slightly, their lavish minds got slightly too big for my liking.

If I'm honest, this part of the day is what I am looking forward to the most. This is our private ceremony that is just for our family and friends. We will not be legally married, as the church ceremony we will have an hour later will be for that, but this is for us. The church is so that everyone who matters can sit there, in front of a God that they don't acknowledge unless it's Christmas or they want to atone for their sins, and watch us be married.

Both me and Liam are catholic, but I can't remember the last time I ever stepped foot in a church. It was probably the last time someone died or got married. It's ironic, given that my family is the epitome of sin. My dad is fucking someone less than half his age, and my mother operates on a healthy mix of antidepressants and gin. So, we are not the poster family for the church, but since my parents agreed to let me have the ceremony we wanted, we decided to do the church wedding too.

After that, we will go onto a sit-down meal held in the most beautiful hall, followed by an evening event where we have managed to invite even more people. There are literally a handful of people that I can tolerate in this world, and yet I have just over three hundred people coming to this wedding in total. Thank fuck we don't have to feed them all because there is no way my venue can seat that many.

I go to check on all the rooms first thing, but the assistant my mother hired, who looks literally the most stressed I have ever seen her, has it all in hand. She is all set up and waiting for our beautiful five-tier wedding cake to be delivered. In the meantime, she was instructing people on where to hang lights or put flower arrangements. So, safe in the knowledge that she has everything in hand, I come back to the house, but I feel lost without Liam.

We decided to do things a little traditional and spend the night before apart. Let me tell you now it was fucking torture. I haven't slept a night without Liam since we met, and I had no idea how much I have come to depend on his warmth. I usually lay my head on his chest, listening to his heartbeat, tracing the ridges of his abdomen. At the same time, he strokes my hair, and we just talk until we fall asleep. I'm sure once I am sleeping, he rolls me off his chest. His arm goes dead, if not, but he always curls up behind me to keep me close.

So last night, not only am I at my most fucking stressed, paranoia and fear of every little thing going wrong with the wedding are taking over me. I also don't have the one thing that calms me down and helps me get some sleep, Liam. This morning when I woke up, it's apparent I had less than four hours of sleep. I'm running on fumes, trying to be in a million places at once. As someone who is used to leading, letting others do the jobs for me is hard. I want to make sure they have done it to my specification, which is why I found myself driving to the venue and then rushing back for my hair and make-up.

Mia, Ryleigh, Freya, my mother, and Von are all in my living room. People are milling around, all of them either handing out breakfast pastries and champagne or doing someone's hair and make-up. Everyone is dressed in silk black robes embroidered with their names. They're in various stages of preparation, and the fantastic photographer I managed to grab for the wedding is trying to get as many candid shots as possible. I hired two photographers to work together. One is to capture all the memorable, posed style photos, and another is to take the ones that nobody realises. The one with the genuine reactions. They are the ones Liam and I want to keep.

As I let two people pull, twist, and curl my silky, bright red locks, I can't help but imagine what Liam is doing. He is already at the venue. They usually give the honeymoon suite to the bride to get ready in, but I wanted to be at home. I felt like being in my own surroundings would be better for me, so Liam and Kellan decided to move to the hall for the night. Finn and Evan are meeting them there this morning. I'm surprised Evan has agreed to be in the wedding party, but I'm more shocked Liam asked him to join. However, he says he doesn't ever want his brother to think he has given up on him. He needs to always know that leaving is an option.

My father and Gramps have suits that match Liam's, but they aren't going to the venue to get ready. Unless mother got them their own room, I have no idea. I know they had a massive argument over who would be the one to walk me down the aisle. My mum actually asked me if I could pick who would I want. I didn't even hesitate for a moment. Jimmy. He has been like a father to me my entire life, raising me, caring for me, teaching me to survive this life. On the other hand, Vernon has never really seen me, having consistently underestimated me, even now. However, my choice was not allowed. We finally agreed that Gramps could escort me for our service and Vernon for the official one. Jimmy was assigned to get me to the castle on time, something he strangely did not seem too happy about.

All the bridesmaids are ready and looking absolutely stunning in their deep purple silk dresses that fall off their bodies like a dark waterfall and look absolutely beautiful. I'm genuinely scared that there's no way I will stand out with those next to me. Once the bridesmaids and Von are all ready to go, a car arrives to take them to the venue. I want my dresses to be a surprise, only my mother has seen them, which is why she stays behind to help me dress.

Yes, I did say dresses, as in plural. Another compromise with my mother. I had an idea of what I wanted, and she had an idea of what she wanted. So, I will be wearing a different dress for each ceremony before changing into my party dress for the evening. After watching several bridal shows on TV, I thought I had a clear idea of what I wanted and was sure my appointment would be easy, but it wasn't. I thought I wanted a ballgown, to look like a princess, but as soon as I walked into the shop, I knew which was my dress. A beautiful ivory lace fabric that clung to my body perfectly. The straps and curved bust line hung perfectly and made my boobs look amazing, but it was the back that I fell in love with. The fabric scooped down my spine, exposing my back in the same way that the dress I wore for my engagement party did. Then the material trailed down and behind me, giving the dress a large lace train. I fell in love with it as soon as I tried it on, and I knew Liam would love it too.

I knew I would have to cover up for the more traditional wedding in the chapel, but this was our ceremony. My mother agreed that this part of the wedding could be done however we wanted. So, we even went as far as agreeing to write our own vows. I literally spent hours on them. But as I stood there, staring at myself in the mirror, I knew exactly what I wanted to say to Liam. I wanted to tell him that I love him. I can't believe I still haven't told him. I came close so many times, but the moment never seemed perfect enough. I should never have chickened out of telling him on the Ferris Wheel.

I look over at my mum and see her trying to blot away the tears threatening to fall and ruin her perfectly crafted face. She stares at me with the proudest look I have ever seen, and I can't help but take another look at myself in the mirror. My long red hair had been pulled back off my face and twisted into a half-up and half-down style. The curls are adorned with beautiful diamante and pearls from the hair accessories that have been delicately placed in the small plait that trails down. Over my hair, slid into the hair design is the beautiful veil made from the same lace on the dress, and it trails down to sit with the train. The dress hugs me in all the right places, and the ivory colour compliments my skin perfectly.

My heart is racing, and I can feel tears threatening to make an appearance, but I blink them back. I have never felt so incredibly beautiful as I do in this moment. My mother, not always someone who shows me affection, reaches forward as though to hug me, which I oblige.

"Brianna...I don't have the right words. I can't even begin to tell you how beautiful you look. I'm so incredibly proud of the woman you've grown to be. When I gave birth to a little girl, it was like a deflated moment for everyone around me. They were all hoping for the next heir, a boy. But not me. I looked down at the beautiful little angel I held in my arms, and I knew you could be whoever you wanted. From the minute you gripped onto my finger, refusing to let go, I knew how tough you would be. I'm not going to lie and say I wouldn't prefer you to be in my world instead of your father's. The idea that you will be a target and that your life will constantly be in danger, it physically hurts my heart, but I know it's who you are supposed to be. I am so incredibly proud of you, Angel. I know we never really talked about something old, new, borrowed, and blue, but I wanted to give you this. This necklace has been in my family for generations. It is always worn by the women of the family and passed down to the eldest daughter. I wore it on my wedding day, and I would love it if this could be your 'something borrowed'."

Mum hands over a blue velvet box, and as soon as I open it, I release a breath I didn't realise I'd been holding. Laying on the velvet jewellery pad is the most beautiful, delicate white gold chain. Hanging off it in the centre is a single large pearl that has been shaped to look like a teardrop, with diamonds dotted around the metal frame of the pearl. The glistening white orb looks perfect and knowing the necklace's history, I'm instantly overcome with emotion. I hand it to my mother to put on me, and as I look in the mirror, we both start to well up once more.

"Thank you, Mum. This looks so gorgeous. I love it. I guess my dress can be something new. Now I just need something blue and borrowed," I add with a chuckle. Trust me not to have given the most obvious tradition any thought at all.

"Oh yes, that reminds me. The girls told me to give you this gift box when you are dressed. I am supposed to leave the room when I have given it to you. But please be quick, Angel. We only have about ten minutes until Jimmy will be here." My mother's firm, bossy tone has returned, and she hands me the box before going back into the living room.

Sitting on the bed, I open the box to find two smaller boxes and two cards, along with an extensive instruction page. It states very clearly I'm to open the bigger gift and the smaller card first, making sure to start with the present. Picking up the package, I can't help but admire the beautiful black wrapping paper, but I quickly tear that off, desperate to get inside. There's a gift box, and as I lift the lid, I find the most beautiful blue and white lace garter, the outer edge dotted with tiny ivory pearls.

Opening the card, I see the scribbly handwriting that belongs to Mia.

Dear Bree,
We are so incredibly honoured to stand by your side and watch you marry the man of your dreams. Your relationship may not have started in the most traditional way, but there is no denying your feelings for each other now. You were made for each other, and we just wanted you to know how much we support you both.

*Since you don't have anything blue, we got together and designed
this garter for you. I sewed it together, and I really hope that you like it
and that it fits. I have never wondered how big your thigh is before.
Anyway, thank you for asking us to stand by your side and watch
you marry your soulmate. We love you.
Oh, and Ryleigh would like to state for the record that if she hears
any stories, let alone has to watch her brother take that off your thigh
with his teeth, you will be responsible for paying the therapist bill.
We all love you both so much. Happy wedding day, Bree!!!
Love, Mia, Freya, Ryleigh, and the most beautiful flower girl,
Hallie xxx*

My breath hitches as I reread the letter, laughing at Ryleigh and her typical teenage attitude. I slide the garter up my thigh as best I can, given all the fabric. I have to admit that it makes me feel incredibly sensuous, combined with my sexy white lingerie. I can't wait for Liam to see me in this.

As soon as I've calmed down enough, I pick up the instructions again. This time I am supposed to open the card. There is no writing on the front, so I have no idea who it is from. As soon as I see the front of the card, I know it's from Liam. The card reads, 'To my beautiful penguin' and there's a picture of two macaroni penguins who look like they are kissing.

It's an ongoing joke between us that we are like penguins. They have only one soulmate, and they mate for life. Still, they are different to most other animals in that the male stays behind to care for and nurture the egg, while the female is the one who goes off to hunt for the food. It's a little like us, I am the hunter who brings home the food, and Liam just does whatever I need from him. We work together like we were made for each other. My breath is already hitched, and I bite my lip in a desperate attempt to stop the tears from flowing just by looking at the cover. Whatever is inside the box stands a good chance of causing my make-up to run.

*Bree, My Princess,
I can't believe this day has arrived so quickly. Time seems to have
flown by, yet I feel as though I have known you forever. I didn't realise
I was walking around with a hole in my heart until you came along
and filled it. You are the most fantastic person I have ever met, and
I am so honoured that I get to stand by your side as your husband. I*

*can't wait to watch you conquer the world and show everyone exactly
what you are capable of.
I was told it was my job to get you 'something new' and 'something
borrowed.' The box in the white wrapping paper is from my mum, and
if you like it, you are welcome to use it as your 'something borrowed.'
She said she wore it on her wedding day. Let's hope it brings us a
happier marriage than they fucking have.
The bigger box is from me and is your 'something new.' I hope you
like it, Princess. Now, get your ass ready and come and meet me at the
end of the aisle. I will be the one in a suit looking very nervous. Can't
wait to see your pretty face.
Love, Your Penguin Liam xx*

I open the first package as instructed, and in black silk coating sits the most beautiful bracelet. It's white gold with D shaped rings slotted together into such a delicate chain. Then hanging from one is a larger shaped D with a large diamond sat in the lower curve of the letter. D for Doughty, and I guess I was about to become a Doughty. The bracelet is beautiful, and I set it to the side to get mum to help me put it on. It's the present from Liam that I am desperate to open.

Tearing at the paper, the box is larger than the others, which confuses me as my brain whirls with all the possibilities of what he could have bought me. Opening the beautiful black leather box, my breath hitches as I take in the most stunning, elegant tiara. It's small, and there is only one point where several tiny pearls and diamonds hang elegantly. I never even considered wearing a tiara, but knowing that to Liam, I'm his Princess, I want to be who he sees.

Placing the tiara on my head and standing up to look in the mirror, I can't help the tears that appear. I thought I looked perfect before, but the delicate, little, white gold diadem sits beautifully in my red curls and looks like it belongs there.

Looking over my shoulder, I see Mum, Dad, and Jimmy standing behind me. Mum is almost sobbing, talking about how much of a princess I look like. Even my father looks a bit odd, almost sad. As soon as he catches me looking, he schools his face and plasters on a fake smile. I guess he has never come around to the idea of me marrying Liam. I quickly ask mum to put on the Doughty family bracelet, and she looks at it longingly. She always has admired a beautiful piece of jewellery. Once that is on securely, the tears start welling in my mothers eyes again. Then, without acknowledging me or telling me I look nice, Vernon pulls my mother away. The photographer who has been silently watching us interact directs us into poses by the car. Fairly quickly, my father shoos her off and insists he is leaving with my mother. Maybe he is really unhappy that I am getting married?

Once he has gone, with my mother reluctantly trailing after him, Jimmy steps forward. He also has a strange look on his face. It's almost a mixture of pride and sadness. When he sees me staring, analysing, he also schools his features. He steps towards me and holds his arms open wide for me. Instantly, I step into them. It's so strange to see him in a suit, but he does look very debonair.

His arms fold around me, and when he talks, it's so quiet I struggle to hear his whispered words. "You look so beautiful, Bumblebee. Thank you for inviting me to be part of your special day."

I pull back from his hug but make sure to keep my hands on his arms as I stare at him, determined to show him my conviction. "Jimmy, you have been more of a father to me than anyone. I wish you could have more of a role, but he is my father after all," I chuckle, and I see Jimmy roll his eyes. He is used to me slating my father.

"Bree, are you sure you want to go through with this? It's not too late. I know the threats have been getting more violent in nature. Are you sure this is worth it?" Jimmy asks, and I pull away completely.

"I don't give a shit about people who make threats with no name, hiding behind their anonymity. All that tells me is that they are too chicken shit to tell me who they really are, and that they're too afraid to fight like a man. So the threats mean nothing to me, but Liam does. This stopped being a business arrangement a long time ago. Yes, it is too soon for us to marry for real, but we are doing it anyway. I fucking love him, Jimmy. My heart is racing, but not with nerves; I am excited about becoming his wife. So your question about if it's worth it is really you asking if Liam is worth it, and he is. I would die for him," I say confidently.

The small huff is quickly replaced by a fake smile. I thought once he knew how I truly felt about Liam, he would support the wedding, and it's like he wants to be, but something is stopping him. He can't help but look ominous. Like we are getting into the car to drive towards the apocalypse.

I go to get in first, but Jimmy insists on getting in first, leaving me to climb in afterwards with the photographer leaning through the window to get some shots. I have no idea what they will look like, as Jimmy's haunted mood fills the air around us, and I try to push it away. I take my mind back to a few minutes ago, touching my tiara to remind me that I will always be Liam's Princess. It doesn't take long going down that road to bring the smile back on my face. The photographer climbs into the front seat, and the driver takes off down the driveway. We only live about fifteen minutes from the venue, so we will be there very soon.

After driving for around five minutes, I feel Jimmy become very rigid, and my danger instinct starts to kick in. I don't know what it is, but something doesn't feel right, my stomach is doing flips, and I know I am not all of a sudden becoming nervous about the wedding. Whatever the danger is, Jimmy knows. How had he seen it before me?

Just as I am going to ask him what is going on, the lorry in front of us stops abruptly, causing us to slow down, and out of a hidden side road, a large black vehicle slams into the front driver side of our car. The beautiful black Lexus we are in spins off the road, barreling down into the field next to us. The vehicle hits with such force that I feel my head smash into the glass window next to me. Blood starts to pour out of the wound, and pain ricochets around my body. I quickly use my hands to cover the cut on my head, desperate not to get blood on this beautiful dress.

My head is ringing, and my vision is blurry. I repeatedly blink, hoping the more I do it, the quicker my sight will return. I am disoriented, but I try to look at the others in the car with us.

"Jimmy!" I shout loudly, reaching over with my bloody hand to shake him awake, but he just lays there. I check his pulse and see his breathing is fine. The more my vision returns, the more I stare, looking for any apparent injuries. That's when I notice that his eyes are scrunched together. Like he can't bear to open them and see what has happened. What the fuck is going on?

I try to see if the photographer and driver are alive, but the door I'm leaning on opens, and I'm dragged out of the car. I look to see if a good samaritan has come to help us or if the emergency services managed to get here quickly. Instead, what I find is a man wearing a balaclava. He sees me looking and immediately hits me across the face using the back of his hand.

My hands fly to my cheek as I cry out in pain. My head already feels like a marching band is stopping through whilst playing the most annoying song, and now it is rattling. I feel like my brain is about to burst, the headache is so intense. His ring must have caught my face because a small trail of blood is leaking from my cheek, mixing with the blood still seeping from my head wound. I stand no chance of protecting my dress now.

The scrawny guy who dragged me out of the car wearing a balaclava pulls me into the muddy grass before trying to get hold of my arms. I fight him as much as my body will let me, body thrashing as I try to gain control. I think I would have succeeded if another person wearing a balaclava hadn't arrived holding a gun straight at my head.

"Enough. If you fight, I will shoot you. Now put your arms behind your back like a good little girl." His voice is deep and authoritative, and there's something about the voice that seems familiar to me. Like I have spoken to this person before, but I just can't remember where.

Doing as I am told, I hold my arms as tightly as possible; it's a trick Jimmy taught me. If I tense up my arms and pull them out just slightly, making sure the other person doesn't notice, then when I relax my arms there will be some slack in the knot. Best-case scenario, you can use that slack to get your hands out completely. Worst-case, it leaves the knot slack but not enough to help you escape. At least it means they won't rub on your wrists as much.

"Make sure they are as tight as you can get them without cutting off circulation. Relax your hands, bitch," he sings like he knew I would try that. I mean, I don't profess to be the only one to know that trick, but I am surprised he just knew I was going to do it.

Before I have a chance to try and contemplate more of what is going on, a bag is pulled over my head, and lanky guy number one pulls me up. I wait, listening for signs of his movements, and once he is standing in front of me, I kick him as hard as possible in the leg. His ear-splitting yell rings out, and it would appear I connected with his cock by mistake. Oops.

I smile to myself until I feel the barrel of the gun being pressed against my forehead. "That's strike one. I have a two-strike rule. I will pull this trigger, do you understand?" the loud voice grinds into my ear.

I listen as he helps his partner up, and they both grab one of my arms and drag me towards where the road is. My bruised and aching head takes a moment to mourn the loss of this beautiful dress before allowing the whole situation to register. I hear the man with the gun murmuring, but I can't tell who he is talking to.

"You okay? Sit down, remember the plan. Look, I have a job to do; you knew it would get rough. Now fuck off and let me do my job," he mutters, and at first, I think he must be talking to someone on the phone. But if that were the case, how would he know they were standing up. He is talking to a third person, and I listen intently, trying to find out who is doing this, but they don't talk about it nor say their name.

When we reach the car, it's different to the one that ran us off the road. I must have missed this car pull up in all the chaos. I'm roughly dragged inside, my veil is torn off my hair, but thankfully I don't lose the tiara that Liam gave me. Liam. I breathe deeply as I realise he will be standing at the altar wondering where I am. I hope he doesn't think I changed my mind. I wish I had told him I loved him. Tears stream down my face as thoughts of what I am missing flash through my mind. This should be the happiest day of my fucking life.

It doesn't take long for sadness to be replaced by fucking raging anger. I am going to slaughter everyone for ruining this day for me. Then, using the skills Jimmy taught me, I take my thoughts back to immediately before the crash. I knew something was going to happen, but how?

Jimmy! Jimmy must have known something was going to happen. He made sure I put a seat belt on. He insisted I sat on the side closest to the driver, essentially so he could be as far away from the impact. He must have been who the kidnapper was talking to. It's hard to imagine that he sat there while I worried about him and let me get kidnapped. More than that, am I really saying he was part of it?

That's when the realisation hits. If Jimmy is involved, the most likely scenario is that he is acting on my father's orders. The more I think about it, not only does my head feel like it might explode, but I know I am right. Liam and Kellan both suspected my father of being the one responsible for sending the threats. Then sending us on a wild goose chase to find guns that were never stolen. I should have listened to them.

Fuck, as if I'm being kidnapped by my own fucking father.

Chapter Thirty One
Liam

The morning of the wedding passes by in a blur. I'm surrounded by my brothers and Kellan, and surprisingly we all get on really well, just like we used to do when we were kids. Even Evan loosens up a bit and seems to have a good time. I was shocked he agreed to be a groomsman when I asked him. I wasn't exactly planning on it, but the more I thought about who I wanted by my side when I got married, it just seemed so obvious to have my brothers here.

We deliberately didn't invite my father to get ready with us, not needing that kind of stress. Kellan said when he took Hallie for a walk around the castle grounds this morning to try and calm her down, he was sure he saw Bree's car. That made me chuckle. I knew my little control freak wouldn't be able to hand over the reins completely. I had seen her mother flying around shouting orders before she fled again, no doubt to help Bree get ready.

My mind wanders as I think about the type of dress she will have chosen. Before she started giving me hints, I would have thought I could guess what she would pick, but after hearing the clues, I have no idea. She was using words like tulle, sweetheart neck, A-line, and she lost me. I could just about keep up with words like sexy, lace, and ballgown, but they all didn't exactly mesh together. Kellan thinks she has two dresses. I can't wait to see her.

We get to the Lantern Room early, as I was instructed, and see that the room is all set up for us. We are only having a few close family members or allies that will get pissed if we don't invite them. There are a couple of people milling about, looking a little bit lost because they have come too early.

"Should we see them to their seats?" Finn asks, and I nod in confirmation. As he walks off, Evan follows after him.

Kellan is holding Hallie, and I can't help but admire how fucking beautiful she looks. She has started to grow a little bit of blonde hair now, and we have managed to tie bits of it up into two cute little pigtails with little bows. When Kellan started getting her dressed in the outfit Bree picked, it sounded like she was being murdered. She is just slightly over six months old now, and you can see the little character she is becoming.

Not only can she sit up on her own, but she is also starting to try pushing her body up with her hands. It looks like she is doing a press-up almost as she works out how to crawl. I don't think it will be long. In the meantime, she has discovered a very effective technique for getting around. She basically barrel rolls everywhere. She goes from lying on her back to her front and back again. Over and over until she reaches her destination or vomits from dizziness.

So trying to get her to sit still long enough to get this dress on is a nightmare, and I can hear Kellan getting more stressed. Luckily, Bree has bought a couple of outfits because there is no way this will stay clean. Hallie has started eating proper food now. Well... when I say proper food, I mean anything mashed up, or that shit they put in a pot and stick a baby food label on it. But some of those rice pudding or banana ones she absolutely loves. Although last week Bree made her some mash with mashed up carrots and suede. She vomited that back up very quickly, and I don't blame her. I would have done too. But when I feed her mash covered in melted cheese, she loves it. I may have to listen to a ten-minute lecture from Kellan and Bree about helping kids be healthy, but I just rolled my eyes. It's no wonder I am her favourite.

It's so strange. As I look at Hallie cuddled up to her dad, wearing the most adorable ivory gown with a deep purple sash wrapped around her, she makes me think about the future. What will Bree and my child look like? Will we have children? My brain is whirling with all these possibilities, and my mind is reeling. I do want all those things with Bree. I want to raise a family with her and give her everything she has ever wanted. I guess our future really does start now.

The chairs fill up fast, and it's not long before the car arrives with the bridesmaids in it. That is my queue to get into the room and wait for my bride. I take a moment to look over my sisters and Mia. They all look stunning. Bree didn't want to go with a traditional colour, but she also didn't want it to be completely black. This shade of purple is about one away, and it looks stunning. The black and white calla lily bouquets that they are given really finish the look.

Kellan, looking somewhat reluctant, walks over to Mia. He mutters something that I am guessing is an apology, but she does not look like she is having any of it.

"Look, I have said I am sorry. I don't know what more to do if you chose not to accept my apology. I just need to know that for the next five minutes while I am behind these closed doors, that I can trust you with the most important thing in my life," Kellan states whilst looking down at Hallie. She looks as though she is listening and taking in every word.

"You can trust me," Mia mutters, and I nod my head to tell him to give her a chance.

"We better get inside," I say quickly as Kellan hands Hallie over to Mia. Surprisingly, she goes without complaint and looks quite happy, instantly grabbing hold of some of Mia's black hair. I would say hair pulling is a new thing, but she has been doing it practically since birth. She just didn't always get many chances since Kellan and I were the main people to look after her, and our hair isn't easy to pull. There are some angles where she can get me, but usually, it's Bree who has to live with that.

We walk in, closing the door behind us, and I feel my nerves start to grow, and I don't know why. My heart is racing, my palms are sweating, but at the same time, I am slightly excited. I know I will be more terrified later, having to essentially perform in front of other people, as it's not my favourite thing to do. I am an assassin for a reason, so I don't have to work in a sociable job. Plus, the pay is excellent, but that is beside the point. I shouldn't be getting nervous. This ceremony is just for us, to tell each other how we feel in our own way. Not a performance or a spectacle, just us. But still, something doesn't feel right.

The longer I stand there waiting, the larger the nerves grow.

Kellan and my brothers have both got bored of standing up and have sat on their allocated chairs and are giving me various pep talks to help me calm down. Christ, even my mother is telling me about how she was ten minutes late to marry my father, while he chips in that she shouldn't have bothered turning up at all.

I try to tune everyone out and think of good scenarios for why she might be late. She might be having lots of photos taken. She might even be stuck in traffic. As I look around, it occurs to me that her parents haven't arrived here yet either. So that gives weight to the traffic argument.

Even though that seems like the most logical explanation, I can't help but be overwhelmed by that impending fear of doom that you get at the height of anxiousness. My stomach feels like it's going to drop from under me, and my heart literally can't race any quicker. I don't know how I know, but I just know something terrible is going on here.

"Try ringing Bree, please," I mutter to Kellan. He tries to argue that there is no need, that she might not answer if she is on her way. Most brides don't tend to carry their mobile phones. But he knows not to argue with me when I glare at him.

It rings and rings, and nobody answers. He tries the numbers for Vernon and Jimmy's burner phones he found when scanning their electronic footprint when they came into our house. We didn't tell Bree about what we were doing because she doesn't want to suspect her own family, but we do.

I don't know how, but I know Bree is in danger. Something terrible is happening, and her family are suspiciously the only people missing. However, her grandfather is sitting at the front, looking equally concerned. He, too, is using his phone to try and get through to people, and when he doesn't, he seems more angry than concerned.

"What's going on, Paddy? Where is Bree?" I whisper aggressively, wanting him to know how pissed I am, but not wanting the whole room to worry.

I can hear them talking. They think she has left me, decided not to marry me, but they are wrong. She would never do that. Not just because of how important it is to her to become the Family leader, but because of us. She wanted to marry me for real. We spent the last twenty-five days talking about our life together. We went through so much shit to get here. First, listening to her mother and the wedding disasters she just had to avert, and my father insisting we marry in a church. Then dealing with all the seating disasters of who hates who and can't sit next to one another. We had to deal with all of that on top of investigating and interrogating people about the threats surrounding us. Still, every night when we went to bed, we cuddled up to each other and went to our happy place.

We talked about what rooms would be nurseries and what Hallie would think of our kid. We talked about wanting to get a dog. She told me she wants to have a little pug and to call him Reggie. I told her I always imagined having a little King Charles spaniel named Corky. She laughed. We joked that Reggie would probably need a girlfriend, and we would have to call her Regina because it works so well. As I reminisce about the time we spent together plotting our lives, I feel a pang of sadness. I make a vow right now to make sure when we get this shit hole of a mess sorted, that I will buy her Reggie, Regina, and Corky. She can have them all. Fuck, even if she decides she wants a deaf, mute dog called Peg, she can have whatever she wants.

Picking up the phone, I try ringing her again, and this time the phone is answered. I pull Paddy and Kellan over to the side, and my brothers follow. I put the phone on speaker so they can hear, but nobody else can. I have said hello a couple of times, but no reply. Then, just as someone starts to speak, my father wanders over loudly, asking what's going on. I shush him, only to get an evil glare back in response. Evan fills him in quickly, and shockingly my father looks murderously angry. At least I can rule him and any of his associates out of this.

"We have your fiancée. Sadly, she won't be making it to the wedding today, but I will give you the chance to see her again. I want the rights to the London franchise signed over to me, legally," the distorted voice says. It's the same robotic voice used to call me in the car. Given my father is standing next to me looking fucking furious, I think I may have been wrong in assuming it was him.

"I want to hear my granddaughter's voice now!" shouts Paddy down the phone with more venom than we were expecting. If anyone doubted his love for Bree, he just proved it. And looking at the faces of the men surrounding me, I can tell that each one of them, even my father and Evan most surprisingly, seem to be willing to go to war for her.

"Liam...Liam, is-is that you?" Bree cries through the phone, and my heart breaks. She sounds so lost and broken. If they have harmed one hair on her head, I will cut their dicks off personally and feed it to them before I kill them. I am generally not the vindictive one and leave that shit to Desmond. But there isn't anything I wouldn't do for Bree.

"I'm here, Princess. Are you okay? Have they hurt you?" I ask quickly, only to hear her screams crackle down the phone.

Crack! The sound of skin on skin, like a slap, vibrates through the phone. Followed quickly by Bree's screams and another voice in the distance. "Fucking, bitch. Bite me again, and I will knock all those pretty teeth out. It will be easier for you to choke on my cock then!" he shouts, and instantly we all become tense.

These guys are not fooling around. They are not just threatening my girl with pain; they are threatening rape. I am sure as fuck not going to stand by and let that happen. I hear the sentence replaying over and over in my head like my brain is trying to tell me something. I don't want to listen to the words anymore. That's when it occurs to me; it's not about the words. We just heard a voice in the background, it wasn't distorted by a filter.Most voice distorters only work if you press the button to activate it, he must have taken his finger off. I'm sure the voice is one I have heard before, but I can't place it with all the stress and anxiety going through me right now. I want to talk, to tell him that I will hunt him down and make him eat his own dick, but I just can't find the words. Luckily, Paddy doesn't have that problem.

"Who am I legally transferring the rights over to? I won't be able to do it without the signature of my son, Vernon. Do you have him, too?" he asks calmly. At first, I wonder what the hell he is doing, but when I stop my brain from acting irrationally, I realise he is gathering information.

"Get the paperwork, and I will sign it. Transfer to Vincent Leonardo Marcushio. Do you need me to spell that?" he asks boldly, and I look over at Kellan in confusion. Why would Vinnie use a voice modifier to hide who he is, then offer to literally spell out his name. This makes no sense at all.

"You didn't answer me about Vernon," Paddy pushes, and there is silence on the other end of the phone like it has been muted. Whoever is talking is reading from a script practically, and that was a question they never saw coming.

"Yes...we have Mr O'Keenan. We will arrange a time to meet, and you will transfer it over to me. Get the paperwork ready. We will meet in one hour," the automated voice demands.

"That's not enough time. My lawyer is in Cork. I need to call him, get the stuff faxed over. An hour is unrealistic," Paddy stresses, the fear starting to creep in as his voice cracks at the end.

"That's bullshit. I have done my research, and I know your lawyer is in London. Twister and Lawson's, if I am not mistaken. So, you better make it work because, for every deadline you miss, I will take it out on your granddaughter," he says, and I can't help but pull on my hair in frustration. What the fuck are we going to do? Why is Paddy smiling?

"Okay, I will have the paperwork done, but I will want proof that Bree is unharmed before I do anything," Paddy states, but the electronic voice just laughs.

"You don't get to make the rules, old man, I do. Your time has passed. Now, it's my time," he states most bizarrely. It's almost like he has been trying to be in power for years, but Vinnie is a hormonal seventeen-year-old who is running on revenge fumes. This just doesn't sound like him.

As the phone hangs up, I must voice that thought out loud because everyone is staring at me like I might be going crazy. He did confess with his name, but I don't believe it. Neither does Paddy. "You are right. This is not Marcushio. They may be being used as scapegoats. They maybe even think they are in charge, but they have no idea they are being played. I think I know who has Bree, and if any of them hurts one hair on her head, I will kill them all," Paddy states passionately as he puts the phone in his pocket, but Kellan holds his arm out for it. He wants to run tests, see if he can make the voice audible. Paddy reluctantly hands it over.

A chorus of 'who' echoes from all around me, and Paddy has the most disappointed, sad look on his face as he answers us all. "Vernon and Jimmy."

A chorus of swear words is what rings out this time. Everyone has a different yet equally pissed response.

"I believe you, but I want to know how you know? Are you sure?" I ask, and Paddy reluctantly shakes his head.

"When you told me you suspected my son of being the one sending the parcels, I promised I would look into it, but I couldn't find anything. Things were suspiciously too clean. I also noticed he talked a lot more about how the power would transfer over. He wanted me to transfer mine to him first, then transfer it to Bree and Liam. He thinks he convinced me to sign over the Ireland branch, but the papers are fake. My lawyer really is in Ireland. I suspected Vernon was having me followed, so I made a bullshit appointment with Twister and Lawson, enquiring about their services. Then I drew up the papers to match them. That's why the kidnapper thinks my lawyer is here in London, and I only told that to one person. He is making his move today because he thinks I finally signed Ireland over to him, and he can keep both." The more he speaks, the more pissed he gets, and I don't blame him. I am feeling murderous.

"This might sound like a stupid question, but I don't really live in your world, so it's not that dumb. But if you are an illegal operation, why do you need to legally sign things over?" Kellan asks, and it's a good question, but not one that gets me closer to Bree.

"We need to do it this way as a show of power. We have legal businesses that we use as a front for the illegal, so that's how the power is distributed," Paddy adds.

"All I want to know is how the fuck I get my girl back!" I shout.

"We have to wait for the next call. Then when he gives us a location to meet and sign, that's when we will pounce. I will get Bree back to you, I promise." Paddy makes it sound like he is going alone, and that thought is laughable. Nothing will keep me from finding her.

"Fuck that. When you know where she is, we all go. I am getting my girl back if I have to kill everyone in sight, including her dad. Are you going to get in my way?" I snarl, and he holds his hands up in what should be a calming gesture, but it isn't. To me, I just see something I want to punch. Instead, I feel Kellan place a hand on my shoulder, and I relax slightly.

"Don't you worry. When it comes to my son, I will be the one to deal with him. You can sort Jimmy and get Bree out. But Vernon is my son, therefore my responsibility."

"Well, it sounds like we have a plan. Shall we get some weapons together? I have a feeling today is going to be a fighting day," my father sings, and I can't help but chuckle. Trust him to find peace in the idea of a good fight. Whilst I don't particularly want to fight, I will do whatever it takes to get to Bree, including cutting down anyone who gets in my way.

CHAPTER THIRTY TWO
Bree

As soon as I start to wake up, my head feels so cloudy and groggy. It takes me a while to get my bearings as there is very little light in here. I try to think back to the last thing I remember, but I can't. Thinking about anything other than what is in front of me hurts. I double-check that my body is intact before looking around to figure out how the hell I am getting out of this.

I look down at my body as my left ankle feels the sorest, after my head, obviously. I notice the beautiful gown I am in and how destroyed it is. That's all it takes for the memories to hit me and the tears start to fall. I allow it for one minute, I can show weakness for one more minute, then I need to be strong after that.

Flashes of Liam and what should have been our happily ever after invade my mind, and my heart physically aches. I imagine him standing at the altar, looking handsome in his suit, waiting for me and wondering if I decided I just didn't want to marry him. I'm hoping that he knows me well enough to not even consider that particular scenario.

The dress is tattered and ripped, the lace ruined, not to mention the mud and bloodstains that adorn what once was a beautiful ivory colour. Reaching up into my hair, I realise I am still wearing the tiara that Liam got me. Maybe it's a sign that if that can survive being plunged into a dark sack, then I can survive being put in here.

I discreetly check for my other jewellery and am shocked to find they are both still in place. They are not only family heirlooms, but they are also worth a fucking fortune, so I am surprised the kidnappers didn't take it.

Then again, if the kidnappers were my family, they wouldn't need to.

I pull my dress up slightly to reveal the source of my pain; a metal shackle has been clamped around my ankle. The metal is so tight and abrasive against my skin it has caused the flesh to tear and bleed. I try to reach down, but there is no point in me even looking at how the lock works. There's no getting out of this without a key or a chainsaw, and I have neither.

Just as I am finally getting climatised, having just felt my two possibly broken ribs on my left side, the door groans open, and a flash of light opens up the shithole. I am in a large, cold, stone room. There are no windows, and the only door is a wrought iron one that sounds like it takes someone with muscles to get the damn thing open.

The light initially blinds my sore and disorientated eyes that are still sluggish and slow to react. My head pounds, and nausea rolls over my body. I must have been drugged, but unlike when I was kidnapped by Liam, I just know that I am in danger. I didn't wake up in a bright room on a comfy bed this time, and these shackles tell me whoever has me, isn't pissing about.

Straightening my spine to hold my head up high, I discreetly wipe the tears away from my eyes using the back of my already filthy hand, and try to ignore the make-up that rubs off onto my skin. I shoot fire at the asshole that just walked into the room. "What the fuck do you think you are playing at? Who are you?!" I shout, and the sadistic giggle that responds causes me to recoil.

"What? You don't recognise me?" the voice snarls as he steps forward.

No longer blocking the light, I recoil in shock as it is someone I was not expecting.

"Art?" I ask incredulously. His responding cackle flips my stomach, worsening my nausea. I have been around a lot of men in my life, and more than the odd psychopath. Hell, I stayed at Desmond's house just last month. So, I have a pretty excellent psychopath radar and can usually spot them from a mile away. The guy in front of me has just made my radar explode, and if someone told me he killed puppies in his spare time, I would not have been shocked. What I am confused by is that not only was Art on his last legs when I left him, he also was a harmless meth addict. The furthest you can get from a criminal mastermind.

"Oh sweetheart, don't be such an fucking idiot. We both know you killed Art, so how can I be him?" the sadistic voice sings.

"You look exactly like him," I mutter, just as much to myself as to this asshole.

"I think that might be an insult since my brother was a junkie meth head with blotchy skin, greasy hair, and very few rotten teeth. I'm Luther."

I instantly jump on the most essential part of that sentence. "Art was your brother?"

"Yes, my twin, actually. I am the younger one by sixteen minutes. He had this beautiful, natural birth, whereas I got stuck when my mum pushed to give birth. The only way they could save my life was to cut my mother open and pull me out of the sunroof, as she says. She later summarised that she should have known I would be fucked up since I ripped her open in two places trying to barge my way out. I hardly think I can be blamed for her saggy cunt. All the pimps she fucks for meth probably has something to do with it, but she feels she has to find the reason why I am so fucked up," he spits, no longer sounding carefree but still like a loose cannon.

Luther steps forward, his dark and unnerving eyes now completely visible, and he looks very unstable. He stares at me with deep loathing, and despite being completely unprovoked, he raises his hand and, using the back of it, slaps me across my face.

The power behind the action is immense, and it instantly knocks me from my kneeling position flat onto the floor. The crack of skin on skin rebounds around the room. The pain seems to bounce all around my already aching head. As his hand swept across my face, he must have caught my nose because I can feel the blood gushing from it. I want to reach up to stem the flow, but I hurt so much; even just getting into a sitting position enough to bring my hand up to stop the blood flow is too much. Besides, there's nothing to stop Luther from kicking the shit out of me, and at least in this position, I can still try to protect my major organs.

It sounds stupid, given the dress is already more than ruined, but as I watch the blood drip down and touch the fabric, my heart aches. This was the dress I chose for Liam. Our ceremony should be done, we should be officially married. Maybe he even liked it so much that he helped me out of this dress and ravished me before ceremony number two. Instead, I'm sitting here, curled up into a ball, trying not to die, and crying about stains on my dress. Will Liam know to come and find me?

Falling into my happy place, daydreaming about what today could have been, I must have missed whatever Luther was trying to tell me. A hard kick to my abdomen gets my attention.

Screaming out in pain, I roll myself up into a ball to try and protect myself. Luther is obviously not happy with that, and he kicks me again, three times in quick succession against my back. I scream loudly, sobbing and begging for him to stop. The last one connected with my possible broken rib, and the pain is so intense that my breath catches, and I struggle to breathe fully. Whenever I try to fill my lungs completely, there's a stabbing pain in my chest that stops me. I am reduced to taking short, shallow breaths as I attempt to breathe through the pain.

Realising Luther is trying to talk to me again, I try to block out the pain to focus on his nasty words. Anything to avoid being beaten more.

"Not so tough are you now, little mafia bitch. In what world did you ever think you could rule?" he taunts, and I just lay there, listening to him. "Then again, you're not really going to rule, are you? Everyone knows Liam Doughty is just fucking you so he can take your crown. Did you know he is double-crossing you? Pretending to like you, fucking you, probably making you fall in love with him. All so that he can get what he wants from you in the end. Desmond Doughty has waited patiently for London, and he wants it. Sadly for him, so do we," he chuckles, and my heart feels like it's about to snap.

My mind is whirling as Luther's words penetrate that part of the brain we all have but try to ignore. He is playing on my insecurities, making me believe I am alone and that Liam doesn't really care about me. There's a big part of me that wants to tell him to fuck off. The part that is so sure Liam really cares for me, and with each happy memory, that feeling is confirmed.

But then there's the negative part of my brain. No matter how much I try to silence it, the insecurities and the vulnerable side always somehow manage to sound louder than the happy side.

This picks apart all my happy memories, looking for actions or words Liam may have used that affirm Luther's statement. I already know that Desmond has no issue forcing his sons to marry women to get what he wants. He is forcing Finn to do it as we speak, but that doesn't mean he is doing the same with Liam, does it?

Why is it so easy for me to ignore everything Liam has ever said to me? Every sweet gesture or sexy touch get's replaced by false memories. Why do the memories fall into oblivion just at the mention that he could be using me? I want to trust him. I want to believe he really does care about me, but right now, all I feel is despair.

I'm pulled out of my anguish when I feel Luther roughly grab me by the back of the head, his fingers gripping my hair so tightly that my scalp feels as though it's on fire. He yanks back so quickly it feels like he is going to pull my hair out, and his grip is so tight that he can easily manhandle me back into the kneeling position I was in before he punched me.

Every movement causes more pain to ripple through my body. Breathing is challenging, and it feels like I am breathing in glass every time I inhale. My heart is racing, and I can feel the beat whooshing through my veins. I use my arms as best I can to cradle them around my body to protect my already damaged ribs and stomach. I'm not sure I can take many more blows, but I sure as shit am going to go down fighting.

"How do you know I'm not using Liam? Keep your enemies close and all that," I say, my voice deepened due to the pain.

Luther looks confused, like out of all the conversations he envisaged, maybe even practised us having, this was not one of them.

"Fuck that. Stop trying to mess with me, bitch!" he yells as he slaps me across the face again.

This time I manage to keep my kneeling position, but the pain is still just as bad. My brain feels like it is being knocked around in my skull, almost like it is reverberating off the sides, just waiting for it to happen enough times that it becomes mush, almost like I put my brain in a blender. The pain feels like a raging thunderstorm is taking place in my skull.

Using the hand not cradling my sore ribs, I bring it up to my cheek, slowly trying to massage the painful and most likely red area. As I lick the lower lip, desperately trying to get rid of the dryness, I taste the very recognisable flavour of iron. His hit must have caught my lip. Sure enough, when I probe it using my finger, I find a cut on the lower corner leaking blood. But given the fact I'm covered in dry blood, sweat, tears, and the wedding make-up I had on when I got here, a little bit of new blood is barely fucking noticeable. I'm glad there isn't a mirror nearby because I sure as fuck don't want to see what I look like right now.

"Who do you work for, Luther? Who organised this?" I mutter, needing to know desperately who it is.

I'm almost sure that Jimmy knew this attack was going to happen, but what I need to know is if he looked the other way, or did he help organise this attack on me? Is my father involved, or has Jimmy gone rogue? Either way, everything I have ever believed has been a lie. Jimmy was like a father figure to me, and he led me to think he wanted me to rule, that he would stand by my side. Yet when I needed him the most, he turned away. Everything that happens to me right now is because of him, and I will never forgive that.

"What makes you think that I'm not the leader of this little party. You wouldn't be insulting me now, would you, little bitch?" he sings, kneeling down so that he is eye level with me.

Using the hand still fisted into my hair, he pulls my head back so I'm looking straight at him. No matter how hard I try, he doesn't allow me to look away. Instead, he stares at me with that demented glare, his eyes roaming all over my body. His look of contempt and disgust is still there, but he also now has this hunger that scares me more than anything. As he licks his lips, looking at me like a juicy steak that he is about to demolish, I start to quiver in fear.

I can cope with a lot, suffer and withstand any pain he throws my way, but if it becomes sexual, that's something I am not sure I can recover from mentally. So I have to keep fighting. I have to believe that Liam will come and save me. But more than that, I have to have faith that I can save myself.

"You are not a leader, Luther. You are given instructions, and you follow them. Now tell me, who is in charge?!" I shout angrily, ignoring the pounding it causes in my head.

"Fuck you, bitch," he says with another punch to my stomach.

I try to bend over as I cry out, desperate to protect my exposed abdomen, but I need my arms to steady myself. I need to place my arms out to stop myself from falling, as he will have more of an advantage over me then. No point protecting what is already damaged now anyway. I can't help the tears that continue to flow. No matter how hard I try to stop them, they flow freely.

He reaches out with his other hand and rips the two spaghetti straps holding my beautifully blemished dress up. With nothing to stop them from falling, the front of the dress flops down. Luckily my perky tits act as a shelf, preventing the fabric from falling and exposing them. Given the sneer on Luther's face, he is not happy they aren't visible.

His hand advances slowly, and I know I only have a minute to stop him from exposing me. Once my tits are out, it's a slippery slope, one I'm not sure I can ever come back from. So, just before his hand can connect with the fabric, I pull back and punch him as hard as possible on the nose.

Luther recoils in pain as a delicious crunch causes his nose to explode, blood flying everywhere. I made sure that my hit was at the exact angle needed to fracture the nasal bone across the bridge of his nose. With any luck, I will have deviated the septum or fractured the cartilage too. Both of those will cause lasting effects.

When Luther finally stops literally rolling about in pain, he stands to tower over me. His murderous expression is covered in blood, making him look even more dangerous. He looks like he wants to kill me, which is not great, but at least he doesn't want to take my clothes off anymore. Instead, he continues to yell expletives at me, telling me what a bitch I am and how much he plans on ruining my life. Apparently, he's going to rip me a new asshole.

I know I should be scared, and I definitely am not looking forward to more pain, but that punch reminded me that I can fight back. Until the stupid fuckers realise they need to tie me up entirely, I will do everything I can to fight them.

Luther looks like he is about to advance again, and I tense my muscles and hold my breath, awaiting the impact. Ironically it's a skill Jimmy taught me, a better way to absorb a blow. I push all thoughts of that traitorous scumbag out of my head and focus on Luther.

Before he has a chance to land another blow, another guy runs into the room. He is young, his baby face with little patches of acne makes him look a lot younger than he probably is. I would guess late teens. He looks flustered and a little confused as he stares between Luther and me. He quickly catches up with what has been happening, and although he looks pissed, he also looks a bit scared of Luther.

"What the fuck, man? I thought the plan was that we just leave her in here until we deal with Doughty. You weren't supposed to hurt her," the youngster states, and when Luther turns his murderous glare on him, it's not surprising when he recoils.

"I don't remember agreeing to anything like that. She fucking murdered my brother! Of course, I am going to punish her" Luther shouts.

"Your brother was a rat. He got what he deserved!" I shout.

Upon reflection, taunting a psychopath with a murderous glint in his eye probably wasn't my best move, but I am never one for keeping quiet when I should. Instantly, Luther launches at me, his fist raining down multiple blows all down my body. The pain is excruciating, and he is hitting me in so many places that I have no idea where to block. I try to curl up with my arms covering my face and my legs protecting my stomach, but this just leads to Luther raining blows down on my side and back. My ribs feel like they are cracking further, and my kidneys are about to explode. My voice begins to go hoarse from all the yelling and screaming. I plead with him to get off me, but he is too far gone in such a murderous haze.

If the young lad hadn't been in the room and hadn't been able to pull Luther off me eventually, I probably would be dead. It took three guys in total to be able to pull him away from me, and still, he was snarling and spitting like a feral animal. As I lay here in a ball, watching him being dragged away, I try to catch my breath and hope I can heal from this damage.

My breathing is ragged, and the pain in my chest when I try to inhale is excruciating. I feel as though I can't properly catch my breath. Using short, shallow breaths, I get enough oxygen to function for now. Given the amount of pain I'm in all over, and the blows I just received, I would put money on me having internal bleeding. If I don't get out soon, I am going to die here.

They drag Luther out, and the young boy stays behind. He looks very uncomfortable, shifting from foot to foot as he looks over my broken body.

"What's your name?" My voice is raspy, and it hurts to speak. I try to catch my breath, but the pain is unbearable. My breathing sounds wheezy, almost like it is creaking. I know I am not getting enough oxygen as my vision is starting to waver, and those telltale spots have begun to appear. I try to blink them away, but that just makes me dizzier.

"Vinnie Marcushio," he whispers, and I want to laugh, but my body betrays me. There's no way this is the criminal mastermind behind all the threats.

"Who is behind this, Vinnie? I know you hate Liam, and Luther hates me, but I know neither of you are the brains behind this. Tell me. I'm going to die here, so you may as well." At the mention of my death, his eyes got as wide as saucepans, and he looks genuinely terrified.

"No, you can't die...you can't. That's not a part of the plan," the youngster mumbles, looking around frantically.

"What is the plan?" I pant as I lay there on the floor. I can't even pull myself to sit upright.

"Vernon is going to be pissed," Vinnie mutters, and he is pacing around the small room. He doesn't look at me when he talks; I'm not even convinced he replied to me.

"Vinnie!" I shout as loudly as I can to get his attention, and struggle to catch my breath, which only leads to a dry hacking cough that causes even more pain all over my body. "Listen to me, please. I need to know who is responsible for this," I plead, tears flowing down my cheek as I try unsuccessfully to sit up.

Seeing me struggling, Vinnie holds out his hand to me. I allow him to pull me up, crying out in pain when the movement makes my body feel as though it's on fire.

"Your dad. He doesn't want you to lead. He convinced me to be the face of this shitshow, or he would take his revenge on me. I stole money from my father, but it turned out it was Vernon's money. That's what got my father killed. It was me. But your dad found out the truth and blackmailed me into doing this to work off my debt. Things started going to shit when he brought the crazy twins on board," he replies, and I shake my head as much as the pain will allow. I'm so confused.

"Wait...what do you mean he brought both twins on board?" I ask.

"So, Art owes Vernon a lot of money after he smoked meth he was supposed to sell. To pay off his debt, he had to pretend to be a rat, to place all the blame on me. I'm an obvious choice since Liam killed my father. Plus, it shifts the focus away from him and keeps you distracted. He wanted you and Liam to fight and fall out. He never intends on giving London over to you. He wants the whole business for himself. When Luther found out you killed Art, he went crazy. Jimmy assured him that he would stop you before it went that far. Nobody knew you had it in you to slit his fucking throat. You're a beast," he jokes, looking at me in a mixture of admiration and sadness.

As his words register, I realise the true extent of their betrayal. "I never slit Art's throat. When I left him, he had wounds to the arteries in his legs, and he would have died from them without prompt medical attention. But I can fucking assure you I didn't slit his throat. I marked him as a rat. I wanted people to know I don't fuck about. That message would not have gotten around if I had killed him. Dead people can't talk about their fears," I explain, and this time it's Vinnie's turn to look confused.

"So you didn't kill Art?" he asks, and forgetting about the pain, I shake my head in denial. I soon regret it as it feels like my bruised brain is bouncing around like a football. I try to remain as still as possible.

"No, he was alive when Liam and I left him with Jimmy. If anybody killed him, it was Jimmy. I'm guessing that was the plan all along. To send Luther into a murderous rage, desperate for revenge, the same as you are for your dad. I take it the plan is to keep me here, lure Liam here, and then kill him?" I ask, and he nods.

"Your father says that if Liam is killed, you will not want to try and rule anymore. So he plans to try and suppress you in any way he can. Although he did clarify that if it came to it, the best solution would be to kill you and make it look like Liam killed you. That way, he has an excuse to go to war with Desmond. Desmond is his real threat; he is convinced Liam is working against you," he explains, and the tears start to fall.

"I know my father is ruthless and power-hungry, but I really thought he loved me. I had no idea he would be willing to sacrifice me for power if it came to that." I'm not really talking to Vinnie at this point, just musing out loud and in general. My heart is breaking now that I know the truth. This whole time the real enemy has been my own father.

Vinnie mumbles something that looks like an apology as he shifts around uncomfortably again. He is just a kid, messed up in adult stuff. He should be out enjoying life.

"What's gonna happen next, Vinnie?" I ask, my vision starting to go hazy from all the talking and the shallow breaths.

"Jimmy and Vernon are luring Liam here as we speak. Once he is dead, then they will come and make it look like they are rescuing you. You are not supposed to know any of this. If they think you know, they will slaughter us all. So please...please don't say anything. I need to know I didn't make the wrong decision in telling you. I just want to get out of all this shit. I made a stupid mistake, and now it's messing up my life," he cries, and I can't help but feel so incredibly sorry for him. Now I know he is the scapegoat and not my natural enemy. All I see is a scared little boy. He is no criminal mastermind.

"I promise, I won't say a word, but I do want just one favour," I say, and he looks at me suspiciously. "If you do everything you can to help me and Liam get out of this alive, not only will I free you of whatever debt you owe my Family, I will secure you for life. You want a job; it's yours; you want money, it's yours. But only if we both survive."

Vinnie looks conflicted, but then his face turns to a small smile. "I don't know how much I can help, but I will do whatever I can. You have my word. What can I do? I can't even make a phone call or use the internet. The paranoid fuckers took my phone."

"Are we near anywhere that has CCTV?" I ask, and Vinnie nods.

"There's a supermarket down the street," he explains, and a big smile spreads across my bruised and battered face.

"You see that tiara over there. Take that and very deliberately hold it up in front of a CCTV camera in the middle of the store. Make sure it's visible along with your face. If you can hold up a sign with any information on it, then do that as much as you can, but make it clear,then pull the fire alarm. Leave the tiara outside the house we are in, somewhere that might be visible to an outsider but not to the people here. Can you do that?" I ask, the plan forming in my mind.

"I will try. If they catch me, they will kill me." His voice sounds small and lost, but he's not wrong. Sadly, the moment my father dragged him into this mess, his life was at risk. I, at least, am giving him a chance to live.

"Then don't get caught, kid," I add with a smile. He laughs before leaving the room.

Pulling the door closed behind him, I am once again plunged back into darkness, only the pain overtaking my body to keep my company. Everything in me, every bit of training I have endured, tells me that going to sleep right now is a bad idea, but I can't help it. The darkness creeps in, and I fall into oblivion.

CHAPTER THIRTY THREE

Liam

Kellan and I race back to the house, desperate to get some answers and hoping to find some clues about what the hell is going on. Paddy stormed off on his own, shouting down his phone at only God knows who. He agreed to meet us at the house. Mum and the girls are staying at the venue. We still have the room that Kellan and I stayed in last night booked and they can stay there. Hopefully, they will be safer there. We manage to convince Finn that the best thing for him is to stay and keep them safe. I need ruthlessness for this mission, and he is not that. Desmond and Evan are surprisingly all in.

On the drive over to the house, feeling more than a little antsy, I ask Desmond why he would help us. What is he getting out of saving Bree? My father never does anything if there isn't something in it for him. He may have agreed on a truce with Bree, but a truce is very different from going to war for her.

"Believe it or not, boy, I actually like Bree. I think you are punching above your weight with her for sure. She is a force to be reckoned with, and yes, she is standing in the way of something I desperately want, but like I told her, I'm playing the long game," he explains. I must admit I am a little shocked. I had no fucking idea he really liked Bree. I didn't think he was capable of liking another person, let alone a rival.

"No matter how much you may like her, she is a rival. Agreeing to a truce is one thing, but this could potentially mean going to war for her. I am willing to jump in headfirst because I fucking love her. Why are you really doing it?" I state firmly, and the car erupts into chaos.

"What?"

"You love her?"

"Your relationship is real?"

My father, Evan, and Kellan speak all at once. It is difficult to tell who is saying what, but I get the general idea.

"Yes, our relationship is real. It became real a while ago. Yes, I realised a few weeks back that I love Bree, but stupidly I never told her. I wanted to wait for the perfect moment, and it never came. The closer I got to the wedding, the more I realised this was the perfect opportunity, but now I know it doesn't matter what the hell is going on around you. You don't need the perfect settings or even romance to tell someone you love them. I should have just manned up and told her those three little words. She never got to hear them, and I never got to say it. So, the minute we rescue her, I will spend forever telling her because life is too fucking short."

I can feel all of their eyes on me, even Kellan's, who should be watching the road, something I quickly pointed out to him. I notice Evan appears very sombre and glances down when he sees me looking at him. Maybe what I said hit a little too close to home with Teigan. I hope he pulls his head out of his ass soon.

"Well, I'm not sure I can follow that award-winning pussy moment," my father jokes. I'm reasonably sure everyone in the car rolls their eyes. "But I already told you. Despite what I originally thought, I do think she will be a good leader. Better than that giant cock, Vernon. The fact I get to start something with him after all these years and it not be classed as me going to war with him, that's a massive bonus." I can't help the chuckle that escapes. It's dark and deep, not exactly a laughing situation. Everyone stares at me to make sure I'm not cracking up.

"Wait, so you are here to fight Vernon without any repercussions?" asks Kellan, and Desmond just nods.

"Look, you can call me a monster, but who doesn't capitalise on a situation like this," Desmond sings, and I hear Evan groan out loud. I gasp since I have never seen him go against Father in any way, let alone in public like this.

"Okay, so changing the subject since I appear to have pissed off both my sons. Kellan...what's going on with you and that gorgeous little mouse...the bridesmaid. What's her name?" questions my father, and for once, I'm glad he doesn't know how to keep his mouth shut. I have to admit I am curious to hear the response. They haven't spoken since that shitshow excuse for an interview, as far as I know. But when things were kicking off, and he needed to leave Mia with someone, she was top of his list. Plus, they looked very cosy as he comforted her about Bree.

"Mia is her name," Kellan grinds out like it physically hurts him to talk to Desmond. He was raised by him for a few years too, and although I did everything I could to keep him out of any real danger, he still got in the way at times. He took more than one beating when I was too broken to take one for him. I'm sure he took some for me the way I did him. That's what brothers do for each other after all. Sadly, Desmond just saw him as another mouth to feed that was bringing nothing to the table. I'm glad he has no clue how powerful Kellan really is.

"She seems nice," Evan adds with a small smile. "Hallie looks so beautiful, too. I don't know how you do it, man."

Kellan gives him a small smile in return. Talk of Hallie is always enough to brighten up his day. Desmond, obviously out of the loop, looks confused.

"I don't understand. So the baby she had with her...this Mia, girl. She has your baby, but it isn't her baby? I'm confused," Desmond speculates, and now Kel really laughs.

"I had a baby almost six months ago with my last girlfriend, Shayla. She left Hallie and me just five hours after her birth. So I have been making do since then. I am staying with Liam and Bree because they are helping me with the baby. I said I wanted to hire a nanny, so I could get back to work. Bree recommended Mia. I met with her and did some background information which she did not like. When I then confronted her about it, we had a big argument. As soon as I start thinking about Bree being in danger, and knowing I'm going to put myself in the line of fire to find her, I found myself wanting to talk to Mia. Don't read into shit. I obviously just realised that despite her background, I can tell she is good with Hallie. I didn't even hesitate when she offered to look after her," Kellan muses. He looks like with each new sentence, he is contemplating what the words may mean.

"Fuck, I had no idea Shayla was the mum. How the fuck do

you get over a woman ditching her baby?" Evan asked, and I have to admit I am a little shocked. I thought Evan was lost, that he was too much like my father to ever be redeemed, but here he is discussing feelings and trying to relate to others. While it's clear Desmond is listening for gossip, other than that, he has very much checked out.

Kellan releases a breath I didn't realise he was holding, sounding like a deeply confused huff. "When I find out, I will let you know. I think that is part of the reason why I don't trust women. Well, her and my mother."

Laughter fills the car because both Evan and I know what it's like to have parent issues. My mother may not be an abusive asshole like Desmond. She talks about how she loves us, yet when the timing was most important, she didn't save us. Kellan has always said that now he has Hallie, he sees the world so differently, and I think in a way I'm the same. I always knew what my mother did wasn't right, but I could never see it as the same as when Desmond abused us. However, now I realise that failing to protect is just as bad. She knew that every abusive act could happen, yet she did nothing to protect us from it; she may as well have delivered the blows herself. Both Evan and I must have come to the same realisation as our shared sarcastic laughter lets us know that for once, we agree. Desmond, on the other hand, just rolls his eyes.

We make it back to the house quickly, and I get Desmond and Evan set up in the living room while Kellan runs up to his room. I let him know I will follow him soon. I can't let Desmond upstairs. I can't let him see what Kel does as his life would never be safe again, but he tells me he will risk it to find Bree.

Working with Desmond and Evan downstairs, I set them on a task to track down Vinnie Marcushio. We have to know if he is involved. They are finding out all his known hangouts or safe houses. Once I have that list, Kellan can scour CCTV of the nearby areas. Desmond calls everyone relevant that he knows. Evan uses his phone to scour the internet, and I try to be useful, but my mind is betraying me.

Walking into her bedroom that quickly became ours, I see all the wedding preparations scattered around the room. My heart feels heavy, and for the first time in as long as I can remember, I feel tears start to well in my eyes. I feel an overwhelming sadness for the beautiful girl sitting on the edge of this bed like I am now. It was just two hours ago that she was preparing for what should have been the happiest day of our lives. Unfortunately, I didn't even get to see what she looked like.

Seeing a phone in the middle of the bed, I instantly become confused because I don't recognise it. Opening it up, I realise quickly it's the burner phone that Jimmy owns. I scan through the calls and messages to see if it will give me any leads, but it is entirely blank. I will have to take it to Kellan to see if he can pull anything from it. In our world, deleting things means nothing.

Before I go to stand, I open up the photos folder. I had no real expectations, but I got lucky as the photo gallery loaded. I clicked on the first thumbnail, only to be greeted with the most beautiful picture of Bree that I have ever seen. It was taken this morning, right here in this room. This is the dress that Bree chose to marry me in, and she looks fucking perfect. She managed to find an impeccable balance between looking sexy with the gorgeous low back, and beautiful with the way it hangs off her body. Not to mention that the magnificent train, veil, and my tiara makes her look so elegant. I don't think I have ever seen her look more stunning.

What causes my heart to break is the fact she looks so happy. She has no idea that the people in these pictures with her, the ones she calls family, are really behind her threat. I just fucking hope Jimmy cares enough about Bree to not get her killed.

Scrolling through the pictures, my heart sinks at the loss of our perfect day. Right at the beginning, this phone's first action was to record a video, and given the thumbnail, it is just of Jimmy. Maybe he thinks there is some form of apology that he can offer. Personally, I am desperately pleading with him to see sense, to not punish Bree for something she has not done. If it means keeping her safe, then I won't marry her. But if they think she will give up the throne so easily, they are very fucking wrong.

I press play and Jimmy's voice and face pop onto the screen. "Hey, Bumblebee. If you are watching this, then things really have gone to shit. I am either dead, captured, or in serious danger. I left this phone here, so if the time came that you needed answers, then you could have them. I have to tell you everything."

It looks like he is shuffling around, nerves evident in the way he mumbles. Anger flashes through my body like a wave of heat, as though someone was setting alight my veins with a hot poker. I want to kill him, but I carry on listening for more crucial details.

"First, Bee, you have to know that when your father came up with this plan, the first thing I made him guarantee is that you would come to no harm at all. He gave me his word, but I don't trust it. I have known the man for too long to not be suspicious of his motives. You have to believe me when I say this is not about you. This is about your father and his desire for power. I know you hoped one day that I would switch sides to come and work for you, and fuck, I really do want to. But I have been by Vernon's side for almost twenty years, and he knows all my secrets. Particularly those that if were made public, I would lose everything. So I am staying with him. At least then I can try to keep you safe," he explains, staring into the camera.

I pause for a second to take some big deep breaths. I'm so angry I could throw the phone, but I need to know more, and so I continue the video while trying to regulate my breathing. "I know that if you hear this, you will be feeling incredibly sad at the loss of Liam. I can tell you have started to develop real feelings for this boy, but your father can't let Liam get away with what he did. No matter how much Paddy may forgive him, Vernon can't. Your dad is angry; he feels like Liam is being rewarded for kidnapping you. Instead of being punished, as he should have been for thinking he can kidnap you, he is being rewarded. Not only does he get to marry Vernon's only child, but he gets the power, too. Vernon will not stand by and watch a Doughty rise to power in his place. So yes, we did all of this to take Liam out, to make sure people know not to mess with you again. I'm sure you will be pissed and annoyed at me, but we did the right thing for the company. You will see that one day." His voice almost sounds self-righteous, and I can't help the horrified snort.

This is all for me. This plan is all to lure me into a trap to kill me. But what Vernon doesn't realise is if he had just asked me to step aside and he could guarantee her life, I would have done it in a heartbeat. Hell, I would have shot myself if it meant Bree was safe, but now I am so consumed with hatred. My trigger finger is on edge and fiercely craving some action. So I will make sure I survive just so I can be the one to blow a hole right in the middle of Jimmy's head.

Noticing he still has a short bit left to say, I stand up and start to anxiously pace as I watch the rest of the video. "I know that after today you won't ever trust me again. Fuck, if I know you at all, you will want to be the one to kill me if I'm not already dead. But I want you to know that I love you, I always have. You are the daughter I never had. There are a few things I need you to know before I go, important things, so please listen. Firstly, Vinnie Marcushio is innocent. If he survives this shitshow, do not punish him. He is in a seriously fucked up situation, and Vernon is blackmailing him to take the fall. He's just a scared kid; he didn't want to get revenge against Liam for killing Leon. He genuinely said there's no point spilling more blood. This kid is too good for our world.

"The other main player involved is Luther McManaman. Both Art and Luther have been working for Vernon. When you interrogated Art, he was a diversion, planting information he was told to. He was made to do it to pay off a substantial debt, but we didn't know that Luther is a straight-up psychopath. I killed Art, following Vernon's instructions, and made it look like you took the interrogation too far. Something in Luther snapped, and he's like a grenade with the pin pulled out. We are just waiting for him to explode. Vernon thinks Luther has control, but I do not. I think Luther is angry, and at the moment, all that anger is aimed at you. I will make sure he doesn't lose it on you, but you deserve to know who your real enemies are. You have no idea how much it breaks my heart to stand against you. I truly am sorry, Bumblebee."

His words sound sincere, but they mean nothing. If he truly loved Bree the way he claimed, then there was no way on this Earth he would stand against her. Whatever Vernon holds over him must be big, but it would never be big enough for me. Nothing in this life could make me turn on Bree. Just the idea of it makes me furious. I will let her see this and decide for herself what to do with Jimmy, but if I know Bree like I think I do, she will not stand by her Family after this. Quite the opposite, she will do anything in her power to destroy them all. If I survive this assassination attempt, I will be standing beside her while she rains down hell.

Shouts from Kellan's room pull me out of my daydreams, and I shove the phone in my pocket before running to his door. I see Evan, Desmond, and Paddy running up the stairs. Paddy must have only just got here, but there is no time to find out what he knows. Kellan must have something big. As we all enter his office, I see the stunned look on all their faces.

None of them was expecting to see the room kitted out like this. Kellan has an extra-large U-shaped wooden desk that I helped him build. There are two large computer monitors on each one that all appear to have different images on them. Most programs have flashing things that indicate they are working away in the background. Some are just a black screen with white code flashing through line after line. I have no idea what any of the side computers are doing, but the main one that takes up nearly all of the middle part of the desk has my attention.

"Holy fuck, how did I not know you are a hacker? I let you live in my house rent-free, and you didn't come to work for me because you had no skills that were of use to me, or at least that's what I was told by you two. Only now, I find out you are a hacker, and probably a good one looking at all of this!" my father screeches. His compulsive need to think of himself at times like this is part of the reason I hate him so much. I love that Kellan cares so much about Bree that he was willing to expose his secret to some very important men, but on the other hand, I hate that he had to do this.

"I am not just any hacker. I am probably one of the best in the world. I consult for major security and government agencies. That's how good I am. But I only do the jobs I want to do, the same as Liam. Unlike you, I actually have a conscience. I never wanted to work for you because the idea of you having any kind of influence over me absolutely repulses me. I would hate to become your clone. You have enough of those as it is," Kellan spits out without taking his eyes off the screen in front of him, his fingers continuing to click away on the keyboards.

My father looks full of rage, his face turning an angry shade of purple, and I know I need to de-escalate the tension quickly. He starts to talk, but I interrupt him. "Kel, mate, show me what you have. Have you found Bree?" I ask, the hope and desperation ringing in my voice.

"Not exactly, but I think I have found one hell of a clue. So, I set alerts up for everyone who might be potentially involved, Vinnie Marcushio being one. I also set it to look for Jimmy and Vernon. I am watching all their known hangouts or safe houses, but not only them, I'm also watching the areas around them.

A few minutes ago, the alert I set up for Vinnie got a hit. Facial recognition identified him in a local supermarket, so I hacked the CCTV to follow him, and this is what I saw."

As he finishes speaking, he presses play on the screen, and I watch a black and white image of the small shop Vinnie appears to be in. We watch as a small guy, who definitely doesn't look old enough to be messing around with Vernon O'Keenan, walks into the middle of the store. He doesn't look at any of the aisles like he is shopping. Instead, he makes sure that his face is seen on every camera that they have in there. He then reaches into the front pocket of his hoodie and pulls out two items. The first one almost brings me to my knees. He is holding the tiara that I bought for Bree, especially for our wedding day. The day my Princess finally became my Queen.

There's a part of me that is overwhelmed with sadness. That piece of jewellery should be on the head of my wife right now, but instead, a messed up teenager is holding it. In his other hand is a piece of paper, he holds it straight up to the camera, but it is too far away for us to see anything. Before I even have to ask, Kellan zooms in and cleans up the image. We all lean in a little closer in anticipation of what the note might say.

Bree sent me.
She needs help now.
Follow the tiara.
I'm not your enemy. V is.
V trying to kill L.
This is not the trap, just a warning from Bree.
Please help us.

"**M**otherfucker!" shouts Paddy at the top of his voice, startling us all a little.

"It's not a nice feeling when your son disappoints you, is it?" Desmond adds, and much to my surprise, Evan snorts.

"We could say the same about our dad, but we don't. So leave your bullshit until after we have found Bree, Dad," Evan says confidently, and everyone stands there with their mouths wide open. I can't remember the last time Evan stood up to Desmond, or if he ever has, but something appears to be changing. Finally, he is thinking for himself, and I love it.

While I couldn't agree more with his statement, I know that nothing will stop Desmond from arguing back. The asshole loves to argue. I cut him off right as he opens his mouth once more. The resulting scornful expression tells me he is not happy that I interrupted him for a second time, but I really don't give a shit.

"What happens next? Where does he go?" I ask Kellan, hopeful that this might show us where my girl is.

We all watch the screen as he walks to the back of the building and sets off the fire alarm. He leaves the piece of paper on a shelf, discreetly tucking it away for us to find, and then he walks out with all the other shoppers.

The camera switches to an outside view, and he walks down a road, making sure to point out to the camera which way he is going, but after that, no new feed appears. Instead, we watch as he walks off the screen, disappearing completely.

"Where does he go?" I demand, and Kellan releases a deep sigh, looking sad.

"There's no CCTV around the houses in that area. I have even looked for personal feeds from home owned cameras, even doorbells, but there is none of use. I'm sorry, Liam." He looks dejected, like he has let me down, and I want to comfort him, but my mind is whirling.

The images play on repeat through my brain. I know Bree would ensure that if Vinnie was risking his life that there's an excellent chance we would see this. She would make sure there was a way to find her. But all I can focus on is that she is missing and I can't find her. She is locked up somewhere, hoping I will come to save her, and I can't.

I am interrupted from my spiralling thoughts as Paddy places his hand on my shoulder, reassuring me. "This is fucking great. We may not have enough information, but my girl has done well. Ringing the fire alarm will make it more difficult for the people watching to tell if new people arrive on the street, so we have to move now. We can check out the streets while people are distracted by the fireman. I've already texted an associate who is on his way there. He will start a small fire in the waste bins behind the shop. That should keep everyone distracted. He will also go and retrieve the note. There has to be a reason he left it there. Maybe it has more written on it. Either way, we need to get it before Vernon's men do. We also need to get that kid out of there because if my son finds out what he just did, he'll be dead by morning if not sooner," Paddy explains. His words finally help me to place the missing pieces together. Fuck, Bree really is brilliant.

We are all on our feet, moving towards the door in an instant. I turn to Kellan, who has a matching murderous look on his face like he is ready to do battle. "Kellan, you can't come, brother. I need you to stay here and monitor the feeds. I know you would fight for Bree, but we are walking into a trap. A fucking dangerous trap. You have Hallie to think about. So, I'm sorry, but you are staying here. Please don't argue with me on this. It's not just because I can't have you getting hurt, but I genuinely do need you to monitor the screens for any threats around us," I explain, trying my best to show Kellan how serious I am.

"I will stay because it makes sense for someone to watch the cameras, but I want you to know that I would have fought for Bree and for you. I may not be as ruthless as you or as well trained, but I can fight. You know that. This is not me pussying out, I am thinking of my daughter. She doesn't have anyone else." Kellan still looks ashamed as he talks, his eyes downcast and his cheek flush with a pink tinge.

"It's not pussying out if I give you an order. I know you would fight for us, take a bullet for us, but I would hate for that to happen. Go and watch the monitors. Keep us all safe from there." I pull him in for a short, unexpected hug. He returns it with a few pats on the back. It's not the most affectionate of hugs, but we don't really enjoy talking about our feelings. In my eyes, he is my brother, and just like I do with all my siblings, I need to keep him safe.

Kellan pulls away from the hug and runs back up the stairs. He shouts as he runs, "Use the earplug to keep communication open, please, Liam!" I confirm I have heard him and walk over to the cupboard by the door.

Using my thumbprint to activate the door, it springs open, revealing my complete weapon collection. Each person takes a couple of items, either guns or knives, as well as stocking up on ammo. We all check the safety and condition of our guns before leaving the house. As I place my gun in my back holster, I'm reminded of the night at my father's house when I told Bree this was her gun, and I was just carrying it for her. Hopefully, if I get close enough, she will know it's there and take it when needed.

Picking up the large container that holds my sniper rifle, I put it into the boot of my car. You never know when it might come in handy. We all get into the car, Evan volunteers to drive, Desmond and Paddy slide into the backseats, talking to each other as though they are old friends and not enemies. I take a moment to collect my breath and focus. I know I am walking into a trap, and there's a risk of death, but I would risk it all for her. I will set her free, even if it's the last thing I do.

CHAPTER THIRTY FOUR

Bree

I don't know how long I sleep for, but I am woken up by Vinnie gently pushing against my arm. He is trying to shake me awake without hurting me. Sadly, no matter how hard he tries, the pain is excruciating. Even the softest touch against my arm feels like he is stabbing a knife into me. My head pounds like claps of thunder, and just the slightest movement sends ripples of nausea through my stomach.

"Here, have a bit of water, please. Just some sips," Vinnie whispers as he tips the bottle into my mouth.

As soon as the cold liquid hits my lips, I open my mouth to devour more, desperately gulping it down. But my fragile body can't seem to process too much water in one go, and nausea rips through me again. I start to gag, and Vinnie instantly backs away, splashing water down my chest due to the sudden movement. He looks around the room frantically, he looks torn, as if seeing the bucket in the corner for the first time.

The bucket is all they left me to use as a toilet, but thankfully, I haven't needed to go. Not that I could move my body enough to get to the damn bucket. Vinnie looks to be weighing his options over which he finds more disgusting; picking up the bucket he thinks I have used as a toilet or watching me vomit all over myself and the floor.

Thankfully, he makes his mind up quickly and tentatively

heads for the bucket. When he sees it is clean and unused, he immediately picks it up and holds it at an angle beside my head. He makes it just in time as my body quickly regurgitates the water Vinnie gave me, along with some not so pleasant green bile streaked with brown and black colours. Vinnie stands as far away as possible whilst still being able to hold the bucket for me.

His eyes are firmly shut and stay that way as I continue to wretch, although nothing more comes up. When the retching stops, Vinnie finally opens his eyes. "Oh fuck, should it be that colour?" he asks while covering his mouth with his opposite hand. He places the bucket next to me and moves away from it. He looks like he is trying to control his breathing so he doesn't vomit.

"It's blood. Chances are, I am bleeding internally. I feel like my body is trying to shut down, Vin. My heart is racing, but my body aches. My fingers are blue, which means blood isn't getting to them. I was desperate for water yet vomited it back up because I couldn't cope with it. Slowly, my organs will fail, this dizziness will overtake me, and I will pass out. If I don't get control of the pain and get into theatre soon, I will die," I explain. The more I speak, the more exhausted I become. My head rests against my arm that went numb ages ago. I can feel it's cold and a bit clammy, yet another sign. I desperately try to keep my eyes open; it's vital now. If I close my eyes I may never open them again.

"Bree, listen to me," Vin says as he gently taps my arm again. I must have zoned out. "I did what you said. I'm sure Liam will be here soon, your plan was great and you know he will come for you. I will do what I can until then. Your dad is going to make the follow-up call in a couple of minutes. He has no idea Liam will know it's a trap, but it will be easier for Liam to break in if fewer people are here. Also, I went through Luther's stash and found a fentanyl patch. It's strong, but it should take away some of the pain until I get you to the hospital. I need to put it somewhere that Luther won't see it and take it off."

His eyes rake over my body, but not in the sexualised way I am used to with men. For him, it is purely practical, yet that doesn't stop the slight blush that creeps up onto his cheeks when he makes eye contact with me again.

"Don't be embarrassed. Put it on my hip. Pull up my dress, and I will show you," I instruct, but he doesn't move. Glaring at him with a serious expression, or at least as much as I can muster under my current condition, I give him my consent. "You have to do it, and quickly before we get caught. Just pretend you aren't looking at my bare ass if that helps."

His dark chuckle takes me by surprise. "I will try, but you do have a nice ass," he says as he starts to pull my skirt up. My dress isn't big and poofy, more free-flowing like a waterfall. Still, it is not the easiest to get up, mainly since I can't move around to help.

After a few minutes of struggling, I stop him. "It's going to be easier if you pull it down from the front. They are already ripped."

Wide eyes stare back at me. "If...if I-I do that, your t-tits will come out," he mutters, and I can't stop the short snicker.

"Don't worry. As long as I get them covered straight after, I will be fine. It's a small price to pay if I want to get help with the pain." Every word I speak is laboured and barely above a whisper.

Without another word, Vin grabs hold of the top of the dress and gently shimmies it down until my right ass cheek is exposed. I am lying on my left hip, so there is no way of getting it down any further, but this is far enough. Vin is respectfully trying not to look at my exposed breasts, making my respect for him go up.

Using my hand, I guide him and tell him exactly where to put the patch. He quickly sticks it on, hiding the backing in his hoodie pocket. Then, as he tries to pull the dress back up again, a loud thundering voice fills the room.

"What the fuck is going on here?!" shouts Luther as he eyes the situation. Now that the patch is on, it should start working soon. Even if someone chooses to expose me, I don't think they will be looking at my outer hip. Besides, he placed it over one of my tattoos, and the brightness of the design will make it difficult to notice the patch. I wait patiently to feel even just the slightest bit of relief.

Vinnie freezes, looking at me with his eyes wide open, like a kid who has been caught with his hand in the cookie jar. If I don't think quickly, this asshole will kill Vinnie just because he suspects something.

"Get your hands off me, you pervert. Put your hand near my pussy again, and I will chop it off myself. Then your dick will be next," I growl, schooling my face into a look of anger and hoping Vinnie can play along. At first, he looks confused, but then he looks over at the grin spreading across Luther's face, and he realises what I am doing.

"Shut the fuck up!" he barks at me. It almost sounds believable, except for the slight shake of his voice at the beginning. He stands and looks towards Luther. "Just showing her who is boss, that's all."

Luther's demented cackle sounds like a stereotypical Halloween villain. Obviously, Art wasn't the only one who liked drugs because Luther looks high as a kite at the moment. He seems very unstable, and I want him as far away from Vinnie and me as possible. The only problem with that is, I'm not sure I can have both.

"Look at you, little gangster. How is her pussy? Is she wet? Girls like her always get wet in situations like this," he says like he knows what women like. Fucking idiot.

Despite looking like a deer trapped in headlights, Vin manages to answer him. "I didn't get that far since you interrupted."

"I'm not stopping you. I won't tell anyone if you want a little feel," Luther chirps, his wide, dark eyes staring at me. It's as though he is hoping that his gaze will burn away what's left of my wedding dress until his view is unobstructed.

"No way," Vinnie states, taken aback by Luther's comment. "No way I'm messing around with a girl while you watch, you sick fucker."

Vinnie stands firm, but Luther takes slow, purposeful strides towards him. Each step is like a predator stalking his prey, and once he has him in arms reach, he fists his shirt into his hands and pulls him close enough to whisper in his ear, but I could still hear. "Then get out of my way so I can have some fun."

As soon as the words are out of Luther's mouth, he pushes Vinnie away towards the open door before stalking over to me. In an instant, he grabs hold of my body and roughly moves me into position. He has me lying on my back with my knees bent. Luckily, the tightness of the dress helps me keep my legs together as I look over at Vinnie with fear in my eyes. His eyes are darting around like he has no idea what to do.

I can't even begin to explain the pain I feel in my body as Luther moves me. The fentanyl patch must be working as it feels as though it takes the edge off a bit, but not completely. As I try to catch my breath, desperately gasping for more air that doesn't seem to be coming, Luther takes advantage. He takes a knife out of his back pocket, and I see Vinnie take a step back, his eyes wide with fear, which I am sure is equally reflected in mine.

He slices through my dress using the knife, right down the middle, and I wince when the blade cuts my skin. I would say accidentally, but by the look on Luther's face, it wasn't an accident. The dress falls open to reveal bloody lines down my cleavage and stomach. His expression turns from violent to hungry. He stares at my bruised and battered naked body that is covered in blood like he wants to devour it.

Kneeling in between my legs, he forces them apart. I try to fight him, but I am struggling to even lift my arms. I shout at him violently, making it clear that I will kill him if he touches me, but he just chuckles.

"Dude, I'm not sure we should be doing this. Vernon gave us clear instructions. We aren't supposed to touch her. He will be back soon," Vinnie mutters, and I smile at him. I know it won't do any good, but I am so grateful for him trying to help. I wish there was some way to tell him to leave me here. I don't want him to have to see this. He can't save me now. Nothing can.

"Fuck that, if I want her then I will take the bitch. Fuck what Vernon says. You are lucky I am giving you permission to touch her. I plan on slicing up this sexy body, piece by piece, as I fuck her. Make her bleed and scream, just like she did to my brother," Luther screeches, fury rippled across his face. Vinnie's eyes are wide as saucers, like it has only now dawned on him how truly fucked I am.

Thankfully, the darkness begins to overtake me, and I start to feel incredibly sleepy. Maybe the fentanyl is finally kicking in, or my body is possibly shutting down. I'm not sure I care which it is anymore.

A sharp slap across my cheek brings me firmly back to the present, as the pain gives me a slight adrenaline rush. My cheek stings, my lip is cut open again, but they are the least of my problems. I look down to see Luther staring at my exposed pussy, his knife trailing lazily up and down my thighs.

"Don't pass out yet, bitch. I have big plans for you, and you are going to endure them all. I saw Art's body, covered in slices, and that is exactly what I am going to do to you," he spits as he drags the blade along the inside of my thigh. He starts at my knee and pulls upwards until it stops just before my bikini line. The cut stings lightly, but I'm guessing the patch is killing my pain, or my body is just numb to all the pain it is going through. It's only a flesh wound, but blood leaks out anyway, running down my leg.

Luther looks mesmerised by the blood trailing down towards my shaved public area, and he repeats the process on the other thigh. I don't scream, there's no point. It's just a waste of precious energy and breath. I'm still struggling to breathe, having to take small pants to get even just a bit of oxygen, and screaming would cause me more pain and damage than the knife ever could.

"Luther, come on, man. I don't wanna get in trouble," Vinnie grumbles, and I take my opportunity.

"Then go, coward. Get out of here. He isn't going to stop, so just get out," I force out in between breaths. It takes me longer than it should to get each sentence out. Vinnie looks at me, tears in his eyes as he contemplates what to do. I give him a small smile to let him know I am okay with him going.

"Fuck, no. You aren't going to miss the best bit. I wanna see how much she is enjoying this," Luther asserts, making it clear that Vinnie is not allowed to leave.

"Just remember that everything you do to me, I will return to you tenfold," I threaten, very aware there is not much more I can do in my current state.

Luther just laughs sadistically before taking his knife and putting it down at the side of him. He doesn't even question if this is safe or not. He knows I can't move, and he doesn't even suspect Vinnie is not on his side. Plus, he would notice if Vinnie suddenly lunged for it. Although, I see Vin considering it, and I stare at him, hoping he can read the massive no I am throwing his way with my eyes. He looks down, and I release the breath I didn't know I was holding.

Sadly, my lungs can't cope with that, and a dry, hacking cough starts. Tears stream down my eyes as my lungs begin to burn, and it feels like I am drowning with no air. Vinnie drops to his knees beside my head and gives me some water from the bottle he brought in earlier. He only lets me have a couple of sips this time, but it's enough to stop the hacking.

"What the fuck are you doing?" Luther asks, looking at Vinnie with disgust.

"I don't want her to die before you get your chance with her," he rushes out, sounding a little unsure as to whether or not that was the answer Luther was looking for.

The tension in the air is palpable, and when Luther finally smiles, Vinnie lets out the huff of breath he was holding. Luther then wastes no time in getting back to what he was doing.

Using his cold, calloused fingers, he parts my pussy lips before sliding a finger down my slit and then back up. He gets no response, and I know my pussy is as dry as the Sahara desert, but that doesn't stop him. He prods around at the top of my hood; I'm assuming he is trying to find my clit, and failing. Giving up quickly, he slides his finger back down the slit again before roughly shoving two fingers into my hole.

I cry out in pain as his fingers roughly penetrate me, and the sensation of skin on skin, chafing and ripping is excruciating. "You like that, don't you, bitch? I told you she would. All bitches like it rough. You just gotta show them who's boss," Luther says proudly to Vinnie, who is trying to look anywhere but at the assault happening in front of him.

Obviously, I don't bother to reply. Luther is living in his own little world if he thinks there is any chance of me enjoying this abuse. However, he continues to pump his fingers rough and deep into my pussy. Each time it feels like a new part of my inside is tearing, and I have actually reached the point where I am begging to get wet just so a bit of lubrication would make this hurt less.

"Tell me you like it, bitch!" he shouts. Before I have a chance to answer, he takes his free hand and simultaneously slaps his hand on my nipples, one after the other. It stings like fuck, but when he hits the second one, where the possibly broken ribs are, the pain is immense. Black spots start to invade my vision, and the whole situation seems so far away.

I know I need to stay away, to fight, but I can't. So, why not let the darkness take me, so I don't even have to know what he forces me to endure.

Just as the darkness is starting to take me, Luther slaps me awake again. "Is this what you want?" he asks as he takes my hair roughly into his hand, fists it tightly before pulling my chin against my chest so that I can look down at what he is doing to me.

The first thing I notice is my body has various shades of bruising. There is blood and dirt smeared all over me, and I'm covered in cuts. I try to ignore my exposed tits, hating how he has pulled on the nipples until they are taut. When my gaze finally reaches my open legs and waiting pussy, I see that Luther has taken his fingers out, but he is now preparing his cock.

Sat between my legs, Luther opens his jeans, pulls out his cock, and strokes it with his free hand. He didn't have much to work with before, but it appears to be growing a bit. His under average-sized penis says an awful fucking lot about Luther. No wonder he is so fucking angry; he is overcompensating.

Apparently, because my body doesn't know whether it is coming or going, I didn't exactly think of that last comment. Instead, I voiced it out loud. Luther doesn't take too kindly to having someone he is about to fuck insult the size of his cock. Without hesitation, he slaps me again, and before I have time to register the pain from that impact, he begins hitting my stomach.

Pain explodes throughout my body, and darkness begins to consume me. With every punch, it becomes harder to breathe. Those telltale spots float into my vision once more, and I'm sure I start hearing things. My imagination is making me think things are happening that aren't, and I am so confused that my brain quite literally hurts.

I am imagining Liam bursting in here to rescue me, him taking me far away from here. I pray to a God I haven't spoken to in a long time, one I am made to talk to at religious holidays only. Most of that is because my mother wants to keep up appearances with the church ladies, but now, while I am at my closest to death, I reach out to him. I pray for him to save me, to help Liam to find me. But most of all, I pray that I don't die. I want to live. I want to live my life with Liam. Unfortunately, at this moment, that is not looking likely.

I feel like my brain is playing tricks on me, that the lights flashing in front of my eyes are more than just the manifestation of my pain. A loud but distant bang sounds, my brain tells me it sounds like gunshots, and that's when I know I must be hallucinating. I hear a commotion and look over at the door, struggling to keep my eyes open.

A large dark figure stands in the doorway, and I can't help but smile. In my final moments, my brain shows me what it looked like the first time I met Liam. When he burst through my bedroom door, blocking the doorway the same as now. Only the last time actually happened. I hear noises from behind me. I know it's Vinnie, and I try to look behind me to make sure he is okay, forcing my brain to concentrate.

"No...don't shoot...I'm not the enemy. I swear, I have been t-trying to help her," Vinnie sobs, and that's when my brain seems to clear for a moment. This is real.

The realisation that the figure in the doorway really is Liam gives me some renewed hope. I try to call out to him, but I can't. My breathing is coming in short gasps.

"BREE!" I hear Liam shouting my name as a sharp pain pierces through my abdomen. I look down slightly and see that Luther has plunged his knife right into my stomach on the right side. A piercing scream I didn't know I could produce leaves my body, almost like I have no control anymore and am just watching from a distance. Then as soon as the pain starts to settle, the darkness begins to descend.

My eyes close, and I hear a gunshot followed by feet pounding closer to me. I can hear Liam, his voice and his sobs. His fingers tentatively touch my body, but as soon as I wince, he backs away. I try to open my eyes, to talk, but I can't. Coldness slides all over my body, and numbness spreads all over. Liam's voice as he shouts for an ambulance and his sobs feel like they are becoming distant.

I try to fight, to let him know I am here. I want him to know I am fighting to be with him, but it's hard. I feel him gently slide his arm under my neck to curl my body up against his. The warmth from his body against my advancing cold and clammy skin feels incredible. I feel his breath against my cheek and wetness from his tears as they leak onto my face.

I want to see him, to take away his pain, but breathing has become too hard.

Everything has become too hard.

The gloominess cascades over me, and this time I can't stop it.

"I love you, Bree. Please don't leave me." Those are the last words I hear before my body gives in, and I can't fight anymore.

The world goes black.

Chapter Thirty Five

Liam

Finding the right house is easy. Vinnie did a fantastic job of leading us directly to it. The piece of paper he hid had the road name on it. After that, it was easy to find the house since he left the tiara hidden outside in a bush. It didn't take us long to come up with a plan; we are ready to storm.

The man Paddy sent to collect the note said that Jimmy and Vernon left about ten minutes ago and have yet to return. That's when we realise the time has come for them to ring and set their plan in motion, but no way am I waiting for them to plan my trap. We are getting my girl out of there before there's any chance she could get hurt.

I do feel some level of reassurance, given that Jimmy's video made it very clear that the plan was not to harm Bree in any way, but that doesn't mean that she couldn't get caught up in the crossfire. I want an ambulance to arrive on-site as soon as we breach the house. Not a minute before, and for fuck sake, no sirens. It's better to say they are not needed than to waste valuable time if someone does get injured.

Using the fancy earpiece Kellan insisted we get, I pass my instructions on to him before turning to address everyone else. "We shoot to kill. The only people in that house that do not get a bullet are Bree and Vinnie. If she says he is innocent, then I will believe that, for now. I can always kill him at a later date if he is lying to me. Understood?"

Nods of confirmation are all I need. "What about Vernon and this Jimmy guy?" asks Evan, and I look at Paddy for instructions.

"I will deal with Vernon. I think that we need to find out from Bree what she wants to do with Jimmy. He meant a lot to her, and I have no idea how she will feel after this betrayal," he says with a heavy heart.

"She will shoot him herself," I mumble, and everyone lightly chuckles. They all know my girl isn't afraid of using her trigger finger if she needs to.

"Even so, it's her decision. You go in first, Liam, then Evan and Desmond will follow you. I will stay here and make sure nobody enters or exits," he says as he instructs the man standing next to him to guard the door. All I know is that this guy was who Paddy sent to secure the scene and set up a diversion. He doesn't argue, just moves into position next to the door, and I honestly don't give a shit that Paddy doesn't have the manners to introduce his man. I just want my girl back, and an extra set of hands is always a good thing. We haven't called for more men, it's better to have five well-trained men breach quietly than have loads who make a scene and risk getting people killed in the crossfire.

We stand in position outside of the main door. We have already memorised our plan of attack. This is where Kellan really shines. Not only did he find us an old map of the building, so we know the entire layout. He also hacked the government satellite that can use infrared to determine how many people are alive inside and where.

Just as we are about to breach, Kellan's voice comes over the communications devices that we all have, and everybody stands still to listen to what he has to say.

"Fuck, Liam. You need to go now. The infrared reading for Bree shows her temperature is flickering into the dangerously low zone. Plus, there is some asshole towering over here in a position that does not look appropriate," Kellan states. I barely let him finish the sentence before I kick the door in and shout that we are breaching.

"So much for doing this methodically," mutters Desmond as he charges in behind me. This approach was his idea to start with. Whenever I suggested that we needed to slow down and plan to ensure there were no casualties, he stopped listening. But now, I just need to get to Bree. Her temperature shouldn't be dropping.

She shouldn't be injured. Maybe Kellan is wrong and it's not her? I know that is fucking wishful thinking, Kellan is never wrong. But it's easier to think he made a mistake than that my girl could be gone.

Listening to the instructions in my ear, I know that despite my little wobble a second ago, I really do trust Kellan completely. I let him guide me through the house, trusting my dad and brother to have my back. The irony of that sentence is not lost on me. Not two months ago, I had been disowned and didn't have any family, now I have a giant, fucked up family of misfits, but they are mine. United in their love for one girl who makes it easy to love her.

I get into the room I was aiming for, and the door is already open. I do a quick sweep of the room's perimeter to make sure I wasn't in any danger. Movement in the corner catches my eye, I see a young boy cowering in the corner. I knew Vinnie wasn't a threat. I had seen pictures of him when I was doing my research to kill his father. So, when Kellan distributed his photo, we all knew what he looked like and not to shoot him. Once I identified he wasn't a threat, I cast my eyes into the middle of the room at my sweet Bree.

Bree's lying in the middle of the room, her body looking battered and bruised. Her skin is ashen in the patches that are not covered in black or blood. Cuts and slices of all different shapes and thicknesses cover her beautiful body. She is completely naked, and a man is in between her spread legs while he fists his tiny cock in his hands.

Seeing me in the doorway, taking up some of the light, he turns to face me. Obviously, he doesn't see me as a threat because he continues pumping that piss-poor excuse for a dick. That's his mistake.

I see red, and rage spreads through my body so badly I can hear my heart pulsing in my head. I don't hesitate, I pull out my gun, but then again, neither does he. As soon as he realises I'm a real threat, he picks up the knife lying by his side and plunges it into the right side of her abdomen. I scream for her, hoping that she can hear me as I make the shot. Then, aiming straight into his tiny little brain, I squeeze the trigger. It's a shot I could make in my sleep. Even the fury and pain I feel at seeing what this guy has done to Bree isn't enough to cause my hand to waver.

Instead, it remains perfectly still as the bullet leaves the gun and hits precisely in the centre of his forehead.

He falls to the floor, but I don't give a shit about him. All I can see is my bloodied and broken girl, her eyes shut and lying there like she won't ever open them again.

I fall to my knees right beside Bree. I want to touch her, to cradle her so that she knows I am here, but there's not one part of her body that doesn't look damaged. Even her gorgeous face is swollen and bruised. A violent frenzy I have never felt before starts to build up. It's painful, and I want to make everyone who had a hand in this hurt.

"Kellan, get that fucking ambulance in here now! She's dying. Oh fuck...I can't lose her! She can't die," I shout and then block out the responses when everyone else starts talking.

I hear footsteps heading our way, but I'm not entirely sure if the ambulance is even here yet. I curl up next to Bree. I try not to touch her too much but am desperate to pass some of my warmth to her. Anything I can do to help. Her eyelids look like they are trying to flutter open, but they don't quite make it. Maybe she is still in there and can hear me.

I watch as her breathing becomes more shallow and more laboured. I can feel her heart rate starting to slow down. It feels like she is giving up, and I can't let her. She has to know what she has got to live for.

"Bree, I love you. Please don't leave me," I whisper into her ear before pressing my lips to her cold, cracked lips.

I sit there, cradling the love of my life and watch as her breathing slows down until it's hardly anything. I throw out a prayer to anyone who is listening and wants to take a chance on a desperate man. I would do anything to have this girl back. I need her. Please do not take away the one shred of happiness I have in my world.

I may not have known her for long, but it's like I can't even remember my life without her in it. It's like I was living in black and white until she brought the colour. She brightened my world, and I would do anything to be able to keep her.

As my tears fall onto her face, I watch helplessly as her breathing slows to a stop.

Before I can even register what is happening around me, my father and brother are pulling me away from Bree. The paramedics arrive and try to work on her, but I'm in a trance, not able to let her go. Evan holds me, half for restraint but also for support. He allows me to lean on him literally while I cry for the girl I love. Even my father, who I didn't think could care for another person, places my arm around his neck to share the burden of my weight.

Paddy is standing on the opposite corner of the room, and I watch as his legs collapse under him and he slides down the wall into a crumpled heap. We all watch as the paramedics start chest compressions on the girl we all love.

Very quickly, they are able to get her heart back into a normal rhythm, but they don't sound confident it won't happen again. "We need to get her to the hospital straight away. We also need to contact her next of kin, as they will probably need permission for surgery," explains one of the paramedics.

"I'm her fiancé. Today should have been our wedding day. Can I come in the ambulance, please?" I ask respectfully, the desperation evident in my voice.

The female paramedic is standing, making notes, while the male one checks all of Bree's vitals and replies. "Of course. I'm sorry to hear that, but unfortunately, you are not legally her next of kin. What about her parents?"

"Unfortunately, they are not available or able to give consent. I am her grandfather. I have a document proving I am her legal next of kin. I can get you it if needed," Paddy replies calmly. I look over at him, confusion evident on my face. With a subtle shake of his head and a quick text to his on-call forger, I assume the document will no doubt make it to the hospital before we do.

Before we even know what's happening, Bree is loaded into the ambulance. Paddy's man is staying to cover the mess we have made. Paddy, Evan, and Desmond all make a run for the car, but as I am getting in the ambulance, I remember something. I apologise to the female paramedic who is securing Bree in the rig. Making sure all her wires are working, fluids are going in, and so much more.

"Evan, get Vinnie over there and look after him! Make sure no harm comes to him. Bring him to the hospital, okay?" I shout, and my brother nods in confirmation before heading back towards the house to find the boy we left cowering in the blood-soaked room.

I strap myself into the ambulance and take hold of Bree's hand. I spent the whole journey talking to her, telling her all about what we should have been doing right now. We should be married, but I tell her not to worry because as soon as she is just the slightest bit better, I will be marrying this girl. The idea that I could lose her is terrifying, and I don't ever want to feel that again.

We arrive at the hospital just in time as Bree's heart stops again. The female paramedic climbs onto the gurney, straddling my girl and begins to press down on her chest while people help to wheel them both through the hospital. I try to help, but I feel like I am falling over my own feet. They push through a door, and a little woman dressed in a nurse's uniform stops me.

"I'm sorry, Sir. No one is allowed past this point. Let me show you into the waiting room, and when we know more, we will update you," she says politely.

I want to argue. I want to tell her to go fuck the waiting room. I want to storm past her to be with Bree. But I don't do any of that, instead, I follow patiently and allow her to lead me into a plain cream waiting room with the ugliest shade of green chairs I have ever seen. She tells me I can wait for her here, and I just break down into tears. The horror of seeing the person you love stop breathing, their heart stops beating, it's terrifying. The nurse gives me a light hug. It's the best she can manage, given our height difference. I am grateful to her for caring. She sits me down just in time for the others to arrive. They take up their seats around me. It's not long before Kellan, Mia, and Hallie show up too.

That gorgeous baby girl always seems to know when I am at my lowest. Or she can sense the general sombre silence in the room because, except for the odd coo from my arms, she remains quiet and settled. I notice that Kellan and Mia are sitting together, talking to each other like civilised humans.

We all sit in comfortable silence until Paddy is the first to break it. "Got you, you fucker!" Paddy shouts. It had been silent for a while, and nobody was expecting someone to talk, and so when he did, everyone jumped. Even Hallie makes a gurgling noise, expressing her displeasure at us all for waking her when she had just fallen asleep.

We all look up to him to explain further. "My guys have caught Vernon and Jimmy. There was some fighting, but I had better men, and they could take them alive. They have them right there if you want me to put them on speaker," he asks, and I nod my head. I have no idea what I'm going to say to them, but I know I need to.

I hand Hallie over to Kellan, who passes her to Mia, without even thinking about it. Paddy brings the phone over to me, and we wait for it to ring. Once they are on speakerphone, I can't find the right words to use.

"I don't even know what to say to you both. You, Vernon, I can understand. I've always known you are a power-hungry asshole. I just had no idea the lengths you were willing to go to so you can get what you want. But you...Jimmy. You betrayed Bree in a way that you can never undo. If she dies, I will hunt you both down and make you pay, painfully," I spit, meaning each and every word.

"W-what do you...what do you mean if she dies?" asks both Vernon and Jimmy at the same time, though it's Jimmy's voice that quivers and shakes.

"That psychopath you left her with? Luther? Well, he beat the shit out of her. Carved her up like a turkey at Christmas. Then stabbed her in the stomach before I got a chance to put a bullet between his eyes. Her heart has stopped twice since we found her. They are pumping blood into her just as quickly as she is pumping it out. Her organs are at risk of shutting down. She is in the operating theatre at the moment." I make sure to list everything they have done to her, every little hurt they have caused. I want them to feel shame for the pain they have caused someone who is supposed to mean the world to them.

Initially, we are met with just silence, then sobs. "We never intended for her to get hurt," cries Jimmy.

"Well, she is fucking hurt. Do you know that Bree once told me that you were the only guy she ever trusted before she met me? She thought you would never hurt her. Now, look. Even if she does wake up, I have no idea what damage has been done, not just physically but mentally and emotionally. Luther was in between her spread open legs when I got there with his cock in his hand. The death he got was too good, in my opinion. Yours will not be as easy," I state, and I hear gasps all around the room when I tell them about the horror I saw in the room.

The only person who looks truly as horrified as me is Vinnie. I give him a small smile. I don't want anyone to know he is here. His life could be in danger, and so he is under our protection. Because of him, I may have got to Bree just in time.

"How fucking dare you threaten me? I am still the leader of the

London base, and you are in London. So, I rule. Remember your place, or I will put you in it, boy!" shouts Vernon.

"Don't you dare threaten my son, you psychopathic piece of shit! Just because you don't give a shit about your daughter and her life doesn't mean we don't. You even think about talking shit to Liam again, and I will rain holy hell down on you until you beg me to stop!" Desmond yells, shocking us all.

"Are you fucking kidding me? Parenting advice from the guy who disowned his son, only to let him back in the Family now there's a chance of power?" adds Vernon, much to Desmond's amusement.

"Actually, since we are stating facts, I didn't kick Liam out of the Family; he left. He chose to work for himself instead of for me. When he introduced that spitfire of a daughter to us, we all knew she would make a better fucking leader than you. I have never hidden that I think I could rule better than you do, but I'm not ashamed to admit that I can't fucking wait to see what that girl can do. I think she will make a hell of a leader, which is why we came to a truce. Thanks to Bree, my sons now communicate with each other again. They are happier than I've seen them in a long time. Not to mention that I have never seen Liam as happy as he is with Bree. So, I may be a shit parent, but I know when to back down," my father replies vehemently. For the first time, possibly ever, I am incredibly proud of my dad.

"Vernon, you are my responsibility, and I will issue the punishment when the time is right. However, I need to be here with Bree and find out what happens to her first, then I will decide. As for you, Jimmy, that will be down to Bree to decide what she wants to happen. But as far as your employment goes, you can very much consider yourself fired," Paddy spits as he hangs up the phone, no longer needing to hear any more from them.

Time passes so slowly as we all just slowly move around each other in the small waiting room. Some pace while others sit in silence. Some offer to go and get coffee and food. But mostly, we just wait, our heads bobbing up and down with every passing person wearing scrubs, hoping that this person will be the one to come in and give us news.

We sit in that small room for eight whole hours with no news, and all of us slowly start to get antsy. Finally, Kellan takes Hallie home to sleep, and Mia goes with them. My father goes back to the hotel, he says it's to update Finn, Mum, and the girls, but we both know that's not the real reason. Shit is getting real, and he is scared. I know because I am too.

Evan and Paddy fall asleep in their chairs, but I can't sleep. Not until I have her in my arms. Not long after they fall asleep, an older man with a bright white beard comes into the room wearing scrubs in an ugly shade of blue.

"Are you the family of Brianna O'Keenan?" he asks politely.

"Yes, I am her fiancé, that is my brother, and he is her grandad." I point to the two sleeping figures in the corner.

"Yes, it was very smart of Bree to legally name you as next of kin when you got engaged. We have the paperwork on file," he states, and I want to smile at Paddy and his ability to make anything materialise. I also want to thank him for trusting me enough to name me. I know Bree would have if given a choice, but he didn't have to.

"That's just Bree. Please, doctor, I have to know how she is," I plead, and he pats my shoulder before leading us over to the two seats in the corner, opposite of Evan and Paddy.

"Bree sustained some pretty horrific injuries, and as you know, she has undergone an extremely complicated surgery. She had several parts of her bowel damaged from the knife wound, including her liver and spleen. We removed part of the liver, as well as her gallbladder and spleen. We struggled to locate all the places she was bleeding internally, but think we have got them all. We have sewn up most of her cuts and have glued others. She has multiple rib fractures, and one of those ribs had punctured her lung. She has a chest tube in place and a machine breathing for her at the moment. She lost her body's blood volume and is currently having it replaced. What Bree's body has been through is horrific, and she is still not out of the woods yet, but I am hopeful. She seems like a very strong young lady," he states, and I can't help but smile. He has only ever known the unconscious version of Bree, and he can still tell she is a fighter.

Looking up at him, I can see there is more he is deliberately not telling me, and that scares me. "What aren't you saying?"

"Unfortunately, no matter how hard we tried, we were unable to save the baby," he says, and I feel like the world drops out from under me, and I don't know which way is which. Bree was pregnant? Did she know? Why didn't she tell me? "She was only a few weeks along. She might not have even known, not that it makes it any easier, of course. I am very sorry."

"Thank you, I have no idea what to say. I didn't know Bree was pregnant, and I'm not convinced she knew either, but I still feel like something has been stolen from us. Can she get pregnant again when the time is right?" I ask, hopeful.

"I am very hopeful, yes. However, it may prove a little difficult as we had to remove one of her ovaries because of the damage. Nevertheless, she could get some help with IVF, if it is needed," he explains, and I give him a small smile.

"I would sell a kidney if it meant her getting anything she ever wanted. Please, can I see her?" I joke and then ask, and he chuckles.

"Well, I don't think I can legally take your kidney, but she is fortunate to have a man like you who would do anything for her. We are just getting her settled in intensive care. You can come in one at a time to see her," he explains, and it's my turn to smile.

"That's where you are wrong. I'm the lucky one because I found her. I will be staying with her, the visitors won't be a problem. We want her to rest and get better."

"Okay, a nurse will be through shortly to show you where Bree is. She will probably sleep most of the night, but that's what we want. We want her body to heal itself," he explains before walking out of the waiting room.

I wake up the guys and fill them in on everything except the baby. Bree deserves to know that before everyone else. I need to make sure the nurses know that it is confidential information. I tell them about the one visitor rule and that it's not up for negotiation. I am going in and not leaving that room until she does. If anyone else wants to visit then they will have to break the one visitor rule, I will not compromise. Paddy tuts when I tell him that and storms out to find someone in charge. He will either throw money at someone, or he will threaten them. Either way, he will get what he wants. When he eventually returns, he confirms that Bree will have extended visiting allowed during the day only. I smile at his confidence.

The same nurse who hugged me earlier is back for her second shift, and she walks me to see Bree. I politely ask Paddy to give me a few minutes alone with her, and he agrees.

Walking into the room and seeing my flame-haired Princess looking so battered and bruised, not to mention so incredibly small on the hospital bed, breaks my heart. I sit down beside her and gently take her hand in mine. She doesn't respond in any way, but I don't care. I just want to be near her. So I talk to her. I tell her about all the shit that went down. I tell her as many times as I can that I love her and that I can't fucking wait to make a life with her.

Time passes a lot quicker with her nearby. Everyone we know and love comes by to visit. The only one I had a problem with was her mother, but she assures me she had no idea what Vernon and Jimmy were planning. She only realised when it was too late, and by then, she was terrified of Vernon. I warned her that I couldn't guarantee I wouldn't kill her husband. She said neither could she. So I let her in. She didn't stay long, uncomfortable with the silence.

Everyone who came spoke to her and tried to lure her into waking up. Hell, even my dad threatened her, but she still didn't wake. Finally, nighttime came around, and the nurses stopped asking me if I wanted to go home. I don't want to be anywhere that Bree isn't. They turned down Bree's sedative a few hours ago. The nurses thought she should be awake by now, so they called in the same doctor from last night, the specialist who operated on her.

In the meantime, having lost feeling in my ass about four hours ago, I very carefully, as to not hurt Bree at all or pull out any of her leads, climb into the bed beside her. I slide my arm under her head and around her shoulders, positioning her body up against mine. I hate feeling her so limp against me, but at least she is still alive.

Stroking the hair off her cheek and tucking it behind her ears, I gently pepper her face with kisses before telling her how much I love her. I need to tell her for real, while she is awake. I must have got very comfortable because I fell asleep, until suddenly someone coughs and startles me awake. I look at the girl in the bed next to me, and once the coughing stops, all I see is the most beautiful girl in the world. I reach over with my free hand, grabbing her water glass, and put in the straw to help her take tiny sips.

"Hey, beautiful," I smile at her, probably the biggest, most genuine smile I have ever had.

"I missed our wedding," she says with a hoarse cry, and literal tears streaming down her face.

"We can do it anytime you want, Princess. I am all yours forever," I stress, making sure she knows how much I care for her.

"I heard you, you know," she states, and I wonder what she is talking about. "I love you, too." Her words go straight to my heart and make it grow impossibly larger.

Leaning down, I press my lips against hers but am careful not to press too hard given all her injuries. We sit together like that for hours. We talk, she sleeps, and she gets better, but most importantly, we get to laugh together. I have lost count of the amount of times I have told her that I love her, but I can tell you now, I won't ever stop. She deserves to have me tell her this for eternity, and I plan to.

We touch briefly on the decision she had to make regarding Vernon and Jimmy. She says she wants to work that out when she gets home, but for now, she wants to concentrate on getting better. We also decide to use these few days to make sure we organise and, even better, a more personal wedding than before. You see, we are still desperate to marry each other, and we sure as shit don't want to wait. Life is short, and almost losing Bree helped me to see that.

Now I just need to find the right moment to tell her about the baby.

CHAPTER THIRTY SIX
Bree

I'm woken by the strangest sensation. It's like I am no really in my body. Instead, I'm watching from above. Like my brain is awake but my body isn't. The beeping from a nearby machine feels as though it is ricocheting through my brain. Each beep causes me a new boost of pain.

My whole body feels stiff, as though I have been in the same position for far too long. I try to move, but I can't. I feel like I am completely numb all over. This is such a surreal experience, but am ready for it to be over. I want to...no, I need to wake up.

I try to force my eyelids open, or even just move a tiny little bi of my body, anything to know that I am still alive because righ now, I'm not all that sure.

As I do a mental checklist of all the parts of my body, making sure to try them all, I am distracted by a voice. His voice.

"Morning, Princess. So it's another day; I don't even know what to talk to you about. The nurses say that I should talk to you the same as I do at home because they don't know if you really can hear me. Fuck, I hope you can hear me. I hope my voice is waking you up and that you come back to me. I miss you so fucking much. I miss your laugh, you telling me to pick my clothes up when I leave them lying around, your touch...fuck, miss how soft you are. Please, you have to wake up. I don't know if I can live my life without you." His voice feels so far away. I'll it can feel the pain and the heartbreak that echoes with every word.

I want him to know I am trying. I want to get back to our life... for him. I never knew that anything was missing in my life until I met Liam. It's like there was a hole in my heart that I didn't know anything about. But when I met him, I suddenly felt full. Like Liam completed me. I can't believe I never got the chance to tell him I love him. I hear him say it all the time now. If only he'd told me while I was actually awake.

Time seems to continue like this for far too long. There are times when I can hear Liam. His voice soothes me like a child listening to a lullaby. That smell that is all Liam envelopes all around me and I can't get enough. No matter how much breathing hurts, it's worth it to inhale his intoxicating scent. There are times when I hear the voices of the people who mean the most to me, but I am so tired that I can't focus on what they are saying. My heart swells just at the knowledge they have shown up for me, and I am desperate to get back to them.

I don't know how long this routine continues, but each time I feel like I get a little closer to letting him know I am here. Every time I fail, every time they leave not knowing I can hear them, I become consumed with the idea that it won't be long until Liam realises I'm a lost cause. I become convinced that it's only a matter of time until he leaves me. Except that day never comes. If anything, I hear more discussion from others telling Liam that it isn't healthy for him to remain in this room for too long. Still, he doesn't leave. His hand never unlaces with mine.

After my last set of visitors for the day, Mia, Kellan, and Hallie, Liam sets in to tell me all about the gossip that I have missed. He lays on the bed with me, our hands clasped together, and for the first time in a long time, I feel warm. I would say it's his body heat, but he has laid next to me every day since we first got here. The nurses have stopped telling him not to do it now, knowing which battles to pick.

Liam's voice fills the room and it's that soothing drawl I have come to depend upon. "I bet you are as shocked as me to see those two even being in the same room as each other after that shitshow of an interview. But weirdly, Kellan needed someone to look after Hallie while he helped me locate you, and he didn't even blink. She was the person he called. I am sure they still argue, and Mia looks at Kellan with such frustration at times it's laughable. I know if you were here, you would be telling me all about their sexual chemistry and how they might be good together, and I would give you a lecture that you do not meddle in our friends' lives. Particularly their love lives. Hallie seems to really like her too. You know what that little demon is like. She is very picky with who she shows affection towards, but she seems to go to Mia with great ease. I'm just glad Kellan has help with Hallie while we are at work. There's a really big fucking part of me that doesn't want him to fuck her. He needs a nanny more than anything else. He has a tendency to just barge right in and not think about the consequences. I wish you were awake, baby. You need to see this and be involved in this. I really want to be able to tell you not to meddle right now."

A power I haven't felt in a long time overcomes my body, and with every ounce of strength I have, I squeeze Liam's hand. His breath is in my ear, causing a shiver to run down my spine as he talks. "Princess...Bree. Did you do that? Can you hear me? Squeeze my hand again if you can hear me."

I do as I am asked, squeezing his hand as hard as I can, and then I feel him. He roughly presses his lips to mine. It's a desperate but short kiss that causes my heart to race. I mean literally. The beeping from the heart machine becomes louder as the room fills with proof of how much Liam's touch affects me.

Things become crazy after that. Liam keeps hold of my hand, but the room fills with doctors and nurses. They do numerous tests on me to determine that I am really here, and Liam didn't imagine things. I do all the tasks the doctors ask of me, and listen to the older, more gravelly voice of who I have come to learn is Dr. Mariton, the man who operated on me when I first came here. He gives me hope that it won't be long until I am awake properly.

I have no idea how much time passes, everything moves so quickly. It's hard to keep track of how often I come and go, in and out of consciousness, and I can't exactly look at a watch. I know that I spend more time asleep than I do awake, no matter how hard I push.

Finally I'm able, even if it's only for a few seconds, to open my eyes. As I look around I realise it's most likely nighttime as the nurses are all a lot quieter, and Liam is lying beside me, with me curled up in his arms. It's an act he has perfected now to ensure he doesn't catch any wire or tubing, and I can still sleep curled up on his chest. But now I don't want to sleep, I want to see Liam. Sadly my body doesn't agree and I fall back to sleep.

My eyelids flutter open, again, and they feel so heavy as I work hard to keep them open this time. The small hospital room is mostly in darkness, lit up slightly by the light from the corridor seeping in through the gap where the door is open. Initially, the artificial light from the corridor is bright enough to hurt my overly-sensitive eyes. But, gradually they adjust. I take in the bleak hospital room and see some of Liam's things draped over the chair in the corner. The table in front of me has been decorated with pictures of my family and friends. There's Liam and me from our funfair date, a couple of Kellan and Mia, alongside ones from the engagement party with Liam and his family.

My breath catches when I see the most prominent photo in a frame in the middle of all the others. The picture has obviously been edited, but it's so beautiful. The image is of Liam standing at the bottom of the aisle, waiting for me to walk down to meet him. The room is decorated beautifully, and all our closest people are sitting looking on. Liam looks a little apprehensive, but it has been made to look like he is looking at me entering the room. The photographer must have taken a picture of what my dress looked like from behind, the train trailing behind, the beautiful open back visible through the veil. That image of me had been placed in the corner of the picture. It genuinely looks like I'm walking down the aisle to meet him.

My eyes fill with tears as I remember what was torn from us. That beautiful day was ruined, and I could have been taken from Liam for good. Anger rises within me as I remember who is responsible, and I will make them pay.

Trying to blink away the pain, I quickly realise that my mouth is still dry no matter how many times I rub my lips together. That cotton wool feeling becomes overwhelming. I notice a glass of water on the table, and I lift my arm to reach for it, trying my hardest not to disrupt Liam. He looks so peaceful when he is sleeping, and the bags under his eyes tell me he hasn't been doing a whole host of that. I should have known he would be in tune with the slightest movement my body makes.

As soon as he feels my arm start to move, he freezes. He feels like a hard rock lying underneath me. He doesn't say or do anything, just waits. I open my mouth to say something, but it's too dry. So instead, I turn my head just slightly so he can see my face as I try hard to give him a smile. My face must be bruised or swollen because it's painful, but as soon as his smile lights up his face, I know it was worth it.

He shuffles us slightly so I can look at him easier. I make sure the grip I have on him doesn't falter. He is never leaving my side again.

"Fuck, Princess. Are you really awake? I feel like I'm dreaming," his raspy voice is like music to my ear. The hand not clasped tightly with mine comes up and lightly strokes my face, pushing my hair behind my ears. I don't even want to think about how much of a mess I look. The way Liam looks at me like I'm a rare artefact he didn't believe existed, but now he has it in his hands, he stares at me with the same awe.

"I'm...here. W-water..." I force out, my voice sounding scratchy and hoarse.

Instantly, Liam reaches forward, bringing the water glass forward and placing the straw in my mouth. I take in a big gulp, and a flash enters my mind. It's like I see parts of a movie, like a trailer of what happened to me, but I don't want to remember it all. I remember enough though. My brain sadly doesn't seem to give a shit, and the memory of Vinnie giving me water only for me to vomit it back up after gulping too hard floods my brain. It's like my body can remember it more than I can as my stomach rolls and nausea overcomes me. I take just a few small sips of the water, just enough to wet my mouth.

"Liam...I—" I don't even know what I want to say to him or how to word it. How do I tell him that I don't remember much of what happened, but I know my father and Jimmy played some part. I want to know how much they betrayed me, but there's still a part of me too terrified to find out everything. Flashes of pain, beatings, and degradation flash in my mind, and I can feel myself becoming overwhelmed. My heart races and the accompanying beeping from the machine letting everyone know that I am freaking the fuck out does nothing to help the situation.

Liam gently strokes my face, and whispers shushing noises to me as he lightly kisses my forehead. The feel of his lips on my skin and his touch sweeping over my body is enough for me to calm my breathing. I try to take a big deep breath, only to wince in pain as I cannot breathe deeply. I try to move my hand to my side, needing to know what's causing the sharp pain I feel near my ribs. It feels like it's preventing my lungs from expanding fully.

Liam grabs hold of my hand before I can get to the source of the pain. "No, Bree. Stay still, please, Princess. I have called for the nurse to come in. You have tubes in your body. The one you were just trying to reach for is because your lung collapsed after a piece of fractured rib pierced it. The tube is preventing the build-up of air. Your lung will feel a bit sore for a while, but honestly, this is helping you. So please don't touch it." His voice is deep and pleading, but of course, I listen to him and let him guide my hand to rest on his chest instead.

"What happened to me, Liam? I don't remember it all," I whisper, and his face pales. His eyes are as wide as saucers. I'm not sure he knows what to tell me.

"Bree, I..." Luckily Liam is cut off when a young, blonde nurse enters the room. She smiles the biggest smile at Liam, taking in his beautiful exposed chest.

"Liam, what have I told you about sitting on the bed. You don't want to get me in trouble, do you?" she giggles. Then she, honest to God, flips her hair back like you see girls do in terrible rom coms when they are trying to get a guy's attention.

As she progresses closer to us, she thrusts her impressive sized chest out, enhancing it further. Her nurse's uniform already looks a tad too small. I don't say that in a bitchy fat-shaming way. Simply that she has obviously chosen to wear a uniform that is a size too small to show off her fantastic figure. Nurses' dresses don't tend to be flattering, but she has added a belt and a good bra, so her curves look great. Fuck, I may be a little jealous, but I have no need to be.

The entire time I am lying here, I stare daggers at Nurse Big Tits, getting angry at her for looking so amazing and flirting with my man, particularly when I look like shit and can't compete. I needn't have worried because Liam's eyes never leave me. I don't think he is even aware she is a girl, let alone how hot she looks. He gently slides out of bed, but I keep our hands clasped together, ensuring he doesn't go too far.

The next couple of hours pass by in a blur. They give me medication to help with the pain, and I doze in and out of sleep for a while, but generally, they are happy I am out of the woods. But that is just physically. Mentally is a whole other story. The flashes of memories are driving me crazy, and I can feel the fear overtaking my body. I think not knowing what really happened is worse than what I am imagining.

It takes a couple of days for me to fully come around from all the medication. When I am beginning to feel more like myself, and with Liam's help, I begin to get up and move around. That's when they make the decision to take out all of my tubes. I am pleased because this is the first step in my journey to getting home.

Almost two weeks after the incident happened, the nurses are finally happy with my progress. The doctors think I should be able to go home the next day if I can manage without extra painkillers overnight. They think I can't handle the pain, which is why I have been asking for additional overnight. They think I am using them for pain, I am not. Instead, I am using them to help me get to sleep. I can't close my eyes without seeing the flashes, let alone the pain I feel when my brain releases new information. Nighttime is always the worst because I have no idea what is real and what's a dream. That's why I have been trying to get help with sleep, but tonight I am determined to be able to go home. No matter how many nightmare's I get, I will be going without tonight. This is the last night Liam and I spend away from our own bed.

Liam has known for a while that there is something wrong. I accidentally wake him up in the middle of the night, he finds me sobbing and shaking, but he doesn't ask me about it. Instead, he holds me and whispers reassuring words into my ear. He tells me to talk to him whenever I am ready, which makes me love him even more. I don't deserve this beautiful man. So, I need to be honest with him.

The darkness of the room acts as a protector for me, and with my head resting on his chest, I know I can avoid eye contact. "Liam...I need to know what happened. My brain is creating all sorts of scenarios. I need to know what's real," I whisper, but I know he can hear me.

His breath hitches. "I have been waiting for you to ask. Do you remember who organised your kidnapping?" he asks, his hand stroking down my arm with a featherlight touch that he knows relaxes me instantly.

"I remember that my father and Jimmy were involved. They were setting up Vinnie...fuck. What happened to Vinnie? He helped me. Is he okay?" How had I forgotten about the scared young lad who got in over his head? He fucking saved my life. How can I remember all the bad shit that happened but not the good?

"Relax, Princess. He is fine. We let everyone believe that he died in the rescue. He's got a new identity, and I have sent him to school with Ryleigh. Kid needs the chance to finish his education and become whoever he wants to be. I owe him for everything he did for you, and I promised I would take care of him." The brightest smile crosses my lips as he speaks. I definitely picked a good man here.

"What about my father and Jimmy? I know you shot that asshole, Luther. Did he die?" I ask. My brain remembers him taking a shot between the eyes, but I don't know how much is reality and how much is wishful thinking.

"He did die. A death too quick and good for him, if you ask me. I'm sorry I took that death away from you. As for your father and Jimmy, they're still alive. Your father organised the whole thing. He wants the entire estate. He planned on taking Ireland from your Gramps and then forcing you to hand over London. He's power-mad. Jimmy left you a video message, explaining his motives. You can watch it whenever you are ready. Your grandfather has them both secured in his house, waiting for when you are ready to pass judgement. When you feel up to it, you will get the London Family business signed over to you. As far as Vernon's men are concerned, most saw what you went through and how you still came out strong, and they are rethinking their views on women. Most have come to pledge their allegiance, but I have Kellan vetting them first. I am so sorry, Princess. You had to get the shit kicked out of you so that people would see how fucking strong you are." His statement is powerful, and it makes me feel about seven feet tall. Liam has this incredible ability to not only say the right things but to give me a confidence boost that I didn't know I needed.

"My instinct is to put a bullet in both their brains," I spit and Liam chuckles, causing my head to vibrate. With the added confidence he gave me, I sat up and turned to face him. His face is illuminated by the corridor lights and he looks more like Liam now. The messy beginnings of a beard have been replaced by the subtle splatterings of stubble that I am used to. The bags around his sunken eyes have also gone. They now look as bright and warm as they have always been.

"I will pass you the gun, Princess. It's the least they deserve. But they are still your family. Nobody will think less of you if you decide to punish them in another way," Liam adds with a smile. He acknowledges the tiny part of me that I tried to keep hidden. The little girl who has been let down by the two men who meant the most to her. How do I kill the people who helped raise me? But, do they really deserve to live?

I push that out of my mind but carry on the conversation, needing desperately to fill in more blanks. I know what I need to ask, but I'm terrified of finding out the answer. I take in a few deep breaths. The slight twinge I get from breathing in too deeply is just a regular occurrence now. I live for the pain, as it distracts me from the mental pain.

"Did he rape me?" I rush out, the words all mumbling together into one sentence, but I know Liam heard because he freezes. His hand that was stroking lazy circles around my thigh stopped its soothing motion. A rush of air releases from his mouth along with what sounds like a groan. Fuck, I don't think I am going to like this answer. Flashes of Luther standing between my legs with his cock hanging out have been crippling my memory and driving my nightmares for the last two weeks. I need to know.

"No, not fully. I think he did use his fingers, and if I could break each and everyone that touched you, I would. I'm so sorry, Bree. You had some small tears from the force and scratches from his nails but no sign of full penetration. Something Vinnie confirmed. He said he will tell you anything you want to know," Liam says so gently, but his words break me.

Tears flood my eyes, and no matter how much I try, I can't keep them from falling. Liam tries to pull me into his arms without any trace of hesitation, but I pull away as the sobs overcome me. My whole body vibrates with pain as I cry for everything that happened.

"Don't pull away from me, Princess. I am here. Let me be here for you," Liam states, his face caring and steadfast. I struggle to believe that he doesn't see me differently after what I have just been through.

"How are you not repulsed that someone else touched me?" I sob, holding my face in my hands as I desperately try to hide him from seeing my darkness.

"Brianna, look at me," he states loudly, and I am shocked to hear him call me by my full name. I look up and see there is no pity in his eyes, only sadness. "I could never view you differently. No matter how many scars you have, physical or mental, they are your war wounds, and I am so fucking proud of you. You survived. That's something a lot of people wouldn't be able to do."

His fingers lace through mine as I finally allow him to take my hands. The certainty on his face tells me he is very fucking serious. "I have a lot of scars," I add, and his resulting chuckle makes me smile.

"Bree, there is something I haven't told you about what happened. I wanted to make sure you were strong enough to hear it first. I'm sorry for keeping this from you, but please know I had your best intention at heart." He looks so sombre, and I am starting to freak out, so I tell him to get on with it. "You were pregnant at the time of the attack. Just a few weeks along, but sadly the baby was too small to survive what your body went through. That sick fucker will burn in hell for taking something so precious from us, I promise you that."

With each word he speaks, the pit in my stomach gets larger. My heart is racing, and I feel like I can't catch my breath. The panic is overwhelming. I have suffered so much pain, but nothing can compare to the pain of hearing what he just told me. The tears fall freely, and I cry. Sobs wrack my body once more as Liam pulls me closer. I don't need to see his tears to know they are there. I can feel the wetness leak onto my cheek. We both lost so much.

I'm not sure how long we just hold each other, but the tears dry up with time. Now that I know everything, I can compartmentalise it all. I know what issues I need to deal with and what I can put to bed here and now. I don't think I will ever get over having a baby taken from me, that's a pain I never want to experience again. But even as the loss begins to consume me, I know that with Liam by my side, we will get through this. Not to forget, but to learn to live again.

That's when I remember the vow I made while I was unconscious. The one promise I made that I fully intend to keep. Pulling my head off his chest, I lean close to Liam, our faces so close I can feel his breath. "I wanted to tell you this on our wedding day, but better late than never. I love you, Liam

Doughty. You are the best thing that has ever happened to me. I am so fortunate that I will be your wife, and when we do decide to have a baby, I know how much it will be loved. You will be an amazing father. I love you," I say and mean every word.

"Fuck, I have waited forever to say those words to you. I love you too, Bree. I can't wait until we are ready to have a little flame-haired mini-princess who looks just like her beautiful mother. I can't wait to marry you, Bree. This time, we will make it down the aisle," he jokes, and I can't help but laugh. The irony is that we never wanted a real wedding. Who knew that a marriage of convenience that stemmed from a kidnapping could become the real deal?

"You did tell me. I heard you tell me it every day. Those were the words that helped me fight every day to get back to you," I explain, and without missing a beat, Liam pulls me in for a searing kiss. This is so much more than the chaste kisses he has been giving me since I woke up. This is desperate and heady, and my arms cling to him, desperate for more. I open my mouth, giving him the access his tongue demands, and I let him take what he wants. Ignoring the bruising and the pain, I pull him even closer, desperately craving his touch.

Just as things are about to go a whole lot further, the distant sound of a hospital call bell reminds us of exactly where we are, and I start to laugh. I feel like naughty school girl, doing something she knows she shouldn't be, but fuck does it feel so right. I can't wait to be discharged home. It's time for me and Liam to start our lives together.

The text from Gramps yesterday confirmed that as soon as I'm out of the hospital and well enough, the running of London is mine. I have already been announced as leader. My Gramps is sending his young prodigy Kian O'Shay over from Cork to help me and Liam learn the business. He has been training under my Gramps for a while. He is loyal enough to want to help rather than take the lead. From what I have heard, he could be a good right-hand man, if I can trust him. Kellan is running a thorough check for me. I want all the information before I meet him.

I know I need to deal with my dad and Jimmy, and they will be dealt with when the time is right. But for now, I plan on going home and being with Liam. We have another wedding to plan. This time, there will be no announcements, and no big frills. Just me and Liam, and our closest family. I want to start my life with him, and I am done waiting.

I am ready to stand tall, to show all the people who don't think I am capable that I can fucking rule. Liam will stand by my side as we declare our love to the world, then once we are married, he will stand by my side in business too. I thought I just needed him to get what I wanted and be given the power, which is still valid. I definitely could rule without him, but I don't want to. He makes me stronger, better. If I was forced to be reckoned with before, then together we are unstoppable.

EPILOGUE
Liam

I can't believe that the time has finally come, yet again, only this time I know, we will come out of it together. Having Bree back home for the last few weeks has been a challenge. The girl has no idea what the word rest means. She constantly wants to be doing something. Kellan and I have literally been following her around, trying to do her jobs, or physically making her sit down. Of course, having the wedding to plan has helped.

I'm so incredibly proud of how she dealt with the pain she went through. I know there are still moments when darkness overcomes her, and she goes in on herself, focusing on the breathing techniques her counsellor taught her. She has been much better after having someone to talk to about how she feels.

I have to admit, as I pull on the suit jacket, which is different from last time, I can't control the flashbacks that overtake me. The pain I felt waiting at the end of the aisle, only for her to not show. The photo we have of the moment, the artificially created version, is one that we both still hold onto. It might not be our wedding day, but it's still a day that has great significance to us. Most people wouldn't want to remember that kind of trauma, but we do. We want to own it and use it.

This wedding is entirely different to the last. We are getting married in a large barn that has been decorated full of black and white flowers. It looks beautifully gothic. Nobody knew the location until I texted it to them this morning. They were all told a rough area, but we wanted the location to be secret. But standing here now, as I look over at the people sitting around me, I can see that everyone made it.

As I am looking over the people who we both love, and wanted to have here, I quickly realise that we can't have it set up like this. Finn, my usher, has asked people to sit either on the bride's side or the groom's, depending on who they knew. But all I can see is the people missing from Bree's side, which is why I tell people to spread out.

Paddy is seated on Bree's side, along with his wife, Clodagh. She suffers from bad arthritis, and we didn't know if she would be able to make the journey from Ireland, but I know Bree will be pleased she came. Next to him is Kian, the new kid from Cork who has been sent to help Bree and me learn the ropes. He seems like a nice kid, a bit rough around the edges, which is a given in our world. My good thoughts about him disappear rapidly when I catch him eying up my sister Freya. He's fighting a losing battle there. Freya is not interested in guys like him. She's always telling me there is no way in hell she will end up with a guy from our world. She will meet a good guy someday, that's what she deserves.

When I say I want more people to sit on Bree's side, Vinnie, or Shane, as he is now called, instantly stands to move to her side. Ryleigh doesn't hesitate in moving over to sit with Shane. They have become really close since he started attending Ryleigh's school. I'm pleased that he has someone he can call a friend. He had to leave his entire Marcushio life behind, but at least with Ryleigh, he will never need to lie. Kellan jokes that they will end up together, but I don't think so. Ryleigh seems to want to give me a heart attack with her choice of assholes. Shane is too much of a good kid for her.

Finn, Evan, and Kellan remain sitting over on my side; they are my groomsmen, after all. Mia stands from her place next to Kellan and goes to sit next to Ryleigh. I watch as Kellan's eyes follow her every move. It's obvious how he feels, and I would be astonished if she didn't feel the same way too. But at the same time, Mia has a secret, and we don't know what it is. Until Kellan finds out, he will never trust her implicitly, which is what he needs for any relationship to work.

The door to the barn opens, surprising us all because everyone who was invited is already here. My father grumbles a wildly inappropriate joke about Bree standing me up again. I don't think he realises how much anxiety I am going through after losing her once. I can't do it again. Choosing to ignore my father, I focus on the woman dressed in a light pink trouser suit. She looks elegant as usual, but I wasn't expecting to see Shona here at all.

When Bree was kidnapped, Vernon was in the other car with Shona. Everyone assumed she knew what was happening, but she claims she didn't know. She only realised when they weren't driving to the venue. As soon as she found out what was happening, she did what she could to get free, but it didn't work. Or at least that's the story she told Bree. Their relationship has been strained since Bree felt Shona was more interested in making things about her own pain rather than Bree's. Bree didn't invite her for a reason. I step towards her, ready to tell her to leave, when Paddy stands and places a hand on my shoulder.

"She won't cause any trouble. She just wants to see her daughter get married," he says quietly, and with a head nod, she takes a seat at the back.

I'm about to take a seat, anxiety building as she is now ten minutes late, when Kellan stands in front of me. Hallie reaches out for me on instinct. She does it every time she is close enough to reach me. I take hold of her little hand in mine, and she lets out the cutest little chuckle. She is dressed in this beautiful white princess dress with a sash around it. I just know that later she will be shuffling around with her nappy-padded ass in the air and skirt up near her ears.

"Action everyone!" Kellan shouts as he slides the phone he was holding back into his pocket, and everyone runs to get into their positions. Bree must have texted to say she is here. My heart starts to gallop and I beg for time to speed up, so I can have her next to me.

I watch as Paddy slips out the side door along with my sisters. Mia walks over to collect Hallie before heading in the same direction. Kellan comes to stand by my side, my two brothers next to me. A photographer, who has been here the whole time but I hadn't noticed, gets up close and personal for some staged shots before getting into position behind the registrar. An older woman stands behind the wooden table currently holding the wedding register, a bright smile on her face.

I take in the few remaining faces of my family and Bree's, and I never thought I could feel grateful for them. I thought I was done with my family long ago, but Bree gave me another chance. We both know that Desmond will be a threat to us one day, but for now, having him as our ally is better.

The music starts, pulling me out of my daydreams, and the doors open. The first to enter is Ryleigh, sauntering with the biggest smile on her face. She looks beautiful in the deep purple dress that Bree chose. It is so close to black while still having an element of colour. I don't miss the smile Ry throws towards Shane. Looks like that is something I am going to have to keep an eye on after all.

Freya moves a lot quicker down the aisle, hating the attention but smiling when she reaches me. She moves to the side in time for Mia to start walking down the aisle. She is holding Hallie, and together they are throwing dark coloured rose petals all along the aisle. Every so often, Hallie will grab a handful of flowers and throw them with the biggest giggle, but then other times, she tries to put them in her mouth.

Mia is doing an incredible job with Hallie, something I don't think is lost on my best friend. If the way his eyes rake over Mia's body is anything to go by, I would say he is very interested. I am less sure about her. She is always so quiet and shy, even more so after we found out she has some kind of secret.

When they reach the top of the aisle, Kellan leans down to place a soft kiss on Hallie's head. I don't miss the moment's hesitation. For a second, I thought he was going to kiss Mia, and given that she froze, and everyone around us gasped, we all thought the same thing. It is like watching a soap opera, waiting for them to get together. I just hope he waits until he trusts her before he fucks her. He really cannot screw this up.

Suddenly the music changes, and the door opens again. "Everything I Do" by Bryan Adams fills the room, and the most beautiful sight beholds me. Bree stands in the doorway, her Gramps linking arms with her, and I can't get over how fucking stunning she looks. She didn't want a dress that reminded her of the one she lost, and this is the complete opposite. She originally bought it as a reception dress for the first wedding, but it seems so much more appropriate now.

The long black dress is so fitting for the occasion. It hugs her tightly around her chest and waist, emphasising her beautiful curves before flaring out. The material looks like that of a ballerina's tutu; I believe it's called tulle. With every step she takes towards me, the dress looks more stunning. Lace with flowers and other patterns becomes more visible. Her flame-red hair is curled and hangs loosely around her bare shoulders. She has a long train that drapes behind her as she moves down the aisle. The closer she gets, the bigger both our smiles are.

It seems to take forever, but when she finally reaches my side, Paddy gives me her hand. "Look after my girl, Liam," he says, and with a smile and a nod, I give him my word.

As we face each other, the registrar begins. I am so busy looking at how beautiful Bree looks I forget to listen to her words. The next thing I know, Bree pinches me and gestures her head towards the registrar, who has obviously just asked me something. "Your vows?" the old woman asks, and I realise it's the part of the ceremony I had been dreading the most.

When Bree said she wanted to write her own vows, I was very much against it. I do not like public speaking, nor do I want to express how I feel in front of everyone, but I would do anything for her, give her anything she wants. But as she stands here in front of me, I don't even need the words I wrote down.

"I'm not great with telling you how I feel. You had to be unconscious before I could tell you I love you for the first time," I start, hearing the chuckles around the room. "But standing here right now, I have never been more sure. Bree, you are my whole world. You are so strong and so determined, whilst also having the kindest heart. I know you could rule this world alone, but it's an honour to stand by your side. I promise to love you, fight with you, protect you, and care for you, always. You are everything to me, and I promise I will spend every day for the rest of my life showing you how much you mean to me. I love you, and I will love you until I take my final breath, and probably even after that. I love you, Princess." I stutter on the last few words, emotion clogging up my throat. Her bright silver eyes look like beautiful reflective pools as they fill with unshed tears. Her smile is so beautiful.

The registrar announces it's time for Bree's vows and I take a breath as she begins to speak just for me. "Liam, when you steamrollered your way into my world, I never knew you would become this person to me. I had lived every day before meeting you, or so I thought. I realised I had just been existing until you brought me to life. You give me the confidence I didn't even know I didn't have. I feel stronger just because I have you near. You are my rock, my penguin, and my soulmate. I am so excited to explore our lives together. I promise to love you and be true to you, forever."

Her words cause my heart to beat furiously like a drum. The love she has for me is overwhelming. I smile a bright smile, and the registrar takes us through the final process. The words we have to say by law, and the books we need to sign. As we slide the rings onto each other's fingers, my heart soars.

Once all that is sorted, the registrar says the words I have been aching to hear for the past ten weeks.

"Ladies and gentlemen, friends and family, I ask you to stand united, to show your love for the new Mr. and Mrs. Doughtry-O'Keenan," she says, addressing our guests before turning to Bree and me. "You may now kiss your bride."

I didn't need to be asked twice. I literally fucking couldn't wait. I lean in and take her lips in a bruising kiss. My hand riding lower on her back than is probably appropriate in front of our family, but I don't care. Catcalls and the 'get a room' I hear from my father are enough to cause us to break apart. We turn to face our audience, smiling and laughing along with them. Before we start our journey down the aisle together, I lean in and whisper in her ear. "I can't wait to get you home and out of that dress. I have waited a long fucking time for this, and I think we should celebrate. Your ass is mine tonight. Happy wedding day, Princess."

Bree's reply is instant, her smile coy. "Fine, but afterwards, I need you to do me a favour. I want you to take me to my grandfather's house. I have made my decision. I thought about it a lot as I was getting ready. They have ruined too many of my days. I'm taking back control. Jimmy has seen his last sunrise. He dies tonight. As for my father, he is banished from the UK and Ireland. If I even catch word that he is in the country, there will be a kill order against him. My mother asked me to spare his life. She is being banished along with him. I agreed she could come to the wedding as a goodbye. It may not be the outcome everyone wanted, and it may have taken me weeks to decide, but

I am happy with my choice. So, let's go party and live our lives together. What better way to start our married life than helping each other bury a body."

The End

Do you want more?
You can now pre-order book two!

Trust In Me is Kellan and Mia's story.
Pre-order here:
https://books2read.com/trustinmeBB2

AUTHOR NOTE

So, what did you think?

Whose story do you want to see next?

Was Black Wedding everything you were hoping for and more? I really hope so because this book means so much to me.

Please do use the following stalker links to tell me the answers to these questions. I can't wait to hear what you think!!

When I started writing Black Wedding, I had the cover and a brief idea, but that was all. I planned on it being a 70k standalone, but the more I wrote, the more the world came to life. I fell in love with Liam and Bree, and all the other Doughty family members. I am so excited to bring all of their stories to life. I can't wait for you to see what I have planned.

If you enjoyed the book, please do consider leaving an honest review. Here are the links to where you can review:

Amazon
https://bit.ly/BlackWeddingBB1

Goodreads
https://bit.ly/BWGRreview

Bookbub
https://bit.ly/BWBbreviews

Reviews are essential to authors and if you are able to leave one that would be much appreciated.

ACKNOWLEDGEMENTS

This book couldn't have happened if it wasn't for the amazing people who helped and supported me during the writing process. The biggest help of all was without a doubt Polly, my amazing editor. She worked so hard to push me and help make sure I put out the best version I could. I am forever grateful.

Tash at Dazed Designs - thank you for creating such a beautiful cover. It was the inspiration that this whole series has been created around and it was an absolute pleasure working with you. I'm looking forward to seeing the others.

Zoe-Amelia - for being such an amazing Beta reader, and reading at the last minute for me. Your love of my characters gave me the confidence to keep going on days when I didn't want to.

Ena and Amanda at Enticing Journey - thank you for helping me to get Black Wedding into the hands of more people. It has been great to work with you.

To all my author girls who have helped me on the really crappy days - Erin, Jess, and Maddison - you have been a rock for me some days! Sam - as always, I couldn't do this without you. You are stuck with me from now on!

To all my family, particularly Mr Luna. Hopefully one day you will make me the happiest little author in the world by asking me to have our own little Black Wedding. But until then, thanks for always supporting me.

To all my readers - thank you for waiting for me. I know it's taken eight months for me to release this book, and I am so grateful that you have waited. I hope it has been worth the wait!

ABOUT
Emma Luna

Emma Luna is a midwife and lecturer who lives in Cambridgeshire, UK, despite her heart still very much being Northern. She lives surrounded by her crazy family; her Mum, who is her best friend and biggest fan; her Dad who helps her remember to always laugh; her Grandparents and Brother who can never read what she writes and her long suffering man-child Boyfriend who she couldn't live without (but don't tell him that!).

In her spare time she likes to create new worlds and tell the stories of the characters that are constantly shouting in her head. She also loves falling into the worlds created by other authors and escaping for a while through reading.

When she's not adulting or chasing her writing dream she loves dog-napping her Mums shih-tzu Hector, chilling curled up on the sofa with her Boyfriend binge watching the latest series or movie, drinking too much diet coke (it's her drug of choice), buying too many novelty notebooks, and completing adult colouring books as a form of relaxation. Oh and she is a massive hardcore Harry Potter geek. Ravenclaw for life!

Thank you for taking a chance on a newbie author - hope you enjoy and come back for more!

STALK ME LINKS

If you have enjoyed Black Wedding and want to find out more about what books I have available, and also what books I have coming up then you have to stalk me!

Join my Facebook Readers Group - Emma's LUNAtic's:
https://www.facebook.com/groups/emmaslunatics

Subscribe to my newsletter by visiting my website:
https://www.emmalunaauthor.com/

Like my Facebook Page:
https://facebook.com/EmmaLunaAuthor

Follow me on Instagram:
https://facebook.com/EmmaLunaAuthor

Follow me on Bookbub:
https://bookbub.com/profile/emma-luna

Follow me on Amazon:
https://www.amazon.com/author/emmalunaauthor

Follow me on Goodreads:
https://amazon.com/author/Emma--Luna/

More Books
Books By
Emma Luna

AVAILABLE TO BUY OR READ ON KU NOW

Sins of our Father Duet
Broken (Book 1)
https://books2read.com/brokenbook1
Retribution (Book 2) - *Coming Soon*

Mischief Managed Series
Piper
https://books2read.com/pipermm

Beautifully Brutal Series of Standalones
Black Wedding - Bree and Liam's story
https://books2read.com/blackwedding
Trust in Me - Kellan and Mia's story - *Coming Soon*
https://books2read.com/trustinmebb2

AVAILABLE FOR PRE-ORDER NOW
Limited edition Anthologies
Hate to Want You - 14th September
2021 Once Upon a Broken Crown - March 2022
Cover Up - May 2022
Once Upon a Bite - September 2022

THANKS FOR READING!!